THE BLOOD MOON CURSE

Chronicles Cataclysm - Book 2

L. Wolfram

KDP

This book is dedicated to my family, for their support, and to my editors, for their hard work. This book is for those who helped to paint The Magical Realm, in hopes that those who read will be thirsty for more.

- L. Wolfram

CHAPTER 1
Peccatum Irae

Dark clouds churned in the sky above and thunder growled in its hidden abyss. Some look into the stormy skies with fear. But to the one out on this night, the lightning was nothing but a response to anger. The sky, a part of him so to speak, does his bidding.

When the clear sunny skies turned dark and ominous, mortals nodded their heads and spoke about the awful weather. Citizens in the magical realm were confused for a moment but decided they had simply not noticed the approaching storm and chose to go about their business.

Some knew the meaning of the dark sky and were concerned, for this was a different breed of storm approaching. The one who remains laughs to itself. It knows exactly the cause of the storm. The storm will roar, the wind will howl, and the rain will pour.

The being to whom the skies respond is indeed feeling anxious, and for the first time in centuries, thoroughly frightened. Therefore, the sky above was darker than night.

The whisper of a cloak was the only indication of movement. The sky mirrored concern through distant thunder. A light rain trickled from above, a crack before the break of a mighty dam.

The cloaked figure ran briskly up the steep rocky slope of the mountain, praying they were wrong, numbly allowing its legs to drag itself closer to where it needed to be. It could almost hear the laughter of what remained, a choking cackling sound.

The cloaked figure disappeared in a bright silver flash and a crack of thunder. Simultaneously, it reappeared upon a hidden doorstep, far above. With another brilliant flash of silver, it reached the mountain cave.

The figure hesitated but knocked its fist against the door. There was a brief silence. The sky hesitated. The rain withheld. Its heart beat faster as it forced the door open. The cloaked figure stepped inside. Red eyes scanned the surroundings.

An overturned table, broken chairs, toppled bookshelves, and blood. It seeped through the cracks of the stone, and ran onto the ground. *Much more will come,* the figure thought.

The figure threw off the hood and a concerned face caught sight of disaster. Fornacem walked slowly towards the unmoving figure.

He shook his head, "No, Heimdall…" He kneeled, placing a hand to his neck. Fornacem stood, taking a few paces backward. "What does this mean? What do I do, Heimdall?"

No answer was returned. The wind carried the scent of ozone and lavender. The smell of a storm, the smell of death, and the smell of murder. The temperature outside dropped, and the rain withheld a moment more.

Lord Fornacem caught sight of something hidden beneath the crimson fold of Heimdall's robes. He reached down and moved the cloak. Sitting upon the stone, an object glinted.

It was a small knife, looking as if it were made of glass. The surface of the knife glinted purple, and Fornacem saw static buzzing across the blade. He reached downward and prodded it. A sharp pain shot through his head, and he quickly retracted his hand. The object resembled a knife. However, it was not merely a stained blade. It pulsated, wanting to become part of him. A slow heartbeat made the object rattle against the floor, frost gathering around it.

Some time ago, this may have been a knife, but it was consumed by what remained. What remained cackled in its darkness and buzzed across the side of the object. What remained had been the death of poor Heimdall.

Fornacem did not move when a brilliant silver summoning circle blazed to life above the object. There was a silver flash, a piercing crack, and a quiet strained scream. Fornacem looked down. There was static, and that was what remained.

Fornacem moved away from the cold corpse, deeper into the cave. He passed more smears of blood, smashed potion bottles, and a cracked stone cauldron. Upon a single piece of paper, black words were scratched through the parchment, and into the table. They read *'the fall of the mighty seer.'*

Walking deeper into the cave, Fornacem froze, looking onto a cold stone wall. He gasped, taking a few steps backward. He collided with a small lamp, which fell to the ground, shattering.

What remained, frost, and blood formed on the wall's surface. It oozed from the cracks and ran to the floor. There, revealed with shock and the misery, were the words Lord Fornacem had been dreading to find.

Dried blood was etched upon the stone wall, *'The blood of their enemy pools in the valley of the fall tree. The angel shall meet her final breath, reborn through blood and death. The Blood Moon Curse has been initiated.'*

What remained crackled against the stone floor and still Fornacem was frozen with fear. His dread poured from the sky above. He was too late.

The wind howled, the thunder rolled, and the rain was

driving. Happy families called to their loved ones to come inside. They sat in peace to eat their meals, blissfully unaware.

What is to come? Fornacem asked the invisible stranger. No one smiled, no one cackled in the endless darkness, and no one comforted young Fortem.

Little Fortem needs his mother, a dark voice chided, *poor, weak, little Fortem!* Laughter surrounded him, orbiting, taunting. He bowed his head, accepting. Suddenly, a loud crack shattered the silence.

A shaking fist drove into the stone in front of Fornacem, silver electricity crackled across his skin. He gulped heaving breaths, his hand shaking, and the voices retreated. It waved sarcastically and smiled. *"See you later little Fortem,"* it cackled.

We move now to a place of darkness and evil. Home to no one; home to what remained. Darkness hung over a hanger of a mortal military base, where many minds had been removed, surprisingly without violence, but gone just the same. Large trucks are delivering gigantic crates. A man yells at the workers, his voice hoarse from the effort.

Within a storage room outside the hangar, a being appeared from thick black smoke. He had dark hair and black eyes and held a staff in a shaking hand. A tattoo was etched into his neck, a hammer smashing into a skull.

He shook his head, throwing his staff to the floor and grabbed his hair with his hands. "Idiots, I work with idiots!" He kicked a nearby table, scattering papers to the floor. He yelled and a spell of darkness crackled in the air.

From an open door, a new figure entered. No mortal being, its skin was smooth dark grey stone. It wore a simple white button-up shirt, tucked into brown pants finished with a black tie. A small moon slowly orbited its head. Its eyes resembled a swirling purple nebula. The figure floated above the earth, defying gravity. A phone was clipped at its waist and in its hand was a simple clip board. It approached the angry figure, "E-Er, are you alright, mister Lapsus?"

Lapsus took a deep breath, "Yes, Atom, just a little stressed. Um, do you have the reports?"

Atom quickly shifted through his clipboard, "Er, yes. They just came in twelve minutes ago, please, follow me."

Lapsus followed Atom out of the room and deeper into the military base. Blank eyed mortals were working, operating forklifts, making charts, caging the Fallen, and disassembling equipment. A large forklift transported a venator in a cage. It howled, scratching at the bars of the cage. It reached a snake head between the cage bars and grabbed an unsuspecting worker. Lapsus looked away as the screams were silenced.

Atom said, "Er, fifty orders of Furnace Fallen came in today. There are twenty orders of venators. There are shipments of the carnifices from overseas, as well as several more boxes of auceps from Mexico. Er, we lost seventeen, er, eighteen more workers, along with six trucks. New ones are on their way. We also intercepted three distress signals. No one knows that this base has been infiltrated. I also have the list of metropolitan areas with high populations."

Atom handed a stack of papers to Lapsus, who scanned the pages.

"Huntington Beach?" Lapsus glanced upward, "I already have to be on Earth, why should I visit a *beach* in California?"

Atom hesitated, "Er, well, Huntington Beach is a highly populated area. Er, it may be autumn, but the area should still be populated. I figured that it was as good a place as any to start."

Lapsus stared at Atom, "That's coming from the same individual who tried to convince me that *the moon* had a high population. You're not trying to postpone the sacrifices are you, Atom?"

Atom looked downward, "I wish that I was, but no, Huntington Beach is a heavily populated area. Also, I do not support mass human homicide!"

Lapsus sighed, "Well, I, never mind. Did the Elder Fallen come in?"

Atom said, "Er, one moment." He pressed a button on the phone, and said, "Er, yes, it just came in."

Lapsus said, "Good, I want to see it now." Atom sighed but nodded. He led Lapsus into the airplane hangar, where a black truck was carrying a large monster on a bent trailer. The monster stepped off the trailer. The trailer groaned, and the ground cracked under the monster's weight.

Atom said, "E-Er, this is it. It was just recently made. So, there shouldn't be a problem with control. All you must do is say the commands in Latin."

Lapsus stared at the Elder Fallen, "Um, why don't we store that monster for now?" Atom filed through his clipboard.

"Er, there are no available hangars open, sir."

Lapsus said, "Oh, well, um, I'll just tell it to stand where the tanks are." He turned to the Elder Fallen and pointed to the corner of the hangar, "Er, *sta illic!*" The eyes of the golden monster flashed, and it slowly walked to the other side of the hangar leaving cracks in its wake.

Lapsus shook his head, "I *hate* those things, what else?"

Atom glanced at his clipboard, "Er, five hundred magician soldiers, five hundred Fallen magicians, one thousand mortal workers, seventy orders of steel, and one thousand days' worth of meals. There were also seven more orders of Furnace Fallen, as well as eleven orders of venators. I also have fifty orders of everything else on standby."

Lapsus nodded, "Excellent, I want a team waiting at Huntington Beach. Now, what of the enemy?"

Atom said, "They have no idea where we are or what we're planning." Lapsus nodded, "Excellent, and what about the other army?"

Atom said, "Er, they're stationed on top of the mountains. They've surrounded the Fall Tree Academy; they await your command."

Lapsus ran a hand through his hair, "Good, can you get me something to drink?"

Atom said, "Er, coffee?"

Lapsus shook his head, "Stronger."

Atom nodded, "Ah, I'll order that now sir. Er, you also have several meetings to attend."

Lapsus groaned, "Whatever, I must have my enemies' blood running into the soil by the end of the month. I want two more copies of the population reports by the end of the day."

Atom nodded, "Very well sir. I'll get that done."

Atom left Lapsus in the hangar. In a few minutes, Lapsus left as well. He entered his office, or rather, what was supposed to be an office. Lapsus sat in his chair wearily, *one more grueling month*, he thought, *one more month of hell, and I can be done.*

He caught a glimpse of something red out of the corner of his eye. His heart leaped into his throat. He whipped around, but it was only a mug. He sighed with relief, but as he did, dread filled him.

He had not caught any glimpse of the Blood Moon Curse. He hoped it meant nothing, but he knew better. The week had gone by without a single magic thing happening. Lapsus numbly accepted the fact that he would have to kill people. He didn't have any other option, if he didn't, if he... didn't...

Lapsus' vision went red, and he pulled his fist from the wall. A framed picture fell from his desk. He slowly reached down and grabbed it. Glass fell from the frame as he lifted it from the floor.

In the picture was a man, a woman, and a smaller girl. The man had dark hair and black eyes shining with happiness. The woman had brown hair, green eyes, and a shimmering

ring on her finger. The girl had the man's eyes, but the woman's hair. This man used to be happy and free, but he fell into darkness. He made bad choices, now his family... Lapsus stared at the picture for a minute, then folded it and put it in his pocket.

He stood from the chair, grabbing a wooden staff from the corner of the room. He opened the door and yelled, "Atom! Get someone to fix the *damn* hole in my office wall!"

He slammed the door behind him. A single pencil rolled off the desk and onto the floor, then all was still.

Elsewhere, a dark figure shifted through a rooftop of leaves. It sneered as it saw many young mortals walking below. Since the opening of the Fall Tree Academy, Umbra Mortis hadn't been able to roam freely. It did once, not realizing the risk, and several children fired spells at it. Of course, Umbra Mortis could have killed all of them, but its master was in charge of the little beasts.

Umbra Mortis noticed many changes since the beginning of the school. There were many more children. They flooded the hallways, talking and laughing. How annoying.

Umbra Mortis didn't know what an academy was, but it was all magic training. The rooms above the main room were fully occupied. They were separated by gender, then age, as more and more students joined.

His master had tried to describe Umbra Mortis to the students as a *free spirit*. Well, that was not inaccurate.

Umbra Mortis had surprising amounts of fun scaring said students. In the library, the dining room, the hallways, it had been the most fun Umbra Mortis had in centuries. Overall, it was a peaceful month at the Fall Tree Academy.

Now though, something was in motion, something dark and evil. No one but Umbra Mortis saw. It knew something evil was lurking. It manifested on the walls as static and blood. It crawled behind the walls, lurking within the shadows.

The mark of the Blood Moon Curse manifested within the academy. However, it went unnoticed by most within the establishment. Only one individual had seen it, many times now. The mark of the Blood Moon Curse had been haunting one individual for a month now. It plagued her dreams and appeared when she was alone. She tried to ignore it, since not only did she have a class to teach, but she had plans to look forward to.

Umbra Mortis overheard conversations between Gloria, Ignis, Dux, Njord, Arthur, Julia, Amber, and even Fornacem himself. Only Njord and Dux thought Gloria had anything to worry about.

It was after a class, when Njord dismissed his students, that Gloria asked for a word. She described the mark, worrying about its hauntings.

Umbra Mortis heard Njord say, "Well, I have been investigating the topic of the Blood Moon Curse thoroughly, Gloria. I am not implying you are incorrect, however, there has *never* been documentation of the *Blood Moon Curse* following one individual. Throughout history, it has followed many individuals, then unexpectedly ceased. Er, are you sure that you are not, er, stressed?"

Umbra Mortis saw Gloria sigh, "Um, I'm not sure anymore. Maybe these classes are starting to get to my head. Just makes me even more excited about getting a break."

Umbra Mortis shook its head. That was the *worst* thing the humans have decided thus far. You should *never* ignore the mark of the Blood Moon Curse. However, since it wasn't in Umbra Mortis's place to say, it couldn't warn them. That being said, the next turn of events should be *very* interesting.

Umbra Mortis heard Gloria bid Njord goodnight and walk off. Making a split-second decision, Umbra Mortis followed, shifting quietly through the leaves. As Gloria turned the corner, the mark manifested. The beast crept through the wall and peered at Gloria hungrily, goading her to come closer.

A red summoning circle blazed on the wall, and the gruesome face of a demon snarled at Gloria. Black stars drifted from the circle and faded from existence. Static buzzed angrily around the mark; blood dripping from the wall.

Umbra Mortis felt the temperature drop as a golden summoning circle appeared in front of Gloria's hand and a comet of ice froze the wall. With a faint hissing and quiet laughter, the mark disappeared.

Umbra Mortis saw Gloria set her head in her hands, "Maybe he's right, I should get some rest." She walked briskly to her room, shutting the door quietly behind her.

By this point, even Umbra Mortis was confused. The mark of the Blood Moon Curse was manifesting stronger and stronger because the time grew near... right? Massacre is unavoidable, it always was. Between both realms there had been a several Blood Moon curses. Each time, blood was spilled. Did the mortals know what was happening around them?

Umbra Mortis had discovered the army just last week, but it remained unnoticed by the others. On the last visit to the camp, Umber Mortis had heard a deep voice say, "We have everything in place sir. We organized several waves of attack, as well as numerous strategies. We are ready whenever you are sir."

Day after day, more troops, supplies, and monsters appeared atop the mountain. Umbra Mortis shifted through the camp and saw monsters not seen in centuries.

A guard ran forward, "General! We have more than eighty percent of our attack forces in place. We outnumber them one hundred to one. The troops are ready whenever you are."

The general nodded, "Excellent, inform the camp that we will attack in thirty-six hours."

The man nodded, "Yes sir!" He turned and ran back into the camp.

Umbra Mortis sighed. It personally couldn't wait for the fight to break out. It could truly prove its worth to its master. That was a little more than a day ago.

Umbra Mortis shifted through the leaves and glimpsed outside. Far above on the mountain peaks, something gathered. They caged monsters, prepared spells, and made weapons. They yearned to spill blood and would soon be ready. When they did strike, they would strike hard. A fierce battle was approaching. Blades would fall, screams sound, and blood spill. But where would the curse commence, and who would be damned to suffer bloody hands?

Umbra Mortis thought about war. It had killed many monsters and the enemy fell before it. Maybe Umbra Mortis would have a chance to protect its master after all.

The moon was full, the first phase of the Blood Moon Curse. The night will be eternal. Armies will gather and the moon wait for blood. Next, the moon will turn crimson, and the ground will be painted red. Screams will initiate the process and blood will fuel the curse.

And yet, something was wrong. An army is many, yet the curse needs but one. The ultimate goal may fail, Umbra Mortis thought. While many may perish, the forgotten lord will not expect failure. The silver blade glints wickedly in the light of the moon above an unexpecting person. But will the blade slip? Was a fault hidden in its edge? It may taste blood, but not its true target.

The Fall Tree must call to arms. Blood can be saved, and souls will stay anchored. The mortals will take notice too late. Umbra Mortis expects another day before they are aware. Exactly another day too late. This entire situation was comical. Nevertheless, Umber Mortis will help when the time comes. Did it remember its spells?

Umbra Mortis found an empty classroom and swirled

into its tiny humanoid form. It thought back to the war and decided on something simple. A summoning circle made of static crackled to life. A strand of black electricity shot a hole in the wall. Umbra Mortis scowled. It was still imprinted to Fornacem?

It tried again, the summoning circle crackled, and a small burst of black flames sputtered to life. It held for a second and died. It tried again, and the flames held. Umbra Mortis held the fire in the palm of its hand. It takes practice. Magic responds to power, isn't that what the humans said? Umbra Mortis never thought about what caused magic to materialize. It closed its hand and extinguished the flame.

Umbra Mortis yearned to be... something closer to human. After its fall, it disliked humans. Yet a secret envy had consumed what remained of Umbra Mortis. It had been an eon since it had given up on being human. Humans are stubborn, maybe it was worth another try.

Umbra Mortis shifted and its form grew larger and crackled with static. It flinched, shrinking in pain. It tried again and power fluctuated. It was beginning to affect the air. Papers fell to the floor, the windows cracked. An ink-like substance swirled around it. Its form changed, it grew larger, and finally, Umbra Mortis changed.

It whipped around and faced a cracked mirror. It stopped and gasped. It had eyes in an actual face? That's new. It had formed a face, hands, even hair. It resembled a child. How ironic. This form was the closest to human Umbra Mortis had been in eons.

An unfamiliar emotion manifested. What was falling from its eyes? A clear liquid, what *was* this? Umbra Mortis reached up and wiped the liquid away. Was this possibly... emotion? *Real* human emotion? Could it be human?

Umbra Mortis saw its reflection smile. Something inside it swelled. It felt happy, it felt ludicrously happy. This burden was known as emotion, and it felt *great*. Umbra Mortis laughed. It waved a hand and dark fire circled Umbra Mortis. Umbra Mortis hovered upward, laughing. A pulse of power incinerated the furniture.

No. Umbra Mortis was male in its lifetime. *He* was Umbra Mortis, and *he* was one step closer to humanity.

Let the army come! Umbra Mortis will execute the enemy. They *dare* try to take something as valuable as life away from *him*? They had another thing coming.

Umbra Mortis heard the door creak open. He swirled around and saw Ignis and Amber staring at him. He laughed, a deep sound. "Hello, Ignis, Amber, how nice it is to *actually* see you."

Ignis's eyes widened as he took a step forward, "Holy... Umbra Mortis?"

He nodded, a smile spreading across his face, "*Yes*?" Umbra Mortis didn't know what would happen when the blade fell. He just knew that he was in for a good time.

CHAPTER 2: GLORIA
To the Pacificus Residence

Gloria stood in infinite darkness. By now, she was used to the dreams. She expected some message from Fornacem, but she was sorely mistaken.

Gloria blinked and waited. She noticed a dull red circle of light. Gloria looked upward and gasped. A red moon glared at her. She took a step backward and hit something solid. She yelped, whipping around.

A man she'd never seen before reached out to Gloria, blood pooling from his mouth. He spoke in a hoarse voice, *"Our angel, why?"*

Gloria shook her head, "No, I-I didn't-"

The man fell to the floor, as blood pooled from his mouth.

A gold light surrounded Gloria. She looked up, and a strange figure of light stared at her. Gloria saw a halo above its head. Shimmering wings opened behind it. Gloria would have thought it was an angel, but something was wrong. Its eyes were red, and its hands were soaked in blood. Gloria gasped as it pointed to her and disappeared.

Gloria felt something touch her head. All around her, it rained blood. Gloria stumbled back and tripped. She looked down and screamed at the cold corpse staring back at her. She stood in a bloody battlefield. Fires raged around her, screams plagued the silence. She was in the center of it all. Gloria saw a red moon in the sky above. It shifted to the mark of the Blood Moon Curse.

Black stars swirled around her as she screamed, "Leave me alone!" The mark bellowed with laughter as Gloria's vision turned red. The ground turned into black clouds. Gloria screamed, as she fell from the sky.

Gloria heard a dark voice laughing, *"Poor angel, you've lost your wings. You cannot escape your fate, your destiny."* As the ground raced closer, Gloria's vision went black.

Without knowing how she got there, Gloria found herself kneeling in the center of a thousand corpses. The smell of lavender burned around her. Blood soaked the soil beneath her knees

An alarm blared, Gloria yelped and fell out of bed. A golden comet of ice froze her alarm. Gloria stood quickly, "I hate alarms, why do I still *have* this thing?" She sighed and got ready for the day.

She left her room, taking the stairs straight to the teacher's lounge. There she saw Uncle Dux, Julia, and Arbor. Julia smiled and gestured to her to sit. As Gloria sat, a plate of pancakes was set in front of her.

Uncle Dux took a sip from his coffee, "Ah, you're awake. Njord's in his classroom, just so you know. You two got your bags packed?"

Gloria had just taken a large bite of pancake, so she nodded.

Julia said, "Just so you know, your father *still* thinks that *we* are going to the capital, so, don't say anything otherwise."

Gloria swallowed, "Um, are you sure that we should be *lying* to dad?"

Uncle Dux scoffed, "That's the only way to get *anything* past Arthur. Don't worry, your mother and I have been doing this for *years*." Gloria laughed.

Uncle Dux checked his watch, "Alright, Njord dismisses his class in five minutes, so go!"

Gloria nodded, taking one last sip of her drink, and walked outside. Just as she opened the door, she ducked to avoid a spell.

Gloria called over her shoulder, "No magic outside of class please!"

The last month at the Fall Tree Academy has been a little strange. She suddenly found herself in a room of twenty plus children, all very eager for her every word. She had gotten into a rhythm. She put her studies, and Uncle Dux's teachings, into her work and it was going very well. They were helping Elementalists learn about themselves, their abilities, and so much more.

The hallways were always full of students, running to the library, the training room, or to their rooms for neglected books. Gloria had been enjoying herself. Arbor was a remarkable help. In the first week, he fixed the training room a hundred times. Gloria and Amber had become very good friends. Nothing could be better.

Gloria approached Njord's classroom. She heard him speaking as she opened the door. Njord was holding five books, four with his tentacles and another in his hand. Since he was a Cecaelia, he could do that. He was writing on a chalkboard while reading the books. He had his reading glasses on, as well as a white button-up shirt with a blue tie. He had a young professor vibe. He was describing advanced magic to his students.

"Now, be extremely cautious when manifesting this. Command spells such as *advance* allow the user to fabricate numerous spells before utilization. You could potentially enhance other spells with this tactic since it accelerates the summoning process. You must be aware of all the effects of the spell before doing this. Failure to do so may result in extreme bodily harm."

Gloria quietly stood next to the door and noticed a few of the students snickered as she entered.

Njord spoke again, "Now, I trust that you will *not* attempt magic of this magnitude without proper teacher consultation. This magic is deliberately hazardous without proper instruction. If there are no further questions, this lesson is finished. Please do not forget your personal belongings."

Gloria walked around the desks toward the front of the room and noted a few students lagging behind, pointing. As Gloria approached Njord, she saw that he was talking to himself and reading three books while taking a quick note on a small notepad.

"Er, I should remember that, as well as that. I should request a session in the training room as well..."

Gloria said, "Njord?"

He jumped and dropped everything. A book fell on his foot, and he knocked over a stack of papers. The students laughed and Gloria turned to them, "Alright, everyone out!"

The students left the room, snickering. Njord stood abruptly, his glasses crooked.

"Er, Gloria! Sincerest apologies, I was overly immersed. I was not conscious of your presence." He muttered a spell and a salty wind swirled. The papers flew onto his desk in a neat stack and the books flew back to their shelves.

Njord removed his glasses, and set them in his pocket, "Er, is it time?"

Gloria smiled. Njord nodded and took a deep breath, "V-Very well, I am still psychologically preparing myself, er, I will be ready in a few minutes."

Gloria nodded. Njord said, "Er, why did I have to package

personal belongings?"

Gloria said, "Um, my dad thinks that my *mother* and I are going to the capital. It'll be fine, don't worry."

Njord stared at Gloria, "When you say that I always worry. I do not approve of lying, however…, very well, I will be right back."

Gloria left for the living room, and Njord for his bedroom.

Gloria walked to the end of the hall and knocked on the wall, "Yo, Arbor? Can you take me to the living room?" Gloria stood back as the wall unraveled into branches. A tree root spiraled into a surface, and she stepped onto it. Gloria went through the wall and descended. Gloria loved doing this, she never got tired of the tree's core.

Just outside the rooms was a space where the rooms were suspended by large roots. It was dark, but there were green buds the size of boulders giving off a green light. They all collected in the center where orbs of light traveled along glowing branches.

Gloria imagined it like Arbor's brain and nervous system. Fireflies glowed randomly throughout. Gloria breathed in the smell of fresh air. After a few minutes, the wall opened, and Gloria stepped into the living room.

Gloria tensed as she saw her father and mother arguing, Uncle Dux was leaning against the wall, biting his lip. She heard her father say, "If you're going to the capital then I want to go! It's dangerous out there, Julia!"

Her mother replied, "Arthur, you're needed here! Gloria and I will be just fine on our own."

Arthur sighed, "Can you at least stay in contact with me?"

Julia shook her head, "You *know* that our messages will be intercepted, the less the enemy knows the better."

Julia caught Gloria's eye and nodded. Gloria sighed with

relief and walked to her bag. She smirked. Njord's bag was disguised as Julia's bag, adjourned with large flowers. How her father did *not* suspect something, Gloria didn't know.

Arthur walked over, "Gloria, I don't like you and your mother going alone... Just promise me you will both be safe."

Gloria nodded, "Of course! We'll be fine, dad." She gasped as Njord appeared and quickly said, "Oh! Uh, Dad, um, I just wanted to say that I love you."

Julia snuck over and whispered in Njord's ear. Gloria saw Njord flinch, then disappear.

Arthur smiled, "I love you too, now, please remember, be safe." Gloria nodded; Julia picked up the other bag and they walked out the door.

After the door shut, Julia held the bag in open air, where Njord grabbed it from her hands.

Julia said, "Just like your father said, it is extremely dangerous out there. I trust that Njord will follow the rules, so Gloria, be safe. Contact us *only* in emergencies, once you leave the Pacificus residence, come *straight* home, understand?"

Njord reappeared and nodded, "Absolutely, I completely understand Mrs. Factorem."

"I told you that you can call me Julia. Bye now." She said as she smiled and walked around to the back door.

Njord shouldered the backpack, "Alright, are you all right, Gloria?" Gloria nodded, "Definitely."

They set off for the pond on the north side of the tree. Gloria heard an explosion and remembered that Amber's class was outside today.

She saw Amber flying through the air. "Come on people! Aim is key!" She dodged a glowing comet and smiled, "Excellent!" She caught sight of Gloria and Njord, "Oh, yo people! Take five!"

She swooped down and landed in front of Gloria, "Hey! Did you think you were leaving without saying goodbye? If you two need any help, contact us. I'll drag Ignis if I have to." She smiled and gave Gloria a hug as she whispered in her ear, "No detours, right?"

Gloria punched Amber on the shoulder, "Quiet, you."

Gloria caught sight of Uncle Dux over Amber's shoulder. He stopped in front of them, breathing heavily. "Glad I caught you! Arthur talking about the Capital got me worried." He saw Amber and said, "Uh, hey Amber." He stood up straight. "Anyways, they're right, it's very dangerous. As your personal teacher and acquaintance of Njord, I have no doubt that he- ah- *you'll* be safe. But I sorta worry."

From his pocket, Uncle Dux pulled two strange items. They were small green orbs the size of marbles. One had a black halo in the center and the other a black octopus.

Uncle Dux said, "Took me ages to get a hold of these. They are powerful relics. They allow *combination animarum.*"

Njord blushed, "Er, I understand that you are uneasy, however, do you not think that this is slightly, as they say, overkill? As well as slightly improper? It is similar to operating a tank to travel to the grocery store."

Gloria said, "Um, what is *combination*- whatever it was?"

Uncle Dux said, "*Combination animarum* is a powerful combination spell. It allows two individuals to briefly become one. This essentially combines their powers, skills, minds, and souls. Sure, it is usually for people who are more, er, comfortable. However, in case you're cornered by something like an *Elder Fallen,* you can use these. All you have to do is hold them and say, *simul.* I'd feel better knowing that you had these, Julia as well."

Njord shook his head, "I do not disagree with additional safety measures. However, I would prefer not to use it. However, I could be comfortable using them if Gloria was."

Gloria suddenly remembered that strange dream. She shrugged, taking one of the orbs from Uncle Dux's hand, "Uh, it's fine, we probably won't use it, but just in case."

Njord reluctantly took the other orb. Uncle Dux said, "Alright, Arthur would kill me if he knew that I gave you those."

Gloria said, "Wait, what?"

Uncle Dux ran back to the Tree, "See you later!"

Njord shook his head whispering, "Extra safety measure, this provides more options..."

Gloria elbowed him. He yelped, "Right!" He whipped around and walked toward the small pond. Amber and Gloria waved at each other as they walked away.

The pond was put there by Uncle Dux and mostly used by Njord, but it was a portal that connected all water related areas in the magical realm. At least, that's what Gloria thought. It had a small palm tree hanging over the water and a single lily pad carried a toad. As they approached the lily pad, the toad spoke, "Where to?"

Njord said, "Er, Njord Pacificus and Gloria Factorem, the kingdom of hydro." The toad nodded. Njord turned to Gloria, "E-Er, I require your hand." Gloria nodded and took his hand. Together they walked into the pond and stood in waist deep water.

Njord said, "This may be disorienting, please consider holding your breath."

Gloria gasped as the water rose. She took a deep breath as her head submerged. Gloria opened her eyes, and they were floating in what Gloria thought was deep water. She felt as though a large drain was pulling them down. She saw a light beneath them, and her vision changed.

Gloria and Njord stood in a small cave. Outside the cave was water with multicolored lights glowing from deep beneath the surface. The small pond was just behind them. They both flinched as the toad spoke again, "Have a nice day."

Njord quickly let go of Gloria's hand, "E-Er, here we are."

Njord walked towards the water, "Ah, right, you cannot breathe underwater." Njord reached into his bag and grabbed what Gloria thought was a pearl.

Njord said, "Er, you require consummation of this."

Gloria frowned, "Um, what is that?"

Njord said, "It is an object I borrowed from Dux. It is a sea pearl imbued with mermaid magic. It will allow you to breathe, see, speak, and travel underwater, for as long as you are in water."

Gloria grabbed the pearl and popped it in her mouth.

Njord said, "Er, do not chew, it may taste unpleasant." Gloria swallowed the pearl, but nothing happened.

She said, "Did it work?"

Njord said, "Yes, once you make contact with the water, it will activate. Now, let us continue." He led the way into the water and Gloria followed. They swam down through a cave opening and Gloria recognized the kingdom of hydro.

Njord said, "Er, I suppose that we should visit Cook."

Gloria nodded and they swam to Cook's restaurant. *It hasn't changed at all*, Gloria thought. The bar looked cleaned and polished. Barstools floated a few inches off the ground.

Cook emerged from the kitchen, caught sight of them, and smiled. "Njord! Gloria! Nice to see you two!" Cook said, "What'll it be, eh?"

Njord said, "Er, I have a favor to ask you..."

Cook said, "Anything Njord!"

Njord said, "Er, I recently discovered that my family survived-"

They both jumped as Cook said, "Good for you, Njord!"

Njord continued, "Er, they have not been able to acquire much currently, nor do they have occupations. Could you please supply them with nourishment?"

Cook said, "Of course! Just tell them where I am! It'll

be on-the-house whenever they want! Besides, not many folks around eat here anyways."

Njord sighed with relief, "You have my gratitude Cook."

Cook bellowed with laughter, "Any time Njord! In fact, why don't I make them something?" Without another word, he disappeared behind the curtain.

Gloria and Njord sat on the barstools. Gloria heard Cook humming in the kitchen. Gloria swiveled her chair and looked around. She saw Mer children playing games and laughing.

Gloria turned to Njord, "By the way, you know how to get to your parent's place?"

Njord flinched as though caught off guard by the question. With a thoughtful expression, he answered, "Well, technicality, no. I have received vague directions from letters, and Fornacem. I am not familiar with their new establishment."

Gloria nodded, "I'm sure it'll be fine."

Njord nodded. A small soccer ball-like object bounced off his head and Njord grabbed it.

Gloria heard a child's voice, "Sorry!" Gloria chuckled.

Njord said, "That is alright." He tossed it back to the children.

Gloria said, "First coins and now soccer balls?"

Njord said, "That will not be a habit."

Gloria laughed, Njord smiled. Gloria thought she heard something behind her. She turned around where bubbles drifted from behind the bar. The next second, Cook reappeared carrying two large crates in a bag.

Njord said, "Oh... Cook-"

Cook interrupted, "Don't say anything, I've been in a position like theirs before. I put all kinds of stuff in here. Uh, no calamari."

Gloria took the bag; it didn't feel heavy, probably because they were underwater.

Njord said, "You have my gratitude, Cook."

Cook smiled, "Don't mention it, anyways, see you two later!" He waved and disappeared into the kitchen.

Njord shook his head, "He is very generous."

Gloria said, "Where to from here?"

Njord pulled a map from his pocket, along with his reading glasses. He was silent for a moment and started to point left. He jumped and pointed right, "Er, that way."

They swam forward, then downward. Gloria saw a large hole in the wall.

Njord said, "Er, this way." They swam forward, passing large stone columns that went to the roof of the cavern.

Gloria swam beneath a patch of seaweed, "This seems remote."

Njord spoke without looking away from the map, "Er, my father has become extremely paranoid. Mostly due to the Capital's attempt to capture us. He has never completely believed they were safe, which is the reason behind hidden, secluded areas."

Gloria nodded and she saw something in the distance, "Is that it?"

Njord looked up from his map and froze, "Er, yes, it is."

They stopped at a small metal gate in a small fence which surrounded a wooden shack. The boards were waterlogged and covered with moss. The roof seemed ready to collapse and a crooked chimney coughed out smoke. There were a few cracked windows of different size and shape. Gloria saw an empty battered trash can beyond the door. Gloria also saw a small sand pit holding small plastic shovels, buckets, and other toys. Gloria could hear quiet voices from inside.

Njord stood there for a moment, Gloria turned to him, "Njord?"

He flinched, slowly putting his glasses and map in his pocket.

Gloria said, "Are you alright?"

He was silent for a few more moments and then he said, "This establishment holds identical aspects of our first home." Njord took a deep breath, "E-Er, I am not ready. What will I say? What will they do? How will they respond by seeing both of us?"

Gloria set a hand on his shoulder, "Njord, calm down! It'll be fine, they'll be happy to see you." She grabbed his arm and slowly led him through the gate. It creaked as it swung shut. They walked up a withered stone path to the door. Gloria saw a few fish dart from the grass. She stepped on something, looked down and saw a soaked box of crayons.

Njord said, "Maria loves drawing."

Gloria nudged Njord and they continued walking. They stopped in front of the door. Njord raised his hand to knock, but he hesitated.

He took a step backwards, "What if this is wrong? What if they are angry? I should have sent more letters!"

Gloria took his arm and pulled him back, "Come on Njord, they're your family, they love you, and they miss you. How do you think little Maria felt when you disappeared?"

Njord's face turned grim. Gloria said, "How would *you* have felt if it was *Maria* that disappeared?"

Njord said, "I would have been devastated! I would have been worried sick! I-"

Gloria said, "Now imagine receiving a letter from her years later."

Njord was silent for a moment, he said, "I... I would be ecstatic-"

Gloria said, "Then that will be how your family feels. Now, are you ready?" Njord was silent for a minute. He nodded.

He raised a hand to the door and hesitated. Gloria nudged him, Njord said, "Er, can you please-?" Gloria chuckled, raised a hand, and knocked on the door. There was silence for a moment.

Njord said, "Do I look presentable? Did I brush my teeth? How is my hair?"

Before Gloria could respond, she heard a voice from inside, "Maria, could you please get the door?" Gloria heard a small click and the door swung inward.

Maria was a young Cecaelia. She looked no older than seven. Gloria noticed gray spots along her arms and tentacles, which were yellow. She had bright yellow eyes. There was a small flower braided in her dark blonde hair. She wore a shirt with a smiley face drawn on the front and she was holding a single crayon in her hand.

There was silence, Gloria said, "Ooh! Is this Maria? She is *so* cute!"

Njord said, "Er, Hello Maria, I have returned." Gloria saw Maria drop the crayon she was holding. There was a long silence and Maria suddenly darted down the hallway. She yelled, "Mama! Papa! Njord brought a pretty lady home!"

Njord jumped, he said, "Wha- wait a moment!" He swam into the house, Gloria just behind him.

Gloria shut the door behind her and turned to the hallway. She counted six drawings of flowers in crayon on the walls. She was standing on a weathered pink rug. The hall ended in a T just ahead, Gloria saw Maria swim to the right.

Gloria and Njord followed Maria into the kitchen, where Gloria saw another figure with gray tentacles and black spots running up his arms and legs. He had gray hair. Gloria assumed this was Njord's father.

The Cecaelia tensed and stood abruptly. "How could I have forgotten? Njord and Gloria?"

Njord hesitated.

Gloria said, "Um, Hello."

The Cecaelia swam to Njord and said, "Has my son really returned?" He hugged Njord, "Welcome home."

Gloria saw Njord smile, "Father, I-"

The Cecaelia said, "No more, Njord."

He turned to Gloria, "My name is Oceanus Pacificus. It is a pleasure to meet you." Gloria heard steps from the other room and a new figure ran in.

The woman was human. She had dark blonde hair with green eyes. She was wearing an old pair of jeans with a tie dye shirt. It looked like a sunset.

She stood there a moment. Njord said, "Mother-"

The lady whipped one of her sandals off her feet. Maria swam behind Oceanus. The lady stormed towards Njord and glared at him, "*Where* have you *been*? You show up after *all* these years? Do you have *any* idea how worried *sick* I have been?"

Njord's eyes started glowing and he kept an eye on the sandal, "I-I was under the impression that you knew that I was visiting-"

The lady smacked Njord upside the head with her sandal as she hugged him. Tears formed in her eyes. "Don't you *ever* leave us like that again, do you *understand* me, Njord Pacificus?" Njord nodded frantically.

Oceanus said, "My love-" The lady stormed towards him.

She waved her sandal threateningly, "And as for *you*, why didn't you give me *any* sort of heads up! I could have been cooking! Or cleaning! Or *literally anything* that would have helped! Do you have *any* idea *why* I'm angry? How could *anything* with a brain have as *little* common sense?"

Oceanus said, "I-I forgot..." The lady took a deep breath, she turned towards Gloria.

"Terribly sorry that you had to see that. I'm Njord's mother, Caribe Pacificus, how are you?"

Gloria said, "Um, I'm good..."

Caribe said, "Now, why don't we take a seat?"

◆ ◆ ◆

They sat at a round wooden dinner table. Gloria had unpacked the food from Cook, which Caribe hurriedly reheated and served. As they sat around the table Maria said, "I've never seen so much food before!" She smiled at Gloria, "Thank you, pretty lady!"

Caribe said, "Maria, she has a name, don't be rude. Now, Gloria, is it? Tell me about yourself."

Gloria nodded, "Um, originally I'm from Earth-"

Oceanus nodded, "A mortal? Forgive me, I mistook you for a witch."

Caribe scowled at him, "It's rude to interrupt! Please, continue."

Gloria found herself describing her time in the magical realm.

Caribe scowled, "When I see whoever this *Fornacem* is, I'll make sure he knows fury."

Gloria saw that Caribe had regained her sandal. She also noted that every Cecaelia in the room was looking away, their eyes were glowing.

Gloria said, "Oh, I just realized, Njord told me that he had a sandal phobia."

They all flinched. Caribe laughed and waved the sandal around, "Unfortunately, the sandal is the only way to get Caecilians to pay attention. Sometimes they need a good whack upside the head. Right?"

Oceanus said, "E-Er, yes."

Caribe leaned over the table, "If you ever need to straighten a Cecaelia out, consider threatening them with a shoe."

Gloria smiled, Njord said, "E-Er, I also would like to mention. There is a person I am acquainted with. He possesses a food stand. He is inclined to provide sustenance if needed."

Caribe smiled, "I missed the way you talk. Well, we will definitely take that offer. Maria hasn't seen a meal like this in a while."

Gloria watched as Maria ate fish. Gloria found Maria's happy smile infectious.

Oceanus said, "Njord, if I may ask, can you please tell me what happened all those years ago."

Njord grimaced, but nodded, "Er, v-very well."

Njord described the attack on the city, the Elder Fallen, and the Capital in disturbing detail. Gloria noticed he neglected to mention the torture section of the story.

Caribe stood and held her sandal in her hand. She scowled, "If I ever lay eyes of this Fornacem, I'll whack him where the sun don't shine!"

Njord said, "Mother! Please, he is one of the ten kings!"

Caribe said, "King or not, this sandal will taste blood! Ooh, I swear to the lords above-"

At this point her argument descended into rapid Spanish, so Gloria missed a few key details. She did notice that Oceanus covered Maria's ears during the first half of Caribe's yelling.

As Njord was trying to get Caribe under control, Gloria heard a voice in her head, "Gloria! It's Ignis-"

Gloria gasped, "Ignis?"

The arguing stopped abruptly. Gloria stood, she heard Ignis again, "Gloria!"

Njord stood as well. He said, "What is wrong? Are you alright Gloria?"

Gloria shook her head, "I don't know! I just heard Ignis, I think somethings wrong!"

Njord said, "Er, communication magic is enhanced through magic in the air. Activate your aura, Gloria!"

Gloria did. Maria said, "Ooh, pretty!"

Gloria heard Ignis again, "Gloria! It's Ignis! There's a big problem at the Tree! Lapsus sent an army. We're in battle right now! They said something about California, a beach named Huntington.

Don't try to come here! They destroyed all the portals and declared war! We don't know why but I-I think this has something to do with the Blood Moon Curse!

Uncle Dux thinks Lapsus intends to activate the curse. He said that you and Njord are the only ones who can stop it! Go to Huntington Beach, hurry-"

Gloria heard a loud explosion, "Shoot, gotta go! Amber! Hold that thing back-"

His voice suddenly cut off, Njord said, "Gloria, what happened?"

Gloria looked to Njord, "We have a serious problem Njord."

Gloria ran out of the shack without much explanation. The Pacificus family chased after her.

Njord said, "Wait! We arrived forty minutes ago! Where are we going?"

Gloria shook her head, "Huntington Beach, California. Lapsus is up to something. We need to get there, now!"

Njord said, "What of the others? Are they alright? Will they assist us?"

Gloria said, "They are in a battle apparently and we're all stuck. They destroyed the portals in the valley. All I know is I'm going to seriously hurt Lapsus."

Caribe said, "Wait."

Gloria stopped just short of the gate. Caribe handed Njord their bags. "You'll need these. I added a few sandwiches."

She added in a whisper, "As well as a pair of sandals, they

are surprisingly effective against things without feet."

Njord said, "Wait! We do not have any propositions! What will we do? What will we encounter?"

Oceanus said, "Your friends are in danger, Njord. You are strong enough to help. We will see you when you are successful."

Gloria jumped and looked down where Maria was hugging her leg, "Visit us again, pretty lady!"

Njord looked helplessly to Gloria, "I-I do not wish to abandon my family again."

Caribe hugged him, "You will not. After you're done with, whatever it is you're doing, send us a message."

Njord hesitated, Caribe yelled, "Go! We'll be fine."

Njord sighed, "V-Very well."

CHAPTER 3: GLORIA
An Elaborate Scheme

After five minutes of hugs, an additional twenty minutes of wrong turns, and ten more to find a portal, Gloria found herself on Earth in front of a busy Walmart. She looked around but didn't see Njord.

Immediately, she heard his voice, "One would find it reasonable that the sighting of a creature such as me would raise concern."

Gloria said, "Can't you do that human transformation thingy?"

Njord was silent for a moment. He said quietly, "Er, I require proper human clothes for that. I only possess a shirt." Gloria sighed and they walked into the Walmart, Njord still invisible.

Half an hour later, Gloria was sitting on a beach under an umbrella. Njord had brought two towels, a pair of boxers, as well as boardshorts. He accidentally forgot to pay for them. They were sitting staring at the ocean. Gloria had to support Njord to stand at first, since he wasn't used to human legs.

Gloria was slightly bitter. She had always dreamed of taking Njord to a beach, but under these circumstances, they weren't going to enjoy themselves. They had a small laugh when Gloria noticed Njord staring at a few seagulls. Njord paled when Gloria had put on Caribe's sandals.

Now though, Gloria was starting to remember a few details. Ignis mentioned an army and a battle. Ignis just mentioned an attack on Huntington Beach. But the beach was *huge*, there was no telling what may happen where.

A heat wave had settled over the town, despite it being November. Njord decided that this wasn't a coincidence. The beach was densely crowded with many people enjoying the waves.

Njord said, "Er, I can understand how the beach may be pleasant. There is the, er, sand, the sea, you are able to construct miniature structures from the sand. It *is* pleasant here, however, I feel as though the seagulls are observing me rather intensively."

Gloria snorted, "A *single* seagull lands next to you *one time*, Njord."

Njord scowled, "It was attempting murder!"

Gloria laughed, Njord smiled. Gloria said, "We've been here a while and there's no telling what may happen. We have no way of contacting the others. If Ignis is right, and Lapsus is trying to achieve the Blood Moon Curse... um, what do you think?"

Njord gained a thoughtful expression, "Well, the Blood Moon Curse requires numerous sacrifices. Therefore, my theory is that Lapsus plans to execute humans in order to achieve this. Given the staggering number of sacrifices required, it would be expected that Lapsus would target densely populated areas. We have no way of telling *where* he may target. Our only solid idea is that he is planning to attack here. The only plan of action possible is to observe what happens during the encounter, then evaluate our next objective."

Gloria nodded, "Um, makes sense, I guess."

Njord suddenly sat up straight, "There is a magical

anomaly manifesting one hundred feet in front of us! We need to evacuate the people immediately!"

Gloria said, "Ah, alright, why would people leave the beach... Oh! Njord, make a storm! A big one, lots of flashing lightning, loud thunder!"

Njord said, "I do not fully understand your logic, but very well!"

Njord put a hand behind his back and Gloria saw a small black summoning circle blaze in his palm. Njord said, "*Kraken, iratum mare.*"

Gloria saw the white clouds above turn inky black. They swirled into a large storm cloud that covered the entire beach. A giant flash of thunder lit up the horizon and a loud crack of thunder made Gloria flinch.

After a few minutes, Gloria heard a voice crackle from a megaphone, "Due to the approaching storm, the beach is now closed. Everyone please evacuate, immediately."

A strong wind blew into Gloria, as locals ran past. She stared at Njord, "I said storm, *not* hurricane."

Njord smiled sheepishly, "It is not a hurricane."

Gloria opened her mouth and a large wave of salty water crashed into her face. Her vision swirled and she felt something wrap around her ankle. The next thing she knew, she was standing next to Njord, fifty feet from where they had been.

Njord pointed to the sea. Gloria saw the water boil and a large golden figure appeared from the waves. Its golden skin was slick with water and the waves came to its knees. The sand groaned under its weight. Its golden eyes flashed, and blue flames danced from inside it.

Gloria groaned angrily, "I *hate* those things! Why couldn't it have been a few Furnace Fallen? Or a fiery snake? I *freaking hate* these things!"

Njord said, "Look out!"

Gloria looked up as she heard a dreadfully familiar *clunk*. She saw a wave of blue flames roaring towards her.

"HO-!" She threw up a wall of ice and a large cloud of steam bellowed around her.

She heard Njord yell, "Woah! *Kraken, fulgur percutiens, antecessum!*"

A clap of thunder exploded like a cannon shot behind Gloria. She peered out from behind her barricade and saw Njord fighting the Elder Fallen, who made a clunking noise.

Njord ducked under its swing, "Combat is extremely divergent with legs!"

Gloria said, "Hang on!"

She flared her aura and heard a familiar chiming. She looked down and was using her angelic aura. After discovering a name for it, the attack aura, Gloria decided to name it something else. Gloria jumped. For a moment her vision was red. She looked down and saw her hands shining with blood. A strange buzzing filled her ears.

She heard Njord yell, "Gloria! Assistance would be appreciated!"

Gloria blinked and her vision returned to normal.

She leaped towards the Elder Fallen but veered over its head, "Wha-woah!" She crashed into the ocean and the water froze around her.

She sat up and shook sand from her hair, "Njord! What happened?"

Njord was blocking the Elder Fallen's fists, but he yelled, "Within the magical realm, magicules are densely packed in the atmosphere. On Earth, there are none! Therefore, your normal fighting strategies may be off. It is similar to transitioning from swimming in water, to swimming in oil."

Gloria said, "Talk about a pain!"

Njord said, "Communicate your thoughts *following* the defeat of this monster!"

Gloria scrambled to stand, "Oh! Right! Sorry!"

She threw her hands forward, "Been wanting to try this, *sanctus Calix!*"

A small ball of ice appeared out of nowhere. Instantly, the water surrounding Gloria froze solid. A golden summoning circle appeared around the comet. Gloria urged the ball forward and it surged from her hands. The sand was thrown in either direction. When it hit the Elder Fallen, it exploded. The Elder Fallen was catapulted into a nearby bathhouse.

Gloria gasped, Njord was frozen solid. She ran to him, "Oh, Njord! I didn't realize what that was! I'm sorry!"

Gloria touched the surface of the ice and absorbed it into her palm with a flash of light.

Njord fell to the ground shivering, "For future reference, announce a warning before utilizing fourth tier magic."

Gloria flinched, "*Fourth? Really?*"

Gloria whipped toward the bathhouse as the rubble shifted. The Elder Fallen stood, shaking dust from its head.

Gloria stamped her foot, "*Sure!* Send one of the *only* monsters that can't be killed by ice! Njord-" He flinched as she said his name, "Hit it with lightning!"

Njord shook his head, "Er, how intense-?"

Gloria yelled, causing Njord to flinch, "If it moves it wasn't strong enough!"

Njord said, "If you say so!"

Njord stood and closed his eyes. Gloria saw the clouds swirl above his head. Njord waved his hand and a large black summoning circle blazed around his feet. Thunder cracked, the wind howled, lightning crackled through Njord's hair. He opened his eyes; they were glowing solid green.

He said, "This will be primed in one minute."

Gloria said almost hysterically, "I didn't ask for a warmup!"

Njord flinched, "I- wha- er- sincerest apo-"

Gloria stamped her foot, "Never mind! Just make sure it works!"

The Elder Fallen stepped closer. Gloria said, "Try this! Uh, *duratus, crescit, antecessum!*"

A ball of ice formed in her hand, grew slightly and started to spin, then rocketed toward the Elder Fallen. It collided with its shoulder, freezing its arm in place. It made a clunking noise and the ice shattered. It stepped towards Gloria before it suddenly stopped.

Gloria hesitated then threw a comet of ice, but it ducked before standing upright again. Gloria turned towards Njord, "Hey, Njord-?"

There was a blinding flash and a rippling explosion. Gloria was thrown head over heels. She landed in the sea, spitting salt water out of her mouth. She saw Njord in front of her, offering her a hand, "I did not mean to affect you. I apologize."

Gloria took his hand and stood. That was when she looked towards the Elder Fallen.

There was a large crater, twenty feet in diameter and ten foot deep. The sand surrounding it had been turned into glass. The Elder Fallen lie smoking in the center of the crater.

Gloria said, "Do you think that worked?"

Gloria saw a ripple of darkness above the Elder Fallen. Njord said, "Unfortunately, I do not."

Gloria saw a strange figure appear from the portal. Gloria had to blink, she thought it was an alien. It had gray skin and colorful solid eyes, but it was wearing human clothes. Gloria saw it was holding a clipboard. There was a small moon-like object slowly orbiting its head.

The figure said, "Ah, not good. I need to report this-"

He saw Gloria and Njord and froze, "Oh, er, greetings humans. I am *Atom.*"

Gloria said, "Um, do you work for Lapsus?"

Atom hesitated, "Er, *who*?" He ducked as a comet of ice flew over his head, "Wait!" He dodged another spell, shot upward into the air and hovered. He said, "You humans are so aggressive!" He said, "Er, sorry, *impetum*."

Gloria heard a clunk, and the Elder Fallen leaped from the crater, charging towards them.

Njord said, "*Fluctus!*" A wave of water briefly blinded the Elder Fallen and Njord ducked under its legs.

Gloria heard Atom say, "Humans can use magic? I must take a note!"

Gloria saw him scribble onto the clipboard. She launched another comet at him.

He looked upward and yelped. He ducked and the clipboard fell from his hands. Gloria saw it land on the ground and scooped it up.

Gloria stuck it in her backpack, "Heh, *yoink*." Then she ran back towards the battle.

Njord ducked under the Elder Fallen's swing and hit it with another bolt of lightning.

Gloria heard Atom say, "Oh no! Where is it?" Gloria suddenly didn't feel her feet on the ground. She looked downward, she was running on air.

Gloria said, "Uh, *what*?" She felt something tug her backwards, she turned around and saw Atom. He pointed a hand to her, he said, "You must have it. Can I please have that back?"

Gloria screamed, "Njord!" Gloria saw Atom's eyes widen, and she saw him wave his hand. Immediately, Gloria fell towards the ground. She looked upward and saw that the Elder Fallen had been launched at Atom.

She felt Njord catch her, and they ran from the beach. They stopped behind a bathroom and Gloria took the clipboard from her backpack.

Njord glanced at her and gained a confused expression, "What is that?"

Gloria said, "I don't know, but that thing dropped it." She saw the words Huntington Beach on the front.

Gloria said, "Oh! Njord! I think this belongs to Lapsus!" Before Njord could say anything, the bathhouse exploded behind them. They landed on the road and Gloria looked up to see the alien floating there.

Orbiting him were cars, bricks, and large pieces of buildings, he said, "I tried to be nice! I do not like hurting humans... but you two seem to be advanced."

Gloria said, "Um, Adam's angry."

Atom sighed, "It's *Atom*! A-T-O-M, you humans are annoying!"

Gloria saw one of the cars shoot towards them, Gloria grabbed Njord's arm and yanked him out of the way, "Good lord!" She yelled.

They staggered to a stop as a van crashed in front of them; the Elder Fallen stomped towards them. As they ran behind an overturned bus, Gloria said, "What do we do, Njord?"

Njord said, "Atom is observing from the air while the Elder Fallen attacks us from the ground. Since ice does not affect Elder Fallen, I will preoccupy it, can you attend to Atom?"

Gloria nodded, "Got it, in case things go south, uh, yell a safe word."

Njord said, "What is a safe word?"

Gloria said, "A word that secretly lets me know something. If we need to run, yell... calamari."

Njord scowled, "Does it necessarily *have* to be *calamari*?"

Gloria smiled, "Yes." She ran from behind the bus.

Gloria yelled up to the alien, "Yo, Adam! Let's dance!"

Atom scowled, "It's *Atom*!"

Gloria saw another volley of cars soar towards her. She blasted them out of the sky and launched a spear of ice towards Atom. Gloria saw it veer right, orbit Atom, and launch back at her.

Gloria leaped sideways, "*No* good!" The spear embedded itself in the road. Gloria said, "Warning! *Angelus Mortis!*"

A black figure appeared from nowhere, shaped like an angel, but made of black flames. Uncle Dux had taught Gloria this spell. He said that it was a dark spell invented by Ice Elementalists. He said that it was mainly used to hold off Elder Fallen in the war. They were supposedly unkillable, the more elemental power the caster had, the longer the curse would last.

Gloria said, "*Impetum!*"

The angel split into two and screamed. They dived for the *Elder Fallen*. Gloria shouted, "Now Njord! Run!"

She saw Njord jump over a car, and they both ran up the street. Another car fell in front of them as they dived into a plaza.

Gloria recognized the Walmart from earlier, "Njord! Behind the store!"

They ran to the back of the Walmart and collapsed behind a dumpster. As Gloria sat down black spots appeared in her vision.

Njord said, "While the angel of death spell is rather effective, it did not appear to be able to engage Atom. Er, are you alright?"

Gloria shook her head, "Yeah, fine, I don't know how many more spells I'll be able to use. I'll be stuck with normal elemental attacks soon."

Njord said, "It is enervating to use spells here, due to the deficiency of magicules."

Gloria said, "*Noticed.*"

She heard a scream, "Well, the angel of death wore out,

now what?"

Njord said, "I do not know, combat with an Elder Fallen is something that we are both rather experienced with. However, Atom adds various complications, we do not know what he may be capable of. From what I can gather, he can distort and alter gravity, this includes orbits, gravitational fields, and the force of the mass of an object."

Gloria said, "*Lovely*, sometimes I'm glad you're a nerd."

Njord shook his head, Gloria said, "Again, *now what*?"

Before Njord could answer, he shot upward as though caught on a fish hook.

Gloria stood abruptly, "*Njord?*" She felt large hands clamp around her arms. She was lifted into the air in the hands of the Elder Fallen.

She kicked her feet, "*How* is something so *heavy,* so *quiet*?" She screamed. Atom appeared over the roof.

He said, "I truly am sorry, you seem like nice people."

Gloria saw Njord struggling against the air next to him.

Gloria said, "Let him go!"

Atom said, "Unfortunately I cannot. You have something of mine. Also, my master wishes to speak with you."

Gloria said, "If you don't, I'll have to use my... secret weapon."

Njord and Atom both gained confused expressions, Atom said, "I have studied humans thoroughly. While you may be slightly different, there is nothing about humans that I do not know."

Gloria said, "If you don't let us go, I'll... explode your brain telepathically!"

Njord and Atom both gained frightened looks, Atom said, "H-Humans possess no such ability."

Gloria said, "But did you study *both* genders of humans?"

Atom hesitated, "I... did not."

Gloria said, "*Then*, you wouldn't know that women *have* such a thing. It's called *calamari*."

Njord gained an even more confused expression, then gasped, and nodded, "Yes! Humans have used calamari for many bloody incidents! It is quite horrific!"

As Njord was speaking, Gloria chanted under her breath, "*Occisio execratione maledicta congessit, antecessum.*"

From her hands, a black light streaked into the Elder Fallen. Spreading from its hands, its golden skin started to turn black. It made a clunking noise, and it staggered, but it still held Gloria.

This was a risky, last resort, an advanced killing curse. All that it did was absorb the magicules out of the target. The risk was that it also absorbed the magical energy from the caster. The more the killing curse worked, the more magicules it used, completely draining the caster. If this didn't work...

Atom said, "How have humans become so advanced? There are many species that I know of that can't do that!"

Njord nodded, Gloria noticed a black summoning circle in the palm of his hand. Njord said, "Yes! Beware the deadly calamari!"

Gloria began to feel the effects of the curse. The dark spots danced in her eyes, something red dripped from her hands. She shook her head, holding herself upright. The Elder Fallen made another clunking noise as the curse covered its whole body. Gloria felt its grip loosen and she let herself slip to the ground.

Atom turned towards Gloria, "Wait-"

Njord interrupted, "There is another human ability that you neglected. *Human ingenuity*." Njord said, "*Fulgur*." A fork of lightning arced from the sky and struck Atom. He fell to the roof.

Njord dropped next to Gloria. Njord tapped her shoulder,

"Gloria? Gloria!"

She groaned, sitting upright, "Am I dead?"

Njord smiled, "No. You are quite alive." Njord pointed to the Elder Fallen, "You did quite a lot of damage."

Gloria turned towards the Elder Fallen, the blue flames inside it were flickering weakly and the ice had turned black. It fell to its knees, and it didn't move again.

Njord said, "I predict that we have had our tolerance of combat for today. I suggest that we locate a place to rest."

Gloria nodded, "Yeah, of course. Just give me a moment."

It took them a while, but they finally found a motel.

Gloria stopped Njord at the door, "Ah, why don't you turn invisible?"

Njord said, "Why is that? Is it not human custom to inform the clerk?"

Gloria avoided Njord's eyes, she said, "Ok, you're *very* nice, and *innocent*, so you wouldn't understand *why* two *teenagers* renting a motel room *alone* is *not* good."

Njord said, "I do not understand. I will trust your opinion however."

Gloria saw him vanish, and she heard him say, "Do not worry, I will not leave your side."

Gloria said, "Kay, good, let's go." They entered the lobby.

A desk clerk said, "Welcome to hotel 39 Westminster. How can I help you?"

Gloria noticed that the clerk was slightly suspicious, he was glancing at Gloria's worn clothes. Gloria reasoned that if a dirty, ragged, and tired teenager staggered into *her* lobby, she'd give them looks too.

Gloria said, "Um, room for t- er, one."

Gloria set money on the desk, the clerk said, "Umm, do

you need anything else?"

Gloria said, "No thanks." The clerk hesitated but took the money and gave Gloria a room key.

"Um, room thirteen. Have a nice night."

Gloria took the key and exited the lobby. She found their room down an outdoor hallway. Gloria opened the door, set the key on the nightstand and jumped on the closest bed.

The door swung shut and Njord appeared out of thin air.

Njord said, "E-Er, I managed to salvage your bag, as well as your other pair of clothing. I also retrieved the clipboard that Atom dropped."

Gloria sighed, "Well, that's good. I'm gonna take a shower and crash."

She heard Njord say as she shut the door, "Er, very well."

The next morning, Gloria woke to a knock on the door. She jumped and scanned the room, finding Njord sprawled on the other bed. Gloria scooped up her sandal and threw it at him. He yelped as it smacked his face. A lady's voice said, "Housekeeping." Njord disappeared as the door opened.

Gloria said, "We- I'm good! Come back later!"

The lady nodded and shut the door, which Gloria ran to and locked.

Njord reappeared, "That person frightened me, I held the concept that it was an unfriendly individual."

Gloria sighed. After they brushed their teeth and raided the mini fridge, they sat on the beds to plan. Njord grabbed the clipboard and filed through it. He pulled his reading glasses from his pocket and started to pace.

He said, "Oh, er, hmm…"

Gloria said, "*Details*?"

Njord said, "Yes. From what I am understanding, Lapsus

targeted a few places in both realms. The first one was Huntington Beach, California."

Gloria nodded, "Well, crisis averted, I guess."

Njord said, "*Impossible*, he plans to attack... *A Bestia city*? Why would he attempt an attack with Lord Behemoth in such close proximity?"

Gloria said, "Wait... A Bestia city?"

Njord said, "Well, sector seventy-eight, C-Four. But, why would he do that? There are population numbers for there as well as Huntington Beach. Does this mean that if he was not successful here, he plans to attack there?"

Njord gasped and Gloria said, "What? What is it?"

Njord took off his glasses, "Lapsus... If the attack on the Bestia city fails... He plans to attack the Fall Tree Academy."

Gloria gasped, "Does that mean that he already attacked the Bestia city? Ignis said that they were fighting an army."

Njord shook his head, "I do not think so. The attack on Huntington Beach has just now been unsuccessful. This means that Lapsus intends to engage the Bestia city next."

Gloria said, "Then... Why is there an army fighting at the Fall Tree Academy?"

Njord closed his eyes and started tapping his glasses on his chin. He stood there for a moment like that.

He scowled, opened his eyes and said, "No, this does not compute! What is the logic behind organizing a premature attack? This does not make sense!"

Gloria said, "What do you mean?"

Njord huffed, "I mean to say, I can identify absolutely no logic or anything to gain with this premature attack. If anything, it only warned us of endangerment. It is as though Lapsus acted upon a whim."

Gloria shook her head, "So, now what?"

Njord started to pace, stubbed his toe on the bedpost and tripped.

Gloria ran to his side, "Are you alright?"

Njord sat upward, "Yes, I am... Wait a moment..."

Njord stood upward and walked to the wall. He grabbed a stray marker from a table and started drawing on the wall.

Gloria said, "Um, I'm not sure housekeeping will appreciate that."

Njord ignored her and continued drawing. After a few minutes, Gloria sighed and sat on the bed. Gloria watched as maps, equations, and charts appeared. They soon covered every wall. Njord stood in the center, looking at them.

He suddenly gasped. Gloria, who had dozed off on the bed, awoke with a yelp to find Njord standing next to her, staring at the wall.

Gloria said, "What's wrong?"

Njord shook his head, "It is in the center."

Gloria said, "What?"

Njord turned to Gloria, "The Fall Tree Academy is in the center! It is precisely corresponding with five different locations. With the Fall Tree Academy in *the center*! Lapsus has already held attacks previously!"

Gloria said, "Um, you lost me."

Njord sighed, took Gloria's hand and pulled her to the wall.

He pointed to one of his maps, "Gloria, what do you notice when you see this map?"

Gloria said, "Oh! I know this one! It's a map!"

Njord said, "No! Observe closely!" Gloria rolled her eyes, then stared at the map. Gloria saw scribbled markings that surrounded the Fall Tree Academy. Exactly five locations... Exactly the same distance apart...

Njord said, "Do you recall the reports of terrorist attacks over the last fortnight?"

Gloria vaguely remembered, the reporters had little to no information. Uncle Dux had increased the security by the

Tree tenfold.

Gloria said, "Yeah?"

Njord grabbed a marker, "Are they not in a strange pattern?"

Gloria nodded. There had been an attack within the celestial forests, a goblin massacre by the sounds of it, as well as an explosion in the swamps, missing reports in two villages, and finally a large magnitude earthquake in a small city. Just as Njord said, they all surrounded the valley. One in the south, one east, one west, one in the north east, and the final one north west.

Njord said, "Do you remember our students' discussion about blood circles?"

Gloria nodded, "Of course, they were trying to summon minor demons as a prank."

Njord said, "What do you require for this?"

Gloria said, "Something connecting in a pentagram pattern, salt, chalk, magic-"

Njord interrupted, "Magic, that is correct! What do blood circles do?"

Gloria said, "Summon demons and curses."

Njord said, "What initiates a blood circle?"

Gloria said, "Blood? Ugh! what are you trying to say, Njord?"

Njord said, "This-" He pointed to the map, "This is a careful, elaborate, and gruesome scheme. Lapsus requires blood and a curse. He attacked the forests-"

Njord touched the marker to the celestial forests. "The city-"

He traced the marker across the valley to the city. "The swamp-"

As Njord traced the marker back to the swamps, Gloria gasped silently, she took a few steps back.

Njord said, "And the villages." He traced from the swamp to the villages, Gloria gasped. A red pentagram glared at her from the wall, the Fall Tree Academy was right in the center.

Njord set the marker on the table next to him, "Lapsus has created a sacrificial circle that covers the entire valley. Meaning that any blood spilled within the circle... will contribute to a curse, the Blood Moon Curse."

Gloria jumped to her feet, "Oh my lord! We should go!"

Njord said, "Wait a moment. Even if Lapsus plans to do this... I do not think this would affect the curse. He is blindly attacking... Does he require human blood?"

Njord stood there for a moment lost in thought. Finally, he said, "I predict that Lapsus is heavily underestimating the Bestia. Even if Lapsus attacks the Behemoth Capital, they have the most advanced armies and defenses of the entire magical realm. I predict that he is not aware of this. He is solely focused on cities of high populations. The populations of the Bestia city are vast, more than enough for his requirements."

Gloria said, "So...?"

Njord said, "Even if we were not there, I doubt that he could harm the Bestia, most adults are capable of combat..." Njord gasped, "Of course! Lapsus plans to distract the most advanced army in the magical realm! Leaving the Fall Tree Academy *vulnerable*!"

Gloria said slowly, "What do you mean?"

Njord said, "The ten kings are on high alert. The most powerful king, army, and nation would be preoccupied by an attack. The only other defense we would have is ourselves!"

Gloria said, "Woah, boy, be that as it may, we have Fornacem, Umbra Mortis, Ignis, Amber, you, me, and the rest of my family. That's more than enough power to slaughter any monster Lapsus has."

Njord said, "He would certainly know this. The only reason he would attack the Fall Tree Academy and its magic users would be if he had discovered a superior force." Njord said, "I predict that we may be able to stop him."

Gloria said, "That sounds too simple for you. What if we capture him?"

Njord said, "I- er- I am not sure."

Gloria said, "We should at least warn them! Maybe keep an eye on the streets until we see something. If we can help, then that would be good too."

Njord hesitated, but nodded, "V-Very well."

Gloria said, "Wait, are there any other places before the Bestia city?"

Njord looked through the clipboard again, "Er, this copy does not seem to possess further information. The terrorist locations are the only other locations."

Gloria nodded, "Alright, so now we have a plan, right?"

Njord took his glasses off and stared at Gloria for a moment, "Er, I would not label a speculation as a proposition."

Gloria said, "Alright, so what do we do?"

Njord took a breath then said, "We are not aware of the numerical levels of our enemies... We do not know of their power either... If they are in possession of another Elder Fallen... We do not know what they will do... therefore..." Njord closed his eyes, tapping his glasses on his forehead, he said, "There is not a high probability of another Elder Fallen... We could effortlessly neutralize any standard enemy as well..." Njord turned to Gloria, "Alright, here is my opinion, we should travel to the Bestia city. If any aggressive individuals should emerge, our assistance may not be required, however, we will be there. Afterwards, I propose we attempt to travel to the Fall Tree Academy."

Gloria nodded, "What'll we do about supplies?"

Njord said, "Er, we may require you to disguise yourself, considering humans are not authorized within the Bestia Capital. As for the supplies, we will be able to restore these in the city."

Gloria nodded, she stood from the bed, "Then what are we waiting for? Let's move!" She ran for the door and ran outside.

Njord jumped, "Wait a moment!" He put his reading glasses in his pocket and ran for the door.

CHAPTER 4: IGNIS
Combination Animarum

Ignis filed through a clipboard as his class settled into seats. He said, "Alright! Quiet please! Calling roll." He started rattling names off of his clipboard, each time he heard his students acknowledgment.

"Kelly?"

"Here."

"Cassie?"

"Present."

"Carl?"

"Unfortunately."

"*Carl*?"

"*Here.*"

"Right." Ignis set his clipboard on the desk as the door opened next to him. Ignis saw Amber appear in the door, she smiled shiftily.

She stared at the ground, "Um, Ignis? Bad news..."

Ignis's heart sank, "Don't tell me... We're doubling up on class again?"

Amber said nothing, she sighed, Ignis's class cheered.

Ignis groaned, "My dad has *got* to move on. My mom has been trying to get his mind off it for *days*."

Amber said, "Well, in all fairness, literally everyone in his family *lied* to him. And now his daughter is lost, with a boy, lord knows where."

Ignis sighed, "What's the syllabus?"

Amber smiled, "Oh... dueling and *combination animarum*."

Ignis said, "Lovely, I'm so excited to get beat up in front of forty kids."

Amber grinned, she yelled to the ceiling, "Yo Arbor! Classrooms three and four request a training room!"

The students all stood from their seats and stood on roots that gathered into spirals. The classroom broke into branches and roots. Desks were taken into the leaf ceiling, and everyone stepped onto the ground.

As Ignis landed on the ground a gust of wind hit his face and Amber appeared next to him. Ignis saw that Amber's class was already there. They sat on the rug and waited.

Ignis said to his class, "Right, everyone on the rug then."

He waited for a few seconds as they got settled.

Amber whispered to Ignis, "So... you gonna be alright?"

Ignis said, "Oh *yeah*, a Dragonborn warrior is about to tear me to shreds in a duel. *And*, I have to try to describe *combination animarum*."

Amber smiled, "See? You'll be fine!"

Ignis rolled his eyes, "You do roll already?" Amber nodded, Ignis set his clipboard on a desk in the corner of the room and stood next to Amber.

Almost eighty eyes stared at them. Ignis was always nervous when he started teaching. It was new to be in the front of a class of kids eager for his every word.

Ignis turned to Amber, "What should we start with?"

Amber said, "Um, the importance of physical ability?"

Ignis nodded, "Ok, um, alright people!"

Everyone waited with bated breath, Ignis continued, "Um, how to start... Ok, who's familiar with close combat?"

Everyone raised their hands, Ignis said, "Right, um..." Ignis scrambled to try and find the words.

Amber glanced at him, she said, "Ok kiddos, picture this-"

Ignis sighed with relief, he had no idea what he was going to say next. Every time there was more than Ignis's class together, it made him nervous. And every time, Amber helped him through his stage fright.

Amber said, "You're a sniper shooter, you're a small, hard to hit, target."

Ignis remembered Uncle Dux describing this to him. Ignis said, "Ah, thank you, right, picture that." Ignis said, "Now, what would happen if you lost your gun?"

Ignis saw the whole class thinking, Ignis continued, "If you become too dependent on your magical ability, then your physical ability will plummet. That's why it's important to have a plan in case you can't use magic."

Ignis heard a voice say, "What if our physical ability is better than our magic?"

Ignis said, "Then vice versa, you can't become too dependent on any one thing alone. One day you may need one more than the other."

Ignis glanced at Amber, who smiled and nodded. It was Amber who told that to Ignis. She said that this thought was how the Dragonborn army became so powerful. Besides their physical ability being powerful already; it was useless against magic.

Ignis said, "Right, everyone pair up and choose a square. Arbor, can you double the room size?"

As the children paired up, the room extended outward, and small roots formed forty large rectangles spread throughout the room.

Ignis said, "Right, you know the rules; knock the other person out to win. However, you can't use magic." At this the entire class groaned, Ignis said, "Begin, and please be careful."

Ignis walked over towards a chalkboard and grabbed a book to look busy.

Amber came up from behind him, "Ignis?"

Ignis turned around and saw Amber smiling. She said, "What next?"

Ignis felt his heart plunge, "I was going to ask *you* that."

Amber said, "What if we give them a show?"

Ignis sighed, "I'd lose in this situation. The only reason that we keep on getting draws is because I kept my distance. You'd take my head off if you punched me."

Amber smiled, "No, I mean something else."

Ignis said, "Um, like what?"

Amber held out her hand and Ignis saw two small green orbs. There was a black dragon in one and a flame in the other.

Amber said, "Dux made them."

Ignis said, "Umm, what are they?"

Amber giggled, and quickly covered her mouth, "Um, these are the keys to *combination animarum*."

Ignis said, "They are?"

Amber said, "Um, why don't we put a pin in that for now?"

Ignis turned over and saw everyone was staring at them.

Ignis said, "Um, right, next-"

Ignis heard a girl yell, "Miss Amber, do a magic duel with Ignis!"

Ignis didn't recognize that voice; he thought it was someone from Amber's class. However, the other students were agreeing.

One from Ignis's class shouted, "Yeah! I've been wondering about that!"

Ignis saw where this was going. He sighed, Amber turned to him, "You up for another round?"

Ignis smiled, *"Totally."*

Ignis and Amber stood in a large rectangle in the center of the room. Ignis had ushered everyone else behind a ten foot thick barrier. He could still see their eyes peeping over the top of the wall. Ignis realized that the students had never seen them duel. The last time they dueled was during the long weeks they waited for students to arrive.

Ignis heard Amber say, "Y'know what I realized?"

Ignis said, "We've never dueled in front of an audience? Yeah, I know."

Amber said, "Eh, let's not let that bother us. Yo, Bruce! Ref please!"

Ignis saw one of her students run towards the side of the battle grounds.

He said, "Um, ready?"

Ignis saw Amber draw a silver sword from her back. It was shaped like a four-foot-tall U attached to a one-foot-long handle. It was Amber's personal weapon. Its surface glinted in the light reminding Ignis of car oil. Ignis remembered Amber showing Ignis this sword. It was a gift from her father. She said other stuff that Ignis didn't understand, but he knew that Amber really loved that sword.

Bruce said, "Set?"

Ignis flared his aura. A few students stumbled from the small shockwave. He heard a few words of admiration.

Bruce said, "Oh boy, FIGHT!"

Ignis and Amber shot towards each other. Ignis set his hands on fire and caught Amber's sword. Three different shockwaves blasted out simultaneously, one from Ignis, one from Amber, and one from the sword.

A strong wall of wind sent furniture flying. Ignis heard a few yelps and a few noises of excitement. Amber smiled and threw her sword back and swiped it sideways. Ignis recognized this move, Amber always started with it.

Ignis deflected the blade and ducked under it. He quickly sent a torrent of fire at Amber and leaped backwards. Before the next second, a crater formed where Ignis was just standing. Amber retraced her fist.

Ignis said, "No punching!"

Amber grinned, "Better hope you dodge then!"

Amber flew towards him, Ignis said, "Ah boy, solaris ruptis!"

With a bright flash and a loud bang, Ignis flew into the air as the ground below him was sliced in half by Amber.

Ignis pointed downward, "*Scintilla iecit, solaris ruptis, antececum!*"

As he was speaking, a summoning circle blazed into existence, the light intensified, and a ball of fire shot towards Amber.

Amber deflected it off her sword, "Really? Layered magic is too slow-WOAH!"

She barely dodged a spear of fire, raised her sword and caught Ignis's fist. Another shockwave exploded around them.

Ignis groaned. Amber smiled, "Good one, but it won't work on me!"

Amber knocked him aside and he fell to the ground. Amber spread her wings outward, and shot back, Ignis barely kept his balance.

Amber smiled, "Layered magic? Sure." She raised her hand and chanted, "*Draconis spiritus, furorem, terebrare-*"

As Amber spoke, the summoning circle grew larger. With a red flash, Ignis saw two more appear behind it, with another red flash, four more appeared around the sides.

Ignis said, "Oh boy."

Amber said, "*Antecessum!*"

A column of red and green flames barreled towards Ignis.

With hardly a second to think, Ignis said, "*Obstructionum.*"

A disk of flames appeared in front of him and hissed as they collided. Ignis saw a glint of light and a silver sword sliced the disk in half. Ignis ducked as Amber swiped her sword again. She swept her leg out and kicked Ignis in the chest. Ignis felt as though he was hit by a speeding train. He flew back and landed hard in the dirt.

He heard Amber say, "Come on, Ignis! You can do better than that! You're not *weak,* are you?"

Secretly, Amber knew that she was the only one that could annoy Ignis. She used this to her advantage to make him fight harder.

Ignis smiled, "Oh, you shouldn't have said that." Ignis raised his hands, "*Paratus!*" A small ball of fire formed in his hands, Ignis said, "*Et Portae Inferi!*"

The smile slid from Amber's face, "Oh no."

She dived to the ground as hundreds of fireballs shot towards her. She yelped, and flew upward, dived again, spinning in mid-air, dodging, and deflecting the projectiles.

She heard Ignis' voice behind her, "Going down?" Ignis said, "*Solaris ruptis!*"

With an explosion, Amber was flung to the ground. Amber sat up, rubbing her head. She gasped at the small scrape there. She looked at her hand and saw blood.

Ignis saw Amber smile, "Excellent. Now let's kick this up a notch!"

She sheathed her sword, Ignis's heart sank. "Oh, great." Ignis widened his stance, there was only one reason that Amber would sheath her weapon.

Amber closed her eyes, the ground around her cracked in

all directions, and her aura flared to life.

Ignis would describe Amber's aura like a vibrant lava lamp. It started out dark red, but it slowly turned green on the edges. It was precisely the same size as his own aura.

Amber smiled, "Oh, Ignis? Ready?" Amber's aura swelled, Ignis poured power into his aura, which flared with intensity.

"Always."

Amber yelled, a red summoning circle appeared in front of her hand.

Ignis threw his hand forward, "*Solaris soluti!*"

Amber yelled, "*Spiritus draconis!*"

Simultaneously, they yelled, "*Antecessum!*"

A dark red beam of light intercepted blue fire. As they collided, an intense explosion rippled from the center. An orb of purple and green light began to swell from the center. Ignis saw red and blue lightning crackling from the beams.

Ignis and Amber yelled. The light intensified and the ground cracked all around them. Branches fell from the ceiling. The walls began to groan under the pressure.

Ignis increased his aura, which reached the ceiling, and the orb of purple light doubled in size. It slowly started to move towards Amber. She gasped and increased her aura as well. It also reached the ceiling. The orb of purple light fell back and stayed suspended in the center of the beams. Green stars of light appeared around the orb. They swirled around it as another pulse of power exploded.

Suddenly, a bright silver bolt of lightning struck the orb. With a crackling explosion, the orb imploded, throwing everyone to the ground.

Ignis sat upward with a groan and saw Amber do the same. Ignis heard the whole class cheer.

Ignis heard an annoyed voice say, "Can you little *shits* keep it down? I haven't felt that much power in a century!"

Ignis saw Fornacem standing in the center of the battle grounds. He had an expression that spelled fury on his face.

He said, "The *worst part?* Neither of you won! Again!"

Ignis looked behind him, sure enough, he wasn't over the boundary, and neither was Amber.

Fornacem groaned, "Take it outside if you're gonna let it loose! If I have to do this again, I'm tossing bolts all around, y' hear?"

Ignis nodded, "Sorry Fornacem. Don't like getting rusty."

Fornacem huffed and disappeared with a bright silver flash. As Ignis stood, he couldn't help feeling sheepish. That was the fourth time that Ignis and Amber had gotten carried away.

Ignis walked over to Amber and offered her his hand, "You alright?"

Amber beamed, "Are you *kidding*? That was the best fight I've had in a *long* time! Let's keep it going, outside everyone!"

As the students appeared from behind the barrier, which resembled a large pile of cinders, Ignis saw only ecstatic looks.

A gentle breeze blew through Ignis's hair, Amber was pouting.

He nudged her shoulder, "Hey, don't be mad, if we fight again, then we'll never cover *combination animarum*. We really should have *started* with that."

Amber huffed, "We had such a good rhythm though. I suppose I can teach them quick."

Ignis said, "In detail."

Amber sighed, "Fine, in detail, then we duel again."

Ignis smiled, "Sounds good."

He turned towards the students, "Right, we'll finish covering duels after *combination animarum*. We'll be outside for the rest of the time, partially because the training room is fried, but mostly because I don't want Fornacem killing me."

The students chuckled and one of them said, "What's *combination animarum*?"

Ignis nodded, "Right, um, Amber?"

She smiled, "Well, *combination animarum* is also known as *the combination of souls*. Basically, with the right preparations, two forces can briefly become one. Combining the mind, body, soul, and powers of both individuals." There were a few gasps of surprise, Amber continued, "Not only is this *extremely* hard to achieve, making the keys for it is very hard to do. Deadly to get wrong, which is why I got Dux to do it!"

Amber once again held out the two green orbs, Ignis flinched, "Wait a second, do you mean-"

Ignis heard a bunch of different words of excitement from the others. Ignis whispered to Amber, "I've never done *combination animarum* before. How in the world do you think we'll be able to pull that off?"

Amber smiled, "Simple, because I believe we can. Also, I know you better than you think, and that helps a bit. Come on, I'll teach you the ritual."

Ignis allowed himself to be dragged ten feet away from the students. Amber pulled him closer and whispered, "Ok, since I know a *bit* more about this stuff, I'm going to handle the complicated stuff. So, you will be in charge of the body."

Ignis tried to process what she said, "Huh?"

Amber rolled her eyes, "Ok, um, I will be in charge of the mind, the power, and soul, while you handle the body, got it?"

Ignis felt that he didn't, Amber said, "Look, this stuff is *really* hard to pull off, chances are that nothing happens. *However*, *combination animarum* responds to compatibility. The better we understand each other, then the easier it will be to pull off. So, lastly, are you ok with this?"

Ignis nodded, "I trust you, let's try it."

Amber smiled, "That's the spirit. Alright, first, hold this."

Amber handed Ignis one of the small green orbs, it felt strangely warm. Amber held the other, she muttered a spell, and they were surrounded by a green circle.

Amber turned to Ignis, "Alright, now, all you have to do is say this, *simul*, ready? At the same time now-"

Amber raised her hand upward, and slowly counted to three, "One, two… three-"

At the same time, Ignis and Amber said, "*Simul.*" Ignis felt his orb grow warmer, and his vision was lost in a brilliant green light.

Just as fast as it happened, the light disappeared.

"Did it not work? *Amber?*"

Ignis looked around, but he didn't see Amber. Ignis saw the students, they were all staring in shock.

Ignis took a step forward, "What's wrong?"

Ignis saw Bruce step forward, "Um, can you hear me?"

Ignis nodded, Bruce said, "You can understand me?"

Ignis nodded, Bruce said, "Um, I think it worked."

Ignis said, "What do you mean?"

Bruce said, "Um, I'll get a mirror, please keep calm."

Ignis jumped. A stranger was staring back at him.

Ignis saw a reflection that wasn't his, whoever it was looked completely different. They had short dark blue hair and were slightly taller than Ignis. They were wearing Ignis's clothes but had Amber's armor. They had dark blue wings sprouting from their back and a tail. Two horns curled from their head. What were they?

Bruce said, "Um, Miss Amber told me to read off a few questions if this happened. Should I continue?"

The strange creature nodded. Bruce said, "Firstly, what is your name?"

The creature was puzzled, there was a name in its mind, alien, yet, correct. The being said, "I am *Spiritus Inferni*. You can call me Spiritus."

Bruce's eyes widened, "A-Alright, what do you remember?"

Spiritus said, "I... I have memories that are not mine. It's strange."

Bruce said, "Um, favorite color?"

Spiritus scowled, "*What*?"

Bruce shrugged, "It's one of the questions!"

Once again, Spiritus held an answer that seemed unfamiliar, and yet it knew it well.

"Purple."

Bruce said, "Wow, alright, um, are you able to use magic?"

Spiritus shrugged, "Let's find out."

Bruce said, "Oh boy, everyone find cover quickly!"

Large wings unfolded behind Spiritus, and it flew into the air. There was a familiar excitement within Spiritus which it recognized as someone else's.

They stopped, suspended in the air. A familiar excited voice spoke within its mind, "*Ooh! We should start with our aura! That'll be cool right?*"

Spiritus said aloud, "I suppose."

They concentrated. The children below gasped as a shockwave knocked them off their feet. A brilliant aura surrounded Spiritus, it was a dark green that faded into a purple color. Random yellow stars flashed around the nebula of color.

Spiritus thought, h*ow is this possible? Where am I?*

A familiar voice spoke gently, *it's alright, keep calm.*

Spiritus grinned, "This is fun."

Far below Bruce squinted skyward, "Is that them? It?

What are they?"

A shockwave knocked Bruce to the ground. There was a flash of silver lightning.

Bruce gasped as Fornacem said, "What in the unholy *hell* is going... on?" Fornacem saw the figure above, "Who the-who's that?" He turned to Bruce, "What the hell is that?"

Bruce shrugged, "They... it... Spiritus?"

Fornacem's eyes widened, "*Oooh*, I got *dibs*."

He disappeared, and Bruce flinched as a crack of thunder lit up the ground.

Bruce complained, "I am surrounded by too much power!"

Spiritus saw a figure hovering ten feet away smiling wickedly, dark red eyes gleaming, "Yo, how do you do?"

Spiritus said, "I know you, but I don't recall where from."

Fornacem laughed, "Holy *shit!* You guys are awesome! You like duels, right?"

Spiritus grinned, "Obviously."

Fornacem said, "That sounds like Amber, and yet you hesitate like Ignis, oh man! I'm excited now! You don't seem like an equilibrium, but still! You want to go a round?"

Spiritus said, "For some reason, I think I do."

Fornacem smiled wickedly, "Names Fornacem, yours?"

Spiritus said, "I am *Spiritus Inferni,* you can call me Spiritus for short."

Spiritus frowned as Fornacem reared his head back and bellowed with laughter, "*This* is going to be *good*."

Down below, Bruce squinted upward at the two figures. A student shook his shoulder, "What's going on up there Bruce?"

They all gasped as two auras flared to life. Bruce's heart sank, "Get somebody, we need to stop this."

The student said, "Who?"

Bruce started to take a step back, "Anyone! Get anyone now!"

Fornacem grinned wickedly, "Ready?"

Spiritus smiled, "Set?"

Simultaneously, they said, "Go."

They both shouted spells at the same time, Fornacem roared, "*Argentum Mico!*"

Spiritus said, "*Portas Inferi!*"

A sliver crack of energy was intercepted by a red circle. It slowly expanded, a black beam of light shot out. Fornacem smiled and was engulfed by the light.

Flesh grew from thin air, Fornacem laughed, "Wow! That stung! Let me feel it again!"

He swiped his hand outward, and his aura flashed, and tripled in size.

Way down below, the grass started smoking. Bruce yelled to the students, "Everyone out of here now! Run!"

As they ran towards the tree, Bruce looked up as a shockwave tore past him. Spiritus aura flared, matching Fornacem's.

Bruce said, "Oh man." They disappeared from his sight and a force sent Bruce flying backward.

Fornacem ducked under Spiritus swing but gasped as a fist appeared in his stomach.

He smiled wider, "Yes! Better!"

He shot to the ground. Spiritus followed. They landed with such a force that they created craters and they shot towards each other again, dodging, blocking, attacking. The ground peeled upward, flying in the wind.

The door of the academy shot open, and Dux, Arbor, Arthur, and Julia ran out. Dux found Bruce and helped him to his feet.

He yelled over the noise, "What in the hell is going

on?" Dux saw his mouth move, but he didn't hear words. Dux muttered a spell, and they were surrounded by a dome white light.

The wind died and Bruce said, "You have to stop them!"

Dux said, "*You don't say!* What happened?"

Bruce said, "I don't know, we were covering *combination animarum*, and that guy appeared out of nowhere!"

Dux said, "What *guy*?"

Bruce pointed, Dux followed Bruce's view, his eyes widened. "No way. You said *combination animarum?*"

Bruce nodded, Dux turned to Arthur, "There's a humanoid thing in the tree, it looks like it's made of ink, tell it to get out here now."

Arthur nodded, "Uh, sure!" He ran through the barrier and into the tree.

Dux said to Julia, "Get in the tree and don't come out until I say, go!"

She nodded and ran for the tree as well. Dux flinched as a shockwave shattered the dome.

Fornacem dodged a fist, then a ray of light, but was caught by leg sweep. A sword appeared next to his face, embedded in the ground.

He smiled, "*That's* Amber's!"

He shot a spell that hit Spiritus in the face. He flew upward, landing twenty feet away.

Fornacem appeared in front, smiled, and a large summoning circle blazed to life. A bolt of lightning intercepted a beam of green and red fire. An explosion ripped from the center. Spiritus yelled and swung the sword, slicing at Fornacem's face.

Suddenly, they froze. Spiritus heard a voice say, "My word, you two are truly remarkable."

Spiritus felt the spell dissipate and a dark figure stood before it. It was a humanoid figure, an ink-like substance made its form. It had irises the color of static. It smiled, revealing shadowy teeth.

"You two have caused *quite* enough commotion. Or should I say you *three*? As always, I'm sure the fighting didn't *mean* to get to this point. Who's in charge anyways? *Ignis*? *Amber*?"

Spiritus felt an enormous sense of Deja vu, everything that Umbra Mortis was saying sounded so familiar, how did he even know its name?

Umbra Mortis nodded, "I see, Amber doesn't know how to separate from you? That's easy, just think about your own bodies, then say *we*."

Two separate voices said, *"We?"*

There was a bright green flash. Amber and Ignis fell to the ground

Ignis didn't remember anything that happened, random pictures filled his head, but he didn't know anything about them.

Amber was almost sobbing. She cried to Ignis, "I'm so sorry! I didn't even think we'd succeed! I didn't- I-"

Ignis smiled, "Don't worry Amber! No one is hurt and personally, I feel great."

It was true, Ignis felt as though he just got a long night's sleep.

Amber stared at the ground, "That's because *I* took the taxing stuff!"

Ignis laughed, Amber stared at him in shock, Ignis said, "Well, from what I heard, I *think* we covered *combination animarum* well."

Amber snorted, *"Oh, you think?"*

They both laughed as a door opened, Uncle Dux

appeared in the doorway, "If you're both ready, we have a council to attend."

Soon, Ignis was sitting at a large table, Amber to his right, while Arbor was on his left. Trays of random food covered the table surface.

As they were sitting, Uncle Dux started, "All right, we stopped an early doomsday. Now, on other topics, in the future, *Fornacem, don't* engage mysterious figures!"

Fornacem roared with laughter, "Oh *come on* Dux! They were *brimming* with power! I haven't had that much fun in decades!"

Uncle Dux scowled, "That is *precisely* why you shouldn't! We didn't know Spiritus's power. You're lucky that no one got hurt, *you damn-*"

Arthur interrupted, "As much as I like cursing at Fornacem, we have other matters to discuss."

Uncle Dux sighed, "I suppose. Umbra Mortis just reported back, the army is showing signs of activity."

Ignis flinched, "Woah, wait, what army?"

Uncle Dux said, "Ah boy, right, side effects of, what's called, *one sided combination* can have that effect. Well, let's catch Ignis up... *again.*"

Ignis saw Amber stare at the ground sheepishly, Uncle Dux said, "You've forgotten Ignis, but an army has completely surrounded us."

Ignis flinched, "*What*? When? How?"

Uncle Dux said, "We noticed last week. *Anyways,* what you *really* didn't know is that Arthur finally believes that this is why Gloria and Njord haven't returned."

Arthur opened his mouth, Uncle Dux cut him off. Arthur grumbled as Uncle Dux summoned a map of the valley.

The peaks of the mountains glowed red, Uncle Dux said, "We've started to feel the effects of the army. There have been rumors of monster roars at night, as well as explosions silenced by magic. I'm assuming that we're in agreement, Lapsus is behind this."

Ignis said, "So… we're surrounded, bad, what do we do?"

Uncle Dux said, "Well, it's not like they have anything we can't handle, not with Fornacem, Amber, Umbra Mortis, and you, Ignis. I mean, we also have the Behemoth army in case things go south. Nevertheless, the fact that they plan on attacking is a bit suspicious. What could they *possibly* have that could harm us?"

Fornacem grinned, "That was *quite* a mouthful Dux."

Uncle Dux pointed at him, "One more word and I'm sewing your mouth shut. Anyways, what should we do?"

Amber said, "Is there any success in opening portals?"

Uncle Dux shook his head, "For some reason, the only portal magic that worked was the special type that Njord used. So, we're stuck here. We need to find a way to contact Gloria and Njord to tell them what's going on."

Arthur said, "Why don't we use phones?"

Uncle Dux scowled, "*Hmm, why didn't I think of that? Oh,* I know! Because phones don't *work here*! If I could have called them then I would have *ages* ago!"

Arthur stood, "You don't have to snap at me!" They started bickering.

Julia tried to calm them, "Please! Arguing won't help!"

Ignis saw Amber slowly lower her head onto the table. Uncle Dux stood, and they started yelling louder. Ignis felt the table rattle slightly and he realized that Amber was hitting her head against the table.

Uncle Dux yelled, "I am trying my *best* Arthur!"

Arthur scowled, "I know that! But sometimes you could *try* to be more responsible!"

They all jumped, with a loud crack, a silver flash lit the room.

Fornacem said, "Why not just cast a small anti magic

barrier and use a phone to hijack one of Gloria's thoughts?"

Fornacem took a bite out of a doughnut before he added, "*Dumbasses.*"

Before anyone could say anything else, Ignis saw a student enter the room.

Uncle Dux said, "We're in a meeting, please come back later."

The student said, "It's the army, they're doing something."

Uncle Dux said, "What?"

The student said, "Uh, you all should see for yourself."

They followed the student and as they walked to a wall, it opened into a balcony.

Ignis heard Uncle Dux mutter a spell, he yelped, "Holy-! We've got a situation!"

Uncle Dux passed Ignis a pair of binoculars. Ignis stared at the mountain and saw a cloud of translucent magic slowly forming. He noticed this happening all around them. On every mountain top, the clouds were slowly billowing towards them.

Uncle Dux said, "Those are all anti magic barriers, which means no magic soon." He muttered a spell, and Ignis found him shoving a burner phone in his hand. Uncle Dux said, "Right, after we drive the enemy away, use that to call Gloria. Don't know how it'll work, might end up being a video call- LOOK OUT!"

He threw his hand up and a wall of white light exploded against a large rock. The barrier faded, Uncle Dux said, "They have catapults? *Seriously?* Alright, all students to your rooms! Everyone else, prepare for battle!"

CHAPTER 5: GLORIA
The Corrupted Hunter

Gloria and Njord were panting heavily, well, Njord was anyway. Gloria had run down the road, until they stopped at a nearby gas station.

Njord spoke between breaths, "Are you even… aware of where… we are traveling to?"

Gloria winced, she turned to Njord, "Oh, I'm sorry Njord."

Njord shook his head, "Your apology is accepted. Now, may we please do what I excel in? Fabricate a plan? Please?"

Gloria laughed, "Yeah."

They bought some supplies at the gas station, then hid behind the store. Gloria sat on an old crate while Njord started to explain the plan. Njord made a map out of green light, it showed the west side of the United States.

Njord took a sip from a water bottle and said, "Alright, the portal with the closest proximity is just outside of Las Vegas, Nevada. It is approximately two hundred fifty miles from here. We have no mode of transportation that qualifies. Magic and elements should be avoided, when possible, in order to not confuse humans, as well as to avoid the attention of roaming monsters. We require a mortal fashion of transport."

Gloria nodded, "Well, what if we find the highway first,

then we can figure out the transportation later."

Njord hesitated, then sighed, "Very well. What of the Bestia city?"

Gloria said, "Well, what do the defenses look like? What should I know?"

Njord thought for a moment, "Well, they have extremely harsh laws. There are usually no exceptions. Humans are captured, if not, executed upon visual contact."

Gloria said, "Good to know."

Njord said, "Anyone who violates law of any sort is immediately exiled. Well, after they become of adult age."

Gloria nodded, Njord thought for a moment, "Er, there are twelve counties within twenty six districts. For example, the city B-six, or Z-ten. I am not sure which city, county, or district we will arrive in. There are very few portals near the Bestia Capital."

Gloria nodded, "So, what would we do when we get there?"

Njord said, "We would require your concealment, most likely utilizing a combination of light and illusion magic."

Gloria said, "Cool, and... what about buying supplies? Do we have their currency?"

Njord nodded, "Amber was kind enough to provide such supplies in advance."

Gloria nodded, "Alright, now, where is the interstate?"

Njord sighed, "That is the question."

They walked from the gas station, following road signs to the highway. A few cars passed them, once a car honked at them. At one point a speeding car tossed a soda bottle out the window. Njord scoffed, muttering about unsanitary mortals. They passed an old deer carcass rotting on the road. They came upon a large rest area just before the highway. After getting water from a couple of vending machines, they sat on a bench.

Gloria said, "Now what?"

Njord said, "Er… I am not sure. We do not possess a vehicle, even if we did, we are not legally permitted to drive."

Gloria sighed, overhead, a bird defecated in front of them.

They both watched as a large semi-truck pulled into the lot. The trailer was white with colorful words on the side spelling Las Vegas. The trucker cursed as he got out of the semi and walked to the rest area.

Gloria's eyes widened as she turned to Njord, "How do you feel about trailers?"

Njord said, "Er… Pardon?"

Gloria ran to the back of the semi-trailer, Njord hastily following. Gloria found a padlock with the key still in it.

Njord shook his head as Gloria grabbed the lock, "How irresponsible. What if the trailer door opened? It creates an extremely hazardous scenario for other vehicle operators!"

Gloria opened the lock and the trailer and pointed inside, "Our chariot awaits."

Njord shook his head, "This is not an ethical plan, what will the human say following the discovery of two dirty teenagers in his vehicle?"

Gloria shrugged, "We'll cross that bridge when we get to it."

Njord muttered as he jumped into the trailer, "That did not answer my question, or solve the problem."

Gloria jumped up and shut the trailer door. They were in complete darkness.

Njord said, "This will not do, *mare lux*."

A soft green light burned into existence. Gloria looked around. They were surrounded by boxes. Njord took a seat near the front where a small AC unit was cranking out air. The floor was slippery. Gloria saw water in small pools all around them.

Gloria heard a voice, "Oops, that's where that key went, could have been bad." She heard the lock click.

Njord said, "However, it is too late to have uncertainty."

The truck engine sputtered to life. Njord said, "I recommend that you locate a seat. You may lose your stance."

Gloria nodded and took a seat across from him, as the truck carried them onto the expressway.

Even with the rattling AC working, it still got hot in the trailer.

Gloria wiped her forehead, "Yeah, this won't do."

She made a small chunk of ice to cool the inside. They drifted in and out of sleep, but between the bumps in the road and the car horns, they couldn't get much rest.

They were both lying on boxes when Gloria heard a familiar tune. The driver was singing loudly.

Gloria started to sing along, "*Viva Las Vegas, Viva Las Vegas-*"

Two voices rang out from within the trailer, "*Viva, Viva, Las Vegas!*" The same voices rang out in laughter.

Gloria turned to Njord, "Hey, how long have we been on the road?"

Njord said, "Approximately one hour, forty six minutes."

Gloria scoffed, "Really? This is taking forever. Talk to me Njord."

Njord said, "Er, what topic are you-"

Gloria said, "Anything, I guess. Strategy, plans, etcetera."

Njord thought for a moment, "Well... I suppose that it would not be a negative proposal... Er-"

Before Njord could say anything else, Gloria heard the brakes screech. Suddenly, Gloria and Njord pitched forward, and the boxes flew everywhere.

Gloria heard Njord mutter a spell and daylight blinded her.

She felt Njord drag her away, "We need to move, Gloria!"

Gloria looked behind her and saw the truck was overturned. The trailer had a large hole in the roof. Another car swerved to avoid the trailer, honking their horn.

Gloria said, "What happened? Is the driver ok?"

Gloria flinched as she heard a loud yell, Njord said, "Er, I do not believe so."

Gloria saw a monster leap onto the overturned trailer, its claws sunk into the tire with a loud hiss. A Venator snarled at them, fresh blood dripping from its black lips.

Gloria made a snarl of her own, "That mutt! That guy was innocent!"

The monster growled and leaped at them, Njord said, "*Fluctus*."

A wave of water slammed the monster to the ground, cracking the road beneath it.

Njord said, "As effective as these creatures are, they really struggle with capture. Let us move, I am sure that there are more monsters nearby. We are not too far from-"

He froze, Gloria followed his gaze.

The monster moved. It bent its broken arm straight with a loud crack. It twitched and stood. Gloria noticed that its skin was bubbling with a static like substance.

Njord took a step back, "Er, strange... I was under the impression-"

Gloria gasped as something shot from the monster's chest. An arm broke through it, it had hair made of static and shining black claws. Static poured from the wound and the monster mutated.

Its golden fur turned black, static crackling across its body. Its head ripped from its shoulders and two more appeared beside the first. It grew in size as two more legs tore from its side and met the ground.

Njord said quietly, "Ah, *corruption*."

The monster roared, leaving Gloria nearly deaf.

Njord yelled, *"Oceanus aestus."* As a charred claw shot towards them, a wall of green light formed before them. The claw ripped straight through as though it was not there. Static buzzed from the arm. Njord yelped and dodged the claw as it cracked the asphalt.

Gloria grabbed his hand, hauling him up the road, "What is that thing?"

Njord said, "It is a *Consumptus,* a Corrupted Hunter beast. Magic and elements have no effect on them!"

Gloria gasped, "What? How do we kill it?"

Njord said, "Mortal methods! Ammunition or dynamite, either would be excellent!"

A claw extended from the monster, barely missing Gloria. Njord said, "Avoid contact no matter what! They can extend their limbs thirty times their normal size!"

Gloria said, "What a pain!"

They ran on the off ramp, the monster just behind them. Gloria yelped as a claw shot over her head. Njord ripped a sign from the ground and threw it like a spear at the monster. It pierced the monster's shoulder, but it kept coming after them. Gloria threw a wall of ice and dragged Njord behind her. She caught sight of an old gas station across the road and bolted for it. The monster walked straight through the ice, liquid static pouring from its shoulders.

Gloria and Njord were crouched behind the dumpsters. Gloria saw Njord's eyes were glowing.

He said, "I have not studied this species thoroughly enough! How do we engage in combat against it? Utilizing magic or elements is ineffective!"

Gloria said, "You said mortal methods, right?"

Njord nodded, Gloria said, "What about fire?"

Njord scoffed, "It would require being entirely engulfed in flames." Njord said, "Why do you ask?" He shook his head,

"As a matter of fact, I should probably now be afraid to ask."

In front of the gas station, the monster lifted a car onto its side. It snarled, dropping it onto the ground. An alarm blared from the car, the monster smashed it, and the sound died. A rubber tire bounced off the monster's head. It roared and whipped around.

Njord threw another tire, "Greetings! I hope you appreciate these tires!" Njord heaved a car at the monster as well.

Gloria crouched on the other side of the gas station. She grabbed a nozzle from the pump and squeezed the lever.

The machine beeped, Gloria read aloud, "Select payment method? Shoot!"

She jabbed the cash button and sprayed the nozzle. She turned the nozzle towards the monster, "Now Njord!"

Njord ripped the cap off the underground gas tank and tossed it at the monster.

Gloria sprayed gasoline at the monster, "Yo, ugly! Take a bath!"

She sprayed gasoline as the monster roared and lunged. She dropped the nozzle and ducked, the monster barely missing her. It crashed into the gas pump and Gloria saw a few new leaks from the pump. The monster roared and leaped after her.

Gloria turned around and saw a clawed hand reaching for her. She screamed, and a brilliant red truck sailed through the air and slammed into the monster. Gloria saw it stumble and slip into the underground gas storage tank. Njord set the tank lid and part of the cement around it, over the hole.

Njord said, "Do we possess a lighter? Or a match?" Gloria gasped as the tank lid jerked a bit when the monster rammed into it. Gloria swung the backpack from her shoulder and found a pack of matches in the back pocket.

She lit one and said, "After I drop it, we need to run,

ASAP."

Njord nodded, "You are correct. On three."

Njord wrapped an arm around her, preparing a spell under them.

Njord counted, "One, two...three!"

Njord lifted the cover, and Gloria threw the match into the tank. Before Gloria could say anything, they shot skyward, as a rumble sounded beneath them. Gloria heard a loud rip and a stray shard of metal from the canopy caught her backpack. It fell from her shoulder.

Just after they cleared the canopy, an explosion ripped the entire area apart. Cement chunks the size of cars flew from the explosion. The gas station was incinerated. Glass and car parts were thrown from the explosion. A cement chunk, the size of a softball, clipped Njord's forehead. Gloria gasped as they started to fall.

Gloria grabbed Njord's foot and blasted ice directly under them until they landed in a pile of golden snow, which quickly melted, leaving Gloria soaked and cold on the ground. She found Njord a few feet to her left.

She ran to him, "Njord! Wake up! Come on!" She nudged his arm, but he didn't move. Gloria panicked and reared back, slapping his face.

Njord jolted upward, "Ouch! Why would you do that? That was painful-"

Gloria punched him on the shoulder, "Why didn't you think about the debris?"

Njord said, "I was under the impression that this was *your* plan. If you require me to, I could list *seventy four* reasons why this was an idiotic course of action!"

Gloria burst into laughter, and Njord smiled. Gloria offered him a hand and pulled him up.

The gas station was now a wall of flames fifty feet high. A smoking car hood fell in front of them.

Gloria nodded, "Think that did it?"

Njord said, "Well, as effective as it may have seemed, an explosion of this caliber would have a ninety percent chance of success."

Gloria cheered, "So we're good?"

A roar made them both flinch, Gloria screamed hysterically, "I thought you just said ninety! *Ninety*, Njord!"

Njord said, "Then there was still a ten percent chance of failure! Do not inculpate me!"

Gloria turned toward the explosion and saw a boney figure leering at them. Gloria could see ribs, blackened organs dripping inky blood, and static. It was missing two heads, the one remaining was missing the side of its face and fire burned in the eye hole. A skeletal hand reached towards them. A chunk of ash crumbled from its hand. It was missing a leg. Two red eyes glared at them.

Gloria shuttered, "Major Terminator vibe, I usually get with the Elder Fallen, and it's *terrifying*!"

Njord said, "It should not be able to extend its limbs. Do not make contact. We need to run again!" He grabbed Gloria, and jarred her out of the way, as a flaming car rolled towards them.

Gloria yelled, "With how dead it looks, it still is capable enough to throw *cars*? I *hate* monsters!"

The monster raised another car over its head and threw it. Gloria and Njord leaped over as it skidded past.

Gloria yelled as they dodged a flaming barrel, "Donkey Kong called! HE WANTS HIS TRADEMARK BACK!"

They ducked under another barrel, Njord said, "I do not understand what you mean, however, I do not believe that provocation is the best alternative."

Gloria fumed, "Well then, let's just *run*!"

Before Njord could say anything else, Gloria grabbed his arm and tugged him along. The monster was slower, so distance grew between them. It scrapped charred claws along the road, leaving lines of ashes behind.

Gloria sent another wall of ice behind them, deflecting the latest projectile car. They stopped behind a fast food sign.

Gloria said, "If mortal weapons work best, then we'll think more mortally. What if we stab its heart?"

Njord said, "That is extremely strenuous when we are not able to make physical contact."

Gloria stamped her foot, "Well I don't hear *you* making any suggestions!"

Njord crossed his arms, "You do not have to be impolite. I am trying my best."

Gloria sighed, "Fine, I'm sorry."

Njord nodded, "You are forgiven. Now, if we have either a way to project something from a distance, we may be able to defeat it."

Gloria said, "Gun?"

Njord said, "Not only do neither of us have the knowledge, or skill, to operate one, I do not desire to attract authorities. More so than we may have already."

Gloria nodded, "True, what about, HO MY LORD!"

She sent a barrier of ice above them as a Big Boy statue crumbled against the ice. A cracking voice said, "Welcome to Big Boy, how can I take your-" The speaker buzzed, and the voice died.

Gloria muttered darkly, "I am going to kill Fornacem for making the *Fallen*."

She shattered the ice and pulled Njord farther up the road.

She pointed to a nearby car, "Njord! Fire with fire! Throw some cars!"

Njord said, "That has a six percent probability of-"

Gloria yelled, "*Njord!*"

Njord flinched. He ran to the curb and lifted a bus over his shoulder with a grunt.

He said, "I will at least raise the probability to nineteen!"

He hurled the bus at the monster. It snarled and batted the bus aside. It spun in the air, landing with a crash.

Gloria said, "That didn't work."

Njord forced her head down as a fire hydrant flew over their heads, "What brought you to *that* conclusion?" he yelled.

They ran further up the street, Gloria spotted a construction area. An orange sign said, *drying asphalt.*

Gloria pointed, "Idea! Njord, there!"

She dragged Njord towards the construction zone. She leaped over the drying cement, Njord following suit.

A construction worker yelled at them, "Hey! What are you doing?"

Gloria yelled back, "I'd run if you don't want to die!"

They entered a half built house, cement blocks rose eight feet into the air.

Gloria ran forward as Njord shouted, "Wait a moment!"

Gloria felt herself falling, there was no ground in front of her. She yelped as Njord caught her arm and pulled her up. Gloria looked down, there were long rebars sticking from the ground. She imagined the bed of spikes would have killed her.

Gloria muttered, "The *irony*."

Njord said, "Are you-"

They both flinched as a roar shook the building around them. Construction workers ran from the entrance, leaping through open windows. Gloria grabbed Njord's arm and pulled him behind a nearby wall. Gloria peeked through a large square hole into the front yard.

The monster was stuck in the drying cement patch in the front. It roared, trying to dislodge itself, shredding the ground.

Gloria nodded, "Right, we have a few minutes, what do we do?"

Njord did a quick look around, his eyes met a few nearby rebars. Njord picked one up, "How is your accuracy?"

Gloria picked up a rebar, "Better than nothing."

Njord sighed, "You really make me experience agitation when you declare that. I recommend fabricating a verified plan of action."

Gloria looked at the front yard. The monster had dislodged one foot and it started to shred the ground around the other.

Gloria said, "No time, distract it until we find a way to kill it!"

Gloria saw that Njord's eyes were glowing again. He shook his head with a sigh, "This is *very* unprofessional."

Gloria laughed, "Since when have *I ever* been *professional*?"

Njord muttered, "Instructing, sleeping, I assume-"

Gloria laughed, she peeked through the hole again.

The monster had torn the ground around it apart. Its feet were covered with dust, and it was sniffing at the cement patch. Gloria climbed onto a pile of bricks, jumping onto the top of the wall. She gave a piercing taxi cab whistle and the monster's head shot in her direction.

Gloria yelled, "Catch!"

She threw the rebar like a spear, hoping to hit its head or heart. The monster caught it in the middle and gave an unamused sniff.

Gloria yelped as the monster threw it back at her, "I didn't mean that literally!"

She ducked. With a crack, the rebar went through the cement wall.

Njord said, "Your angle was-"

Gloria yelled, "I'm not about to die with someone telling me my math was wrong! You try it!"

There was a blue flash, Gloria saw that Njord had reverted back into a Cecaelia.

Njord folded his clothes and put them into his bag. He picked up several rebars, "It will only physically only be able to catch two. Well, I expect."

Gloria grabbed a few, "Right, we'll ambush it, good?"

Njord nodded, "That plan is satisfactory."

Gloria hesitated, she shouted, "Now!"

Gloria jumped off the stack of bricks and jumped onto the wall. Njord simultaneously leaped upward, throwing six rebars at once.

The monster caught Gloria's again, but three of Njord's hit home. One went through its shoulder, one through its leg, and the last through its neck. Blood like used car oil spilled from the wounds, especially the neck injury. The monster roared, and ran at Njord

He yelped, "W- *Ventus!*" He shot into the air as the monster barely missed his leg.

The monster landed and skidded, its claws leaving scratches in the concrete. A brick exploded into pieces against its head and the monster roared as another brick hit it. Gloria picked up another and pelted it at the monster.

Njord landed next to her as a human, saying, "As you would say, good idea." Then, *"Oceanum ventum!"*

The entire stack of bricks lifted into the air, swirling around them. The wooden pallet under the stack flew at the monster. It roared, batting it aside, Gloria saw it crash into a small yellow forklift.

Njord yelled, and the storm of bricks flew towards the monster. He ducked as a section of wall flew towards him. The monster roared. There was a skidding noise, and a bright yellow fork lift plowed into the monster. It's prongs stabbing into its chest.

Gloria yelled, "Need a lift?" She floored the gas, placing a brick on it, and jumped out of the forklift.

The forklift kept moving, along with the monster. With a large crash, it careened into a construction pit. Gloria landed on the other side.

She watched as Njord ran to her, "Are you alright?"

Gloria nodded, "I'm lovely, help me up."

Njord pulled her from the ground, "Remind me to never allow you to operate a vehicle."

Gloria dusted herself off, "Yeah, yeah, whatever. I don't want to hear that from someone who wears their shorts *backwards*."

After Njord fixed his clothes, they walked to the edge of the pit. The monster was trying to scratch at the fork lift. Gloria saw rebars piercing its body. The forklift was smoking from on top of the monster.

Gloria collapsed to the ground, "Cool."

Njord said, "It has not been eliminated."

Gloria looked around and spotted a large white truck, "One moment."

She walked to the truck. Njord looked down towards the monster and shuddered. The large white truck backed towards him, stopping just in front of the pit.

Gloria got out and shut the door, "Good thing that's automatic, can't drive a stick shift."

Njord shook his head, "Pardon?"

Gloria shook her head, "Never mind."

She walked over to the side of the vehicle with Njord following. They looked down towards the monster.

Njord said, "Er, any last words?"

Gloria spat at the monster, "*Good riddance.*"

She pressed a button and the truck poured cement into

the pit. The monster roared, but as the cement buried it, it became muffled.

Njord said, "One, remind me never to make you angry. Two, you are extremely ruthless."

Gloria nodded, "Sounds about right."

Gloria sighed and walked away from the pit and sat down on an overturned crate. Njord hesitated before sitting next to her.

Njord said, "Er-"

Gloria stared as the construction pit overflowed with cement. "Now what? I lost all our stuff," she said.

Njord said, "Do not accuse yourself. We were struck with a dangerous situation. What is important is that we are both alive."

Gloria set her head in her hands, then shook her head, "What are we going to do? We have nothing! No map, compass, food-"

Njord yelled, "*Excuse me!*"

Gloria flinched, she had never heard Njord raise his voice before.

Njord stood in front of Gloria with crossed arms, "Affirmative, we possess no supplies, it is true that we possess no nourishment. However, I have memorized every map of California, and perceive that we are facing east. We in fact do *not* have nothing!"

Njord took a breath, "We have each other! I have you and you have me! If you were to question me, I would conclude that this is more than satisfactory! I will defend you, support you, as well as whatever else you may require. Not because I require it, but because I am your companion!"

Njord continued, "Do not *ever* doubt yourself! You have to be one of the bravest, kindest, and smartest people that I know. *Never* have I seen you hesitate in the face of danger. *Never* have I seen you retreat from a fight. And *never* have I seen you give up!

You push, you try, and you succeed! You never show fear! You never give in! With this knowledge I know that we can- no, we *will* succeed! If we fail, then I will be satisfied as long as I know that we both tried!"

Njord pointed to Gloria, "Now! Are you going to sit there? Or are you going to stand up, and assist me to the Bestia Capital?"

Gloria was stunned, struck speechless. She never thought about what Njord thought of her. Was he being flattering? No, he was saying what he believed, Njord thought that *she* was all of those things?

Gloria smiled and stood, "You know who you're talking to."

Njord nodded, but suddenly threw himself to the ground, "I thought that I was extremely disrespectful! I was yelling, I interrupted you-"

Gloria burst out laughing, "Good lord, calm down Njord. I appreciated the reminder, thank you."

They both flinched as a voice said, "Aren't you two lively."

They both spun around and saw an old man. He smiled, "I remember when I was your age." Laughing to himself, he walked back into the building.

It took a while, but eventually they found the portal hidden behind an abandoned McDonalds. There was no issue with the Sleeping Fallen. After an hour, Gloria stood before a wall as large as the one surrounding the Capital.

However, unlike the Capital wall, this wall was much more fortified. Iron spikes as large as smart cars covered the top of the wall. Gloria felt uneasy as she noticed a skeleton impaled on one of them. Watch towers rose up every five hundred feet. Njord pointed to a gate. Two Dragonborn guards stood on either side.

Gloria said, "By the way, how will a human like me enter a human hating city like this?"

Njord said, "Er, Dux gave me an idea. It is not a deficient idea, I assure you. We will have to disguise you."

Gloria said, "Um, how do we do that?"

They both retreated into the bushes, Njord said, "I will utilize illusion magic, as well as a few spells. It is a certain type of magic, there is an issue, however. We require you to disguise yourself as a Bestia Human hybrid."

Gloria said, "How is that a problem?"

Njord said, "Er, the more indistinguishable the illusion, the better. Er, I mean, the more indistinguishable it is from your normal state, the longer the magic will last."

Gloria said, "Why is that?"

Njord said, "Well, the human body is the base of most beings. Two arms, two legs, a head, two eyes, comprise most mythical creatures. They show similar human traits."

Gloria said, "So... what would be fitting?"

Njord said, "Well..."

He stared at Gloria for a moment, just long enough for Gloria to feel uneasy.

Njord said, "I would predict that a Bull Bestia would be rather simple. I discovered that City C-Four is a Bull Bestia city. You would be required to abandon your sandals, however. Yes, this may work."

Gloria took a nervous step backwards, "Woah, boy. I'm *not* having a cow's head."

Njord said, "You are describing the minotaur more than a Bestia, do not worry, this will match your original form by eighty five percent."

Gloria sighed, "Well, if it'll work, then, do what you must..." Gloria closed her eyes as a bright white light flashed in

THE BLOOD MOON CURSE

front of her.

Gloria opened her eyes, but she didn't feel any different.

Njord said, "Well, the process was successful. You look like a Bull Bestia."

Gloria said, "How do I look?"

Njord muttered a spell and a reflective surface appeared. She flinched when she saw herself. The only noticeable features were the horns curling a foot above her head and round hooves for feet.

Gloria reached towards her head, but she didn't feel the horns there, her hands went through them. She said, "Wow, they'll think these are real?"

Njord nodded, "Yes."

Gloria said, "What about your disguise?"

Njord said, "Given that I am a Cecaelian, I do not require one."

Gloria said, "Ah, right, should we go then?"

Njord nodded and they ran from the bushes towards the gates.

The guards didn't even look twice. One pulled a lever and the gates swung in. As they passed, the gate swung shut. After a small stone hallway, they entered a stone circular chamber. Gloria saw two Bull Bestia standing in front of another gate, though these guards seemed different.

Njord said, "Oh no."

Gloria whispered, "What's wrong?"

Njord whispered back, "There is a slight chance that Bull Bestia of their caliber may be able to identify your disguise as faulty."

Gloria sighed, "Never can be easy, huh?"

CHAPTER 6: GLORIA
The Mighty Bestia Capital

The guards were slightly smaller than the Dragonborn outside. One was slightly shorter than the other. The one on the right held a long spear. Gloria saw horns and hooves.

The Bestia holding the spear was built like a long distance runner. She had brown eyes and hair, which was neatly clipped at her shoulders. Gloria saw she wore gray leather leggings, with a steel guard on her left shoulder. Her eyes reminded Gloria of Amber's, glowing with excitement.

The Bull Bestia on Gloria's left looked similar, to the point that Gloria decided they were twins. He was more heavily built. His arms were crossed, and his gray eyes gave a defensive look. He had short brown hair and a small gold ring hung in a necklace around his neck. He wore a brown kilt, with leather leggings.

Gloria concluded that either of these guards were strong enough to break her neck. However, they looked just slightly older than her and Njord.

The female Bestia nudged the others' shoulder, Gloria heard her say, "Bo, look! A Bull Bestia!"

A male voice said, "Don't judge a book by its cover, Bele."

Bele said, "Oh don't be so strict! I haven't seen a Bull

Bestia since graduation!"

She turned to Gloria, "Hello! My name is Cybele, though most call me Bele-"

The other guard said, "Bele!"

Cybele gestured to the other guard, "And this is Bovi!"

Gloria said, "Bowey?"

Cybele laughed, "It's Latin, it's spelled with a V and pronounced as a W."

Bovi nudged Cybele, "We're not supposed to socialize Bele."

Cybele sighed, "I know, but I get bored standing here!"

Bovi said, "I *know* that, I just don't want to lose our jobs-" He flinched, "Um, anyways! State your purpose!"

Cybele elbowed him, "Let off! Have you ever seen a criminal or human ever enter?"

Bovi said, "No-"

Cybele said, "Then let loose a little! They would need to be out of their minds to try and enter the Bestia Capital."

Bovi sighed, "It's protocol Bele!"

Cybele said, "I want to at least know their names!"

Bovi said, "What if they're wanted? Or human-"

Gloria said, "My name is Gloria, and this is Njord."

Njord muttered, "I would have used different names-"

Cybele smiled, "Gloria, what a pretty name! You two go right through! If you're travelers, go to the Golden Ring Inn, mention my name and they'll give you anything for free-"

Bovi said warningly, "Bele-"

Cybele said, "Look at them Bo! They're cut, bruised, and I don't see any bags! They were probably run off by a monster, or an angry human mob."

Well, she's not wrong, Gloria thought.

Cybele turned back to Gloria, "That's the Golden Ring Inn, mention Bele, get whatever you need. If you need us, we're in district C, county four, C-Four. Look for the twin rings and our names above an arch."

Bovi set his face in his hand, "You're being too nice again Bele-"

Gloria said, "Thank you so much! We really appreciate it!"

Gloria took Njord's hand and started for the exit, Cybele waved, Gloria waved back.

Njord said, "She was extremely kind."

Gloria nodded, "I actually feel bad for lying now."

Njord said, "Do I need to remind you of how Bestia perceive humans?"

They exited the tunnel, and Gloria gasped as they entered the Bestia Capital. Gloria thought that they must have been in an area that was mostly populated with Bull Bestia. Everywhere Gloria looked, she mostly saw Bull Bestia of all ages. Then Gloria reminded herself that they were in a Bull Bestia city. There were shops, houses, markets surrounding them. The shops were stacked on top of each other with clerks trying to sell various items to the passing crowds. They were walking on tan colored bricks that made the road. Gloria watched little children Bestia playing. There were lanterns with colorful fires drifting above the road.

Gloria looked up. Behind them she saw two golden rings surrounding the words, *the Bull Twins*, Gloria also saw their names in small letters.

Gloria said, "Why are they displayed like that?"

Njord said, "According to Amber, citizens are allowed to challenge what are called *gatekeepers*, as an attempt to replace them in their jobs. From what I am informed, a gatekeeper is one of the highest paying jobs in the entire capital."

Gloria said, "And what happens to the old guards?"

Njord said, "If they have not perished, then they are unemployed and publicly shamed."

Gloria said, "That must be a little stressful."

Njord said, "They retire after a certain age. It is a permanent occupation, you are not allowed to quit."

They walked under a bridge, Gloria saw a few Bestia children playing what seemed to be hopscotch. A few others were kicking a ball around, while two were wrestling.

After passing the bridge, Gloria spotted a large gold ring. There were large bold letters spelling the Gold Ring Inn. It was a tall clean brown brick building, with balconies on every room. A neon sign pictured a large bull sleeping, with Z's floating upward.

Gloria pointed, "Bingo, that's where we stop, Njord." Njord nodded, Gloria said as she pushed open the door, "And Bele was kind enough to help us."

The desk clerk was also a Bull Bestia, they smiled, "Welcome to the Golden Ring Inn, how can I help you?"

Gloria said, "Er, we'd like two rooms, also, Bele said that we could get supplies here?"

The clerk laughed, "Bele, huh? She's nice to everyone, tied in rank with Bovi for gatekeepers you know! The town is so happy for her, for them I mean. As for the supplies, sure! Anything you need, I'll get you."

Gloria nodded, "Er, clothes, food, water, camping supplies, and bags please."

The clerk nodded, "We'll deliver it to your room shortly." The clerk handed Gloria a set of keys attached by a small ring, "Enjoy your stay."

Gloria and Njord found stairs and walked a few stories upward. Gloria couldn't help but notice that this inn was much cleaner than the inn at the Kingdom of Hydro, or the one on Earth.

Gloria opened her door and sighed happily. She collapsed onto the nearest bed, sinking into it. Njord checked the windows, locking them. He found that the rooms were joined by a door. He disappeared into his room while Gloria found a television remote.

Njord returned and frowned when he saw Gloria watching the tv.

Njord said, "Er, I will occupy the neighboring room. I recommend a shower-"

He flinched when Gloria glared at him, "Are you saying I *stink*?"

Njord quickly shook his head, "I did not intend to be offending! However, you do appear to possess an unpleasant aroma-" His eyes widened, and he ducked behind the door as ice froze over it.

Gloria yelled, "You *don't* tell a girl that she smells, unless it's a *complement*!"

Njord resurfaced, his eyes glowing slightly, "A-Apologies!" He shut the door.

Gloria shook her head, "*Unpleasant aroma, honestly.*" She smiled, "Sometimes, he's plain hopeless." She looked around the room, hesitatingly smelling under her arm. She recoiled, "But he's *never* wrong."

She stood from the bed and walked briskly to the bathroom

Gloria awoke slowly and sat up rubbing her eyes. She had slept like the dead. She realized that she and Njord haven't slept a full night since the Fall Tree Academy. She stood up, stretching and noticed two yellow bags next to her bed.

She rummaged through them, finding maps, compasses, flashlights, a tent, sleeping bags, bug spray, sun screen, two folding knives, and other useful supplies. Gloria smiled as she found changes of clothes. She had slept in a bathrobe. She also found a stack of money.

"That's nice." she said. There was also toiletries and a

touring pamphlet.

She walked to the next room, knocked, then opened the door. She saw Njord asleep in his bed.

She said, "Njord! Wake up dude!"

Njord flinched, yelping as he fell out of his bed. Gloria said, "Bele really paid off! We got everything we needed! I even found first aid and some magic supplies!"

Njord muttered, "Yes, yes, very excellent. However, why did you have to-"

He reappeared from behind the bed, his eyes blazed green. His hands shot over his eyes, "Why- P-Please acquire proper c-clothing!"

Gloria looked down. She burst out laughing, "*Sorry*, you didn't have to over react, it's just a *robe, weirdo.*"

She shut the door behind her and Njord lowered his hands, "I-It was n-not an overreaction, if a-anything it was proper ethics."

A few minutes later, Gloria heard a knock on the door, "E-Er, are you alright?"

Gloria said, "Come in."

When Njord entered, Gloria saw that he was wearing new clothes from his bag. He adjusted the collar of the gray shirt. "There was a pair of pants that were with this. Needless to say, I neglected them."

Gloria said, "Cecaelia don't wear pants, now do they?"

Njord blushed slightly, "I recommend you attempt to fabricate a flexible eight legged garment! It is surprisingly difficult!"

Gloria laughed, "I'm just messing with you. Now, let's see what we need to do."

Njord reluctantly joined her on the bed. Gloria opened a map from the bag which showed the entire Bestia capital.

Gloria said, "Now that I think about it, why did we end up here? In lovely C-Four? Bull Bestia city? Right where Lapsus wanted to attack?"

Njord said, "Well, the portal automatically sends users to the most used portal. City C-Four is also the second largest district in the Bestia capital, next to the Dragonborn districts A and B. Therefore, the portal sent us here by default, where most users go."

Gloria said, "Wait, isn't Lapsus aiming to kill as many as possible? With these defenses, why would he attack here?"

Njord thought for a moment, "Well... Er... that... That actually is not a bad question."

They both jumped as a loud explosion sounded from the window. They ran to the balcony and looked at the road. Gloria smiled, it seemed as though a parade had started. Bull Bestia were throwing fireworks into the air. There were numerous dancers, some were doing tricks with spears as they walked by.

Gloria laughed, "How cool, what is this?"

Njord said, "Er, my knowledge of specific Bestia traditions is vague, however, I recognize this as *the Fire Bull March*. They march along the main street, activating numerous fireworks to celebrate the establishment of their city."

Gloria recognized Cybele and Bovi aloft large floats. Bovi stood with his arms crossed, occasionally smiling at the crowd, while Cybele was enthusiastically waving.

Gloria pointed, "Hey look! It's the bull twins!" Gloria called out, "Hey, Bele!" She saw Bele look up at her and wave. She suddenly frowned, squinting her eyes at Gloria.

Njord yelped, forcing Gloria's head down while he muttered a spell. Gloria saw a bright white flash. Njord pulled her back up, waving downward.

Gloria whispered, "What-"

Njord muttered, "You were not disguised!"

Gloria inhaled sharply. She waved back at Bele, who reluctantly waved back, shaking her head, as if denying a thought.

Gloria walked into the room, "I totally forgot! That was too close, thanks Njord."

Njord nodded, "Do not worry, however, we need to be cautious. Do you recall what I said yesterday? I claimed that another Bull Bestia could possibly interfere with your disguise. Fortunately, this may only happen during... er... Bull Bestia tend to initiate challenges by butting heads. In your case, you would suffer from severe head trauma, if not death."

Gloria nodded, "Good to know."

Gloria walked towards her nightstand, taking the brochure from the top. Gloria scanned through it, Njord came up behind her.

Gloria shoved the map into his hands, "You read, you're quicker, determine what we should do. I'll gather our things."

Gloria went into Njord's room first. She grabbed his bag, some water, a few books, and a smaller black notebook from his desk.

She opened his bag, "Woah."

Everything was neatly organized. Gloria suspected Njord could have fit another load of things and still have space. Gloria's bag was almost bursting. She had just folded and shoved everything back.

Gloria found where Njord's things went, and zipped his bag shut. She realized that she had forgotten that small black notebook.

She picked it up, reading the front, "*Captain's log?*"

She figured that she shouldn't go sneaking through his things, though her curiosity almost made her. She dropped it in his bag and met him in her room.

Njord was standing, muttering to himself, Gloria said, "Anything?"

Njord said, "Well, I determined the chances of Lapsus attacking highly populated locations within this city. However, locations such as academies, restaurants, and suburban accommodations are each surprisingly heavily guarded. The schools being the heaviest with protection."

Gloria waited, Njord said, "I have discovered that the Fire Bull March concludes at the city's amphitheater. Afterwards, there will be the main celebration. I predict that most of the population will be located there." Njord shook his head, "The probability of Lapsus attacking that location is approximately seventy six percent. What I do not understand is *why*. If all of the city's population will be there, then the security will be at the highest point. Therefore, there is a high probability that he is underestimating the Bestia."

Gloria said, "So... what should we do?"

Njord said, "Regarding the numbers, I predict that we should attend this festival. If Lapsus attacks, then we would be there to capture him, as well as subdue any threat. If it is a magical threat, then we would be the only ones able to defeat them."

Njord realized that Gloria was staring at him, Njord looked towards the ground, "E-Er, you are staring rather intensively."

He caught his backpack in surprise, Gloria said, "Just admiring your thought process. Let's go to a festival."

They exited their rooms, bade the desk clerk goodbye, and left the inn. It wasn't too difficult to find the amphitheater, with the advertisements, the locals, the signs, and the brochure. They passed a large market just before the amphitheater's gates.

One seller pointed to Gloria, "You there! You're a pretty lass! Why not decorate that pretty neck of yours?" Gloria respectively declined the vendors and eventually they were at the gates.

The amphitheater was a large stadium-like settlement. The walls were made of smooth white stone, with large lights pointing into the center.

They stood in a steadily moving line. When they got near the front Gloria gasped. The guards next to the entrances were waving metal detecting devices around the Bestia. Once it beeped, and the Bestia sighed, fishing a crystal ball-like object that floated in his hand.

The guard said, "No magic of any kind in the amphitheater, hand it over, you'll get it back afterwards."

Gloria tugged on Njord's sleeve, "Problem, problem, problem!"

Njord followed Gloria's hand, gasping at the sight of the guards, "Those are magicule detectors, they sense magic of any kind. They would discover your disguise!"

Gloria said, "What do we do?"

That was when Gloria heard a familiar voice, "Hey, isn't that- it is! Gloria? Njord?"

Gloria and Njord turned to see Cybele waving at them. She dragged Bovi behind her. She smiled at Gloria, "How are you guys? Did you like the inn?"

Gloria inwardly signed with relief, "Oh, yeah it was nice."

Cybele said, "Did the desk clerk give you any trouble?"

Gloria shook her head, "He was more than happy to help."

Gloria thought she saw Bovi glance at the top of her head out of her peripheral vision. When she looked at him, he was staring at Cybele.

Cybele said, "Say, me and Bovi are supposed to go up to a security booth, you two want to come and sit with us?"

Bovi said, "Bele, we're not supposed to offer that to the public!"

Cybele elbowed Bovi, "Come on! We need more people to talk to! This is the first female Bull Bestia I've *talked* to in *ages*." Bovi sighed.

Gloria said, "Um, sure."

Cybele beamed, "Awesome!"

They led the way, Gloria glanced at Njord and followed.

They reached the guard, who said, "Lady Bele, sir Bovi, welcome."

Bele waved and walked through the gate. The guard eyed Gloria and Njord but didn't say anything.

They followed the bull twins through the crowds, finally reaching a door in the walls. They entered an elevator and entered what Gloria thought was the booth. There were six movie theater-like seats in front of a large glass window. There was a clean red carpet that made the floor. They were high above the stadium and overlooked the many Bestia filling the amphitheater. There was a drone of conversations and quiet music filling the silence.

Cybele sat next to Bovi and gestured to Gloria to sit on her other side. Njord took a seat to Gloria's right. Cybele set her spear on the floor in front of her.

She groaned, "I can't wait for all these security measures to end! I've had to escort seven royals, surveillance ten meetings, and even a *birthday* party! I am *so* tired."

Bovi said, "Doesn't help that the moderator is up our tails."

Cybele threw her hands upward, "I know! Random inspection this, and strength test that! If I have to demonstrate combination animarum *one more time* to that weasel." Cybele scratched her head, "Speaking of tails, did you hear that they added a tail grooming law? I need to get a tail brush now."

Gloria decided to take a brave stab at conversation, "So, uh, you and Bovi are gatekeepers?"

Bele nodded, "Yeah, good money, but I should have just been a regular guard. Took my parents' entire savings to afford the training. I'd give *anything* to just disappear. Go see the world, actually make friends."

Bovi looked at Cybele, "I wish we could too, Bele."

Gloria said, "What's a moderator?"

Cybele said, "A snotty dude who makes sure Bovi and I follow the laws. Bragging about his *authority*." Cybele spoke in a mocking voice, "*Oh look at this! A law that allows me to execute gatekeepers? Well, glad I won't ever have to use that! Right, you two?*" She groaned, "So annoying!"

Bele looked at Gloria, "What about you two? Where are you from, the Celestial forests? No, you wouldn't have been chased out of there... right?"

Gloria said, "Um, around that area, yeah."

Bele gasped, "You're near the humans?"

Gloria saw Njord glance away. She thought she saw a green glow against the wall in front of him.

Gloria said, "Yeah?"

Cybele said, "Isn't that a little dangerous?"

Gloria thought for a moment, "Well, the humans I am near are... friendly."

Cybele scoffed, Gloria said, "No really! The magicians helped the fairies loads of times."

This was true, Gloria and Uncle Dux visited quite often. They usually helped a few animals out of traps and chased the occasional magician from the woods. Mostly anything the fairies and the elves reported.

Cybele said, "Magicians aren't nice, they hate Bestia. Me and Bovi have been chased by one mob too many." She nudged Bovi, "You remember that, right?"

Bovi grunted, "They wanted our skin for their coats. I gladly sent them to a hospital."

Cybele looked at Gloria, she said, "You sound like you know these humans though."

Gloria felt Njord nudge her, though he still stared at the wall. Gloria said, "Um, from what I heard...the magicians there are really nice. They opened a school for other magicians and

Elementalists."

Bovi and Cybele both looked shocked, "They opened a school for *Elementalists*?"

Gloria nodded.

Cybele thought for a moment, she said, "Wow, that's... different. Are the founders all Elementalists?"

Gloria said, "No, there's only two, but they're the founders."

Bovi said, "From what I heard, humans and magicians alike hate Bestia. I guess they still hold a grudge from the war. Even though it was *them* who killed the Bestia king."

Gloria said, "I've seen a Dragonborn in their midst."

Bovi and Cybele snorted, Cybele said, "No offense, Gloria, but Dragonborn *hate* humans. Even more so than Bestia, I would bet my job and all my savings that no Dragonborn would ever be caught *dead* with a human."

Gloria shrugged, Cybele said, "Maybe these humans *are* good?"

Bovi said, "I doubt it. It sounds like plain insanity, Dragonborn and *Humans*? You must have seen an illusion or something." However, both seemed lost in thought.

Gloria turned to Njord. She whispered, "I want to tell them."

Njord whispered back, "*Pardon*?"

Gloria said, "I don't like lying to them! I want to warn them about the attack!"

Njord said, "They would eliminate you if you were to revea- do you know what! We are not required to make companions here!"

Gloria said, "If the two best guards in the city are, well, on guard, then they could help us!"

Njord said, "I understand your reasoning, however it is too precarious. They are required *by law* to... *execute* humans."

Gloria said, "We'll cross that bridge when we get to it."

Njord said, "I dislike what you are saying."

Gloria stood, Cybele said, "Um, what's wrong Gloria?"

Gloria caught Njord's eye. He was shaking his head, Gloria said, "Cybele, Bovi, there's something I should tell you."

Bovi stood up straight, Cybele said, "What?"

Gloria said, "If I were to say... this amphitheater has a high chance of being attacked and Njord and I are the only ones who can stop it..."

Bovi stood, Cybele caught his wrist, "Bo, no!"

Cybele turned to Gloria, "What are you saying?"

Njord stood as well, "A-Apologies! Gloria and I have come to warn this city! We plead with you to neglect asking how we possess this information."

Cybele glanced at Bovi. She turned to Gloria, "We'll overlook it, what is going to happen?"

Gloria said, "An evil magician named Lapsus is planning to attack here. We're not sure when, or where, but he plans to kill as many people as possible. We decided to come here, to stop him from hurting anyone!"

Bovi said, "Magician?"

Cybele elbowed him, "I believe you Gloria! We'll help! Tell us more!"

Gloria said, "We think that he'll summon the Fallen, or some form of magic-"

Bovi scoffed, "*Please*! Bele, why should we believe them? *The Fallen*?" He gave her a slightly knowing look.

Cybele said, "I know *every* Bestia in this city, *except* her! I have to believe her! We were informed that something might happen, this might just be it!"

Bovi said, "How would they know? Why are they telling us?"

Cybele said, "We won't ask!"

Bovi glared at Gloria and Njord, "There is something off about them, Bele."

Gloria said, "We promise that our only objective is to help!"

Cybele glared at Bovi, "*Bo.*" Bovi squirmed a bit, Cybele said, "Bo!"

Bovi said, "Alright fine! But what if the Capital hears about this?"

Cybele said, "What they don't know won't hurt them."

Bovi sighed, "Oh boy."

Cybele turned to Gloria, "What must you do?"

Gloria faintly heard a voice through a speaker system from below. It sounded like the show was about to start. Gloria couldn't make out the words, but the crowd cheered loudly. Gloria saw a few fireworks light up the room. Bovi and Cybele were both staring at Gloria intently.

Gloria hesitated, all she knew was that they had a very vague idea of where Lapsus would attack. They didn't know his power or capability, they couldn't afford to be wrong.

Gloria turned to Njord, "What would you do?"

Njord thought for a moment, "Well, since we do not have a confirmed theory of what Lapsus will utilize, the most that we could do for now is summon a photonic magicule sensor. This will allow us to know where he may appear if he uses magic. It would alert us precisely up to five minutes in advance if it were a vortex."

Before Gloria could ask, Njord said, "A vortex is a magician portal that connects with the magical transportation system."

Gloria nodded, Cybele said, "Could you please do this? If you aren't lying, then it sounds like we'll be facing a magician."

Njord said, "In all technicalities, it would be a Fallen magician with unknown capabilities."

Bovi said, "Then what are we waiting for? There's a

hatch that leads on top of this booth."

They stood. Bovi being the closest, opened the hatch and went first, followed by Njord, then Gloria and Cybele. Below, a performer was singing while the Bestia cheered.

Bovi shouted over the noise, "Cecaelian, use your magic, I will inform other guards to stand down." Bovi brought his hand to his ear, where Gloria saw a small device like an earpiece.

Gloria saw Njord's eyes glow, "Er, right."

Njord brought his hands outward, "Er, *inspicere, translatio-*"

While Njord was muttering, Gloria thought she saw Bovi tighten his fists. Cybele set an arm on his shoulder.

A small white spark spluttered into view and shot upward straight over the crowd, into the center of the amphitheater.

Njord said, "In approximately two minutes four seconds, a vortex connecting from Earth will appear there."

Gloria said, "That's all you can tell?"

Njord's eyes glowed brighter, "I have never utilized this system of magic before."

Gloria said, "We need to empty the amphitheater, who *knows* what he might bring here." Gloria said to Cybele, "Can we do that?"

Cybele said, "The only reason that they would empty the amphitheater is if a category three or four threat were to occur. A vortex is considered two."

Gloria said, "What about evil magicians?"

Cybele said, "Depending on the numbers, one to ten is one, ten to forty is two, fifty and up is three."

Gloria said, "What about monsters? Like the Fallen?"

Cybele said, "Any sort of Fallen is a three."

Njord said, "One minute!"

Gloria said, "What if it's an Elder Fallen?"

Bovi said, "You seem to know a *lot* about our enemy."

Cybele elbowed him, "Stop it."

Gloria said, "Let's just say that I've dealt with him in the past."

Cybele said, "Look, there's not much that the Bestia can't handle. Worst comes to worse, someone gets an injury or two. We'll evacuate if it's worse."

Njord said, "Thirty seconds!"

Gloria said, "Fine, no matter what happens, just know that Njord and I are not your enemy."

Before Bovi or Cybele could say anything else, a large purple cloud formed in the sky. Gloria saw a human figure drop from the cloud.

Gloria scowled, "It's him."

Lapsus shot spells at the speakers and his own voice echoed through the amphitheater.

"Filthy beasts, know who you stand before! I am your destiny, your death. Kneel before me! Your death will help nurture your new lord. Honor your savior, for I have come to save you all."

Gloria said, "What is he even talking about?"

Lapsus ducked as a spear flew over his head, "Silence! Comply peacefully, and I will not level this city!" He was clipped in the head with a small rock.

Dark waves of light swirled around him, "I said, SILENCE!"

He threw his hands out, a wave of black light exploded in the amphitheater. When the smoke cleared, Gloria saw that the entire amphitheater was coated with a thick black ice.

Cybele made a noise of anger, "He dares use magic against Bestia? That goes against the ancient laws signed after the second war!"

Gloria spoke to Cybele, "Stay here, Njord and I will handle this."

Gloria nodded to Njord. He wrapped an arm around her, muttered a spell, and they flew down into the arena.

When they were gone, Bovi turned to Cybele and said, "I know you like them, Cybele. I will support you in what you do. I know that you know what they are hiding. You must decide to follow the law or turn a blind eye."

Cybele sighed, "I know Bovi, I know."

Gloria and Njord landed a few yards away from Lapsus. He appeared different, his eyes were filled with static. His clothes were rags and he had not shaved in a few days. His voice sounded different, it simultaneously carried a menacing tone and a chilling freeze.

"You two? I should skin him, I thought he lost those papers" He pointed to them, "I hope you have come to surrender. I've been rather *busy*."

The large cloud above churned faster. Roars and groans echoed from the tempest's center. Tendrils of smoke drifted from the cloud, orbiting it, then rejoining the mass. Black electricity crackled from the cloud.

Gloria snarled, "How dare you attack my home! My friends, and my family! If the Bestia don't kill you, I sure as heck will!"

Lapsus sneered, "You are as fiery as I was told, it seems you've found a look that makes you even more brutish than before. He did not think that was possible."

Gloria charged forward, Njord held her back, "Wait a moment-"

Lapsus laughed, "You are all imbeciles! Scattered, confused, and as always, you have no idea what is to come."

Gloria yelled, "So bring out whatever *grand* thing it is that Njord and I have to destroy!"

Lapsus scoffed, "As you so desire." He raised his hand

upward and bellowed into the clouds, "*Vocavit!*"

The cloud rumbled, and a large figure dropped from the cloud, directly in front of Gloria and Njord.

It was tall, almost twenty feet. It towered over them. It was very skinny with charred skin crumbling from its form. Gloria noticed a large cleaver-like weapon fused to its bony wrist. It was a blade the size of a Cadillac and it glinted with a blue light. The other hand was also a blade, but much smaller, it looked like a kitchen knife. The monster's head had skin too large for its face, as though someone pulled the skin up and a revolting mass hung from the back of its head. It had no skin on its bottom jaw which was wired to the top jaw. There were random knife shaped spikes jutting from its back. The creature groaned and roared through its teeth. Black blood pooled from its mouth as smoke drifted from its nose.

Gloria shuddered, "*What is that?*"

Njord said, "It... It is the *Carnifex, the butcher.*"

The creature groaned, blood bubbling from its maw.

Lapsus said, "Observe closely, lesser beings, it is infused with the Flames of Destruction, enhanced with magic."

Njord gasped, Lapsus smiled widely. Gloria said, "What's wrong?"

Njord said, "This creature is enhanced, meaning that it will be difficult to defeat it with magic. However, a fair match would be utilizing...the Golden Ice."

Gloria gasped, Njord said, "He predicts that you are not able to use it without revealing yourself."

The butcher snarled and steam hissed from its mouth.

Lapsus said, "I predicted that your breed would be here. You have been a nuisance for far too long. Now perish, *impetum!*"

The butcher struck its hands together, sparks flying from the blades.

CHAPTER 7: IGNIS
The Initiation

"**A**ny other activity?" Ignis asked. Uncle Dux replied, "No, it doesn't seem like it. Come inside Ignis, we have a few things to go over."

Ignis set the binoculars in Uncle Dux's hands and followed him to the dining room. Ignis saw his parents, Fornacem, Umbra Mortis, Arbor, and Amber sitting around the table. Uncle Dux took the head of the table, while Ignis sat next to Amber. Fornacem jolted awake as Uncle Dux started.

Uncle Dux said, "Right, we still don't have magic. We need to know what we can do without it." Uncle Dux said, "Let's see, we have Amber's physical strength, and she can fly. We also have Fornacem and Umbra Mortis's physical strength..." He suddenly groaned, "It's just not enough! There are enough Fallen up there to fill a super bowl stadium! Fornacem call them off!"

Fornacem said, "No can do, the Fallen aren't as dumb as they seem. They've been promised blood and they don't forget that."

Amber said, "Also, don't go bragging about our physical strength, there's only so much that we can do."

Umbra Mortis said, "I feel as though you are only including *yourself* in that situation."

Amber sighed, "Fine, disregarding the *deities* in the room, *I* can only do so much."

Umbra Mortis grinned, "At least you know who your lords are."

Fornacem said, "*Damn* straight."

Uncle Dux gave a loud taxi cab whistle, "Listen, your Holinesses! Amber out performs all of us here with her sword capabilities. Also don't claim to be gods when you *both* can actually die."

Fornacem said, "Eh, fair enough."

Umbra Mortis said, "Mortals can't come back from death though."

Ignis spoke and everyone turned to look at him, "Listen! We have to work together! We need to figure out a way to contact the others and defeat the enemy! Is there any word from any of the others?"

Uncle Dux said, "No, any messages get intercepted. We're on our own."

Ignis sighed, the enemy had fired at them using catapults. Just before the barrier sealed over them, Arbor managed to sneak the students into an underground bunker, one hundred feet in the ground. He grew apple trees and sent a river through the room. Ignis felt better knowing the students were secure. Now, they had to find a way to protect themselves. They had not been able to contact Gloria or Njord and the silence made Ignis uneasy. Arthurs occasional outbursts didn't help either.

Arthur said, "We need to call the others! That should be the priority, Dux!"

Uncle Dux said, "Look, they're most likely going to attack again very soon. We need to find a way to protect ourselves. What have we got so far?"

Amber said, "I can fly around with my sword."

Uncle Dux nodded, Arbor said, "I still control the valley."

Uncle Dux said, "Very good."

Arthur said, "Why can't we just use magic? Or the elements?"

Uncle Dux shook his head, "As I mentioned before. There is an anti-magic barrier above us. Simply said, no magic or elements."

Umbra Mortis snickered, everyone stared at him, Uncle Dux said, "Any comments from the *peanut* gallery?"

Umbra Mortis grinned, "You humans are *so* simple minded. Who says you need *magicules* to perform magic?"

Uncle Dux slammed a hand to the table, "If you're going to say something, demon, then say it."

Umbra Mortis rested his head on his hand, "My, my, what a *terrible attitude*, Dux. Say the magic word."

Uncle Dux scoffed. Ignis sighed and said, "Please, Umbra Mortis?"

Umbra Mortis floated upwards, humming. He snuffed out a candle on the chandelier.

After a moment he grinned, "Back in the old days, and I mean the *old, old* days, humans used to be *so* ingenious. They built structures that lasted millennia, and even worshiped gods." He tilted his head backwards, "*Well*, they still *died*, but all humans are fragile. Nevertheless, they made sacrifices to the gods, praying for whatever they needed." He stared back down at them, "Some would even say they discovered how to use magic."

Uncle Dux said, "Yeah? So what?"

Umbra Mortis appeared next to Dux, who flinched as Umbra Mortis flicked his ear, "*Patience*, mortal. Point is, there were no *magicules* back then. What an *asinine* excuse, back when *I* was human, we *pitied* those who relied on magicules. Dead magic floating around, disgusting thought to have all that *shit* flowing inside you."

Ignis said, "What do you mean?"

Umbra Mortis said, "Oh, long story short, you can perform magic and elemental spells without magicules."

Uncle Dux scoffed, "*Horseshit*, that's not possible."

Umbra Mortis gave a sarcastic look of shock and drifted upward again. When he spoke next, it was in an affronted tone, "*No*? The thousand plus year old deity is *wrong*? *Well*, why'd I waste my time *here*? No one *appreciates* my help."

Ignis stood, "No, wait, please tell us."

Umbra Mortis smiled widely, "If the *tightwad* over there apologizes, hmm, I'll possibly reconsider."

Uncle Dux shook his head, then realized that everyone was staring at him.

He scowled, "Wha- you can't be serious! Magic without magicules? The thought is ridiculous!" Uncle Dux made a noise of indigency, as Umbra Mortis flipped him off.

Ignis said, "Come on Uncle Dux."

Uncle Dux spluttered, "What? We- I- We're about to *die*, and now I have to apologize to *that prick*?"

Julia smacked his arm, "Language, Dux! And yes, you do!"

Uncle Dux groaned, "*Fine*, I'm sorry."

Umbra Mortis appeared behind Amber, who yelped as Umbra Mortis plucked a hair from her head, "*Right*." He appeared back over the table, "Magic lies in everything. Only problem is, objects don't have the ability to live, so they can't use magic. *Humans* however..." Umbra Mortis took the hair, dropped it, and it stayed suspended. He thought for a moment, "Hmm, right, *vita*."

The hair blared a bright orange color and arced, spinning in a fast circle.

Ignis stared in shock. Amber said, "How is he doing that?"

Umbra Mortis dropped his hand, and it stayed spinning, "Amber, could you say... *simul?*"

Amber looked concerned, but she said, "Um, *simul?*"

The hair froze, and shot to Amber's head, where it fused back to her scalp.

Umbra Mortis said, "Magic hid within the hair and little Amber had no clue. Now, you want to use *magic?* For starters, all of you who have an aura. Is that *not raw* power? Hmm, why wasn't that thought of, hmm, *eh Dux?*"

He grinned wickedly at Uncle Dux, who stared at the table.

Ignis said, "Is... there a problem Uncle Dux?"

Uncle Dux said nothing, Umbra Mortis cackled, "*Poor* old Dux is going to have to swallow his pride and use aura magic!" He cackled again, pausing only to scoop a doughnut from the table, "Summary, auras are *not,* as magicians say, *used magic,* but the opposite. Anyhoo, I'm done for now, tell me when there are humans to kill. I'll be taking a bath."

He disappeared with a loud hiss, Uncle Dux sighed. Ignis said, "Uncle Dux?"

Julia patted Uncle Dux's back, "While your uncle is very skilled in magic, aura magic... was just something he never grasped."

Uncle Dux stood suddenly, "Alright! So, I can't use *child* level magic! Big deal!"

Ignis turned to Amber. She said, "Aura magic is the simplest kind of magic. It was incorrectly thought of as what remained after magic was used."

Arthur said, "And someone who never used it, doesn't know how."

Ignis was lost in thought. *There was a possibility for magic?* If there was, then they could be at a large advantage. Their magic was very advanced. If they could somehow tap into their magic, they'd have no problem defending themselves.

Wait, Ignis thought, *is that even possible?*

Ignis said, "That aside, can we really use magic and elements?"

Uncle Dux nodded, "I had hoped never to do it, it's embarrassing. I mean, the barrier will still weaken our magic."

Ignis stood, "So, what do we have to do?"

Arthur said, "Basically, we have to use our auras when fighting. It'll be difficult, but we can do it. The enemy would never see it coming."

Uncle Dux said, "That's because it's a *desperate* thing to do!"

Arthur smacked his arm lightly, standing from his seat. "Alright you big baby, let's teach an old dog, even older tricks.

Just like they warned, magic without magicules was hard. Ignis's aura flared meekly, but it stayed in his vision. Ignis was reminded of when he first summoned his aura, except Uncle Dux was doing worse. A shimmering white aura briefly appeared around Uncle Dux, but it faded away.

Julia said, "Don't worry Dux, you're getting the hang of it."

Ignis had decided that using magic without magicules was similar to removing swimming fins. Amber had described it as a reverse filter. The magicules allowed magic to move freely around you. Without it, magic liked to cling to other magic, so it liked to stay within you.

They were inside the training room. Fornacem was lounging on an old couch, while everyone else was trying to achieve their magic. Ignis stood on the red rug, trying to concentrate on Umbra Mortis's words.

Amber appeared next to Ignis, with a heavy gust of wind. "You're almost there. Basically, magic is a spoiled brat that wants to be fed a treat before doing anything."

Ignis smirked, after a while, his aura was back to normal

size.

Amber flared her aura, it flickered, "Woah, it *is* harder."

Ignis saw that his father achieved his aura almost immediately. It was identical to Ignis's.

He said, "Been a while, but it's like riding a bike."

Ignis felt a small wave of power and he saw Uncle Dux maintain his aura. It was a shining white light, surrounded by drifting stars of gray.

Uncle Dux shivered, "Oh that's *so* weird!"

Julia said, "You get used to it. Now, try channeling more power."

Uncle Dux concentrated, and his aura flared.

Julia said, "Good! Now, try a basic spell."

Uncle Dux raised a hand, "*Scintilla.*"

A small white flare shot from his finger, before fading from existence.

Julia smiled, "That's it! Keep it up!"

Umbra Mortis appeared out of nowhere. Fornacem grinned, "Afternoon."

Umbra Mortis snorted, "I remember when my aura was that pathetic. I don't think mine could fit in the valley."

Uncle Dux said, "I'm surprised your *ego* can."

Umbra Mortis cackled, "Focus on your meek little aura Dux. You still have a bit to go."

After a while, Ignis was firing elemental spells, teleporting, and moving just as quickly as before.

Arthur said, "You know, practicing without magicules is almost like lifting weights, but in reverse."

Umbra Mortis appeared next to him, "What an excellent example Arthur!"

Uncle Dux closed his eyes. A staff appeared in his hand, and he laughed, "Look! I summoned something!"

Umbra Mortis said, "Isn't it nice to remove those

training wheels?"

Uncle Dux ignored him and twirled the staff. A ball of fire followed the end. Uncle Dux swiped it sideways, and a burst of fire exploded in front of him.

Umbra Mortis appeared in front of them, "Here's a neat trick, if a spell is coming at you, summon a simple negative vortex. Dux, if you will?"

Uncle Dux nodded. A small green swirl of light appeared in front of his hand.

Umbra Mortis pointed at him, an orb of dark light began to swell from his finger. Umbra Mortis said, "Don't flinch now!"

The bullet surged from his finger and disappeared into the vortex.

Uncle Dux's jaw dropped, "*What? How?*"

Umbra Mortis said, "Vortexes connect directly to the caster. A regular vortex projects energy to transport the caster. So, a negative vortex-"

Ignis said, "Transports magic energy into the caster."

Umbra Mortis nodded, "Free energy!"

Uncle Dux said, "Wait, I thought you had to cast a spell to use magic."

Fornacem said, "Well, more powerful users don't need to do that. Usually, people think of the spells in their heads. The magic responds to them through their power. Making it difficult to tell what they'll do."

Ignis sat on the rug, taking a drink from his water bottle. Uncle Dux walked over to him, looking rather pleased with himself. Afterwards, they held another council.

Once again, Ignis found himself sitting at the table.

Uncle Dux said, "Alright, we can sort of do magic. We have loads more options now."

Arthur said, "Magic or no, there are still only seven of us. Sure, most of us have overpowering magic abilities, but we have to keep the damage within the valley."

Fornacem said, "Well, if it's numbers, you're worrying about, why not rally the kids downstairs?"

Uncle Dux shook his head, "Absolutely not. If Lapsus needs blood for a curse... The less blood there is, the better. Also, you would most likely use them for sacrifices, or entertainment."

Fornacem said, "Fair enough."

Umbra Mortis said, "Hmm, do I still *have* blood? That's a theory I have to test."

Uncle Dux ignored him. It took him a few attempts, but he summoned a map of the valley. Ignis saw that the red marks on the peaks of the mountain had grown larger and a darker red color.

Uncle Dux said, "Right, the enemy is growing and expanded their camp into the valley. Fornacem senses millions of Fallen, while Umbra Mortis thinks thousands of Fallen magicians may be there."

Fornacem smiled, "I remember your reactions to the first butcher. HA! I wish I had taken a picture! Dux almost pissed his pants!"

Uncle Dux sighed and pointed to the map, where white marks of light slowly appeared in the valley. "Which is why we need to surprise the enemy at every turn. I'm talking traps, basic elemental surges, vortexes to trip them up. That'll be phase one. Phase two, Arbor's security will kick in. He'll uproot rocks, control roots, and cause some earthquakes. If they get past that, then they'll meet us at phase three. The last hundred yards to the tree, we'll be there keeping them back."

Umbra Mortis looked bored. He nabbed a cookie from a tray, "You mean I don't get first pickings of the magicians? That sucks." He took a bite of his cookie, "I want dark blood!"

Uncle Dux said, "We're getting there. Now, is there anything that they might have that may cause a problem?"

Fornacem said, "Obviously, they have the Fallen.

Furnace Fallen, Golden Guardians, hunters, even a few butchers, which I haven't seen in a hundred years. I even saw a trapper."

Uncle Dux shuttered, "I hate trappers, though not more than butchers. Right, what else?"

Umbra Mortis said, "Dark spells, probably up to fifth tier magic. A few snacks for me then."

Uncle Dux said, "Right, going from what Umbra Mortis said, we need our auras around us at all times for magic, spells, elemental stuff. I will send messages through telepathy spells."

Uncle Dux pointed to Ignis and Amber, "You two however, when the enemy starts to attack, you call Gloria with that phone. Got it?"

Amber gave a thumbs up, "Can do."

Uncle Dux nodded, "Right, if there's no other questions, I suggest we put those traps up quickly."

The next hour, they prepared for the enemy. With Fornacem and Umbra Mortis's help, Uncle Dux made a bunch of traps, a few more deadly than he planned. Arbor summoned roots larger than trains, making an intricate, hard to navigate, terrain. If magicians touched them, they would be thrown away from the tree. Ignis saw gigantic plants resembling fly catchers.

Finally, there were the seven of them, the final line. They would wait one hundred yards from the tree and blast spells, magic, and curses at anything making it past the traps. Fornacem and Umbra Mortis would be on opposite sides of the valley, spreading their strength.

All that was left was to contact the others and await the enemy. They were stationed in pairs around the tree. Arbor was busy controlling the valley underground. Arthur was with Uncle Dux, facing the south. Ignis was stationed with Amber facing north. Julia went with Arbor to protect the children. Fornacem faced the west side of the valley and Umbra Mortis had the east.

They stood there, Amber kicking a small rock.

She turned to Ignis, "Hey, are you nervous?"

Ignis said, "I mean, millions of monsters essentially want to eat us, and magicians want to torture us to death or sacrifice us to a demon. Just another day."

Amber snorted, "Right, what if we do that thing again?"

Ignis said, "You don't mean *combination animarum,* do you?"

Amber nodded, "We have magic and relics! Why not use them?"

Ignis said, "Well, Spiritus almost destroyed the valley last time. It's better to have more numbers for now. Also, we don't know what we're doing. But, if there's a *giant* threat, I'm down."

Amber smiled, "Alright, fine."

Ignis heard Uncle Dux's voice in his ear, "Checking, does this work?"

Ignis heard his family respond. Amber said, "Yes sir."

Uncle Dux said, "Perfect, now, the enemy will likely attack after the sun sets. The valley will be dark in a few minutes. There are a few spells that'll signal the enemy's advance. Green is the traps, yellow is Arbor's maze, and red is when you'll see them. Defeat them or turn them to ash. Any problems, let us know."

Ignis said, "Got it."

As the sun set, Amber took a deep breath. "Here we go."

Ignis gasped as a green flare shot up in front of him.

Ignis said, "I've got a green flare over here!"

Uncle Dux said, "Brace yourselves, I just got a green too!"

After a while, Ignis heard the traps kick in. Screams and roars sounded in the distance. Ignis saw a magician float up in the air. After thirty minutes, Uncle Dux said, "Woah! I got yellow!"

Ignis saw a yellow flare shoot over his head, "Make that two." Ignis said.

Umbra Mortis and Fornacem said at the same time, "Green."

Uncle Dux yelped, "Woah! They're on my side now! Damn, I *hate* butchers!"

Fornacem cackled, "I made them *especially* for small targets you know."

Uncle Dux said, "When they're twenty feet tall, *every* target is a small target!"

Fornacem said, "That's the point! Ooh, I got yellow."

Umbra Mortis complained, "I *just now* got it! *Come on*, I want blood!"

Ignis said, "Quit arguing, please, oh boy." A red flare had shot upward in front of Ignis. "Red! We got red! It's a Fallen.... what the heck is that?"

Ignis saw a strange looking Fallen, a small shriveled being. Ignis saw long arms carrying many chains. It was dragging its feet, groaning in agony. It lifted its head and bared its teeth. Sections of barbed wire were sunk in the monster's charred skin.

Amber said, "Oh, that's an *Auceps.*"

Ignis yelped as a length of chain flew over his head.

Ignis said, "Trapper?" He jumped as a device resembling a bear trap snapped shut at his feet. Ignis realized the traps and the chain were not metal. Ignis gagged at the fleshy nail material. They moved as a part of the monster.

Ignis flared his aura and sent a ball of flame forward. It passed straight through the monster's chest. It screamed in agony, disintegrating as it fell to its knees.

Amber shuttered, "I don't like those."

Ignis heard Uncle Dux yell, "Ooh! I hate the *Reptans*! Gross!"

Ignis said, "What?"

A red flare shot into the sky, and Ignis saw a monster appear from the maze. It looked like a large four legged spider with large spikes for hands and legs. It had many red and beady eyes. It had six rows of needle-like teeth. Ignis groaned as he saw a tuft of blue fire emitting from a large wound on its side.

Ignis said, "Fire creature, I can't kill it."

Amber grinned, "I'll get it!"

She unsheathed her sword and charged. She flew in the air, slicing straight downward. The monster roared and dodged the strike.

Ignis heard Fornacem say, "Oh, right, the *Reptans*, spider-like creatures with devastatingly poisonous teeth. They can make a web that's also poisonous. They can see a few seconds into the future. Unless they're made with ice, then they can paralyze you with one glance. You know, I remember testing that poison on myself, it almost killed me! It took my arms and legs, and I almost suffocated in my own saliva."

Uncle Dux yelled, "Happy times!"

Umbra Mortis said, "Ooh, my sacrifices have arrived. I bid thee adieu."

Amber dodged the monster's strike, sweeping her sword sideways. She sliced one of the monster's eyes. It roared, firing a web directly at her. The web caught her, sending her backwards, where she stuck to the tree.

Ignis said, "Are you alright?"

Amber grinned, "Poison doesn't affect me!" She struggled against the webs, "Though, this stuff does."

Ignis heard a hiss and whirled around. The monster bared its teeth at him.

Ignis said, "Alright spidey, I can't kill you, you can't kill me. Well, not as long as you don't use those mighty fine teeth of yours. Why don't we relax and talk or something?"

The monster snarled. Poison dripped from its fangs,

where it hissed on the ground, the grass dying instantly.

Ignis said, "No? Well, that's unfortunate."

He saw Amber writhing to escape the prison. Her blade slipped from her fingers. Ignis moved a foot to the right, the monster followed.

Ignis said, "I have a question. What has four legs and is bleeding out?" Ignis took a few steps back as the monster hissed.

A silver blade dropped from above, piercing the monster's throat. It roared, stumbling backward, as blood poured from the wound.

Ignis said, "In case you didn't know, it was you!"

Amber appeared above it, "Die!"

She tore her sword from the monster's neck and stomped on its head.

Amber wiped her sword off in the grass and sheathed her weapon, "Not bad, eh?"

Ignis said, "You don't worry enough."

Amber said, "You worry too much."

Uncle Dux yelled, "Holy cow! *Furnace Fallen*! Woah! Somebody get those Golden Guardians! Amber! Ignis! Have you called Gloria and Njord yet?"

Ignis gasped, "Whoops!"

A large explosion ripped the silence and Ignis saw a large wave of Golden Guardians. Ignis said, "Not good, I'll try it!"

He pulled the phone from his pocket as another red flare shot upward. Ignis gasped as he saw a bunch of Fallen magicians.

One of them spoke to another, "I heard the boss was attacking Huntington in California. More blood for the gods, eh?"

They stopped short upon seeing Ignis and Amber. The magicians prepared spells, Amber blew fire at them.

She turned to Ignis, "You call Gloria! I got this!" She leaped into the crowd of magicians.

Ignis yelled, "What about those Golden Guardians?"

Ignis turned on the phone, jabbing the call button. He scrolled through the contacts, finding Gloria's name. The Golden Guardians disintegrated as balls of fire hit them.

Ignis muttered as the phone rang, "This is so *dumb!*" he heard a magician scream.

A Fallen magician yelled, "Back you filthy beast! A mere creature like you can't stop the power of the Blood Moon Curse!"

Ignis heard the phone say, *your call has been forwarded to an automatic voice message system-*

Ignis bellowed, "This is so *dumb!*" He jabbed the redial button, bringing it to his ear. Amber dodged spells and ducked under fists. Ignis winced as her sword found an unsuspecting throat.

Well, Ignis thought, *they are trying to kill us.*

Ignis ducked under a Golden Guardian that dove at him. Ignis heard Gloria's panicked voice, "Ignis?"

Ignis flinched, "Gloria! It's Ignis! There's a big problem at the Tree! Lapsus sent an army. We're in battle right now! They said something about California, a beach named Huntington.

Don't try to come! They destroyed all the portals and declared war! We don't know why but I-I think this has something to do with the Blood Moon Curse!

Uncle Dux thinks Lapsus intends to activate the curse. He said that you and Njord are the only ones who can stop it! Go to Huntington Beach, hurry-"

There was a loud explosion, and Amber yelled. An Elder Fallen burst through the maze, breathing fire everywhere, not sparing the magicians. It made a clunking noise as Amber took a small chunk off of it with her sword.

Ignis said, "Shoot, gotta go! Amber! Hold that thing

back!"

Ignis dropped the phone, sending a fireball at the Elder Fallen. It made a clunking noise, charging Ignis. He blasted fire and flew into the air.

Ignis muttered, "Why do they have so many of these things?"

Ignis blasted it in the face as Amber swung her sword again. There was another explosion.

Uncle Dux said, "*Canes,* closing in fast! Arthur-"

Arthur said, "Got them!"

The Elder Fallen swung at Ignis, he ducked and said, "*Limitata, fulminationem!*"

A large blue and black explosion blasted the Elder Fallen, sending it hurtling back into Arbor's maze.

Amber landed next to Ignis, "Nice one." Before Ignis could answer, another explosion ripped around them.

Ignis looked upward, his face fell, "That don't look good."

A large black cloud appeared over the valley, completely obscuring the sky. Black lightning crackled.

Uncle Dux said, "Oh my lord! That's a class A summoning portal! Fornacem, change in plans! Get to the roof and destroy that thing!"

Fornacem said, "Eh, alright."

Ignis flinched as sliver light lit the entire valley. Ignis's heart sank to his stomach as hundreds of monsters dropped from the cloud. There was a blinding black flash, and Arbor's maze, and the traps ahead disappeared.

Ignis yelled, "What happened?"

Uncle Dux said, "They fluctuated the anti-magic barrier! It resets magic in the area, canceling long term magic. And it put Arbor to sleep!"

Ignis groaned as an army of monsters charged at him,

"It's gonna be a *long* night, isn't it?"

Uncle Dux said, "New plan! It's a free for all! Kill every monster and evil magician in sight! Do whatever it takes to keep them away from the tree. I'll protect the tree, sending them back into the fray!"

Umbra Mortis said, "Ooh, with genuine pleasure, Dux."

A bunch of silver lightning bolts flashed from the top of the tree, striking hundreds of monsters. Ignis watched Umbra Mortis fly by, shooting dark spells at monsters and magicians. He saw hundreds of spells shooting between them. Ignis saw a few spells from Arthur as well.

The ground shook, Uncle Dux said, "Ha! Tier four, I've missed you!"

Even with the strong defense, countless monsters continued to spill into the valley. Ignis fired a wave of fire into the monsters and hundreds more took their place.

A black spell shot into the sky and Ignis heard a voice chant, *"Voco te, sentire iram meam, suscipe verba mea, demergat in coccineo mortem!"* There was a chilling cackle, and the spell exploded.

Ignis glanced upward at the moon and gasped. A lunar eclipse was occurring. The moon was surrounded by a dark blue light, the stars turned black and dimmed in brightness. The clouds disappeared, and whispers filled the air. The temperature plummeted and Ignis saw frost gather on his arms. Ignis decided that if the Blood Moon Curse was going to happen, it would happen here, at any minute.

Ignis remembered the signs. The sky turns dark, *check*, the moon prepares for blood, *check*, the stars fade into darkness, *check*.

Ignis would have to watch out for the next phase, because that's when he'll have to hold back. The sky will turn red, and the moon will start collecting blood. Then the whispers will temp Ignis into the curse.

Uncle Dux said, "Oh lovely! The curse is manifesting! It's only phase one people, so killing is tolerated, don't kill when phase two kicks in! That's what Lapsus wants! At least keep the blood off the grass."

Ignis estimated they had twenty four hours before phase two of the Blood Moon Curse. If they live that long, things will start to be harder.

Ignis turned to Amber, "You ready?"

Amber grinned at him, "Always."

Ignis nodded. Together, they jumped into the infinite army of monsters.

CHAPTER 8: GLORIA
Controlled Corruption

The butcher leered at Gloria and Njord, black bubbles frothing from its maw. Gloria's mind raced almost as fast as her heart. She couldn't use the Golden Ice. If she did, the Bestia would kill her.

It was enhanced, meaning that Njord's magic would have little effect. And of course, the only weapon she had was the puny knife in her backpack. Gloria suspected that the monster would lunge as soon as she moved.

Gloria thought, *how do you kill these things?* A smart voice answered back, *Golden Ice?* Gloria scolded herself, *not helping!*

The butcher charged. Gloria gasped and ducked under the blades. As she had expected, the giant blade was extremely slow, but powerful. The blade crashed into the ice, cracking it. The monster unlodged the blade and stomped towards them.

Gloria remembered covering these monsters during her class. Gloria insisted that ice users send spells in its blind spots, behind it, or directly under it.

Gloria said, "No good! Njord do something!"

Njord said, "I am as restricted as you are! Tempest magic would alert the capital, and other magic is insufficient!"

Njord rolled to avoid the blades, Gloria said, "What about the enhanced magic that you do?"

Gloria watched as Njord deflected the large blade into the ground next to him, "That is an idea."

Njord pointed at the monster, "*Torrens pluvia!*"

A black summoning circle blazed in front of Njord, and hundreds of small needle-like rain droplets fired from the circle. They shot through the monster like bullets. It roared and fell backwards, before slowly getting back to its feet.

Gloria saw a green blur, and the monster fell to the ground. After another blur, a large hole appeared in the monster's neck. It roared, swiping sideways. Gloria saw the blur stop a few feet from her and she saw Cybele holding her spear. She had a strange green hue around her.

Cybele spun her spear, "Back off!"

Gloria saw a figure leap from the top of the booth. With a loud crash that sent debris flying, Bovi landed next to her.

Bovi widened his stance, "Never fought a Fallen before."

Gloria ducked under the monster's swing, "Be grateful that you never have!"

The monster got back to its feet and raised its cleaver-like hand.

Cybele said, "*Wow, that's* slow."

As the blade swung down, Cybele disappeared, reappearing under the monster. She jabbed the monster's knees, disappearing with another green blur.

Bovi said, "Not everyone knows self-enhancing magic Bele."

So that was it, Gloria thought, *Cybele knew how to use self-enhancing magic?* Gloria decided to take a mental note.

Bovi punched the ground, picking up a chunk of ice the size of a pickup truck. He threw it at the monster. It roared and sliced the ice in half. Bovi leaped at the monster, punching it square in the jaw.

The monster's neck bent backwards in a sickening angle, and it fell to the ground. Bovi grunted as a spell hit him in the chest.

Lapsus sneered, "Damn beasts, this is a higher beings business." He fired another spell at them, Njord intercepted.

Lapsus snickered, "A duel then, squid?"

Two black summoning circles blazed on the ends of Njord's hands, "I suppose."

Gloria grew frustrated trying to help Bovi and Cybele, but the most she could do was throw ice chunks and trip the monster. Every time it got back up and each time it seemed to grow faster, smarter, stronger and angrier.

Njord and Lapsus were locked in a ferocious duel. Spells were flying in every direction.

Lapsus yelled, "Despair mortals, I have been accepted by a higher power!"

Gloria clipped his forehead with a chunk of ice, "Shut up, dude!"

Lapsus yelled, sending a shockwave and knocking everyone off their feet, including the butcher. Lapsus raised his hands and the cloud above crackled.

"Your childish remarks end here!" He yelled and waved his hand. A dozen monsters fell from the cloud. Gloria gasped, whipped off her backpack, and pulled the knife from her bag.

"I miss magic," she muttered.

The Furnace Fallen stood upright as a bunch of Golden Guardians swooped from the cloud. Gloria groaned as a Furnace Fallen charged. Gloria ran. Finding a large rock, she jumped on it, leaped off, and landed on the monster's back.

It felt like Gloria was riding a bucking bull, except that bull was as hot as a working forge. Gloria stabbed the knife into the monster's head as it ran forward.

Gloria said, "Woah! Bad idea!" Gloria steered the Fallen into the other monsters. Cybele dodged the monster, giving the trampled monsters a quick stab with her spear. She snickered at Gloria as she steered the Furnace Fallen over another monster.

Cybele said "You're nuts Gloria!"

Bovi was wrestling a Furnace Fallen. He grunted, lodging his fist into its side.

Gloria saw that Njord had conjured a storm that was striking any monster that left the area. It sent an occasional lightning bolt at unsuspecting monsters too.

Finally, Gloria's ride slowed down, its skin cooling until it disintegrated.

Gloria took a breath, "That was a horrible idea." She caught sight of another, "So let's do it again!"

Gloria somehow managed to kill a few more Furnace Fallen before she noticed Cybele pulling a Bestia from his seat. "Alert the Capital that there's a Fallen magician attacking."

The Bestia took off out of the amphitheater. Gloria seriously hoped that wouldn't be a problem later.

Bovi lifted the Furnace Fallen and slammed it into the ground, disintegrating it. Gloria heard Njord yelp and fly over her head. Lapsus strode towards her.

He threw his arms open, "Is this not glorious? The anarchy, the chaos."

Gloria backed towards Njord, "Umm, you're nutso, dude."

Lapsus sneered, "You will see that ventures are fruitless. Once I conquer these dull beasts, I will be unstop-"

He grunted as Bovi punched him in the side. Lapsus flew into the wall, making a large crater.

Gloria shuttered, Bovi's punches were equivalent to being hit by a speeding semi.

Gloria shook her head, running to Njord's side, "Njord! Are you ok? Do *not* make me slap you again, mister! Cause I will!"

Njord raised his hands, "Please do not. I am alive."

Gloria said, "Life and death are very close lines, you know!"

Cybele and Bovi appeared next to them. Cybele said, "You are so cool, Gloria! You killed a bunch of those monsters!"

Bovi huffed, "I killed more."

Bovi whipped around, punching a Furnace Fallen so hard his fist went through its face. Monsters surrounded them even as that one disintegrated. They moved as one. Bovi slammed the ground, knocking the monsters over. Cybele slashed their stomachs with her spear. Njord cast a dozen spells, and Gloria lodged a knife in one of them.

As Gloria tore her knife from the monster, the butcher rose again.

Gloria groaned, "Can someone help me?"

Cybele stood beside her and set the head of her spear on the ground. Gloria stood on it. With a grunt, Cybele launched Gloria at the butcher's face. Gloria stuck the knife in its eye, repeatedly stabbing it.

The butcher roared, slashing at her, but ultimately hurting itself. It grew rigid as a spear went through its neck. Gloria leaped to the ground, where Njord caught her.

Gloria hopped down, "Cool-"

Lapsus sprawled on the ground and Gloria saw broken bones snap back into place.

He stood, wincing, "Until his job is finished, he cannot die." He raised his hands and chanted, "*Trado tenebras, essentiam et corruptionem, me devorabit.*"

There was a blinding explosion, and a wave of darkness knocked them to the floor. When the smoke cleared, Gloria saw that Lapsus changed.

Static covered his arms, and small spikes of purple light grew from him. Black stars drifted from his body, fading into the dark skies. One eye was completely black, with his pupil blazing white. The other eye had static buzzing around it.

Njord gasped, "Is that–"

Lapsus bellowed, his voice deeper and more demonic, "Controlled corruption, the ace card of those Fallen Magicians! With this, he shall blow you all to hell!"

He put his hands together and a black ball of darkness collected there. Njord grabbed Gloria around the waist and leaped skyward. Bovi scooped Cybele from the ground and lunged the other way.

A blast of darkness exploded under them. It tore a hole in the amphitheater's wall. With a thunderous rumble, the wall crashed over them. A wall of wind slammed into Gloria as she lost her sight, but she felt Njord's arms around her.

He set her on the ground, "Are you alright?"

Gloria spit dust and coughed, "Peachy, where's Bo and Bele?"

As the dust cleared, Gloria saw Cybele and Bovi fighting Lapsus. Gloria stared at Cybele in awe. She was dodging spells with the grace of a gazelle. She spun her spear so fast that she was deflecting spells. Bovi was too slow to hit Lapsus, but he kept him moving. How Lapsus was able to fight both of them, Gloria didn't know.

Lapsus sent a spell at Cybele, who deflected it and swept her spear low. Lapsus jumped and hit Cybele with a spell. Bovi nailed him in the stomach, and Lapsus was sent flying.

A dark tendril of energy arced from his hand, connecting to the ground. Lapsus flipped back towards the ground, landing on his feet. The static crackled, sending black sparks from its surface.

Lapsus winced, "You damn beasts are proving rather resilient. I suppose I will have to push him harder!"

He yelled, and the static raced up his arms, past his shoulders, covering half his torso. Black stars made small explosions like firecrackers as they hit the ground. The spikes grew larger, and the static on Lapsus' face expanded.

He roared, sending another wave of magic at them.

Njord yelled, *"Thadal undam!"*

A tidal wave intercepted the magic in an explosion. Gloria gasped. She saw Bovi dragging Cybele towards them.

He set her on the ground, "She's using too much magic. It's taking all her energy."

Cybele was unconscious but was still breathing heavily.

Gloria said, "I'll watch her."

Njord said, "Bovi, I will assist you in combat."

Bovi nodded and they charged Lapsus, who activated his aura. With a powerful blast, it exploded into existence. It was a dark purple light, with patches of static buzzing throughout it. He sent a volley of dark spells, which Njord deflected.

He pointed at Lapsus, *"Ad iram augendam, fulgur!"*

A bright bolt of lightning struck Lapsus in the chest. Bovi jumped behind, hitting Lapsus in the back. Lapsus spat blood on the ground and sent spears of darkness towards them.

Njord ducked, sending more spells at Lapsus. Bovi dodged, kicking Lapsus in the stomach. Lapsus threw up more blood, shooting a spell at both of them.

Gloria's attention was brought to Cybele as she muttered, "No, I don't want to, Bo. I-I can't."

Gloria glanced at her. Cybele said, "I don't care what they are. They just seem so… nice." Gloria gasped, does that mean that they know? If they know, then why are they helping?

Before Gloria could conclude anything, Cybele coughed and jolted upward.

Gloria said, "Um, e-easy, you're ok."

Cybele gasped and pointed at Bovi and Njord. "Wha-what about them? I need to help!" She picked up her spear, trying to stand. A weak green hue surrounded her but faded as she collapsed to the ground.

Gloria said, "Rest a second, you took a dark spell straight to the face."

Cybele said, "I-I can't do nothing!"

Gloria grabbed her shoulder, "It's ok, I feel the same way. I can't help either."

Cybele glanced at Gloria. They stared at each other for a minute. A silent understanding drifted between them.

They gasped as Bovi crashed into the wall beside them. Njord shot a spell immediately followed by a lightning bolt. Lapsus dodged the first spell, yelling as the bolt hit him. He bellowed, firing a blade of darkness at Njord. Gloria gasped, Njord's eyes glowed entirely green.

He caught the blade, "*Mandatum, tempestas fluctu.*" The blade of darkness burned green, then surged to Lapsus. It caught his shoulder. He yelled, falling to his knees. Njord raised his hands to prepare another spell.

Lapsus bellowed, "*Emittet!*" A ball of static blasted Njord in the face.

Gloria yelled as Njord fell to the ground, "No!"

Lapsus raised his hand and a blade of darkness blazed. He gasped as a golden spear embedded in his stomach. The color of a dull bronze, it quivered like a fired arrow in a struck target.

Gloria screamed as an alien feeling grew within her. It roared, driving her power to an edge. It was a fury like anger, yet shaky like fear. It was a feeling that Gloria didn't know, but it caused her to act without thought or movement.

A voice echoed through her mind, *remember this feeling, Angelo. Use it when the time comes.*

Lapsus looked down. The spear extended, widening the wound. Spikes of ice tore through his body. Blood pooled. He looked at Gloria, his eyes widening. He whispered something Gloria couldn't hear.

Gloria's scream tore from her throat as the ice spear

drove further into Lapsus' body.

The voice in her mind continued. *To see someone suffer, it is pleasant, isn't it? You cannot deny, Angelo, you will feel this feeling again. Oh yes, and what a time it will be. Use it to drive you to new heights. I'll be waiting, Angelo.*

Lapsus coughed blood and set a hand to the ice. It coated his hand, sending spikes through it. Lapsus' hand fell to his side. Gloria breathed heavily. The ice disappeared with a golden flash, and she ran to Njord's side.

Njord shook his head, "You... revealed yourself."

Gloria tackled him in a hug, "I don't care."

They glanced at Lapsus, crawling slowly away. The static had faded from his body, and he returned to normal. He left a trail of blood. Gloria fought a savage pleasure. Her vision turned red.

A voice whispered in her ear, *Almost, little one, almost.*

Gloria stood, making a spear of ice. Njord set a hand on her shoulder. Gloria hesitated, but the spear disappeared. She watched as Lapsus disappeared in a black smoke.

They flinched as Bovi spoke, "I knew there was something about you."

Gloria spun around. Bovi stood next to Cybele, his arms crossed. They stared at them with a mixture of awe and horror. Njord's eyes started glowing.

Bovi said, "I knew... from the very beginning..." Gloria braced for him to say it. He said, "I knew that you were a decent person."

Cybele, Njord, and Gloria stared at him in shock.

Bovi said, "Just so you know, I am grateful for your help. I will always remember it. However, the next time I see you, I will unfortunately have to arrest you."

Bovi scratched his head, he said, "Oh *shoot*! Looks like we *lost* them, Cybele!"

He bumped Bele's shoulder. Bele said, "Oh! Yes! *How*

unfortunate! *Hmm,* I wonder if they're over *there.* *Why* don't we go check, *Bovi?*"

Bovi said, "Hmm, that's a *great* idea, Bele!"

Cybele was brimming with happiness. She hugged Bo, dragging him out of the amphitheater. She waved at Gloria, before disappearing from her sight.

Njord said, "Did they just... release us?"

Gloria smiled, "I think so, Njord."

Gloria hoped she would be able to befriend them, outside of their duties.

Secretly, Gloria began to scheme a way to bring them to the Fall Tree Academy... Amber could veto any jurisdiction by the capital, since she was the princess.

As Gloria weighed these thoughts in her head, Njord said, "Let us go, we need to depart before the authorities arrive."

Gloria followed him, walking towards the edge of the amphitheater.

They found their bags underneath the rubble, surprisingly intact, and made for the Golden Ring Inn. They found the lobby empty, the clerk snoring at the desk. They found their room, and Gloria crashed onto her bed.

Njord set his bag next to his bed. He found his toothbrush and made for the bathroom.

Gloria couldn't help but wonder, *why did they let them go?* Bovi, who was extremely strict, following laws and years of training, suddenly ignored them? Gloria suspected that Cybele was behind it.

Njord left the bathroom and bade Gloria goodnight.

Gloria lay in her bed, lost in thought. *What was that?* Gloria thought, *controlled corruption?* She would have to ask Njord about it tomorrow morning.

What was that *voice?* Was it... *right?* She didn't know what happened. That voice gave her the feeling from her dreams, the ones connected to the Blood Moon Curse. And that strange winged figure.

Who was that? Gloria thought, *what is happening to me?*

The clock chimed quietly from the corner. *Is it really two o'clock in the morning?* Gloria thought. She decided to go to sleep, so she changed out of her ragged, dirty, and holey clothes, found her toothbrush, and brushed her teeth.

Gloria spat into the sink and absently scratched the top of her head. She gasped and stared into the mirror. There were no Bestia horns there. Gloria glanced at the ground, there were no hooves. She stared in the mirror in wonder. Just how long was she walking around completely undisguised?

Gloria remembered when Lapsus activated that anti-magic stuff. If she remembered correctly, it negates long term magic. *Or,* Gloria thought, *disguises.*

Gloria allowed her hands to drop to her sides and laughed to herself. She began to yearn, a strange and unexplainable yearn. Without proper understanding, Gloria found herself wanting to befriend those strange twins.

Gloria awoke and stretched, switching on the TV. She got dressed as the news droned.

As she brushed her teeth, she heard the news say, "According to eyewitnesses, numerous monsters attacked the Behemoth Amphitheater C-four. Suspects left the scene of the crime before authorities could arrive."

The news continued, "In other news, reports show signs of Elementalists in the area." Gloria choked on her toothpaste, spat it out, tripped over the trash can, and ran to the front of the TV.

A one horned Bull Bestia continued, "Traces of the Golden Ice were found in the amphitheater last night. Ice Elementalist Gloria Factorem is wanted for questioning in regards to the attack. Here is a photo of Gloria Factorem."

Gloria's photo flashed on the screen. "Any knowledge of this individual is to be reported immediately. Those not providing known information will be exiled for treason."

Gloria slumped to her knees. The TV continued, "As a reminder, humans are to be killed on sight. Positions of higher authority shall be exiled if not reported to the Capital. In other news, today is going to be a cool day in lovely C-four-"

Gloria turned off the TV, "Come on!" She felt her little hope dashed. Feeling dejected, she decided to bother Njord.

She knocked on the door and he responded drowsily, "Enter."

Gloria entered, sitting upon his bed. Gloria said, "I have a question for you."

Njord had apparently fallen asleep while reading, because he now removed his reading glasses, setting them on his night stand.

Gloria said, "What is controlled corruption?"

Njord sighed, "Controlled corruption. I dislike this topic."

Gloria waited. Njord said, "Corruption occurs when a magician loses their humanity. Their magicules turn into *what remains,* the complete absence of magic and life. It is a negative force, deadly, essentially anti magic." Njord continued, "Controlled corruption is when a caster voluntarily converts their magic into what remains. It is extremely lethal to cast. It is a horrible curse."

Gloria nodded. She watched him stretch. She said, "By the way, I'm wanted."

Njord sighed, "That is not preferable."

Gloria nodded, "What do we do?"

Njord said, "Either we disguise you in a different matter, or convert you by utilizing invisibility."

Gloria slumped to the ground, "You don't think that

Cybele could help, do you?"

Njord said, "I do not understand why you desire friendship with the bull twins. Also no, they are not permitted to help us."

Gloria said, "It's just a feeling, Njord. I think that they can help us."

Njord got out of his bed, stretching again. After a few minutes, he reappeared in front of Gloria.

He spoke as he adjusted his tie, "I believe we need to plan. We have successfully diverted the crisis. Now, we need to study how to travel back to the Fall Tree Academy. Preventing any crisis there. The problem is how will we get there without getting spotted, without dying, as well as bypassing a barrier of unknown capabilities."

Gloria thought for a moment, "What about teleportation?"

Njord said, "Negative. The barrier absorbs magic, meaning we would be incinerated upon making contact."

Gloria said, "Well, we won't do that then. Um, first things first, we need to escape here. Preferably without getting caught or dying. Cause you know, I don't like dying and stuff."

Njord thought for a moment. Gloria noticed a small packaged mint on Njord's pillow. She unwrapped it and ate it.

Njord said, "The closest exit is through the bull twins chambers."

Gloria said, "But they have to kill us."

Njord finished adjusting his tie and walked over to the mini fridge. "If we were to travel to other exits, we would require bypassing the border patrol, then the gatekeepers for that district."

Gloria said, "So, the quickest route is through the bull twins?"

Njord started rummaging through the fridge, "Who are already in danger for not reporting us to the Capital."

Gloria said, "And may be exiled if they do it again."

Njord nodded. Gloria said, "What if we sneak through invisibly?"

Njord fished two microwavable cinnamon rolls from out of the fridge, "Precarious. Illusion magic of that caliber is not powerful enough."

Gloria said, "What if we ask nicely?"

Njord said, "That has a four percent probability of success."

Njord put the cinnamon rolls in the microwave, setting it for thirty seconds.

Gloria said, "That's more than I thought it would be. Oh!"

Gloria shot to her feet and ran to her room, grabbing a pamphlet from the nightstand. Gloria said, "The gatekeepers have to protect their posts, *right*?"

Njord nodded, Gloria pointed to their names in the pamphlet, "What if they come with us? If they disappear, then other Bestia will take their jobs. I mean, they're posted *right* here."

Njord frowned, "Er... How would that help us?"

Gloria said, "We're fighting a battle at Fall Tree. Bele even *admitted* she didn't like the job! She said that she'd give *anything* to leave!"

Njord said, "The Capital would be short two gatekeepers!"

Gloria scoffed, "They'll be fine. They will have new guards soon. Think about it! They see the world and help us! It's a win-win!"

Njord hesitated and thought for a moment.

Gloria said, "Come on, you can't say that you don't want to help them."

Njord said, "I do wish to help."

Gloria said, "Then let's bust them outta this place!"

Njord collected the cinnamon rolls from the microwave, passing one to Gloria, "Careful, it is hot. What if they do not wish to leave? Do we have the right to ask them to abandon their lives here?"

Gloria said, "Come on, Njord, we know the *king's daughter*, and we sort of know him too. I'm sure he could arrange for something if the twins want to visit."

Njord said, "Be that as it may, what if this is not the right idea? They cannot be discovered assisting a fugitive or leaving the capital. If we are discovered, then we may be forced to combat them!"

Gloria hesitated, "Well, I don't want that..."

Njord said, "Neither do I. They both fought Lapsus, when they were weakened by dark magic. I do not see us being successful against them in battle."

Gloria thought for a moment, taking a few bites from the cinnamon roll.

"Still, they *want* to leave, and I want to help them. They might have a way for us to breach the barrier!"

Njord thought for a moment, "We need to be extremely cautious. One wrong move, and everything may turn disastrous."

Gloria ran to get her bags, leaving Njord spluttering, "Wha- did you not hear me?" He tripped getting out of bed, following Gloria out the door.

Njord pulled Gloria aside to disguise her before a Bestia couple walked past. They left the Golden Ring Inn, heading for the bull twins. They passed a few wanted posters of Lapsus and Gloria on the way. Security had increased tenfold. Guards were everywhere, at every vendor, outside of every building, patrolling every street.

This made Njord extremely nervous. His eyes glowed.

"They have increased security. If they see you…"

Gloria whispered, "Don't worry, it'll be *you* attracting the attention if you're muttering to yourself."

After a few minutes, they arrived at the bull twins gate. They watched to make sure that no one was watching and slipped into the corridor.

Gloria said, "Well, that was surprisingly easy!"

Njord said, "Do not jinx us. The more difficult part is ahead."

They started down the stone corridor. Gloria's heart beat faster, through fear or excitement, Gloria didn't know.

They finally met stone doors and Njord glanced back at Gloria, "We are still able to turn back. Are you sure you wish to proceed?"

Gloria nodded before she could change her mind, "Yeah. Let's do it."

Njord nodded. He muttered, "I have a bad feeling about this."

Njord took a deep breath and pushed the stone doors open. They creaked loudly, and Gloria saw the bull twins.

They were clearly not expecting them to show up. They were standing just past the door. Cybele gasped, pointing excitedly to Bovi, who seemed in shock.

Gloria turned visible, waving, "Um, hey guys."

Cybele smiled. Bovi said, "You should not have come! It's too dangerous-"

Gloria said, "Yo! Proposal, we want you to come with us! We're in a bit of a tight spot."

Gloria described how Lapsus attacked her home. She described what he was planning. It took a while. Bovi flinched at every small sound, glancing at both doors.

"And so." Gloria concluded, "We need your help. Please."

Cybele looked at Bovi excitedly. Bovi hesitated. Gloria

crossed her fingers, silently praying. Bovi said, "As much as I want to Bele, I still don't fully trust humans. We would never be able to return again. What about our family? Or our friends?"

Gloria said, "What if I was good friends with Lord Behemoth's daughter?"

Bovi flinched, "L-Lady Amber? You must be bluffing!"

Gloria shook her head, smiling. Bovi pulled Cybele away for a moment.

He spoke in a hushed tone, "Cybele, I'm ok with whatever you want to do... But Lady Amber? This is sounding suspicious... What if they lead us to a trap?"

Cybele smacked his shoulder, "Why would they save us and our town, *just* to do that Bovi?"

Bovi shook his head, "I am just being cautious. It is the law-"

Cybele said, "Well, I'm tired of the law! I want to be free! If they know Lady Amber, then we could visit whenever!"

Bovi hesitated, Cybele said, "Come on Bo! Please?"

Bovi sighed, "Very... Very well."

Cybele laughed, "Thank you, Bo!"

Bovi said, "When do we leave?"

Cybele said, "All I own is this spear and this stupid armor. Let's leave now!"

They flinched as the stone doors flew open and six Bull Bestia entered. "Look! The bull twins are fighting the fugitive! Let's watch them take them down!"

A small figure entered the room, Cybele and Bovi gasped. The figure was small, shorter than Gloria. Its horns barely topped Gloria's head. It had round glasses and a clipboard in one hand.

The guards said, "Moderator! We discovered the bull twins had the fugitive. We were about to-"

The moderator held up a hand, "Weekly inspection, as you were bull twins."

Cybele looked devastated. Gloria remembered what Cybele said about him.

Didn't Cybele say that he could execute them if they break the law? Gloria started to panic, *they won't be able to spare us in front of him!*

The Moderator took a note, "Well, while we have fugitives here... I would like to go through the normal routine, hmm, yes." He took a quick note, "Demonstrating usual fighting tactics, enhanced magic, and combination animarum, yes, that should suffice."

The moderator set his pen on the clipboard and watched the bull twins intently. The other Bull Bestia awaited.

Gloria whispered, "Who's that?"

Njord whispered, "A moderator, one who is responsible for gatekeepers. They are the ones who punish law breaking gatekeepers."

Gloria gasped. Bovi sighed, Cybele whispered, "Bovi, please don't."

Bovi said, "Gloria Factorem... By the order of the Bestia's capital... I sentence you to death."

CHAPTER 9: GLORIA
Pleasure In Suffering

Gloria's heart sank and she saw Cybele mouth, I'm sorry. She raised her spear and pointed it at Gloria. They took a step back. Njord stepped in front of Gloria.

The moderator looked at his notes, "Hmm, yes, firstly demonstrate your normal combat abilities please. Bovi, Cybele, if you will."

Bovi sighed, but took a step forward, his face grim. Cybele hesitated, the Moderator said, "Is there a problem, Bele?"

Cybele took a step forward. Gloria saw Bovi point three fingers by his side. Gloria saw him lower one, Gloria whispered to Njord, "Get ready! He's about to attack!"

Bovi lowered the last finger and lunged at Gloria and Njord.

They scattered as Bovi cracked the ground where they were. Gloria noticed that Bovi wasn't moving nearly as fast as he was while fighting Lapsus. She didn't know whether or not he was using self-enhancing magic. But Gloria could tell that he didn't want to fight.

The Moderator smiled, "Yes, marvelous strength as always, Bovi. Keep it up."

Cybele charged at Gloria, while Bovi attacked Njord.

Gloria ducked under her spear, deflecting her next strike with ice.

The Moderator said, "Good lords! Elementalists! You mustn't be defeated, twins."

Gloria glanced over Cybele's shoulder. She saw Njord duck under Bovi's fist. Gloria caught Cybele's eye as she swung her spear. Cybele was slower too, she seemed to miss her strikes. Gloria knew fully well she could have hit her. Gloria leaped back as Cybele walked towards her.

The Bestia guards cheered, "Yeah! Get them, bull twins!"

Cybele glanced at the guards. The Moderator said, "Don't distract them! Oh dear, you've already distracted me!"

The moderator waved his hands, "Stop now, stop!" Cybele and Bovi froze, the Moderator said, "I forgot, I need both of you to answer a few questions. Yes, oh well, guards, if you will, kill the fugitives."

Gloria saw Cybele make a regretful face but clipped her spear to her back and walked towards the Moderator. Bovi followed her.

Three guards rushed Gloria. She didn't want to hurt them, but unlike Cybele, these guards would kill Gloria.

Gloria activated her aura, blasting the guards off their feet. The Moderator flew through the air, where Bovi caught him.

"Good lord!" The Moderator scowled, "Kill them!"

A guard attacked Gloria. She ducked under the swing and launched a comet at them. Two other guards charged at the same time. Gloria made an ice barrier and the guards crashed into it. Njord was dodging and firing spells at the guards. Gloria saw that he wasn't using his powerful spells.

Just defeat them, Gloria thought, *easy now.*

The Moderator yelled, "Come on now! It's only two people! Get on with it!"

Gloria leaped over her barrier, shooting ice at the guards

feet. She fired comets at their faces, and the three guards collapsed to the ground.

Gloria heard the Moderator huff, "Now *really*! *Unbelievable!*"

Gloria saw Njord a few feet away. He seemed alright. The three guards were unconscious around him.

The Moderator shook his head, "I suppose *I* will oversee your fight. Twins, finish them, now!"

Cybele sighed and charged at Gloria again. Under the direct eye of the Moderator, Gloria thought that Cybele couldn't afford to go easy on her.

Gloria ducked under her spear, gasping as Cybele hit her with the butt. Gloria leaped backwards to avoid the spear head.

Gloria whispered, "Sorry!" Then yelled, "*Tempestas glacies!*" A wave of golden ice flew towards Cybele, who spun her spear and deflected the ice.

Gloria saw Bovi barely miss Njord. She couldn't tell how well he was doing. Gloria dodged another spear strike. Gloria gasped and heard Njord cry out in pain. Cybele kicked Gloria to the ground and raised a spear to Gloria's throat. Gloria saw Bovi grab Njord by the neck, slamming him into the wall.

The bull twins hesitated. Cybele had her foot on a small stub behind the spear head. Gloria pictured its use in finishing enemies. Bovi froze with a fist raised, both breathing heavily.

The Moderator said, "Excellent, well, no reason to keep them alive, kill them." They didn't move, Bovi's fist wavered.

"Did you not hear me? Finish them!" Cybele took a breath and locked eyes with Gloria. She scowled, raising her foot and slamming it onto the ground.

The Bestia guards began to stir. Cybele turned to the Moderator, "No!"

The Bestia guards stood. The Moderator chuckled, "I think I may have misheard you, did you say-"

Bovi dropped Njord, "She said no."

He walked over and helped Gloria up. The moderator and the Bestia guards stood in shock.

Bovi said, "She said no, and so do I."

The Moderator spluttered, "Wha- What *incompetence*! I would have suspected Cybele, but *you too* Bovi? Never have I-"

The Moderator froze. His eyes turned dark, and he disintegrated. Cybele gasped in shock. Gloria said, "That was unexpected."

A dark voice cackled. They formed a circle, facing the walls, in a fighting stance. The Bestia guards raised their weapons, glancing frantically around the room. Gloria recognized Lapsus' voice.

"I had expected slightly more from the Bestia Capital. I was hoping to watch those dull beasts kill you."

Cybele tightened her grip on her spear, "I know that voice." She muttered.

Lapsus appeared out of a thick smoke. He cast a spell freezing Gloria, Njord, Cybele, and Bovi to the ground. The Bestia guards charged at him. The first one swung an ax at his head. Lapsus sent a spear through his chest and the guard fell to the ground.

Cybele screamed, "Monster! Stop!"

The second guard jabbed Lapsus with a sword and dodged his spell.

Lapsus yelled, "*Crucifige!*"

The poor Bestia guard screamed in agony. His armor melted. His skin was forcefully peeled from his feet over his head, leaving a revolting mass which flew to the wall and stuck there. Gloria felt sick and looked away from the guard. Bovi struggled against the ice, a large crack formed by Gloria's feet.

The next two guards attacked together, one swept a sword at Lapsus' legs, another aimed for his head. Lapsus sliced one in the stomach and his insides spilled to the floor. A dark spear plunged into the other's throat. They fell to the floor. Lapsus sent a spear of darkness behind him, killing another guard.

Lapsus eyed the final guard, who panicked, threw down his weapon, and fled. He slipped on his brethren's blood.

Lapsus said, "I expected more."

He sent a spell of darkness at the guard who melted with a loud scream.

Bovi yelled, breaking the ice around them.

Cybele fell to the floor, tears running down her face, "You... You monster! I'll kill you!"

Cybele charged Lapsus who dodged her spear, "We're not doing this song and dance again, beast."

He sneered as the spear grazed his arm. Gloria thought Cybele's eyes would glow if she were any angrier.

She screamed, "You'll pay for their deaths!" She swung her spear, striking him in the jaw.

Lapsus collapsed and Cybele grabbed him by his collar and punched him in the face. She reared back, and struck again, teeth and blood flying. He chuckled. Cybele struck him again, and he bellowed with laughter.

"You'll never survive! You'll never make it to the valley! You puny mortals know nothing of my power..."

Gloria saw him raise a hand to Cybele's face, Gloria screamed, "Watch out!"

Cybele was struck in the face by a static covered comet, and she fell to the floor. Bovi yelled and charged at Lapsus. He laughed, striking Bovi with the same spell. Bovi groaned but reared back with a fist. Lapsus' smile disappeared as Bovi punched him in the face, hurtling him into the wall.

The bull twins writhed on the ground. Gloria ran to their side, "Cybele, Bovi! No!"

Lapsus laughed, "It is no use girl. Soon, they'll be under *my* command."

Gloria shook Cybele's shoulder, "Fight it Cybele! Bovi!"

Gloria gasped as two black streaks of light struck Cybele and Bovi in the head. They yelped and stopped moving. Njord and Gloria retreated.

Cybele rose, her eyes pitch black. "Filthy humans!"

Bovi struggled and slammed a fist to the ground, but he too arose.

Gloria said, "Oh no."

Lapsus said, "It seems that magic is no match for his strength!"

Lapsus rose unsteadily, an ink-like substance dripped down his face.

He pointed to Gloria, "You cannot stop fate. You may only accept what is to come! There is no stopping destiny! Accept the darkness or be consumed."

Lapsus turned towards Cybele and Bovi, "Bull twins, *Impetum!*"

The bull twins scowled and turned towards Gloria and Njord. Bovi hit his fist into his hand. Cybele spun her spear. Both readied a stance.

Lapsus said, "*Vivere et resipisce!*"

Bovi and Cybele shook their heads. Lapsus laughed. "So long!" He laughed again, disappearing into a cloud of smoke.

Cybele and Bovi crouched down. Cybele whispered to Bovi, "There it is... Look Bo, it's overrun by them! We need to save the citizens!"

Gloria whispered to Njord, "What's happening?"

Njord shook his head, "I... do not know."

Bovi nodded, "I'll distract them in the front. You sneak in through the back and deal with the magicians."

Cybele nodded, "Alright, go!"

The bull twins charged. Cybele leaped onto the far wall, shooting off of it towards Gloria. Bovi attacked Njord directly, bashing the ground with his fists.

Gloria dodged Cybele's spear and yelped as Bovi's fist came at her. Gloria leaped back and Bovi smacked Njord sideways into the far wall.

Gloria gasped as Cybele thrusted her spear, grazing Gloria's arm. Gloria activated her aura. The bull twins hesitated for a moment, then charged. Bovi against Njord and Gloria against Cybele.

Even with her aura, Gloria could just barely dodge Cybele's quick attacks.

Cybele yelled, "Get back human! Get away from him!" She swept her spear, knocking Gloria back. Cybele pointed at Gloria, "This is the last time you'll hurt him!" She charged again, Gloria made a shield out of ice, catching Cybele's spear.

Gloria said, "Cybele it's me! Gloria!"

Cybele shook her head, "You can't fool me, magician!"

She kicked Gloria's legs from under her, thrusting her spear at the ground. Gloria rolled away, the spear just missing her.

Gloria thought wildly, *is she not seeing me?* Gloria said, "Snap out of it, Cybele!"

Cybele used the butt of her spear to hit Gloria, "I said stay back! Bovi, take front!"

Bovi leaped up while Cybele jumped towards Njord.

Bovi crashed in front of Gloria, "You'll pay for what you've done." He demolished the ground under Gloria, sending debris flying. Gloria tried to say something, but her voice failed her. *He may be slower,* Gloria thought, *but he's much stronger!*

Gloria summoned a shield of ice. Bovi punched it, cracking the ice.

Bovi gasped, "Cybele! They've summoned more weapons!"

Cybele turned towards him, "*Seriously*? We'll just have to deal with that later! Keep holding until the reinforcements get here!"

Gloria said, "Huh?"

Njord said, "I recognize this magic! It is a configuring memory spell, they are reliving an old memory from the past. They must see us as enemies!"

Gloria groaned, yelping as Bovi stomped at her.

Gloria said, "Bovi, big ma- er, bull... why don't we talk about this?"

Bovi scowled, "You had your chances to speak, now you die!" He raised his fists over his head, slamming them into the ground.

Gloria said, "Didn't want to do this, "*Carcer!*""

Bovi was frozen in a large block of ice.

Gloria rushed over to Njord. He dodged Cybele's spear, using a spell to deflect a strike. Cybele yelled, thrusting her spear. Gloria threw a comet at her feet, freezing her in place.

Gloria put her hands together, "Sorry Bele!" She froze her in ice as well.

Njord leaned against the wall, "You have my gratitude, she is extremely swift." Gloria heard Bovi's ice prison crack slightly.

Gloria said, "We don't have time, what do we do? Can we get rid of the spell?"

Njord said, "In order to do that, we would have to either render them unconscious, or somehow remove them one hundred miles from the casting point."

Gloria said, "Seriously?"

Gloria glanced at Bovi, the cracks were growing larger, "We need a plan to beat them, at this rate, we'll tire before them!"

Njord said, "I do not know! They are severely advanced warriors! The best that we can do is use more advanced spells."

Gloria shook her head, "I don't want to hurt them!"

Njord said, "They will be fine, there is no other

alternative, they will eliminate us otherwise."

With an explosion, Bovi escaped the ice prison. Gloria and Njord backed against the wall. Bovi stared at them. He twitched, a black spark shot from him. He slowly walked towards Cybele's ice prison. He struck it, cracking it in half and Cybele broke it open.

They stood, glaring at Gloria and Njord. Cybele muttered something and a green hue enveloped her.

Gloria said, "Ho boy."

Cybele disappeared into a green blur, Njord yelped as he was struck.

Gloria leaped out of the way as Bovi tackled the wall, making the room quake. Njord jumped over a green blur. Bovi was moving faster, attacking Gloria more ruthlessly, putting holes in the stone.

Cybele said, "Take front!"

Bovi, grabbed a large stone, whipping it around and hurling it behind him. Cybele slowed to a normal run, jumped up, stabbing her spear into the ground. The rock hit her spear head and she flew upward. She threw her spear at Gloria as she flew.

Gloria yelped, diving to avoid the spear, while Bovi attacked Njord. Cybele tore her spear from the ground, grasped the end of the hilt, and spun in a deadly circle. Gloria ducked, the spear slicing a piece of her hair. She gasped as Cybele kicked her. Gloria flew towards Bovi, who whirled around, caught her, and threw her at Njord.

They crashed to the floor, the bull twins surrounding them.

Gloria flared her aura. Njord and Gloria spoke at the same time.

"*Kraken tempestas!*"

"*Congelatio!*"

Gloria's spell froze them in place, while Njord's spell

threw them into the wall.

The ice broke as they hit the wall, Cybele coughed.

Bovi said, "Are you alright, Bele?"

Cybele nodded, twirling her spear, "Use your enhancing magic Bo, I'll take the-"

She hesitated, shaking her head, "I'll take the other magician, you take that... Bestia." Bovi nodded, "Alright."

Bovi stood, setting his fists together and was surrounded by a red hue.

Gloria blurted, "Expulso, *Angelorum Ira!*"

A bright white light surged from Gloria's hand, and time slowed down. When Gloria blinked, she was standing in darkness.

A cold voice said, "Why hello, *Angelo*. Why have you arrived?"

Gloria couldn't respond, she was frozen. She wanted to scream. *Don't want to be here! Trying not to die!*

The voice said, "Hmm, no answer? Very well, I suppose I should show you your fate..."

Gloria's vision changed. She was looking at the Fall Tree valley. She gasped at the millions of monsters in her view, her family fighting them off. Gloria saw the moon slowly turning red, as though a lunar eclipse was occurring. The sky was black, the air cold.

Gloria saw Amber slice monsters in half in slow motion. She saw one disintegrate and Ignis appear behind it. Hovering over the top of the tree, Gloria saw Fornacem roaring in silent laughter. Silver lightning licked the grounds throughout the valley. He had his whip in his hands and Gloria watched as it slowly inched towards the ground. Gloria saw Umbra Mortis frozen in the air, there was a tendril of dark flame surging into monsters from his fingertips. To Gloria's right, Arthur and Uncle Dux were running from a butcher. Uncle Dux was frozen, a spell just leaving his fingers, while Arthur tripped over something. As they fought, more monsters surged from the mountain peak and through the caves. Their mouths were open in silent roars.

That cold voice whispered, "They need you, *Angelo.* More than you or they realize. Will this be their downfall? Or will you be their savior?" The image rippled before Gloria's eyes, the voice said, "My, my... at this rate, surely, they'll perish. How unfortunate."

A shadow appeared in front of Gloria's vision sitting on a throne, sipping from a wine glass. Two horrible maroon eyes glared at her. There was a darkness in those eyes that seemed as though they had seen thousands of years of bloodshed.

The figure said, "And yet, there is a way to help them, is there not?"

Gloria said, "Who are you?"

The figure laughed, "Isn't it obvious?" A red circle appeared in his palm and Gloria gasped. It was the mark of the Blood Moon Curse. The mark glowed brighter, before disappearing.

The creature said, "Don't worry, this will all be over soon. As soon as I have my sacrifice, it'll all be over."

Gloria said, "Stop this! Leave us alone!"

The figure smiled, blood red teeth gleaming, "No can do, *Angelo.* Blood is just too sweet to bypass, especially human blood. Soon, we will be *bathing* in it, all thanks to you."

He smiled wickedly, Gloria said, "We? What do you mean? Who falls to the curse? When will it be?"

The figure raised a finger to its lips. Gloria's vision turned red, and the figure cackled.

Suddenly, Gloria was watching a scene through someone else's eyes. They approached a wooden door. A cold wolf howl broke the silence. Her vision shifted to the full moon which glared an ugly red. She watched as a pale hand slowly pushed open the wooden door.

A woman turned to her, "Oh! Samael! I've been so worried! They chased you into those horrible woods! Our children have been wondering... Are... Are you alright? What are you doing?"

Gloria saw a silver blade rise from her side. The lady took a step back, "Samael... what... Please, no!"

The blade rose, the woman screamed, and a silver streak drug across her neck. Gloria wanted to look away, but she couldn't. She watched in horror through Samael's eyes.

The man was breathing heavily, the blade gleamed scarlet. A small boy appeared around the corner, the boy said, "Papa?" Gloria wanted to scream at the boy to get away.

The man smiled widely, "My son, please, come here."

Screams filled a peaceful silence. The silver blade took many lives that night. It tasted the blood of many innocent souls.

Gloria caught the man's appearance in a cracked mirror, he wore a black, blood-stained chasuble. In his hand was a single bloody knife. The man's eyes were black, darker than the night. The man killed and killed, until only he remained in the village.

Gloria wanted to close her eyes. *Please,* she begged, *make it stop!*

Samael stared at the moon and laughed. He gasped, dropped the knife, and fell to his knees. "What have I done?"

He looked at his hands, covered in blood. Lavender burned in his nose, and a cackle plagued the silence. A red cloud seeped from the ground in front of Samael. A demon appeared from the smoke. It wore a dark suit. Black horns curled from its head.

It grinned, "You have done well."

The man choked, "My family! My friends! My life! You

took everything from me!"

The demon mused, "*Actually*, you did that *yourself*. Well then, I suppose you have no reason to live, now *do* you?"

The devil seized Samael's throat and drug him away. Samael kicked and screamed, a blood churning, bone chilling sound. Such a sound of terror it made Gloria's hair stand on end. The ground rumbled and large black gates rose from the earth. Fire roared and hissed.

Samael saw the gates and screamed in horror, kicking, and calling for help. The devil smiled. "You don't deserve help, do you? You did this to yourself. After all you said to them, you were right. The devil was there, and he tricked you."

The gates opened and the demon held Samael over the fires. Screams of the tortured, and the sounds of the damned echoed from the flames.

The devil said, "You killed hundreds in cold blood. One would say... are you even alive anymore? Were you ever *really* human?"

Samael begged the demon, "Please... let me live."

The devil purred, "Why should I? You said it yourself, you have nothing."

Samael sobbed. The demon mused, "*Samael*, which was my angel name before I became a demon, I hold a fond longing for it."

The man choked, "You're-You're Lucifer! The Fallen angel! The angel of death!"

Lucifer chuckled, "Yes, yes, I am... and as for you..." Lucifer pulled the man close, his eyes gleamed a dark maroon, "You shall become the incarnation of my wrath..." The devil smiled and dropped Samael. He screamed as he fell into the darkest pits of Hell.

There was a noise that resembled church bells, except far too deep and disturbing to belong in a church.

The demon looked around, "*Finally*, some genuine quiet,

the holy grounds will dissipate after sunrise." He erupted into flames. "I shall take my leave, before *humility* arrives." The demon glanced at the blood soaking into the ground. He stared at Gloria through the flames, "Who is next *Angelo*? Can you tell me who?"

Gloria's vision turned red and once again she stood in front of the demon. He made a sound of longing. "I liked that guy. You wouldn't recognize him now..." He smiled, "But didn't you see? The man begged his people for understanding, what did they do? They ran him out of town, branding him a heretic."

He swiveled the wine in his glass. Gloria suspected that it wasn't wine.

The demon continued, "Despite his holy beliefs, he still extracted revenge. He followed my orders perfectly. How did I repay him?" His eyes gleamed wickedly, "I took his soul. Later, he became a demon manifested from the incarnation of his own revenge and haste. His *Wrath*, if you will."

Gloria said, "Why are you telling me this?"

The demon laughed, "*Why*? Because I *want* to, *Angelo*! I wish to see suffering... As do you."

Gloria took a step back, "No."

The demon nodded, "You desire to slaughter every monster that dares step into your valley, any monster that dares harm your family."

Gloria said, "Killing monsters is not evil! They seek to kill my family, what else am I supposed to do?"

The demon stared at Gloria, as if just now taking in her presence.

He said, "Suffering is still suffering. To kill in defense ends their living. You cause suffering. You cause their pain, and you will cause their death."

Before Gloria could reply, the demon continued, "What did you feel, *Angelo*, when you almost killed Lapsus?"

Gloria looked away. She didn't know what she felt, she just didn't want Njord to die. She... she *did* want Lapsus to feel a small shred of what she felt.

"You wished to hurt him... didn't you? You wanted him to feel the pain that he wrought this past year." The demon stood from his throne and walked towards Gloria. "*You* wanted to hurt him, *you* drew blood, *you* brought him to the brink of death, only to *rip* the relief of death away!"

Gloria started backing away. The demon continued, "You *liked* to watch him suffer. You felt pleasure watching him writhe in agony. Why? Because you're a monster. A mortal who felt so much pain, suffering, and cruelty by his hands, that she wanted to give him a slice of hell."

Gloria felt her back hit something solid. She crumbled to the ground and her voice shook. "No... I didn't-"

The demon bellowed, "YOUR CORRUPTED SOUL WAS BEYOND REPAIR! YOU SHOULD BURN IN THE DEPTHS OF HELL FOR ALL ETERNITY!"

Tears spilled down Gloria's face, the demon towered over her, "*Unless*, you *would* have... had I not put those thoughts into your head. You live up to your namesake enough, and it *disgusts* me."

He turned away from her, "Damn, you know, *Angelo*, demons are supposed to *hate* angels. Angels are creatures of light. They use their holy power to bring good and bless those disgusting humans, *regardless* of their sins." The demon snarled, "They are forgiven, and they are let into heaven." The demon glared at Gloria, "So now the question is, *Angelo*, what will you do now?"

Gloria felt herself fly backwards and Njord yelled, "Gloria, watch out!" She ducked as Bovi struck the stone above her. Gloria yelped, leaping away.

She looked around. Cybele was on the ground, rubbing her head.

She yelled, "Stupid magician! Comply already! You can't beat us!"

Njord yanked Gloria away from Bovi, who narrowly missed Gloria's head.

Gloria yelled, "What happened?"

Njord said, "You were momentarily unconscious!"

Njord ducked under Cybele's spear, Gloria said, "What? Why?"

Njord said, "I do not know! I predict the spell you utilized was overly exerting!"

Gloria would have to worry about that vision later. She saw her family was fighting against long odds. They really needed help.

Cybele leaped at Bovi and set her spear so that the flat side was facing him. Bovi raised his hands, caught the spear handle, and the spear head. He grunted and threw Cybele at Gloria. Cybele spun in mid-air and threw her spear at Gloria, who rolled out of the way as it was embedded in the stone wall.

Gloria looked up. Cybele grabbed her spear and looked at Bovi, "Bovi! There are more by the eastern side!"

Bovi nodded, "Got it!" He ran towards Njord. Cybele dislodged her spear and ran to join him.

Gloria's head spun. *If she's seeing a memory, was I a dead guy? If they're seeing one thing, they can't see us. If Njord and I stop fighting... their sight will clash with the spell!*

Gloria stood, she yelled, "Njord!"

She gasped as Cybele's spear flew towards her.

Njord yelled, *"Kraken ventus!"*

A strong wind knocked Cybele's spear aside, and Gloria formed an ice wall to block Cybele. She landed on the barrier, cracking it, and jumped off. Before Gloria could move, Bovi slammed through the ice. He grabbed Gloria by the throat, lifting her off the ground.

Bovi sneered, "You're going to pay for what you did."

Gloria screamed, "BOVI WAKE UP, IT'S GLORIA! DON'T KILL ME!"

Bovi hesitated, "That... That's not what they said..."

A strange light flickered through Bovi's eyes. A bolt of lightning struck Bovi, and he dropped Gloria. Njord pushed him back with a spell. He skidded to a stop next to Cybele.

Gloria grabbed Njord and pulled him away from them. She forced him to crouch low, next to the left wall. The bull twins attacked again, but Cybele hit only thin air. She swung her spear, leaping backwards again.

Cybele was about to attack when Bovi caught her shoulder. Gloria didn't know who was more surprised, Njord, herself, or Cybele.

Bovi said, "Wait a second Bele."

Cybele said, "What do you mean? What are you doing?"

Bovi said, "Something... doesn't feel right."

Gloria glanced at Njord. He shook his head in wonder. Cybele hesitated, lowering her spear.

She said, "What... what do you mean?"

Bovi said, "I... We've been here before..."

Cybele raised her spear, "Yeah, we've been sent to protect this village multiple times."

Bovi said, "That's not what I mean Bele. I... I killed that magician."

Cybele gave a confused look, "*Yeah?*"

Bovi said, "And yet, they said something. It was a voice I recognized."

Cybele glanced at Bovi, "You're not making any sense... These magicians *killed* innocent Bestia families, remember?"

Cybele flinched, whipping her spear skyward, towards an invisible threat.

Bovi said, "Just now, Bele! There was nothing there! That was when those magicians shot at us from the top of the building!"

Cybele said, "Wait…"

She stood suddenly and turned to Bovi, "If we've been here before…"

Cybele gasped, "Isn't there a giant golden monster next?"

Bovi nodded, "Well yes, but-"

Cybele said, "We need *combination animarum* to defeat it!"

Gloria gasped, Njord said, "Oh… please lords no…"

Bovi said, "That's not what I mean Bele, something's off."

Cybele dug into her pocket. Gloria's heart sank when she recognized a small green orb. Cybele said, "Come on Bovi! Before it's too late! We need to combine!"

Bovi hesitated, "What about the villagers, wait, is this even real?"

Cybele pointed at nothing, "Does that *look* real? Of course, it is!"

Bovi glanced at the wall, "I… there's something off."

Bovi shook his head. Cybele said, "Look at me Bovi."

Bovi stared at Cybele, she said, "This is a top class S threat. If we're going to prove our worth to the Capital, we need to beat it."

Bovi took out his orb. Gloria grabbed Njord's shoulder, "Njord." She said warningly.

Bovi said, "I… I just don't know Cybele."

Cybele smiled, which creeped Gloria out, since her eyes were pitch black. Cybele said, "Trust me Bo… We can do this."

Bovi nodded, "Alright. Let's do it!"

Gloria and Njord started backing up, Njord said, "This may be disastrous!"

Gloria whispered hysterically, "*May?*"

Cybele clipped her spear onto her back. A green circle blazed around the bull twins.

Cybele grabbed Bovi's hand, and they both said, "*Simul! Spiritus tauri!*" Gloria gasped as a bright green light flooded her vision.

CHAPTER 10: IGNIS
Battle at Fall Tree Valley

The enemy had retreated, for now. How long it would last, Ignis didn't know. He felt the retreat was unnecessary. He and the others were worn from the battle. All but Fornacem and Umbra Mortis were either exhausted or injured. For now, they gathered in the dining room. Julia tended to the wounded, while Fornacem loudly bragged about being unscathed.

Arthur rested in a bed in the other room. Ignis was with Amber at the table, tending to a wound on Amber's leg.

He held up a bottle of hydrogen peroxide, "Just so you know Amber, this may hurt."

Amber scoffed, "*Please*, you're talking to the *princess* of the Dragonborn! As if some *mere* mortal product would ever make me- OUCH! OW! Ok, ok, ok, Ow! OW!"

Ignis smiled to himself as he cleaned her wound. Amber drummed her fingers against the table, "It's ok, I'm strong, I can- OW!"

She punched the wall, cracking its surface, Ignis said, "You good?"

Amber exhaled loudly, "*No.*"

Uncle Dux entered the room with an ice pack wrapped around his shoulder. He said, "You two, ok?"

Ignis nodded and held up a bandaged arm, "Mom patched me up earlier. I'm helping Amber with her leg."

Amber said, "Ow! Be gentler, Ignis! Ow!"

Uncle Dux smiled, "Injury, let me guess, a new experience?"

Amber nodded her head, "The last time I was wounded- Ouch! I was fighting an ice golem. It- OW! Watch it, Ignis! It threw me into the mountain, which had a lot of- Ow! Ice spikes." Amber shook her head, "Never used this stuff to clean a wound though!"

Uncle Dux said, "Can't risk healing magic, the barrier makes it unstable. I also suck at it almost as bad as aura magic."

Amber gritted her teeth, "I may want to risk it anyway! Ow!"

They turned towards a cackling voice as Umbra Mortis appeared from thin air, "I remember when I was as fragile as you. What a time it was... I wish I still felt pain. Fornacem's the lucky one."

Fornacem laughed, "Pain, the only reminder of my once human self. Makes me feel so alive."

Ignis rolled his eyes. Amber said, "Pain is being a pain in the- OW! Right now."

Ignis grabbed a bandage and started wrapping her leg. Julia entered the room with water which she passed around.

She spoke to Dux, "Arbor is still asleep. He managed to make a tunnel to the children's room, they're all alright for now."

Uncle Dux nodded, "That's good."

He turned to Ignis, "Any word from Gloria?"

Arthur entered the room as Ignis shook his head, "No, I know she got my message. But she hasn't said a word back. All we can do is hope she made it to Huntington."

Arthur sighed, "I knew I should have gone with them."

Julia scowled, "And leave us with one less person to help?

I don't think so, mister!"

Arthur complained, "But they might need my help!"

Julia said, "They're fine on their own. You just don't trust Njord! You need to have a little faith, Arthur. Who was the one who retaught you about spell tactics?"

Arthur scowled, "That squid-"

Julia said, "Arthur!"

Arthur said, "Fine, Njord did."

Fornacem whistled, "I'm surprised you remembered his name."

Julia continued, "And who helped move your stuff into your room, regardless of injury?"

Arthur crossed his arms. Ignis and Amber glanced at each other then back to Arthur. Arthur grumbled, "Njord did."

Julia whispered, "And who told you about the shortcut to the bathroom?"

Arthur scowled, "Fine! That kid's ok!"

Julia nodded, "More than that, he's helped countless times. So lay off!"

Fornacem snickered, "Got told, didn't you?"

Arthur said, "Shut up, you damn-"

Julia elbowed him. He sighed, shaking his head.

Uncle Dux said, "Well, while everyone's here, let's talk strategy."

Everyone groaned. Uncle Dux said, "I know, war's no fun, but no one wants to die right?"

Fornacem said, "Depends on the moment."

Uncle Dux ignored him and summoned a map. "Now, we roughly killed... er, how many?"

Fornacem started counting on his fingers. "Four thousand, six hundred, eighty-nine Fallen."

Uncle Dux slumped, "Really? How many are left?"

Fornacem shrugged, "The number keeps going up. You

don't want to hear it even if it didn't."

Ignis pulled Amber's bandage tight and helped transport her from the table to a chair. Ignis said, "What about magicians?"

Umbra Mortis said, "I've killed almost a thousand, but there are tens of thousands more for me to snack on."

Uncle Dux shook his head, "The best we can do is rest and wait for them to strike again."

Fornacem said, "We're fighting a losing war, well, you all are anyway."

Uncle Dux said, "For some reason, most of the monsters are fire related, and magically enhanced."

Amber said, "It's as if Lapsus knew that Gloria and Njord weren't here."

Uncle Dux said, "If Gloria was here the monsters would: A) go down easier, and B) *stay* dead."

Julia said, "And with Njord, we would have a better plan."

Fornacem said, "I could use some of that *kraken magus* magic right now."

Umbra Mortis grabbed a muffin from the table. He picked off the bits of blueberry and took a bite of it.

Amber said, "What if we do *combination animarum?*"

Uncle Dux shook his head, "Absolutely not! I don't know how you and Ignis pulled it off the first time, but Spiritus is simply too powerful. You would kill all of us along with the army. You simply don't have enough control."

Amber sighed, "I heard of a gatekeeper couple who use it."

Umbra Mortis said, "I don't know, it wouldn't *exactly* hurt, would it?"

Everyone stared at Umbra Mortis. Uncle Dux said, "Hell no! Are you kidding? They have next to no experience with combination animarum! Who's to say that they'll succeed? Even if they did, who's to say that they'll be able to fight off an army? I know you're shrugging it off, but you're tiring out too!"

Umbra Mortis shrugged, "Just a *suggestion*."

Uncle Dux shook his head, "Besides, that would be one less person to help fight! Numbers are crucial."

Umbra Mortis said, "Would you rather Julia and Arthur have a try at it then?"

Uncle Dux said, "There's not enough time or power right now to make more keys. Besides, Gloria and Njord are the only other ones with keys-"

Uncle Dux froze. Fornacem cackled, "Oh, you gonna get the smoke now boy!"

Arthur spoke in a stiff voice, "What did you say, Dux?"

Julia sighed, "Arthur, Dux and I spoke, and we both agreed. If they came into contact with an Elder Fallen or Lapsus, they should have the keys just in case."

Ignis saw his father scowl. Amber muttered, "Here we go."

"WHAT?" Arthur exploded, "Why in the *world* would you do that?"

Fornacem said, "For the sake of reason, I personally think that it was a good idea. Look at what Ignis and Amber pulled off. They made quite a strong opponent against me."

Julia said, "You were fine with Ignis having one."

Arthur said, "That's because I didn't *know* that he had one!"

Julia said, "And because you actually *trust* Amber!"

Amber blushed, Arthur yelled, "B-Besides the point!"

Umbra Mortis said, "Well if they figure out how to do the ritual, that is. If so, then having two combinations may help extraordinarily." Umbra Mortis grinned, "Then again, you do have extreme trust issues, you stubborn jackass."

Arthur huffed, "Am I the only one who knows how *dangerous* it can be?"

Uncle Dux said, "Of course not! Njord and Gloria are *more* than responsible enough to use it in emergencies!"

Amber shook her head. She made a gagging motion at Ignis, who snorted in laughter.

Umbra Mortis said, "Look, Arthur, we're in the middle of battle. Chances are, they might not even get here in time. Chances are, they won't pull it off. I'd be willing to bet that Njord and Gloria together can get out of any situation. If they use it, great, more power to them."

Julia said, "Our children are growing up in a dangerous world, Arthur. You need to understand that as long as Lapsus is out there, they are in danger. We need to teach them more ways to defend themselves, so that when a crisis occurs, they have more ways to help."

Arthur hesitated, "Why didn't you at least *tell* me?"

Julia slammed her water down, spilling it everywhere, "Because I *knew* you would react like this! This is why I never tell you things! This is why we all lied to you about them traveling to the Pacificus residence!"

Julia continued, "In fact, *Njord* was the only one who *didn't* like the idea of lying to you!" Julia sighed, "He's such a nice boy. Why can't you just be nice to him? There's no reason not to!"

Ignis watched Fornacem play the knife game with a fork. He didn't flinch as it sunk into his hand.

Uncle Dux said, "Can we get back to the *not dying* tactics? What we should *really* worry about is trying to get the others here."

Arthur sighed, "You're right, both of you. What information do we have now?"

Amber looked up from the table. Fornacem was absently stabbing his hand, he seemed bored.

Uncle Dux said, "Right, if we're able to use the smallest shred of magic, we'd be able to open a portal. Problem is, we don't know exactly where Gloria and Njord are."

Arthur said, "Wouldn't they be at the beach?"

Julia shook her head, "If Lapsus was there, then they would have run! We need to think as they would."

Uncle Dux thought for a moment, "I'm not as smart as Njord, but..." He gasped, pointing to the wall, "*Tradendae Terrae!*"

Ignis saw a white line of light extend into a television-like surface. At first the television was covered in static. Then the image shifted to a ruined beach.

Julia said, "What are you doing Dux?"

Uncle Dux said, "If there were a monster attack and people saw it, it would have made the news, here we go!"

Ignis saw a reporter appear on screen, "Just yesterday, residents of Huntington fled in panicked swarms as strange activity closed the beach. Residents describe loud explosions, flashing lights, and a storm system rolling through. Witnesses describe lights and explosions behind the nearby Walmart."

Julia said, "That must be them!"

The reporter continued, "Though no fatalities were reported, hundreds of thousands of dollars in damage was discovered as vehicles, a fast-food restaurant, and a beach bathhouse were destroyed."

Julia muttered, "Oh my."

Pictures of destruction filled the screen. The reporter said, "Here's an eye witness, who happened to be on the beach at the time of the events."

The picture cut to a shirtless guy with thick yellow hair covering his eyes.

"There was a giant, I don't know what! It looked like a giant crystal man, man! These two children were tossing fireworks and crap at them. Then some weird dude appeared and started throwing cars, shooting lasers and stuff."

The reporter said, "While no evidence leads to any loss

of life during the storm, local meteorologists are confused by the sudden appearance of it."

Amber suddenly said, "That'll be Njord!"

The reporter continued, "Strange patches of glass were found surrounding one of the beach craters. Here's what our local police have to say."

The image cut to a bulky officer, "It's nothing out of the ordinary of course. Probably some kids lightin' fireworks just before the storm." The officer scratched his head, "Freak accidents too, fireworks hit the gas tanks, haven't seen a- show like that in years."

The television blurred the man's cursing. The reporter said, "Could these events be linked to similar reports two hundred miles north-east? Find out this and more at our later update. This is ABC news, channel seven, reporting live from Huntington Beach-"

The television turned to static. Julia exclaimed, "Oh, I hope they're alright."

Ignis said, "Sounds like they're heading towards Las Vegas, why would they go there?"

Uncle Dux said, "Well, it's possible, but... there *is* a portal just outside of Las Vegas, it's possible they were heading there." Uncle Dux said, "Fornacem, what kind of monster was at that beach?"

Fornacem said, "Well, we saw glass, either that was Njord's storm magic, or it was a fire monster. But it was surrounding a crater, meaning something strong must have hit it. If it was heat, the monster must be ice related. The only ice-related monster strong enough to cause that much damage is an Elder Fallen."

Julia gasped, Uncle Dux said, "Now, now, there were no signs of fatalities. Let's just keep an ear out for their names on the news stations in the mortal or magical realms." Uncle Dux said, "Why don't we check other news stations."

He flicked through the mortal news and heard about weather, traffic, and robberies.

Amber said, "Try the magical realm."

Uncle Dux nodded and started going through the channels. Ignis heard, "Lovely day in the swamp capital. Residents are shocked to find a magician and elemental attack in Bestia city."

They gasped at images of a demolished amphitheater. Amber said, "Hey! That's C-Four's amphitheater!"

An image of Gloria appeared on screen, the Bull Bestia reporter said, "Ice Elementalist Gloria Factorem is wanted for questioning in regards to the attack last night. Any knowledge of this individual is to be reported immediately. Those possessing information not turned over will be exiled from the capitol for treason. As a reminder, all humans are to be killed on sight. Positions of higher authority shall be exiled if they do not report to the capitol. In other news, today is going to be a cool day in lovely C-four-" The reporter hesitated, "Er, sorry, this just in, witness report sightings of a *Fallen* magician in the area. Bestia reports multiple Fallen sightings as well."

The image faded, as an explosion rattled the tree. Uncle Dux yelled, "Woah! Wave two everybody! Prepare for battle!"

Amber tried to stand, but almost fell over. Ignis caught her, one of her wings hitting his face.

Amber said, "Sorry!"

Ignis said, "Don't worry, can you walk?"

Amber put weight on her leg and nodded. She snatched her sword, which was leaning against the wall.

She turned to Ignis, "Grab my hand a sec, don't let go."

Ignis sighed, "This doesn't sound good."

Ignis just barely grabbed her hand when her wings unfolded. Ignis yelped as Amber tugged him out the nearest window.

Ignis's vision was a bundle of color as he looked onto the

battlefield. "What the heck is that?"

A gargantuan monster was crawling across the valley. It must have been half the length of a football field. Its skin was blackened and char the size of a car roof crumbled from its body. It looked to Ignis like the top half of a man. Blackened organs dragged from the bottom half of the monster leaving the grass behind the color of ink. The monster grabbed the earth in its hand, dragging its body towards the tree. It had glowing eyes, resembling fiery blue pits. Blue fire roared from the top of its head, down its neck, and onto its shoulders, giving Ignis the image of a large man being consumed by fire.

Furnace Fallen followed the giant beast, some eating small pieces of the giant monster's organs, only to disintegrate instantly.

Ignis heard Fornacem's voice, "Oooh, I should have never watched *Moana*."

Uncle Dux yelled, "You *seriously* based a monster on *Taka*? I AM GOING TO MURDER YOU!"

Fornacem said, "No, not *Taka*, I'm not getting sued by Disney. Besides, I made them during the second war. It's *Seniorem Reptans, the Crawling Eldest*."

Ignis said, "Looks aside, how do we kill it?"

Fornacem said, "It's an Elder, you know how tough the Elder Fallen are. It won't be easy at all! We need Gloria now!"

Amber shuddered, "I watched that movie with Gloria, now I wish I hadn't."

The Seniorem Reptans roared and slowly rose into what would be a sitting position. A ball of fire formed in its hands growing to the size of the Eartha model.

Ignis felt his heart sink, "Amber! DIVE, DIVE, DIVE!" The monster threw a blue fireball at Ignis and Amber. But the ball of fire turned into a wisp and absorbed into Ignis's hand. Ignis shook his hand. It burned.

Fornacem said, "Watch out, Ignis. That's a lot of fire

to absorb all at once. Don't absorb too much or you'll disintegrate."

Ignis yelled, "I don't know *how* to *not* absorb it!"

Ignis saw Umbra Mortis dive at the monster, which roared and batted him back. Ignis watched in shock as Umbra Mortis crashed into the other side of the valley.

Ignis said, "Oh yeah, it's tough alright."

Ignis heard Umbra Mortis growl, "Ooh, I may not be able to kill it, but I sure as hell am pissed now."

Ignis heard Uncle Dux say, "Ignis, Amber! We'll handle the Seniorem Reptans, you guys circle the valley and kill the incoming monsters!"

Ignis saw smaller Reptans crawling into the valley.

Ignis gasped, "Hey! They're ice Reptans!"

Uncle Dux laughed, "Good! Then you two will be able to kill them!"

Fornacem said, "Don't let those Reptans look into your eyes. That's as bad as instant death. Watch out for the Seniorem Reptans' organs too. They're extremely toxic, don't touch the blood."

Ignis nodded, "Amber?" She grinned and she dropped Ignis.

Ignis activated his aura which streaked behind him like a comet. He landed in a cluster of Reptans, and an explosion burst around him. The monsters roared, and twenty leaped at him. Ignis threw fireballs, killing half of them. He leaped over one and stomped on top of it. He ducked under another, dragging a fiery blade across its stomach.

Ignis learned that whole weaponry tactic from Gloria. Njord had given Gloria a book on, 'Cyromancing, mastery level' and Ignis a book on 'Molten Mayhem' which both essentially explained how to make weapons out of their elements.

Ignis remembered Gloria's words, "Just concentrate. Feel your element form around your hand and sharpen it." She then sliced an apple neatly in half.

Ignis had made a flimsy string of fire that exploded the apple. He could remember Njord saying, "You are doing excellent, keep rehearsing!"

Ignis sliced the legs off another monster, stabbing straight into its throat before it could bite down. Ignis saw Amber swoop down, slicing, kicking, or setting fire to the Reptans. Ignis's heart leaped to his throat when he saw the Seniorem Reptans turn towards him.

Ignis said, "Oh, please no."

The Seniorem Reptans roared, fell on its stomach, and crawled furiously at Ignis.

Ignis yelped and heard Amber say, "Hang on Ignis!"

Ignis heard a peculiar low-pitched whistle that turned into a higher pitch as it continued. The Seniorem Reptans reached a hand to Ignis but suddenly he was in the air.

Amber grinned down at him, "Hey."

Ignis gasped, the Senior Reptans left deep trenches fifty feet wide behind it. They were quickly filled with black, oil-like blood, making a toxic swamp.

Uncle Dux said, "How can it move so fast?"

Fornacem said, "Well, you know I wanted to give it legs, but then I realized how much lighter it was without them! I watched a documentary about acids in the stomach, and *viola*, one awesome monster!"

Umbra Mortis launched comets of darkness at it, but they did nothing. The Seniorem Reptans roared, batted them aside and they slammed the ground in front of it.

Ignis' vision shifted to the front as a loud screech sounded. A swarm of Golden Guardians flew at them.

Amber screamed, "Hold on!"

Ignis said, "What are you doing- OH LORD!"

Amber sheathed her sword, grabbing Ignis's other hand. She tucked her wings, and they plunged into a steep dive.

Ignis didn't question Amber's flying ability, but... it was a different thing when he was rushing towards the ground at hyper speed with hundreds of hungry monsters behind him.

Amber pulled out of the dive at the last second, and Ignis felt his feet brush the top of the grass. The Golden Guardians could not bank like Amber and rammed into the ground with a crunching sound. Amber flew up with thirty Golden Guardians still following. She raced to the top of the barrier, following its curve down. Ignis fired a comet behind them.

An explosion rose, taking out a few more of the Guardians. Ignis could tell Amber was tiring. As they lost speed, the Golden Guardians were veering closer. Amber swung Ignis backwards, and he fired comets at the monsters. Amber looked back just as a Golden Guardian flew in front of her. They plowed straight through the monster and fell towards the ground at a forty-five-degree angle.

Ignis yelled, "Amber! Fly us out!"

Amber spread her wings and gasped, "I can't! They're covered in monster guts!"

Ignis gasped as ten more of the monsters flew towards them, their mouths wide open. Ignis wrapped an arm around Amber and pointed at the monsters, *"Furor inferni!"*

Fireballs flared and exploded, dropping the monsters one by one, until the last one was only a foot from them. Ignis bellowed, *"Sol percutiens!"*

The monster groaned and exploded in front of them, soaking them in blood and inner remains. Ignis realized they were ten feet from the ground.

He pointed under them and yelled, *"Erumpunt iecit!"* He and Amber shot up one foot before crashing and tumbled onto the ground.

Ignis pushed Amber's wing off him, "You ok, Amber?"

Amber sat up and gagged, "You smell disgusting!"

Ignis wiped a chunk off of Amber's shoulder, "I think *we*

smell disgusting."

As they broke into laughter, Amber said, "You know your shoes are *fried* right?" Ignis looked down. The soles had melted against the barrier, any longer and he would have lost his feet. They broke into laughter again but flinched as an explosion roared behind them.

The Seniorem Reptans fired a volley at the Fall Tree and Ignis saw a wall of darkness intercept the projectiles.

Uncle Dux said, "Hey! Someone take care of those monsters on the east side!"

Amber nodded at Ignis, grabbed him, and flew east. A Furnace Fallen and a Venator were running towards the Fall Tree.

Amber said, "I got left!"

She threw Ignis at the Venator, while she dove for the Furnace Fallen. Ignis landed on the monster's head, kicking with both feet. The monster roared, swiping at Ignis, but he was already on the ground. Ignis sent a spear of flames into its stomach, and it disintegrated.

Amber sliced the Furnace Fallen's arms and hit it at the waist as well. It crumbled into cinders. Amber swung her sword and ran to Ignis.

Amber said, "What now?"

Her eyes got big as she glanced behind Ignis, "Up we go!"

She grabbed his arm, and they flew up, just as the Seniorem Reptans crawled by.

Ignis saw no other monsters in the valley. The Seniorem Reptans roared at them and slowly made its way up the hill, disappearing over its peak.

Uncle Dux sighed with relief, "They retreated, alright, everyone back to the Tree. We have a few things to go over."

As soon as Uncle Dux was in the same room as Fornacem, he punched him hard across the face.

He yelled, "*That* was for making that stupid monstrosity!"

Fornacem howled with laughter, "Not sorry Dux! Those things kicked *ass* in the second war!"

Arthur shuddered, "Don't remind me." They all sat around the dining table once again.

Uncle Dux said, "Alright, so we know where the others are, for now. So, let's focus on trying to reactivate a portal." Uncle Dux pointed to Umbra Mortis, "You have the most magic power here, right? Do you have experience with travel?"

Umbra Mortis blew a raspberry, "Sure I do, but for now, I am *exhausted*. You've been running us like dogs for almost two days, Dux!"

Uncle Dux sighed, "Unless you *want* to die, we must keep fighting. Which brings me back to the subject of finding Njord and Gloria."

Uncle Dux eyed everyone individually, his eyes resting upon Amber, "Amber, what do you know about portals around the Bestia Capital?"

Uncle Dux had caught her by surprise.

She stammered, "Um, well... There are a few by the *heavily* populated cities. Fortunately, that includes one by C-Four."

Uncle Dux nodded, "I think Gloria and Njord found out Lapsus was in the Bestia Capital, traveled there from the portal by Vegas and fought him."

Amber said, "If she's still wanted, that *must* mean she is still alive!"

Uncle Dux nodded, "Exactly. Now, all we have to do is connect a portal to *that* portal and bust them out."

Fornacem said, "Only there's one problem."

Uncle Dux said, "What is it?"

Fornacem said, "Besides the fact that we're out of doughnuts and the shitter's clogged, from inside an anti-magic barrier, you can't connect two magical places."

"*What?*" Said Uncle Dux, "Why not?"

Fornacem said, "Opening a portal draws magic. It requires more magic than we can make. What we would have to do is travel to the mortal realm, maybe Vegas, *then* get Gloria and Njord from the capital."

Uncle Dux slapped a hand to his head, "And the portals would still be resetting."

Fornacem nodded. Julia said, "So what do we *do?*"

They sat in silence for a while. Ignis noticed Amber had a large square box sitting in her lap. Her fingers were covered in a sugary white powder. Ignis accepted a doughnut under the table.

Uncle Dux said, "We just might have to risk opening a portal directly to them..."

Arthur said, "No!"

Fornacem said, "Horrible idea!"

Julia said, "Not only is it indeed a bad idea, anchoring a portal to someone within the magical realm is too risky! You'd risk killing them! There's too much magic around them to pinpoint a safe place to open one!"

Uncle Dux waved a hand angrily, "I know, I know!" Which is *why* I was going to ask for a little help..."

Uncle Dux took a deep breath, "Fornacem, can I borrow some magic?"

Everyone at the table looked shocked. Fornacem said, "Back up a sec, *you* want to borrow magic... from *me*? Are you nuts? The slightest bit too much and you'll spontaneously combust."

Uncle Dux said, "I just need enough to open a portal from two hundred miles away. And enough to sense *exactly* where the others are. I can open a portal in front of them and we can get them."

Arthur stood, "This is a little extreme, even for you, Dux."

Amber said, "I know a thing or two about *magicae opprimi*, it's *not* worth it."

Ignis said, "Woah, wait, what's that?"

Uncle Dux said, "*Magicae opprimi* is when you use someone else's magic to compress your own, making you temporarily more powerful, just long enough for three spells."

Amber said, "And failure?"

Ignis looked at Fornacem as he made a quiet whistle, followed by an explosion. Fornacem said, "Like the fourth of July."

Uncle Dux said, "Look, I'll be fine! It'll be just enough to see the others and make a portal to them."

Fornacem said, "A portal *directly* to them?"

Uncle Dux said, "Where they were last in the magical realm. I'll see them."

Arthur said, "It's a bad idea, Dux."

Uncle Dux said, "Look at what we're facing, Arthur! I don't think we can survive another attack from that Seniorem Reptans! We need Gloria and Njord, there's no time! We need to do it *now*!"

Everyone fell silent. Ignis knew they were tired. The enemy didn't need sleep and had enough numbers to fight for months.

Fornacem shrugged, "What the hell. I'll do it." He walked to the other side of the table.

Arthur stopped him for a moment, "Go easy, please."

Fornacem smiled, "I got it."

He set a hand on Dux's shoulder and glanced around. "You may want to step back." He advised.

Everyone joined Ignis at his side of the table.

Uncle Dux said, "Light me up."

Fornacem lifted his pointer finger and a small silver speck drifted from his finger to Uncle Dux. Ignis saw it disappear, and Uncle Dux gasped, doubling over.

Arthur said, "Woah, Dux!"

Uncle Dux held a hand up, "It's ok, I'm good."

He looked up and Ignis gasped. His eyes were glowing a solid white. Latin words began appearing out of light, orbiting him.

Uncle Dux said, "*Alii ad me.*" His form glowed brighter, and he gasped.

Julia said, "What is it? What's wrong?"

Uncle Dux returned to normal. The silver speck drifted back to Fornacem.

Uncle Dux looked frightened, "It's Gloria and Njord... They... They're not at the Bestia Capital..." He looked at the others. "They're gone."

CHAPTER 11: GLORIA
The Space Between Minds

G loria had a tight grip on Njord's arm, "What do we do?" Njord's eyes were glowing fiercely, "I do not know!" Green light filled the room, nearly blinding. Gloria gasped as she realized two glowing green eyes were staring right at them. A new figure took a step forward.

Gloria didn't recognize them. They wore Bovi's necklace, as well as Cybele's shoulder armor, Bovi's kilt and what resembled Cybele's spear. The blade was larger, and shaped like a simple flame, almost tear shape. The metal twisted in an intricate pattern. They wore green beaded bracelets on their wrists and hanging from their horns. Two normal horns appeared where they should be, and two small ones grew underneath, like a thumb under a pointer finger. Amazingly, they were a foot taller and even heavier built than Bovi. Their eyes were bright green. Gloria watched as a black substance flooded into their eyes. They spun the spear in a circle, slamming the butt of it onto the ground.

The figure snarled, sounding deeper than either of the twins, "We are *Spiritus Tauri, the Spirit of the Bull!*" They took a step forward, "You are our enemy. Perish by our hands!"

Gloria squeaked like a mouse, Spiritus Tauri moved quickly, faster than even an Elder Fallen. Gloria didn't have any time to react. She was swept off her feet and flung to the other side of the room. She gasped in pain, the breath knocked from her lungs. Njord landed next to her.

Spiritus Tauri turned around, "Surrender now and we won't destroy you." Its spear drug on the stone and orange sparks flew from the blade. Gloria gasped for breath. The figure in front of them had all of Bovi's strength and all of Cybele's speed. It was simply too much for Gloria and Njord.

Is this the power of combination animarum? Gloria thought.

Njord muttered, *"Kraken tempestas!"*

A strong salty wind slammed into Spiritus Tauri. It flung back Gloria's hair. Spiritus Tauri didn't move.

They said, "Your spells are no match for us. We are a combination!"

Gloria shook Njord's shoulder, trying to speak, but her voice was a wheeze.

Njord said, "They are too strong. We are not able to defeat them."

Spiritus inched closer and raised their spear. Gloria dove her hand in her pocket, bringing out a small green orb.

Spiritus Tauri froze, "What is this? Is that what we think it is?"

They clipped their weapon onto their back and stood straight, crossing their arms. Gloria couldn't help but notice that they stood like Bovi did.

They said, "Combination? Let us see if you are worthy of the enchantment."

Gloria pointed to the orb, then to Njord. Still wheezing, she coughed.

Njord said, "Are you sure? We may not succeed."

Gloria nodded frantically, tears streaming down her face. She coughed again. In a hoarse voice she said, "S-Say *simul* on three!"

Njord nodded, Gloria said, "Three!"

And they both yelled, "*Simul!*"

Nothing happened, Spiritus Tauri shook their head, "Unfortunately, combination is not as simple as it seems-" They gasped.

A green light burned into existence around Gloria and Njord. As though someone were tracing light into the world. Gloria felt the orb warm, and a green flame started rising from the green circle.

Spiritus Tauri smiled, "Well, you managed to achieve it. Good luck keeping form."

Gloria said, "Huh?" And her vision was lost in a bright green light.

Gloria blinked, she stood in a vast, empty white space. It stretched as far as the eye could see. Gloria looked around. She was alone, panic built in her chest.

She called out, "Njord?"

Her voice echoed around her. Walking forward, Gloria looked around her. *Where the heck am I?* She thought.

Gloria saw something just ahead. She sighed with relief when she saw Njord.

He was wearing his reading glasses, his gray button-up shirt, and his favorite blue tie. There was a pencil above his ear, and he was standing behind a white desk that almost blended in with its surroundings. On the desk were two computers, a pencil holder, a bunch of papers, and other supplies.

Gloria said, "Njord! Thank the lord I found you! Where are-"

Njord smiled blankly, "Hello, Gloria Factorem."

Gloria hesitated, "Um... Njord?"

Gloria watched him shake his head, "No, no, I am

technically not Njord."

Gloria became extremely confused, "Um, what? Where are we? What are you?"

The Njord waved around, "We are in the *spatio inter mentibus, the space between minds.* You are currently in between the subconscious minds of Gloria Factorem, and Njord Pacificus."

Gloria had to think for a moment, "And... what are you?"

The Njord smiled, "I am the Njord best equipped to speak with you."

Gloria stared, "Huh?"

The Njord smiled, shaking his head slightly, "Let me see... have you ever heard the expression? There are hundreds of miniature *'yous'* in your mind? Typically depicted running fax machines, printers, and computers?"

Gloria nodded, The Njord said, "Well, that is partially true. There are thousands of *'Njords'* that run through his mind. Each control functions like moving, thinking, talking, etcetera. I am the Njord who has the highest probability of success when speaking to you currently, Gloria Factorem. I usually control speech when speaking to you."

Gloria's mind ran wild. She thought, *if that's true, then keep it together 'mes'.*

Gloria shook her head, "Wait, wait, wait... Why am I seeing this place like this?"

The Njord said, "This is the simplest, and most accurate, image producible, that will not explode your mind."

Gloria nodded, *"Right*, right, right. And, what's with the whole, *highest probability of success* when talking to me, thing?"

The Njord opened his mouth for a moment, then looked horrified. He quickly grabbed the phone on his desk, and whispered into it, "Send another! Hurry!"

The Njord dropped the phone, stood from his chair, and started walking away. It seemed like he was walking down invisible stairs behind his desk.

Gloria said, "Hey! Wait a moment!"

Simultaneously another Njord walked down invisible steps from just above Gloria.

Gloria said, "Um…"

This Njord was wearing a white button-up shirt and a red tie. He had a blue pen above his ear. His reading glasses were folded and hanging from his shirt pocket.

The Njord smiled, "Hello Gloria."

Gloria blinked, "Um… hi?"

The Njord shuffled papers on the desk. Gloria said, "Um, what Njord are you?"

The Njord smiled, "I am the Njord who best handles crisis in thought."

Gloria made an indignant sound, "Is he really *that* nervous speaking?"

The Njord said, "Only to-" His hand shot over his mouth, "Er, let us pretend that I did not say that."

Before Gloria could grill him on what that meant, the Njord said, "Now, you and Njord Pacificus attempted combination animarum at precisely ten thirty-six a.m."

Gloria said, "Please don't tell me we died."

The Njord chuckled, "No, no, you succeeded!"

Gloria gave a sigh of relief. The Njord brought up a heaping stack of papers from under the desk.

He said, "*Now*, however, you and Njord are currently dividing the responsibilities of combination animarum."

Gloria said, "What are they?"

The Njord said, "Well, pain, thought, speech, body, soul, power, mind, emotions, opinions, breathing-"

Gloria raised her hands, "I get the idea."

The Njord said, "Basically, because you and Njord did not think of it beforehand, you have to decide now."

Gloria said, "How were we successful?"

The Njord said, "Amber told Njord that combination animarum responds to compatibility. That alone seemed to make you successful."

Gloria said, "Huh." Gloria shook her head, "Wait! Where's Njord if I'm here?"

The Njord said, "I will try to simplify the answer as much as possible. He is *here*, but he is not. He is in the *exact* place you are in this current moment, but in his own understanding."

Gloria said, "So, Njord is currently talking to one of thousands of 'mes'?"

The Njord nodded, "Correct."

Gloria said, "Oh, that hurts to think about..."

The Njord pushed the papers closer to Gloria, "Now, you need to sign your name on whatever you wish to take responsibility and control of."

Gloria gaped at the papers, there were at least a hundred. *"Seriously?"*

The Njord nodded, "Yes."

Gloria snatched a pen from the Njord's desk, "If I'd known I'd be doing paperwork..."

Gloria looked at the first page. It said, *by signing this paper, it signifies that (Your Name Here), understands the dangers and responsibilities of combination animarum. Please sign below to assume the responsibility.*

Gloria saw this was the page for controlling... *the mind?* Gloria thought, she flipped a few pages.

"Nervous breakdowns? Burps? Why do I need to sign these?"

The Njord said, "Every possible conscious and unconscious action and thought needs to be controlled by either you or Njord, every heartbeat, every blink, every neuron firing, one of you must control it."

Gloria sighed. She then saw a large stamp just behind the monitor. The handle to the stamp said, *equilibrium*.

Gloria pointed, "What about that?"

The Njord followed her finger. "Equilibrium, this is dividing every action and thought equally, by what best suits the two who are combined."

Gloria dropped her pen, "Let's do that."

The Njord looked nervous, "Are you sure? Equal combination animarum is the most powerful and the hardest to achieve. Once combined, your personality may change exponentially."

Gloria nodded, "It'll be fine."

The Njord nodded, "Very well."

He picked up the stamp and pressed it upon the first piece of paper. Brilliant green ink spelled the word *equilibrium* in bold letters. The Njord went to the next page and stamped, then the next.

The Njord said, "You may take a seat, this will take a bit."

Gloria looked behind her and a large office chair appeared. Gloria sat, watching the Njord stamp the pages. Gloria waited, lifted the chair height, lowered it, spun in circles, and even rolled around the desk a few times. She groaned. Then, she had an idea.

"Hey Njord?"

The Njord spoke without pausing or looking up, "Yes?"

Gloria said, "If you are, er, one one-millionth of Njord, do you still have his thoughts and stuff?"

The Njord adjusted his glasses, "Technically, yes."

Gloria said, "What was in that small black notebook?"

The Njord almost missed the page, his eyes glowing. He cleared his throat, "E-Er, what notebook?"

Gloria said, "It said, *captains log* on it?"

The Njord hesitated, he picked up the phone, "Send

another!"

Gloria watched with a confused expression as the Njord walked down the invisible steps behind his desk, and a new one took his place.

Gloria said, "And you are?"

The Njord said, "I am the Njord best suited for social speech."

Gloria narrowed her eyes, "Meaning?"

The Njord's eyes started glowing. Immediately, he reached for the phone, Gloria said, "Wait! Sorry! Just stamp the papers!"

The Njord pulled on his collar, "Speaking to you is indeed..." The Njord shook his head. He picked up the stamp and started stamping the papers.

Gloria said, "What does Njord think of me?"

The Njord hesitated. He eyed the phone. "Er, you heard his opinion at the construction zone in California."

He stamped a few pages, and Gloria said, "What's in the book?"

The Njord took a breath, "Er, that information is extremely private."

Gloria hesitated, *what extremely private information is Njord keeping from me?* Gloria thought, *also, what's causing Njord's brain to break down trying to talk to me?* She thought, *is it about me?*

Gloria decided to grill the Njord again, "Is it like a journal?" The Njord leaped to his feet, "Er- uh- wha- what made you think of that?"

Gloria mentally nodded, *it's totally a journal.* Gloria said, "Is it about me?"

The Njord swallowed, "E-Er, n-no. Not precisely."

Gloria said, "Does he mention me?"

The Njord dived for the phone, "Send another!"

Gloria roared with laughter as another Njord appeared.

She said, "I didn't know he wrote a journal! Oh, I am *so* going to ask him to read it!"

The Njord raised his hands as though approaching a wild animal, "N-Now, now, let us not be hasty. You-You would be hypocritical. You hated it when Amber and Ignis eavesdropped on you and Njord."

Gloria said, "But Njord and the others wouldn't know that."

The Njord tried to say something, but he fell silent. He sat in his desk chair, apparently thinking.

The Njord said, "I need a moment." He grabbed the phone again, and said, "Er, could you please send the majors? Thank you."

The Njord disappeared down the stairs, and the single desk turned into a large, stretched, high desk and two smaller desks appeared on either side. Four Njord's appeared at the desks.

The one on the far left wore a yellow button-up shirt with a smiley face tie. The Njord to his right wore a red button-up shirt, with a black tie, that wasn't properly fixed. His lips were pressed together. Gloria recognized the expression. Njord wore it every time someone questioned his answers. The one on his right wore a light purple button-up shirt with a white tie. The one on his right wore a blue button-up shirt with a loose gray tie. Two more appeared in the smaller desks on either side, one in a light blue button-up shirt and reading glasses. He held a calculator, several books, and a notepad. A pencil was tucked over his ear. The other wore a green button-up, and he had a pen in the front shirt pocket.

Gloria took a step back, "Woah." It was as though a council of Njords had gathered. It made Gloria think of a courtroom.

The Njord in the yellow said cheerfully, "Hello Gloria! We

are the four main emotions, on my right is Advanced Intellect. We call him A.I. To my far left is Success."

Gloria hesitated, The Njord in the yellow said, "I am Happiness-" He went down the line in order of appearance, "Then Anger, Fear, and Sadness!"

The Njords nodded at Gloria, she blinked a few times, "Um, ok?"

Happiness continued, "Let's see-"

Anger scowled, "We cannot even file *one order*, *seriously*?"

Fear inched away from Anger, "U-Um, why... may we please relax a bit?"

Sadness was twirling the pencil around in his fingers, looking dejected.

Happiness shook his head, "A-Alright, this is ok! We can fill out a *simple equilibrium* combination paper, right?"

Anger huffed, "Once again, half the brain was sent into mental panic from-"

They all flinched, Happiness said, "Anyways! Continuing!"

They all started stamping papers, The Njord on Gloria's far left, A.I., was hastily making calculations. He gasped, taking a paper from the desk. He held it towards the other Njords, "I have a speech pattern with an eighty percent success rate!"

Gloria burst out laughing, "Oh my *lord*, I hope I'm not all scatterbrained when Njord talks to *my* mind." Gloria smiled, "*Get it? Scatterbrained!*"

She doubled over laughing. The Njord crumbled up the paper and threw it into a waste bin. "Never mind."

Gloria wiped a tear from her face, "Wait, wait! Was that about me?"

Happiness said, "Oh, I see the issue. Come on! We are a smart individual, who speaks on a daily basis! We just need to stamp these papers!"

The Njord on Gloria's far right said, "That was a good joke. It's ok, now we need to focus on stamping the papers."

Gloria waved her hand, "Sorry! I'll stop talking now."

The Emotions stared at the Njord, then they continued stamping papers. They flinched as a phone rang.

Happiness picked it up. "Happiness here."

He listened for a while, "Mhmm, I know. Look, we are in the middle of something! Get magic intellect in there then! I have advanced intellect with me now. Mhmm, we will only be a while longer. Thank you. Have a nice day."

The Njord set the phone down, "Something went wrong, Njord just now picked the equilibrium stamp."

Anger growled, "Finally! I skipped eleven papers already!"

Gloria's head started spinning. What the heck was she seeing? A collaboration of Njord's thoughts and emotions banding together? Gloria realized this depicted Njord combining with her. So, this might be the simplest way for her to see it. Still, it turned her head to mush. Would that cause a problem for Njord? Gloria decided to stop thinking before she blew a fuse.

Time passed; Gloria didn't know how much. There was a clock in the corner, but it read in... did that say *nanoseconds*?

Finally, the Emotions filed their papers and gave them to Advanced Intellect. He nodded, and all of the Njord's disappeared. A single Njord appeared in front of Gloria, sitting at a regular desk.

He said, "Alright, almost done... Now, are you alright with this?"

It took a moment, but Gloria realized that he was speaking to her.

She said, "With what?"

The Njord removed his glasses, "Combination

animarum, are you sure you want to go through with it?"

Gloria nodded, "Yes."

The Njord nodded, the papers disappeared. The space around them turned green. A large green button appeared on the desk. It read *equilibrium*.

The Njord said, "All you have to do is press this."

Gloria nodded, "Pretty sure someone would *kill* for this button." Gloria hesitated. She looked at the Njord, "Will I remember any of this?"

The Njord shook his head, "No. The past events have been recorded in nanoseconds. They will not be stored in a memory base and will be discarded."

Gloria said, "What? How am I going to remember all this? I have *so* much to grill Njord about! How he thinks when talking to me, that book, and what he's writing about me!"

The Njord smiled shiftily, "Njord will be glad about that. If that makes you feel better."

Gloria grumbled, "It doesn't."

Gloria pressed the button, the Njord and the desk disappeared. Gloria looked around. From the horizon, a green wall of flames rushed towards Gloria.

Gloria's heart leaped to her throat, "HOLY-" Her words were drowned out as the wall of flames met her.

Two hearts, souls, and minds became one instantaneously. A bright green explosion pushed Spiritus Tauri back, and a new figure arose. Eight tentacles covered in black spots formed its lower half. It sported long golden hair, with black ends and was dressed in an open golden button-up shirt over a flowing gold dress. A glass water tank hung at their back, and a pair of reading glasses covered bright golden eyes. The figure took a breath.

Spiritus Tauri gasped, shaking their head and the black

substance retreated from their eyes, revealing their green color. "Who-Who are you? Where did you come from?"

The figure slung the water tank off her shoulders, and it disappeared in a bright golden light. The figure smiled, "From the void of course!"

Spiritus Tauri spoke in a guarded tone, "What is your name?"

The figure spread her arms, stretching. She smiled widely, waving. "Name's *Aureum Spiritum*, you can call me Rem!"

Tauri replied, "Interesting name. Shall we carry on?"

In a golden flash, eight legs grafted into two human ones. Rem now wore jeans. She spun in a small circle and pointed to Spiritus Tauri, "*Ok!*"

Tauri lunged their spear at Rem, who caught it with her bare hands. It gasped, "Such a powerful form!"

Rem winked, "Aww, you make me blush!" She kicked Tauri, who crashed into the wall. Rem pulled a hair tie from her pocket and whistled as she put her hair in a ponytail. She stuck out her tongue, "Catch me if you can, cow face!"

Tauri growled, throwing the spear. Rem caught it and checked her reflection in the blade. "Ooh! Celestial steel! Grade twelve! I didn't know that combination animarum enhances weapons! That's *so* cool!" Rem thought for a moment, "That would require at *least* eight years' experience. Factoring age, species too..."

Tauri tried to yank the spear from Rem's hands. Rem huffed, "That was *not* nice! You're gonna make me forget what I'm saying!"

They tried again and Rem let go. Tauri flew backwards, collapsing onto the ground, huffing, "If you are going to fight, then fight!"

A bright gold aura fading into shimmering black sprung to life around Rem. "Aaaand, *pew!*" A golden-black comet surged from her finger and exploded against the wall where Spiritus Tauri was standing.

Rem stamped her foot, "Man! I missed? My calculations were *perfect*. I even factored wind, magical resistance, gravity-" She dodged Tauri and returned a punch. "It's rude to interrupt! Sheesh you two! You made me forget what I was going to say!"

Spiritus Tauri struggled to stand. Rem kicked them in the stomach, and they crashed flat on the ground. Rem snapped her fingers. "I got it! I sound like a nerd!" Rem laughed squatting next to them, "Moo?" Tauri swiped, Rem dodged. "*Missed* me!"

Spiritus Tauri groaned, "Stop mocking us! Who is in charge anyways?"

"Well, in all technicalities, we are *both* in charge. Utilizing such tactics as situational awareness, fighting tactics. I forgot what I was saying again! Argh!" She stamped her foot. "Enough rational thinking! Let's combat!"

Spiritus Tauri snarled, "Very well!" and struck a series of rapid blows. Rem caught each volley and flipped them to the ground. "You sort of *stink*."

Spiritus Tauri roared, kicking Rem away. A brilliant green aura flared.

Rem pushed off a section of wall, "*Rude*." She flared her aura and shimmering golden wings burned into existence. A green light formed a halo above her head. Glittering black storm clouds formed around her, flashing with gold lightning.

Rem's eyes flared gold, "*Toro, toro!*" Spiritus Tauri snarled and charged. Rem blasted a gold light, "*Ole!*" She threw a spear of ice. Spiritus Tauri dodged, but a strike of golden lightning brought them to their knees.

Rem walked over slowly, playing a game of hopscotch with the bricks and punched Spiritus Tauri across the face.

Spiritus Tauri yelled, "*Buccina!*"

Rem said, "Nope! *Oceanum aureum!*"

A green light was overpowered by a powerful wave of golden light. Spiritus Tauri crashed into the wall, the spear clattering to the ground.

Rem hummed to herself, skipping over in a quick Karaoke walk.

She pulled Spiritus Tauri's head up by the horns, "Yoo hoo! You two awake in there?" Spiritus Tauri groaned, and Rem giggled, "My, my! I don't know my own strength! It's weird!"

Rem glanced at Spiritus Tauri, they said, "Finish us then."

Rem said, "Hmm?"

Spiritus Tauri yelled, "Finish us! You don't care for us!"

Rem hesitated, "Er...who are you anyways?"

Separate broken voices spoke, "Your friends! It's Bovi and Cybele!"

Rem stammered, "U-Um, you attacked us!"

Spiritus Tauri set their head in their hands, "I know! But you didn't remember us at all!"

The smile slid from Rem's face. Strange memories collaborated and formed a single memory in her head. Two Bull Bestia, Rem saw them smile, reaching out a hand.

Rem shook her head, "No, we didn't- I didn't-"

Spiritus Tauri grabbed the front of Rem's shirt, "The spell forced us to fight you!"

Rem froze, then sighed. "Listen you guys, I'm *very* different from the other two. This is the first time I've been brought from the abyss. I didn't even exist until now. Some memories slipped from me." Rem tapped her head with her fist, "Blondes, huh?"

Spiritus Tauri's eyes narrowed, "The spell is *still* in effect, I still see you as something else."

Rem whistled, "You two make one *powerful* combination then." Spiritus Tauri chuckled.

Rem stood. Her aura faded. She offered a hand to Spiritus Tauri. They hesitated but took her hand.

Rem said, "You know, Gloria wanted to befriend you, even after combining. The two bozos that I am don't know much about it."

Spiritus Tauri said, "They must have incredible compatibility. You are almost a different person."

Rem shrugged, "Two different personalities will do that."

They laughed, Rem said, "Now, we have to get rid of that spell so we can help each other."

Spiritus Tauri hesitated, "I have been using equal combination for a long time. I remember two different memory strands. What do *you* remember?"

Rem shrugged, "Eh, random bits and pieces from both memories."

Spiritus Tauri said, "They mentioned their valley under attack."

Rem snapped her fingers, "Oh, yeah! Will they help?"

Spiritus Tauri nodded, "They certainly will."

Rem smiled, "Then, we must help each other now, Gloria and Njord's friends will find them soon. We just need to teleport far away first."

Rem removed her glasses, tapping them against her jaw. She said, "Ever been to Earth, Spiritus Tauri?"

Spiritus Tauri flinched, "No."

Rem said, "I never tried enhanced arch angel teleportation, nor have I been strong and smart enough to pull it off. *But* I *think* I can manage."

Rem's aura exploded and wings of light spread behind her. She smiled, flicking the green halo over her head, it spun once, resting over her head.

Spiritus Tauri hesitated, "We... we're not sure if Gloria and her friends would appreciate this... I mean, they're so close to the end of their journey."

Rem shrugged, "Well, can't teleport into the barrier and they can't teleport here. They will travel to Earth. Not knowing where we are, it'll default to the least occupied land mass, which happens to be Antarctica. Hope you guys like the cold!"

Spiritus Tauri was sure Rem was talking to herself as well as them. They said, "Alright then. Take us to this… Earth."

Rem smiled, "Alright then!"

Rem's aura intensified. Spiritus Tauri watched as a large golden-black summoning circle occupied the entire floor.

Rem chanted, "*Angeli ius est, per regnum mortale, divina tradenda!*"

The summoning circle turned black, and the temperature of the room plunged. The circle slowly opened from the center. Spiritus Tauri shivered. They saw an infinite mass of a cold white substance. The substance flew on frigid winds. Clouds obscured the sky. The summoning circle pulled the Combinations towards it.

Spiritus Tauri said, "It doesn't look very pleasant…"

Rem smiled, "Well if our friends are smart, they'll try to think like Njord. They'll discover we're not here, and *bingo*, they'll travel to Earth."

Spiritus Tauri said, "How do you know this will work?"

Rem winked, "I don't, but I do have Njord's intellect, and Gloria's abilities. They may or may not help a bit."

Spiritus Tauri glanced towards the portal as a cold wind blew. "Will we survive these challenging lands?"

Rem thought for a moment, "Well, that's really up to the four of them. This portal is going to separate us. Didn't think about that…"

Spiritus Tauri sighed, "How will the four know what happened?"

Rem giggled, "We won't!"

Spiritus Tauri sighed. Rem waved her hands. They

disappeared in a bright golden flash.

CHAPTER 12: GLORIA
Lost in the Frigid Ice

G loria saw a golden flash, then a bright green flash. The next thing she knew, she was falling to the ground. Gloria gasped as she plowed into snow. It was very cold, obviously. Luckily, Gloria landed in a tall snow pile, so her landing was soft. The bad thing was, she was wet and freezing.

Gloria sat up. She was to her shoulders in snow. She shuddered violently. A blizzard roared around her. Looking around, she saw nothing for miles. The skies were a cold black sheet of clouds, no sun or moon to tell time. Gloria sneezed. A loud roar sounded in the distance.

Where am I, Gloria thought. *If I'm on Earth, what the heck was that? Nothing would survive here.*

Deciding she was probably on Earth, Gloria concluded she was either very far north or south. As another roar sounded, she concluded that one thing was for certain, she was in danger. Gloria stood, shivering. Her aura was activated and that was probably keeping her alive.

Where the heck am I?

Gloria was on top of a large snow pile, and she saw three snow covered mounds in the snow below her. Gloria stumbled down, the howling wind making her shudder.

Gloria saw a long spear next to a mound. Gloria dug

under the snow and found a frozen water tank. "Ho!" Gloria stood in what she thought was the center. Gloria yelled, flaring her aura. The snow cleared in a ten feet circle. Njord, Bovi, and Bele appeared from beneath the snow. They were unconscious.

I've got to get them warm! Gloria put her hands to the cold ground and erected a large ice dome around them, leaving a hole in the top. She made a crawl space leading off ten feet before opening. Gloria stood in their makeshift igloo. At her feet, Gloria found matches, a frozen water bottle, Njord's backpack, the remains of her own, and a bundle of supplies.

Gloria gasped as she found the keys for combination animarum safe in her pocket. She sighed with relief, she spoke out loud, "Well, at least those are safe. Now about you guys..."

Gloria found a box in Njord's backpack and emptied it for kindling. She shuddered as a pathetic little fire sputtered and threatened to go out. Gloria wrapped Njord, Bovi, and Cybele in sleeping bags she found in the supplies. She wrapped them separately, since *she* wouldn't want to share a sleeping bag, but dragged them close together for warmth.

Gloria tossed the tent bag into the fire, "Good thing most of this stuff was made of plant material that will burn." Gloria tried to remember what happened but drew a blank. She remembered a green light, then almost nothing. Gloria closed her eyes and images flashed through her mind. The view seemed to be from only one eye. There was a pain behind her eyes, and Gloria shook her head. She'd make no progress on her own.

Gloria tried to wake the others. She had no idea how long before Bestia or Cecaelia would succumb to hyperthermia.

Njord is a sea creature, Gloria thought.

Gloria stumbled over and started with Njord, "Njord! Wake up dude!"

Starting to panic, Gloria thought he might not be

breathing. She set his tank of water over the fire. She tore open Njord's backpack, emptying it. She found a pack of smelling salts in the front pocket.

Gloria took Njord's tank and connected it to him. Gloria put the smelling salt directly under his nose and broke it. Njord's tank gargled like a water machine, and Njord surged forward. He gasped, "What! Wha...Gloria? Where are we?"

Gloria tackled him in a hug, "Good lord! I was so scared, Njord! Your tank froze, and we were all sprawled in the snow-"

Njord set a hand on Gloria's shoulder, "N-Never mind."

Gloria said, "Look, I found the bull twins!"

Njord glanced over, "Oh, why is one of them wrapped in our tent?"

Gloria said, "You were all freezing!"

Njord shivered, "I still am. You are aware that the temperature here is negative fifteen degrees Celsius right? Er, five Fahrenheit? The temperature is steadily rising, however." His breath steamed as he spoke.

Gloria hesitated, "Is it? I did break a sweat dragging you." Gloria shook her head, "I'll try to wake the twins."

Gloria made sure that Cybele wasn't near her spear when she broke the smelling salt. Cybele gasped and looked around frantically, "Where am I? Where's Bovi?"

She saw Gloria, "Oh, Gloria!"

Gloria smiled nervously, "Hey."

Cybele said, "Where's Bovi?"

Gloria pointed to the tent, "Right there."

Cybele said, "Under the tent that's *on fire*?"

Gloria looked over at the tent and yelped. She tore it off of him, throwing it into the fire.

Cybele saw Njord, "Hello Njord."

Njord nodded, "Er, greetings."

Gloria was about to break the smelling salt in front of

Bovi, then remembered how he broke that stone wall.

Gloria dragged Cybele over, "Right, in case he punches, *you* break this."

Cybele held the smelling salt in confusion, "What is this?"

Njord said, "A chemical compound, usually consisting of ammonia, utilized for stirring consciousness. The smell causes the body to automatically breathe, resulting in the regaining of consciousness."

Cybele said, "Oh."

Gloria said, "Just break the thing under his nose."

Cybele did and just as Gloria predicted, Bovi lunged. Cybele was narrowly missed, and his fist slammed into the ice. Bovi said, "Gah! What? Where am-"

Cybele hugged him. Bovi blushed. Cybele backed away, grabbing his shoulders, "Are you ok, Bo?"

Bovi nodded, "Yeah, fine."

Cybele sighed with relief. She flinched, retracting her hands.

Bovi glanced around, "Where... Where are we?"

Gloria sighed, "We don't know. Somewhere cold on Earth."

Njord said, "Why would we be on Earth?"

Gloria shrugged, "I don't know, it's the only place that I think we would go."

Cybele gasped, "Wait! We're not in the capital?" She looked devastated, "That's not how I wanted to leave! Everyone will think we're dead!"

Cybele took a breath, Gloria said, "Look, I don't know how we came here, does anyone else?"

Bovi said, "I think it was your combination."

Gloria and Njord flinched, Njord said, "Apologies."

Cybele smiled warmly. "Don't worry, it was your first

time using combination animarum, right?"

Gloria nodded, "Yeah."

Cybele said, "That happens to a lot of first timers. I've never seen an equal combination done successfully on the first try. You guys are really something."

Gloria felt a pulse of pain in her head, "Why does my *head* hurt so much?"

Bovi said, "If you use combination animarum, you'll get used to it. It's a side effect of sharing a memory."

Gloria said, "You guys seem to know a lot about combination animarum."

Cybele got a faraway look in her eyes. She said, "We've been around it a lot. Back when Bovi and I were just starting as guards, we were sent on a lot of rescue missions, overseen by the Dragonborn. There was a monster the Dragonborn didn't expect. Bovi and I were the only survivors."

Cybele leaned against Bovi. He awkwardly patted her back.

Cybele said, "When Bovi and I returned, we devoted ourselves to getting stronger. We learned self-enhancing magic at twelve."

Gloria said, "Why so young?"

Cybele said, "We are legal adults at eleven. If your family wants you to become a guard, you are sent to training camp the next day." She looked at Bovi and tapped his arm, "That's where I met Bovi."

Gloria hesitated, "Wait a second, aren't you twins?"

Cybele and Bovi looked confused, Cybele said, "*What*? No, not at all. That's just the nickname our town gave us. We didn't have the heart to ask them to change it. They made signs and floats when we were made gatekeepers."

Gloria said, "So... you're dating then?"

The Bull Bestia blushed. Cybele flew off Bovi's shoulder and they looked away from each other.

Gloria said, "Oh, sorry. Um, what happened next?"

Cybele cleared her throat, looking slightly pink. "B-Bovi and I discovered combination animarum during our next mission. Two Dragonborn warriors used it and they became the strongest warrior I've ever seen. They flattened our enemy and destroyed the monster with ease."

Cybele glanced at Bovi, "Bovi and I both were so inspired that in our free time, we worked to learn more. We saved up money to forge the keys and practiced combination, sometimes all night." She laughed, "Bovi, do you remember when we accidentally slept in?"

Bovi smiled, "How could I? The general chewed us out for an hour."

Cybele nodded, "But we did it, we were the youngest Bestia warriors, possibly in all existence, to achieve it. It was years later that became Spiritus Tauri. For a while, we went around, saving Bestia, attending to our guard duties. When we were alone, we used combination animarum on our missions."

Gloria leaned forward, "What happened then?"

Cybele smiled, "Well, we were caught by our general. He gave us an earful, but then he approved of it. A year later, the old gatekeepers retired and had a family together. Bovi and I took over."

Cybele spoke with awe in her voice.

Gloria thought of something, "Hey Bovi, the fire's getting low, can you get firewood?"

Bovi said, "Um, sure."

As Bovi stood, Gloria said, "Just so you know, it's *really, really* cold out."

Bovi said, "That'll be fine, Cybele and I have trained in conditions like this." Bovi left the igloo, trudging through the snow.

Gloria turned to Cybele, "Do all gatekeepers end like the ones you mentioned?"

Cybele avoided Gloria's eyes, "Er, it is common, but ill advised. The capital's reason is that if there is a battle, and one dies, well, it would be easier if you weren't close."

Gloria started to think like her friend Amber. "You totally like him, don't you?"

Cybele flushed red and sat up quickly, "I-what? I- What are you talking about? I could never..."

She came to a halt, noticing Gloria beaming, "You totally do! You like Bovi!"

Cybele shushed Gloria, looking around, "Shh! He might hear you!"

Njord frowned, "What are you talking about, Gloria?"

Gloria said, "Um, let me say this in a way you'll understand... she holds a deep affection for Bovi."

Cybele hid her face in her hands. Njord said, "Oh, that is wonderful then?"

Gloria nodded, facing Cybele, "How long?"

Cybele glanced at Gloria. She sighed and leaned against the wall. resting a hand on her head. "A week after I met him. I've always seen him around, but I didn't feel that way until later."

Gloria said, "Wow, how does he feel?"

Gloria regretted asking. Cybele looked dejected. She unclipped a bracelet from her wrist, staring at it. She said, "I... I've mostly been keeping the feeling to myself. Guards aren't supposed to be like that. I tried to ignore my feelings. But as time wore on, the feelings got stronger. The more jokes he told, the more I wanted to hear. I was always nervous when we were alone guarding the entrance to the capital." Cybele gained a smile, "It started a week after my employment. I was training in a city, and we were raided. I was alone, scared and confused. I watched my brethren fall in front of me.

Then... I met Bovi. I was cowering behind a wall, spells raged the skies around me. I saw Bovi run into the building. He ducked behind the wall in front of me. He saw me and my fear. He saw that I was scared and confused."

Gloria waited. She wasn't usually the one to show interest in these topics, but for some reason, she wanted to hear every word. If possible, she wanted to help.

Cybele said, "Bovi ran to my side and spoke with me. I'll always remember what he said to me." Cybele continued, "He said, *'Hey! What's your name?'* I told him, and he said, *'Hey Cybele, what do you call a sleeping bull?'*

I stared at him in such confusion, there was chaos all around us. Why was he asking a joke?" Cybele laughed, "I said what, and he said *'A bulldozer!'* It was such a bad and corny joke, that I broke into laughter. Immediately, I felt better. He offered a hand and said, *'My name is Bovi. Nice to meet you! The enemies are distracted, let's run'*.

And we did. He protected me from the attackers and helped me all the way to the capital. What made me develop those feelings wasn't that he saved me, and it *definitely* wasn't the joke. But he saw that I was hurting and helped me, not even knowing, or caring who I was.

No one ever did that before, I was always alone at training camp, and even before." Cybele looked at the reflection in her spear, "After that mission, I felt different. I found myself staring at him. I wasn't focusing on my training. I didn't know *what* I was feeling. I didn't have anyone to talk to. No one could help me understand. Some nights I would scream into my pillow in the female ward."

Gloria imagined being her age, confused, and hopeless, and alone.

Cybele sighed, "It was against the rules for two guards to have a relationship. So, I did my best to ignore my feelings." Cybele smiled sheepishly at Gloria, "But... they haven't disappeared." Cybele continued, "Everyone knows the rules, Bovi would never feel the same.

Some of the other female guards discovered how I felt. *You're obvious, you're so hopeless.* If I got on their bad side, they threatened to tell him. I didn't want that! He was the only one who spoke to me, I didn't want him to abandon me."

Gloria scoffed, "How horrible!"

Cybele said, "I wish one day, he might notice my feelings, and possibly feel the same way. We wouldn't know what to do then, but I wouldn't care, as long as he felt the same."

Gloria thought for a second. Bovi was rule-abiding, she could imagine the struggles Cybele had experienced. Gloria processed the story for a moment and realized she had seen Cybele stealing glances at Bovi, during the parade, in the booth even.

Gloria said, "What are you going to do now that you've left the capital?"

Cybele sighed, "I don't know."

Gloria said, "Are you going to tell him how you feel?"

Cybele said, "I don't think he's ready for that... I don't think *I'm* ready for that... I've tried to give him hints, that I wanted something more, sometime later. He never got the hint."

Cybele sighed, Gloria said, "What were your *hints*?"

Cybele blushed, "I... I said he smelled nice once."

Gloria burst out laughing. Cybele blushed, "I had no idea what I was doing!"

Gloria wiped a tear from her face, "I'm sorry! I can't judge, but you have to try better than that! Look, compliments are fine, but the smell thing is a bit creepy. Tell him he's nice, that sort of thing. Has he ever done anything that stood out to you?"

Cybele said, "He gave me his shirt once when it was raining."

Gloria said, "Ok, that's a start." She narrowed her eyes, "*Wait*, what did you do with it?"

Cybele blushed even deeper, "I... kept it."

Gloria sighed, "Wow, you *were* hopeless." Cybele huffed. "Ok, I stink at this kind of stuff. Amber knows *way* more about it."

Cybele said, "L-Lady Amber?"

Gloria nodded, "I'll get her to help you."

Cybele waved her hands, "No, that's ok, you don't have to go to the trouble!"

Gloria said, "I'm helping, take the help."

Cybele smiled, and pointed at Njord, "Not a word of any of this to Bovi. Understand?"

Njord said, "I do not have a complete understanding of the situation. Regardless, I will not inform Bovi."

Gloria whispered to Cybele, "If there is *anyone* who's more hopeless than you, it's Njord. Poor boy didn't know how to brush his teeth."

Njord sighed as Cybele laughed.

Gloria heard loud stomping, and Bovi crawled through the igloo entrance. Gloria noticed Cybele staring, then quickly looked away. Bovi was covered in snow. In his arms, he held enough sticks and branches to make several miniature log cabins. Gloria plucked one from his arms, and broke it into pieces, tossing them into the fire.

Bovi said, "Found a dead tree a few clicks south of here. Where should I put these?"

Gloria said, "Next to the supplies is fine."

Bovi nodded as a stick fell from his bundle. Both he and Cybele reached for it.

They flinched. Cybele retracted her hand as though burned, "Sorry."

Bovi said, "It's fine."

Gloria gestured to Cybele, who stammered, "U-Um! Thank you, Bovi! You-You did a great job!"

Cybele glanced at Gloria, and she gave a thumbs up. It was hard to tell in the light, but Gloria thought Bovi was blushing.

Bovi looked away, "Um, don't mention it." He set the sticks next to the supplies, taking a seat next to Cybele.

Bovi said, "What do we do now?"

Gloria said, "Well. I don't know. Pretty soon, we'll be screwed for supplies. Njord can make water, but for food, we'll need to figure something out. There are no living plants for hundreds of miles." Gloria set her head on her hand, "Maybe we could tunnel under us for water, there may be fish."

Bovi nodded, "What about your family?"

Gloria said, "I don't know. We couldn't travel to them because they're trapped in an anti-magic barrier. The portal from Bestia city wouldn't have worked, besides, it would have had to reset anyway."

Gloria said, "Njord, what do you think?"

"Well, we are not able to travel from here. None of us have the intellect to create a vortex or the energy to find a portal. The others may have no idea where we are. If they are trapped inside of an anti-magic barrier, travel for them would be difficult. For now, we require a secure source of food, since we currently possess water."

Gloria said, "Man, not sounding good."

Njord continued, "We were teleported here, I assume, by our combination. This means that we have a good reason to be here. Given Gloria and my, as well as Cybele and Bovi's combination, must have traveled voluntarily."

Gloria said, "What reason do you think?"

Njord shook his head, "I do not know. From what I am able to determine, we have the best chance of survival and success of reuniting with the others, if we are here. Therefore, I conclude that we require a stable food source. We do not know how long we may be stranded here."

Gloria had been hoping for slightly better news. She said, "Ok, that's fine. What can't two Bestia, a Cecaelia, and an ice Elementalist do? We've all got this!"

They flinched as a roar shook their igloo. Gloria sealed the entrance and made the walls two feet thicker. She made the one side of the wall into a window. Whatever was stomping outside made Gloria's heart stop.

At first Gloria thought it was a Seniorem Reptans, but she realized that it was *much* worse. Instead of fire rolling from its head, large golden ice spikes grew. Ice stalactites hung from its bottom jaw, and golden eyes leered at them, Gloria could see blue fire rolling inside them. Gloria saw frost covered organs spilling from its back end. Its blood had reduced the areas behind it into a toxic wasteland.

It was every ice Elementalists' nightmare. No one spoke, wide eyed with terror.

Gloria said, "That's just great! There's *no* way in heck we're killing *that* thing!"

Cybele said shakily, "What is that thing?"

Gloria said grimly, "It's a *Seniorem Nix Reptans, the Snow Crawling Elder.*" Gloria ran her fingers through her hair, "I only heard *legends* of these things. I had no idea they *actually* existed!"

Njord said, "I remember Fornacem informing me of this creature. He created Seniorem Reptans from both elements of creation. However, they grew to be much stronger than he anticipated.

The Seniorem Nix Reptans battled the fiery Seniorem Reptans. Neither could overcome the other. They caused a lot of damage to Fornacem's castle, so Fornacem cast the Seniorem Nix Reptans population here, to Antarctica."

Cybele gasped, "That's a *Fallen*?"

Gloria nodded, "Yup. If what I've heard is true, Fornacem *himself* had difficulty harming these things. Their skin is as hard as Rex Cataclysmi itself. It's basically impenetrable. They're smarter than the *Elder Fallen*. They can hurl ice comets, spears, and use the magic that ice Elementalists do. There's *no* way any of us are hurting that thing."

The creature stared at them through the wall. It tapped the dome, making it rattle. The Seniorem Nix Reptans stopped and moved so its eye was staring directly in the window.

Gloria said, "There's *no* way it doesn't see us."

The monster made a peculiar clicking noise. Thankfully, it seemed to lose interest. The gargantuan corpse scooped the snow next to their fort and ate it.

Gloria whispered, "Go away, please!"

The monster, however, did not want to. They watched it slowly pile heaping mounds of snow around their fort, making a snow wall five stories high. It made an entrance and rested next to their fort. They watched as it closed its eyes and a rumble told them it was asleep.

Gloria whispered, "The Seniorem Nix Reptans are some of the only Fallen that sleep, so it can save energy."

Bovi whispered, "One thing is for certain. We are not going *anywhere* with that thing outside."

Njord nodded, "Correct."

Gloria quietly made an ice blade and started carving the ground away.

Njord said, "What are you *doing*?"

Gloria said, "I'm digging, to see if we're- yes!"

Underneath, Gloria saw a clear surface. They were over a large frozen lake. Thankfully, the shore was under their igloo, so the monster wasn't risking them falling through the ice. Gloria carved a hole, pulling out a four-foot-tall cylinder of ice.

Gloria looked into the black depths of the waters and turned to Njord, "Think you can swim in that?"

Njord stuck a finger in the water and shivered, "It will be unpleasant, but yes, I can."

Gloria sent Njord to hunt for fish, after describing what to look for. It was just Gloria, Cybele, and Bovi in the igloo. Gloria felt like an enormous third wheel. She pretended to be busy with supplies and tried to read a book.

In the ice reflection, Gloria saw the two Bestia look at each other, then quickly glance away.

Gloria chuckled silently. *Good lord, I need to get them to the others.*

After what seemed like hours, Njord returned with a large cluster of what looked like shelled spiders.

Cybele cringed as Gloria said, "What are those?"

Njord smiled, "King crabs!"

Cybele looked disgusted, "Those are *edible*?" She asked in a horrified voice.

Bovi said, "Maybe they taste better than they look?"

Gloria sharpened the ends of a few sticks to make crude roasting device. Realizing that they couldn't skewer the legs, they wrapped them in tin foil that surprisingly was buried under their stack of supplies. They ate them after they cooled down.

Gloria took a bite and sighed with satisfaction. She scarfed down six legs before she remembered to breathe. Cybele poked at a leg, experimentally. She almost took a bite without removing the shell. Gloria barely stopped her in time, showing her how to crack the shell.

Gloria chuckled, *I'm teaching how to eat again.*

Bovi broke open the shells without effort. He took a bite, his eyes grew wide.

He nudged Cybele, "Try that Bele, it's *so* good."

Cybele glanced at Bovi and took a bite. "Oh, I wish I had these at the training camp!"

Bovi nodded, "Agreed, I think my hooves would have had more taste than that food."

Cybele laughed, smiling at Bovi. He smiled back

sheepishly. Gloria smiled to herself.

They heard a light rumble. Gloria made the ice clear again. A second Seniorem Nix Reptans appeared over the snow wall. This one had a large scrape through a closed eyelid. It roared, shaking the igloo, making a few things fall over.

The other Reptans roared back, raising a hand. They watched as a golden ice spike the size of a small skyscraper grew from its hand. The second Reptans batted it aside, throwing a comet of ice which caught the first monster in the shoulder.

Gloria shuddered, "I hope the others find us soon. There's no way we're escaping with those things outside."

Njord said, "I predict that this shelter is concealing us from the others, but it is attracting monsters."

They jumped as the monsters crashed through the snow wall. One reared back and struck the other in the face. The first launched another comet at the other's good eye. It roared as it fell to the ground.

Bovi said, "This structure will hold up right?"

Gloria nodded, "It should. The ice element can't oppose itself, meaning they can't break this ice. They won't be able to kill us with their ice abilities. That doesn't stop their sheer size from crushing us, or their poison dissolving us."

They winced as the two eyed Reptans scratched the other in the face. It fell to the ground with the sound of an Earthquake. The first grabbed the other's intestines, wrapped them around its neck, and began to strangle it.

Cybele said, "How gruesome."

Bovi nodded, "Best we don't interfere."

Gloria remembered reading about these monsters. They apparently didn't follow directions well. This had been the first Fallen to ignore direct orders. They took countless lives, enemy or not. They were one of the most dangerous Fallen of the second war and were cast away after.

Gloria shuddered. *I can see why Fornacem dropped them here.* Gloria thought *she* would never want to be within one hundred miles of one. The mere thought of two of them battling less than twenty feet away scared her. The roars were like a large magnitude earthquake.

The two-eyed monster pulled tighter on the bloody cord and roared, as the second slowed down. It clawed meekly at the snow drifts and its hand fell to the ground with a mighty crash. The monster rose over the corpse and roared, shaking the igloo.

Then they watched in horror as it started tearing its flesh, eating. Gloria gagged and made the wall solid again. Eating each other made them stronger, larger, and smarter. Gloria felt sick.

Bovi said, "So, what are the names of this family of yours?"

Gloria paused with a crab leg in her mouth. She swallowed and said, "Well, there's my brother Ignis, he's a fire Elementalist. You know Amber, there's my parents, also Elementalists. There is a strange dark being that helps Ignis named Umbra Mortis. There's Arbor, a tree spirit. Then there's... um, Lord Fornacem."

Cybele choked on her crab leg, "What?"

Bovi said, "The *King* of the Fallen is there?"

Gloria nodded, "Unfortunately, we are related. He's turned good now, we think. He's helping to fight off the monsters." Cybele glanced at Bovi. Gloria said, "We're all wanted by the Capital."

Cybele sighed, "Well, that's *one* thing we all have in common now."

They flinched as a loud roar again shook the ground. It seemed the others could not come quickly enough.

CHAPTER 13: IGNIS
To the Cold Barren Waste

J ulia attacked Uncle Dux, "What do you mean they're gone, Dux?" she wailed. Uncle Dux shook his head, dislodging Julia from his sleeve, "They're simply not there! I don't know!"

A frustrated sigh came from the end of the table, "Look, there *must* be a simple reason why they've gone and where." Julia looked away. They stared at Ignis. He continued, "We have to focus on what matters. The bigger problem is the next monster wave and how in the world we're going to deal with that. I for one think it'll be too much for us."

Fornacem said, "We all believe the only way to kill it is with Gloria's help. Julia doesn't have that kind of power anymore, no offense."

Julia lowered her head. Arthur said, "Don't blame yourself, Julia. No one could ask you to fight that thing."

Julia sighed, "I just wish I could help! I hate being stuck in here listening to explosions, not knowing *when* you'll return."

Amber sighed as she eyed a large brown bottle in Ignis's hand. While they were discussing what to do, Ignis pointed out the large scrape on Amber's arm. Ignis found himself with medical supplies once again in his hand.

Ignis discovered that only he could risk helping Amber, since Dragonborn blood was supposedly extremely hot. Arthur said that being her friend, Ignis should be the one to help.

Fornacem added to Ignis in a whisper, "He's *extremely* squeamish." his eyes gleaming.

Amber bit her lip as Ignis set a soaked rag onto her arm. Ignis said, "We need to think harder. *Why* would they leave? They knew something was wrong here after the message. We know they left the beach, went to Vegas, and then the Behemoth Capital."

The others nodded. Uncle Dux said, "It doesn't seem as though Lapsus was caught. Not according to the news. I hope that means he hasn't done something to them. He would have fled back to his base, or to here. The only other option would be to go to Earth, but *why* would they go to Earth?"

Fornacem said, "We could search for them on Earth, right? It is much smaller than the magical realm. Maybe they thought it would be easier for us to follow their auras."

Uncle Dux shook his head, "Earth is still *huge*. They know that searching on Earth isn't much easier. They would have been in a hurry after hearing our message. There is only so far that I can see an aura. Who knows where they would have ended up?"

Fornacem shrugged, "Well, where would they go? Not to Dottie, I hope."

Julia said, "Njord is smart, maybe they knew they couldn't travel directly here from the capital."

Uncle Dux nodded, "I think they're alright. There were no casualties on the news in either realm. And... if that were true... then..."

Fornacem said, "If we knew where they were and we could bring them here, it would be a nasty surprise for Lapsus."

They flinched as Amber yelped, "Sorry, I'm o- OW! I'm

ok."

Umbra Mortis said, "We need to think harder. The portal would have been resetting if they used it to travel to the Bestia Capital. So *how* did they travel to Earth? That would have been extremely difficult from within the capital. They would have set off trillions of alerts in the main castle *if* they succeeded. There's not another portal for a hundred miles. There's no way they got out if they got in." Umbra Mortis continued, "What is the only thing that would be powerful enough to open a vortex *that* quickly?"

Uncle Dux said, "A huge boost of power-"

He gasped, Umbra Mortis nodded, "They must have achieved combination animarum."

Arthur pursed his lips, "If that's the case-"

Julia said, "What would have caused them to do that? That's what I'm worried about."

Uncle Dux said, "It wouldn't have been Lapsus. He was already seen. The whole city would have been after him and would have seen it."

Uncle Dux glanced at Amber, "Um, am I right, Amber?"

Amber squeezed Ignis's hand, causing it to change color. She nodded, speaking through gritted teeth, "Yeah, they would have been at the vortex sight within a minute. No one would have had time to escape."

Julia said, "If we're talking about combination animarum, then doesn't that change a few things?"

Umbra Mortis nodded, "We're talking about a *whole* different being here. Their thoughts would have been *combined*, possibly even *more* complex than Njord's. They may not remember that we were in trouble. If it was their first time achieving combination animarum, was it an equilibrium?"

Uncle Dux scowled, "Impossible."

Amber shook her head, "Not entirely. Combination animarum responds to compatibility. Good friends can combine easily, regardless of having no experience. Of course, they wouldn't have kept their forms, but... if it's an equilibrium-" She winced, taking a quick breath, "Then their personality could be completely different. With Njord's brain, they could be even *smarter*."

Uncle Dux whistled, "A miniature Einstein."

Umbra Mortis said, "Even more, I'm thinking Isaac Newton."

They were lost in thought, though Amber's occasional yelps broke the silence.

Ignis said, "Wait, if they traveled to Earth, they must have been counting on something..."

Fornacem said, "Like what? *Our* stupid *asses*?"

Ignis nodded, "Maybe."

Fornacem looked shocked, "I was joking."

Ignis said, "No, let's think... They *willingly* went to Earth. Uncle Dux, was there an anchored location they were going to?"

Uncle Dux shrugged, "No, it was just a portal to Earth, an anchored vortex would have required a longer preparation time. They disappeared in less than a minute."

Ignis tied Amber's arm in tight bandages and started to pace. He said, "No anchor, meaning... what is the default vortex to Earth?"

Uncle Dux seemed surprised by the question, "Um, it would be the least populated place."

Arthur said, "So... what does that have to do with anything?"

Ignis said, "I think they were counting on us to know that. They knew that we'd be confused with them going to Earth. They knew we could not travel to the Magic Realm because of the barrier."

Fornacem took a sip from a soda, "*So?*"

Ignis said, "They had no ideal location, they just wanted

to go to Earth, right?"

Julia said, "Meaning, they would go to the default Earth location."

Uncle Dux said, "The place with the least amount of people!" Uncle Dux gasped, "They must be in Antarctica!"

Fornacem sprayed his soda, "No way!"

Amber said, "How do you figure?"

Uncle Dux said, "They must have thought that by going to Earth *we'd* be able to reach them!"

Umbra Mortis said, "That was quite a gamble, but it paid off."

Uncle Dux said, "Not quite. We still need a portal."

Fornacem rose and wiped soda off his mouth, "I *really* hope you didn't say *Antarctica.*"

Uncle Dux said, "I did, why?"

Fornacem groaned and threw his soda can at the wall, "*Antarctica* is where I cast the second worst monster ever! Why did it have to be there?"

Uncle Dux said, "The *Elder Fallen*?"

Fornacem shook his head, "No, the *first* elder beings. They were even *more* dangerous than the *Elder Fallen.*"

Uncle Dux said, "How's that possible? I thought that the Elder Fallen were the most dangerous Fallen."

Fornacem shook his head, "Oh no, they are only *one* of an even more dangerous race. I didn't just make an Elder Fallen. I made an *Elder Race.* A new brand of monsters that I kept hidden in case."

Fornacem pointed vaguely out the window, "You saw their fiery brothers earlier, I'm talking about the *Seniorem Nix Reptans*, the *Snow Crawling Elder.*"

Ignis gasped, Uncle Dux scoffed. In fact, even Arthur and Julia seemed doubtful.

Uncle Dux shook his head, "No way. Those things ice

Elementalists told their children as bedtime stories? Those are myths! Parents used them to keep the children from wandering around! A monster like that couldn't possibly exist!"

Fornacem looked grim. Uncle Dux's smile wavered, "Right?"

The look on Fornacem's face reminded Ignis that he was hundreds of years old. He said, "Oh, they're real all right. A crowd of these things could occupy Rex Cataclysmi himself, easily."

Uncle Dux glanced around, his smile faltered, "Wait, you're being *serious*?"

Fornacem nodded, "*They* are the worst monsters I have ever made. They have the capabilities of more advanced ice Elementalists. They know ice Cyromancy, on top of ice Elemental spells. I've seen more advanced ones open vortexes. Their skin is unbreakable. They are smarter, stronger, and angrier than other monsters. I've heard reports of them attacking my enemies, and even I felt bad. One second there's peace, the next... well... they leave no survivors."

Uncle Dux looked horrified. Amber sighed, "Lovely. Anything else we should know?"

Fornacem said, "*Seniorem Nix Reptans* are notorious for not following orders. It was one of the reasons why I lost the second war, they never listened to me. I made them after the Elder Fallen. They made me hesitate before making more of the elder race. They could smell ice Elementalists three hundred miles away."

Ignis said, "Ok, so, most likely, Gloria and Njord will be surrounded by one or two of these things, right?"

Fornacem said, "Actually, they don't get along with each other. They'll make some sort of den around large chunks of Golden Ice. They know that they have some connection with it. Others will try to invade dens for the ice. Once defeated, one will consume the other-" Amber made an audible gagging noise. Fornacem continued, "-and grow stronger. They will reach maximum size after eating five brothers."

Fornacem waved a hand, "One would have picked up Gloria's scent immediately. Knowing how resourceful they are, Gloria would have hunkered down. That is a mistake, the *Reptans* would make a den, and stay there for *years*. They feed the air coming off chunks of Golden Ice. One chunk would keep it there for years."

They all groaned. Uncle Dux stood, "The longer we stay here, the stronger that *Seniorem Nix Reptans* will be, right?"

Fornacem nodded, "Big time. We are mostly fighting fire monsters here. No offense, Ignis and Amber, but you aren't helping much. Sure, Amber can slice the monsters with her sword, but it would be best if you were to help the others get here."

Arthur, Julia, and Uncle Dux stood, arguing and yelling. Ignis gave a piercing whistle, no one stopped.

Amber said, "Let me try."

She opened her mouth, and much to Ignis's surprise, gave a roar so loud it shook the entire room. The others stumbled. Julia caught herself on the table. Arthur flared his aura, and Uncle Dux looked around frantically.

Amber said, "Listen! Gloria and Njord are my friends! I'm not going to sit here while there are monsters prowling around them! If Ignis and I can help, let us go! Gloria, Njord, Ignis and I are strong enough, no matter *what* comes at us!"

Uncle Dux said, "What if they attack with ice monsters after you leave? What if they send an *Elder Fallen*?"

Fornacem huffed, "Then *damn it*, *I'll* kill it! They are the *only* ones who can succeed with this mission! Give them a chance!"

Arthur said, "But-"

A red light gleamed in Fornacem's eyes, "We're *never*

going to get anything done without them! Our number one priority is getting them back here, right? This is the best and quickest option!"

Julia said, "But, even *you* have trouble against monsters like that!"

Fornacem grinned, "That was back in the old days, I'm much stronger now. Believe it or not, I kinda think the four of them might just *barely* match my strength. They don't have to fight it, just get around it."

Everyone but Fornacem, flinched as Umbra Mortis spoke. Ignis had forgotten he was there. "I for one think that Fornacem's right. Let them go, if they think that they can succeed. Any trouble and, well, worse comes to worse, *two* combinations could *destroy* one of them things."

Amber piped up, "Please! I want to save my friends!"

She bumped Ignis, he nodded. "We have to help! We're fighting a losing battle. Nothing will change until we act."

Everyone started at Dux, Julia and Arthur. Julia glanced at Arthur, and they both stared at Uncle Dux.

He glanced around and groaned, "Why is it *always* me that makes the hard decisions? *Fine*, but any trouble and you get back here as soon as possible."

Amber squealed, "Can do!" She and Ignis shared a high five.

Uncle Dux said, "Now, all we have to worry about is rebuilding the portal before the next wave arrives." Uncle Dux motioned around, "Arthur, hold the Tree until the enemy arrives, put the Second Sun on standby." Arthur nodded. Uncle Dux pointed to Julia, "Julia, go downstairs and try to wake Arbor, tell him to kill every monster in the valley if he can." Julia nodded and ran from the room. Uncle Dux pointed to Fornacem, "You, if Arbor doesn't wake, or even if he does, give the monsters *hell*."

Fornacem shrugged, "Eh, nothing better to do." He

grinned and disappeared in a bright silver light.

Uncle Dux pointed to Umbra Mortis, "Follow Fornacem, I'll need you in a second, stay ready." Umbra Mortis nodded grimly and disappeared in a flash of black light. Uncle Dux pointed to Ignis and Amber, "You two, follow me, we have a portal to open."

Ignis and Amber followed Uncle Dux out into the valley. Ignis glanced apprehensively at the mountain peaks. "They're watching us."

Uncle Dux said, "I know, as soon as they figure out what we're doing, they're going to attack. We've got to hurry!"

They snuck through a large trench and ran briskly towards the arch. The top had broken off. The main dais was cracked, black ice covered its surface.

Uncle Dux said, "Amber, if you would?" Uncle Dux turned to Ignis, "We don't want you to use your powers yet, Ignis, they'll sense it and come crashing in."

Amber took a deep breath. When she opened her mouth, Ignis saw a bright ball of fire hovering there. He looked away as it brightened like a welding machine. A roar of fire rolled over the ice, and it started to steam. Uncle Dux took his spell book from his coat pocket, just as Amber paused for another breath, blowing more fire at the ice.

Uncle Dux kneeled in front of Ignis, "Look, I don't like this *Seniorem Nix Reptans*, business. Worst comes to worse, use the Second Sun if you must, just try not to vaporize half the planet."

Uncle Dux grinned. Ignis nodded, feeling queasy, "Ok."

Amber huffed, taking a deep breath, "Done."

Uncle Dux pointed to the main dais, *"Reparare!"*

The stone dais was lost in a flash of white fire, but reappeared, solid. Ignis heard monsters roar and nervously tapped his foot, "Hurry."

Uncle Dux reached out to touch the stone, "Ah, actually,

that'd be a bad idea."

Uncle Dux looked through his spell book, "Um, *supernatet.*"

One of the arch chunks glowed with a faint white light and slowly drifted towards the arch, setting into place. Slowly but steadily, the stone chunks flew into place.

Uncle Dux said, "*Simul.*"

The arch glowed with a bright white light, but one of the chunks slipped.

Uncle Dux said, "Come on! *Simul!*"

Amber glanced apprehensively over her shoulder, making Ignis do the same. Ignis saw small figures huddling around the mountain summit.

Amber said, "Umm."

Ignis said, "Any time, Uncle Dux."

Uncle Dux wiped his forehead, "Little longer, *simul!*"

Ignis heard loud roaring from the mountain peaks.

Uncle Dux cursed and whispered into the communications, "Arthur, Fornacem, the enemy is about to attack. Umbra Mortis, can you come here?" The words barely left Uncle Dux's lips when Umbra Mortis appeared floating over the arch.

"You rang?" Umbra Mortis caught a section of the arch, "I'll speed things up." He set the stone in place, "*Coactus in unum!*" There was a loud click and Umbra Mortis muttered, "*Bitch.*" He said slightly louder, "*I said, coactus in unum!*" The arch shuddered and glowed with a dark green light.

Ignis heard a loud roar and saw the armies run down the mountain side. "Uncle Dux!" he said urgently.

Uncle Dux pointed to the arch, "*Accende et vivere!* Come on!"

Ignis heard Arthur's panicked voice, "Hey! The Seniorem Reptans is back! Get over here *now!*"

Ignis looked over his shoulder, sure enough, the Reptans was crawling over the mountain peak, like Godzilla over a building. It roared and thundered down the mountain side, leaving a poisonous swamp in its wake.

Ignis heard his father mutter, and a bright blue flash made Ignis look back. Arthur's arms resembled magma. Blue fire rolled off his burned sleeves. His eyes glowed with a fierce light. He yelled and leaped at the enemy. He spun, firing twin columns of light in both directions. He flew up, putting his hands together, raining fiery bullets. He ducked under a leaping monster and yelled another spell. A summoning circle blazed to life. A storm of flaming comets rained down on the enemy.

Ignis blinked, "That's… my dad!"

Umbra Mortis said, "Oh this is ridiculous!"

He shoved Uncle Dux aside and raised his arms, "*Expergiscimini!*" He roared, and the arch shuttered. A strange whistle filled the air. Ignis covered his eyes when he thought the arch would explode. There was a deafening crack and a dark surge. A dark green portal swirled into existence.

Uncle Dux yelled, "Go, go, go!"

Amber grabbed Ignis's hand, and they ran through the portal. The last thing Ignis saw was a wave of monsters surrounding them. Umbra Mortis yelled, sending out a dark pulse.

Ignis shook his head, recognizing the Sleeping Fallen. He almost had a heart attack when he saw they were awake. Then he realized they were completely ignoring them. A few pointed, then returned to whatever they were doing.

Amber gripped Ignis's arm a little too tightly, "W-Why are they awake? Why are they awake?"

Ignis shook his head, "Don't worry. They won't attack." Ignis sounded like he was trying to convince himself more than Amber.

Amber shook her head, her wings shuffled, "Never mind! Let's get the others!"

They started forward slowly. Amber whimpered at a loud hissing noise. That strange intoxicating lavender aroma burned Ignis's nose. At first, he thought it was a strange new perfume from Amber, then he remembered this place always smelled that way.

Amber flinched as a Sleeping Fallen snarled, but it didn't attack.

Ignis said, "You don't like these monsters, do you?"

Amber shook her head, "They look too much like people. My dad told me that there are trillions. He fought them off once. He almost died."

Ignis nodded, "Don't worry, they have no reason to attack. In a second, we'll feel the magic set in." After Ignis said it, he felt them slow down, and suddenly, they were standing in front of another arch.

Ignis glanced around for the torch, "Uncle Dux used a-" He gasped, a Sleeping Fallen held it out to him. Ignis took it hesitatingly, "Um, thanks." The Sleeping Fallen nodded and curled back in slumber.

Ignis dropped the torch into the brazier, and the portal swirled into existence. Amber leaped through just before Ignis. He absorbed the flames, and the portal closed

Ignis took one step forward and sunk five feet into the snow. He saw Amber shivering in front of him. She sneezed, nearly setting Ignis's pants on fire. "S-So cold!" She whispered.

Ignis said, "I think we're here."

Amber rolled her eyes. She flew Ignis out of the snow trench, and they landed in a snowy land mass. Ignis scanned their surroundings. The moon hung cold and dark in the sky above. Ignis couldn't see anyone, but immediately spotted a large trench. Ignis pointed to it and Amber nodded and flew them there. Ignis recognized it as the belly mark of a *Seniorem Nix Reptans.*

The ground bubbled from the acidic blood. Far to his right, something lurched. Ignis pointed, Amber nodded. They flew over, and Ignis saw a Seniorem Nix Reptans crawling towards the horizon. If it weren't for its exposed organs, Ignis wouldn't have seen it.

Amber said, "I bet it's heading towards the others, we should follow."

Ignis nodded, and they continued. Ignis noticed that Amber was shivering and started to wonder if Dragonborn were coldblooded. Ignis channeled a little warmth through Amber's hand.

She sighed, "Thanks."

Ignis nodded, "Course."

After what seemed like hours, Ignis spotted a large snow mass. They flew over and saw another monster crawling around a large ice dome.

Ignis pointed, "There's smoke coming from the top, I bet it's the others!"

The Seniorem Nix Reptans sitting in front of the ice dome had four eyes instead of two. One pair just above the first. Golden Ice formed sharp claws. It was sitting like a human and making things out of ice. Ignis saw it stacking large ice squares, shaking its head and knocking them down.

Ignis said, "It... It seems smarter."

Amber nodded, "Fornacem said they get smarter the more of its kind it ate. What's that say?"

Ignis looked where she was pointing. Carved on the inside of the snow wall was *provecta.* Amber said, "That's Latin, it says... *advanced?*"

Ignis said, "It knows that it's an advanced Seniorem Nix Reptans, wonderful."

The second Reptans reached the snow wall and huddled just behind, giving Ignis the impression it was hiding. It peeked over the snow wall, apparently waiting until the larger Reptans' back was turned. Ignis watched as the advanced Seniorem Nix Reptans held ice over the smoke, letting it melt, then eating it.

Ignis told Amber to set them down on top of a nearby snow pile. From the top, Ignis scanned the area.

Amber rubbed her arms with her hands, "Why couldn't they have traveled someplace warm? I really hope Earth isn't *all* like this."

Ignis assured her, "No, we're just in one of the coldest places."

Amber sneezed, "It's not affecting you."

Ignis said, "Must be because I'm a fire Elementalist. Now, what do we do about those monsters?"

Amber said, "I don't know. Eventually we're going to have to fight one if we're not careful."

Ignis shook his head, "I'd rather avoid that."

Amber nodded, "A-Agreed."

Ignis said, "I don't know if a distraction would work. They might see through it, Fornacem *did* say they were smart."

They watched as the first Reptans made furniture out of ice. It scooped snow into a large bowl, there was a flash of gold, and a spoon shaped ice crystal appeared. Ignis's jaw dropped as it took a bite of snow, using the spoon. It smiled, making a noise like an intrigued child. It glanced at a nearby ice tower and shoved it to the ground. Ignis flinched as the ground shook.

Amber said, "Isn't that a big deal for things on your planet? I mean, it's making *tools*."

Ignis waved a hand, "Yes, now what do we do as a diversion?"

Amber said, "We don't want to reveal the others are

literally right next to it."

Ignis shook his head, "No. We don't"

Amber said, "Oh! What if I fly over it and lead it off towards the horizon?"

Ignis shook his head, "Then the second one will take over the base. You'll tire out before that monster does. Also, it's too quick. If it loses interest in you, it'll come straight back here before I could get out with the others. And I might be alone fighting the second one."

Amber sighed. Ignis saw her tail droop, "Yeah, I guess." She shook her head, "What if we send a spell to distract it?"

Ignis shook his head, "No good, it'll discover where we are, and it'll be on guard. That'll be even *more* difficult getting to the others."

Amber nodded. She shivered, hugging her arms for warmth, "Well, whatever it is, let's hurry, I've never been in the cold this long. This weird stuff is soaking my clothes!" She sneezed, making a small flame that melted a patch of snow.

Ignis said, "We want to avoid combat, so a distraction is best. The only question is *what* the heck that'll be."

They both were lost in thought, but an answer appeared in the form of an Earth-shaking roar. They peered over the peak of the snow mound. The two Seniorem Nix Reptans were fighting.

The first roared at the intruder. Ignis saw snow melt as it contacted its organs. The second roared back, swiping the other. Ignis saw golden ice spikes lengthen over its body and its eyes glowed a fierce blue color. Ignis flinched as the first lunged and grabbed the second around the throat. The sound was unbelievable, Ignis thought he might go deaf from the roars.

Amber nudged Ignis, "Well, how's that for a distraction?"

Ignis nodded, "That'll be it. Hurry!"

Creeping down the snow drift was not an easy task, but

eventually Amber and Ignis entered the home of the Seniorem Nix Reptans. They were careful to avoid the pool sized trenches filled with poisonous blood. As they walked closer, Ignis saw a large opening in the front of the snow pile.

It must be the door, Ignis thought.

They crept closer, and closer, then froze as a large golden ice spike flew in front of them. Ignis gasped silently as the snow drift fell, revealing the fighting monsters.

The intruding Reptans sliced the first in the face using lengthened ice claws, but the first shoved it off and threw a comet of ice. The intruder fell to the ground and the defender picked it up by its spine, which was poking out the gaping hole in its backside. The intruding monster roared as it was lifted off the ground. They watched in frozen horror as the defender slammed the intruding monster to the ground. Ignis thought the monster's neck had broken.

They both realized they were running out of time and Ignis ushered Amber behind the cold ice structure. They glanced out and Ignis felt sick.

The triumphant Seniorem Nix Reptans grew an ice knife from its hand, larger than a school bus. Amber covered her mouth with her hands as it dove the knife into its back. Ignis felt sick as it removed the spinal cord with a gurgling noise.

Amber prodded Ignis in the back whispering urgently, "Let's get them and get out of here please!"

Ignis flinched, "Oh, yeah."

They snuck to the entrance of the igloo and knocked on what they thought was the front.

Ignis heard nothing but a loud rumble as the larger Reptans consumed the other. Suddenly, a hand drug Amber and Ignis into the dark. Ignis gasped at the shadow of a tall horned figure leering over them. A male voice growled, "Who are you?"

CHAPTER 14: GLORIA
A Combined Effort

Strong hands drug Ignis into the dark and hung him upside down. A female voice said, "Bovi, wait! It might be Gloria's friends! Ow!" Bovi said, "Are you alright, Bele?" Cybele responded, "Yeah, tripped over an ice block."

Ignis gasped, "You know Gloria?"

Gloria heard that voice, "Ignis?"

Gloria heard Amber whisper, "Gloria?"

Gloria said, "Bovi! You killed the fire when you opened the door!"

"Sorry! I was just being safe," Bovi replied.

Gloria heard Cybele's concerned voice say, "What now?" She heard a sigh, "Oh, this is ridiculous," and fire blazed to life.

Ignis saw Gloria and Njord seemingly sitting on the ceiling. A dead hearth was smoking in front of them. A large Bull Bestia held him and Amber upside down by their feet. Amber clutched her shirt, so it didn't go over her head.

Gloria gasped, "Amber! Ignis!"

Ignis heard the Bull Bestia gasp, "Lady Amber?"

Amber said, "The one and only. Now, unless you want your hides on fire, put me down!"

Ignis and Amber were lowered to the ground. Ignis saw a

female Bull Bestia scurry over, "Oh, Bovi! What did you do?"

Gloria said, "Yeah, that's Ignis, my brother, and Amber... the Behemoth princess."

The Bull Bestia fell to their knees and stammered, "Forgive us, lady Amber! Please accept our humblest apologies!"

Amber grinned and said in a lofty tone, "WHY I NEVER! *Never* have I sustained such disrespectful behavior!"

Gloria smiled, rolling her eyes. Cybele raised her head shakily, "F-Forgive him, my lady! He did not know!"

Amber pointed at Cybele, "*Did* I *say* that you could rise?"

Ignis snickered. Cybele paled and shot back to the ground, "Apologies, my lady!"

Amber huffed and covered her smile. Her voice shook with the effort to hide her laughter, "As-As princess of the Behemoth c-capital, and heir to the throne. I declare thee to be b-beheaded!"

Even Njord smirked as the Bull Bestia quaked. Cybele whimpered, "Please my lady! I-" She froze as everyone burst into laughter. The Bull Bestia rose in uncertainty, staring around in bewilderment.

Amber smiled, wiping a tear from her face, "Just messing with you." Amber dusted snow off her shirt, "You can stand, and you don't have to treat me like a *princess*. I just wanted to do that one more time."

The Bull Bestia slowly rose to their feet.

Gloria tackled Amber, "You guys made it! Thank the lords! We were trapped in here... and we didn't know *what* to do. We had to eat crabs! *Crabs*, Amber, *crabs*!"

Amber hugged Gloria back, "Oh you *poor thing*! You sat here eating luxurious *crab*, while Ignis and I were fighting a *monster war*?" They smiled at each other.

Ignis smiled at Njord, "Good to see you."

Njord smiled, accepting a high five, "Er, you as well."

Gloria gestured at the bull twins, "Anyway, this is Bovi and Cybele. They helped us escape the capital. They're our friends."

Ignis nodded. Cybele gave a small wave, and Bovi a curt nod. They were stealing glances at Amber, as though expecting her to behead them.

Amber pointed to Gloria, "Why the heck did you guys come *here*? To *this* frozen wasteland? We were all so scared when we heard you disappeared from the capital!"

Gloria shrugged, "Heck, I don't know! There was something with combination animarum. The next thing I knew, we were stranded here."

Amber shuddered, "With those horrible monsters outside too."

Gloria said, "Never mind that! How's everyone?"

Ignis made a grim face, "Not great, there are so many fire monsters. Amber and I could barely help at all. We've seen a Seniorem Reptans already. Amber and I barely made it here in time. There were *so* many monsters, Gloria."

Gloria gestured to the damp fire ashes, "Well, don't just stand there! Tell us about it!"

Ignis relit the fire, giving a soft blue light. Amber and Ignis sat on the other side of Gloria and Njord. They all sighed, enjoying the warmth. They sat and listened as Amber and Ignis told them of the fate of the valley.

It took a while, Ignis noticed that the sun never rose from the horizon. Gloria and Cybele gasped in the right places, saying things like, "Oh no!" or "I'll kill that Lapsus." Bovi listened with polite concern. Njord bit his lip, as though making mental notes in his head. As Ignis mentioned the Seniorem Reptans, Gloria's face fell.

Ignis nodded, "With you two, we could kill the monsters! Amber and I can't kill *any* of the fire monsters! We need you!"

Gloria nodded, and Amber said, "They've held off killing us for some reason, leaving just before they overwhelm us. After this wave, I don't know if we can hold them!"

Gloria gasped as Njord's eyes glowed green. He seemed to be deep in thought.

Njord whispered, "That is horrible! We need to depart immediately!"

Amber said, "Only one problem. That Seniorem Nix Reptans made a den around you. We don't know how to get past it. There's a portal about ten miles northwest of your door. We need to sneak there and get to the valley!"

Gloria sat down meekly, "There's no way that we're killing that thing. It's eaten four other Seniorem Nix Reptans already."

Ignis flinched, "*Four*? What do we do?"

Gloria gestured to Cybele and Bovi, "They want to help! They're super strong! They beat Njord and I easily!"

Cybele squirmed, "*After* we used combination animarum, and you didn't use any spells against us."

Amber and Ignis gasped. Ignis knew they were thinking the same thing. Ignis remembered Umbra Mortis words, *we're talking about a whole different being here. Their thoughts would have been combined, possibly even more complex than Njord's. They may not remember that we were in trouble. If it was their first-time achieving combination animarum, was it an equilibrium?*

Ignis recalled what Amber had said. *Not entirely. Combination animarum responds to compatibility. Good friends can combine easily, regardless of having no experience. Of course, they wouldn't have kept their forms, but... if it's an equilibrium... then their personality would be completely different. With Njord's brain, they could be even smarter.*

"What if we do a combination? Amber and I, from what I heard, gave Fornacem a pretty good fight." Ignis blurted.

Cybele gasped, "You fought Fornacem?" She spoke with awe.

Ignis shifted in his seat, "Well, yeah, I guess we did."

Cybele shook her head, "Lady Amber is great!"

Amber smiled, "Drop the Lady part, but compliments are fine."

Bovi said, "Wait a moment, combination animarum is not something to be taken lightly. One wrong step and it could devastate the grounds and kill the users. Best case scenario is nothing happens."

Gloria shook her head, "But, we did it fine the first time."

Bovi explained patently, "Combination automatically responds to compatibility. Compatibility is how well the forces of the users will mix. If there is a disagreement, like wants, opinions, that sort of thing, the combination becomes unstable. The higher your compatibility, the better chance you have of succeeding the first time around."

Cybele nodded, "I mean, it's not easy, but the best type of combination is equilibrium. There are four types of combination, equilibrium combination, one sided combination, unstable combination, and everything else in between, called scaled combination."

Bovi said, "Equilibrium is the strongest and the most stable. This is when the two users are perfectly balanced. They both equally handle everything about the form, giving it max input in everything they do. Perfect combinations like these last as long as the users wish."

Cybele sighed, "It's beautiful to see it mastered in person."

Bovi said absently, "It's what Cybele and I do."

Cybele bit her lip and continued, "Now, one sided combination. This happens when one person takes ninety percent or more of the responsibilities of the combination. Essentially this happens when one person uses another for their own benefit. Or when one user controls one thing and nothing else. These last as long as the main user, the one with more responsibilities, wishes. Essentially imprisoning the second user."

Bovi said, "Then there's unstable combinations where the combination is simply unstable. Either one combiner doesn't wish to combine, or they argue before and during the process. Colliding with functions for the combination. Disrupting the flow of combination. These usually don't last long.

And then there is a scaled combination. This labels all other combinations. Where one person takes slightly more than the other. These are stable enough to work, but the responsibilities are not split equally, causing the combination to perform below full potential. These last as long as both users can manage. It takes a lot of energy to achieve. Equilibrium combinations don't use any energy when done correctly."

Gloria gapped at them, "You guys have *got* to train us. If we can master combination, we could be *so* much more help."

Ignis nodded. Amber said, "After the monsters are dead, you guys have got to teach at the academy. You know about guard training, weaponry, and combination animarum for older classes!"

Cybele and Bovi hesitated. Gloria whispered to Cybele, "I'd be just you and Bovi in a single class if you'd like."

Cybele blushed and spoke to Bovi, "B-Bovi, maybe... maybe it wouldn't be such a bad idea."

Bovi thought for a moment, "Teach *human* children, go *against* the training, teachings, *and* beliefs from the past *seven* years?"

Cybele sighed, "Oh, well-"

Bovi smiled, "As long as you're there, I'd be happy."

Cybele's face glowed like a setting sun. Bovi flinched, "I-

I mean! I w-would be fine with it a-as long as you were t-there!"

Gloria and Amber shared a wide smile. Amber nodded frantically. She mouthed, *they're so cute!*

Amber cleared her throat, "Right, so Ignis and I got the keys."

Amber pulled a small green orb from her pocket, "Going back to the problem at hand, combination? Anyone?"

Ignis saw Cybele's eyes widen, "Lady Amber, I didn't know you could do combination! Forgive my idiocy!"

Amber sighed, "Drop the *lady*, please talk to me normally, I left the capital to *escape* all the royalty. Call me Amber."

Cybele and Bovi nodded, "Yes, Lady Amber!"

Amber sighed. Gloria shook her head, "I don't know if Njord and I could pull it off. I don't know if you guys could either. We know basically *nothing* about it." Gloria looked as though she suddenly had an idea, "Oh! But they do!"

Cybele and Bovi flinched. Gloria said, "You guys could teach us how to do it!"

She pointed to Ignis and Amber, "Ignis is a fire user, their combination is *super* powerful!"

Cybele and Bovi stared at Amber and Ignis in awe. Cybele said "Lady- I mean, Amber willingly combined with a human? That... that is unheard of."

Ignis shook his head, "No way. We almost destroyed the entire valley last time. There's no way we could direct Spiritus in one direction. Not without lots of practice, sorry, but we can't do it."

Gloria saw Njord speak, "I would have to agree with Ignis, it is ill advised to attend battle with little experience."

Bovi leaned towards Ignis, "Do you have *any* idea what he's saying?"

Ignis shook his head, "Most of the time, not really."

Bovi sighed, "Glad I'm not the only one."

Cybele said, "Wait a second." She looked at Ignis and Amber, "You two have succeeded in combination?"

Ignis nodded. Amber said, "Yeah?"

Cybele said, "What type of combination was it?"

Everyone else was stumped, Amber said, "I think Dux said...one sided combination?"

Cybele nodded, "Ok, who was in control of what?"

Ignis cocked his head, "Huh?"

Amber said, "I handled everything but the body."

Cybele sighed, "I'm sorry to say, but without more practice, you two won't be able to succeed in combination animarum."

Gloria gasped, "Why not?"

Cybele said, "Combination animarum is an extremely complicated method. They don't have enough experience. It would seem that, as with you, Gloria, their compatibility was the only thing that made them able to use it. The second time around, compatibility alone won't cut it." Cybele glanced at Gloria, "Equilibrium combination however, might."

Gloria said, "Huh?"

Cybele set her hands on Gloria's shoulder, "You and Njord are the only ones strong enough to be able to achieve combination right now! I've never seen a more compatible fusion!" Bovi cleared his throat, Cybele blushed, "Besides me and Bovi, I mean." Bovi smiled. Cybele shook her head, "B-Beside the point! I think that you and Njord, with a quick refresher, can hold off that Seniorem Nix Reptans long enough for us to escape!"

Njord stood suddenly and opened his mouth as though to speak, but thought better of it, and started to pace.

Gloria said, "But, what if we fail?"

Bovi said, "You and Njord successfully managed equilibrium on the first try, which is unheard of. You are able to fuse whenever you choose, allowing Rem to take over. In the future, it'll take more effort."

Ignis saw Cybele glance away.

Amber frowned, "Um, who's Rem?"

Gloria shook her head. Cybele said, "It's what the combination of Njord and Gloria told us to call her. Rem could distract the Seniorem Nix Reptans out there. Equilibrium matters a lot in combination, please Gloria."

Gloria hesitated, but nodded, "I'll do it!"

Ignis saw Njord freeze next to the wall. "I fabricated a plan in case a combination was going to be used. It did not factor Gloria and I utilizing it."

Gloria extended the space, each holding their breath in case the monster noticed. Cybele stood with Bovi next to the wall. She cleared her throat, "R-Right. Combination animarum, a technique discovered thousands of years ago, passed from one generation to the next."

Bovi said, "It's not an easy thing to do. You need to be in the proper mindset. Let's try something."

Bovi ordered Njord and Gloria to stand next to each other, Bovi said, "Now, Gloria, off the top of your head, what is Njord thinking *right* now?"

Gloria shook her head, "No idea."

Bovi said, "Now, hold your keys up."

Gloria did so. Njord reluctantly following suit.

Bovi said, "Njord, what is Gloria's favorite color?"

Njord flinched, "Er... green?"

Gloria gasped, "How did you know?"

Bovi said, "Now, Gloria, set your free hand on Njord's shoulder."

Gloria did. Bovi said, "Now, what is Njord thinking of?"

Gloria blurted, "How warm my hand is."

Njord jumped. He shrank away from Gloria's hand.

Bovi's eyes widened. "Wow, you two *really* are

compatible."

Njord said, "Wait a moment! What is this concluding? We require traveling to the portal immediately!"

Cybele said, "That was a compatibility test. Bovi and I used to do them all the time for the moderator."

Amber said, "But he's right, we should hurry!"

Cybele thought for a moment, "Ok. When you combine, think of equilibrium and nothing else. Negative emotions, personal thoughts, words like *we*, usually break the connection, don't do that."

Njord nodded. Gloria held out her combination key, "Njord?"

Njord sighed, "Very well. We require haste. There was a sixty seven percent chance of-"

Gloria flicked his ear, "Yeah, we're not diving into *that* rabbit hole. She laughed, Ignis gasped.

A large green ring started to glow around Njord and Gloria even before they did anything.

Gloria said, "On three?" Njord nodded, bringing out a now glowing combination key.

They simultaneously said, "Three, *simul!*"

Ignis felt his hair fly in the wind as a bright green light surged. Comets of green light swirled around the circle. Suddenly he was staring at a new figure.

The figure took a deep breath and flipped their golden-black hair. "Hey, hey!" The figure stretched and smiled, looking around. "Yo, where am I and where's Spiritus Tauri?" The figure saw Cybele and Bovi, "Oh, *hey* you two." She grinned at Ignis, "Hey! What up, man?"

Ignis was baffled as the figure shook his hand vigorously. She readjusted what Ignis realized were Njord's reading glasses. The figure smiled. "Name's Rem. I know you! You're Gloria's brother! I remember reading some of her memory fragments!"

She spotted Amber and darted over. Ignis realized eight golden tentacles were sliding against the ground. As though reading his mind, Rem looked down. "No time for that!"

There was a golden flash, and the tentacles were replaced with human legs in ripped jeans. Rem hugged Amber, "What's up girl? By the way." She pulled Amber close and whispered in her ear, "Gloria wants your help in *that* category over there." She pointed to Cybele and Bovi.

Amber grinned from ear to ear, "Oh my *lord*! *Who are you*? You're not what I thought a combination between Gloria and Njord would be *at all*!"

Rem smiled, "*Equilibrium* on the first go! Can you *imagine*? What did you expect, factoring age, experience, and of course *logic*! There's always that small percentage of failure! But we did it!" Rem smiled, speaking very fast.

Ignis nodded, "Yeah, *now* I see it."

Amber said, "How are you talking about Gloria and Njord without separating?"

Rem nodded, "Well, you know how combination responds to compatibility! That's how they-" She pointed to Bovi and Cybele. "-could stay combined for so long! And that's how Njord and Gloria became *this*. I mean, factoring in no experience or fear of death, but having the keys!"

Rem shook her head, "I'm sounding like Njord again. Let's get to business, now-"

Ignis's jaw dropped as a map appeared in a golden light. Ignis pointed, "How- how did you do that?"

Rem winked, "Well, let's just say that equilibrium is *pretty* cool. *Multiplies* power instead of adding, of course, it's different for everyone." Rem glanced at Cybele and Bovi, "Right, you guys?"

Cybele nodded silently, staring in awe at Rem.

Amber gasped suddenly, "*That's* how you all got here! You and Njord had such good compatibility, that you got equilibrium right off the bat!"

Rem nodded, "By the way, I am *so* glad you paused to think! Everyone else was *clueless*! Sometimes I'm surprised by my own genius." She frowned, "But all we did was guess that they would come here... I *know* that." She must have realized that she was speaking to herself and grinned, "Oops."

Cybele said, "Well, you decided on a whim, risking the chance of them not thinking like you."

Rem said, "Oh *come on*, I wouldn't want to be saved without my helper thinking! What fun would that be? Coincidence? Chance? Luck? Ha! Who invented these things, eh?" Rem snickered, returning to the board, "Now, it is precisely fifty-four thousand, sixty-three feet to the portal. Just over ten miles, we require- um, need, to run there. *I* will distract Ullr." Rem shook her head, "*Require*, now I'm *really* starting to sound like Njord..."

Ignis frowned, "Who the heck is *Ullr*?"

Rem smiled, "The advanced Seniorem Nix Reptans outside, *duh*." She rolled her eyes, as though that was an obvious answer.

"Aaannyhoo, Cybele and Bovi will run with Amber and Ignis. To make things quicker, Amber will fly Ignis, and Bovi will carry Cybele." Ignis thought he saw Rem's eyes flicker in their direction. Cybele opened her mouth to speak, but Rem said, "Now! You all should know to avoid the poison pools, watch out for snow patches, *and*, oh! I got an Ullr to befriend!"

Rem ran to the door, "Funny how those things work... Right! We got a portal to catch! And a valley to save, people!" She disappeared from sight, humming to herself.

Ignis said, "She's a bit... much isn't she?"

Cybele nodded, "A powerful combination indeed. With proper training, they would be an unstoppable force. Come on, we need to hurry."

They followed Rem to the entrance. Ignis saw her tie her

hair into a ponytail.

Rem said, "Now, wait for the signal. Off we go!"

Before they could ask what, the signal was or for a reminder of what they were doing, Rem opened the entrance and flew out the door.

Bovi said, "Anyone else feel like she's a few steps ahead of us?"

Amber said, "I'm sure it'll be fine. Rem must think that we're not as fast as she is." Ignis didn't think she sounded sure.

Rem hovered over the Seniorem Nix Reptans. She called down, "Yoo, hoo! Ullr!"

The Seniorem Nix Reptans flinched, looked at Rem, then hissed. Ignis flinched as the Golden Ice spikes extended, and its eyes blazed. It swiped at Rem. Ignis gasped, she wasn't there.

Amber pointed, "There!"

Ignis saw Rem standing on Ullr's shoulder, gazing into the sky with a hand over her eyes, as though shielding them from the moon. The Seniorem Nix Reptans looked around.

Rem said, "See them?"

It looked at Rem, stared at her for a moment, then roared, swiping at her.

Ignis heard her sing, "*Missed me!*"

Bovi shook his head, "Fighting Rem is like fighting a thousand bees."

Cybele said, "Really annoying, really smart bees."

Rem disappeared again, appearing directly on the Seniorem Nix Reptans nose. She poked it, "Boop!" It swiped at her, "Yo, Ullr! Got your nose!"

Ullr roared again, swiping at her. Cybele, Bovi, Amber, Ignis, and Rem peered from behind the wall.

Ignis said, "Did she just… *bop* his nose?"

Amber said, "*And* take his nose?"

They flinched as Rem yelled, "Signal!" They whirled back

as she disappeared in a golden light.

Ignis said, "Uh, go!"

Bovi nodded. Cybele yelped as he scooped her up and jumped away. Amber grabbed Ignis's hands, and they flew upwards.

Ullr glanced at the others, making a squealing noise. Rem threw a snowball at it. "Ullr! Look here please!" Rem flicked his head, sending him into the opposite snow pile.

Ignis's eyes widened, "They're so strong!"

Amber nodded, "Just imagine their elemental and magic power!"

Ullr rose from the snow and roared, sending a comet at Rem. She didn't move, the comet phased right through her. It stopped in midair behind her, then absorbed into her. Rem dodged as Ullr lunged at her.

Rem snickered as Ullr huffed, "Aww, you seem young! I think I might keep you! You like the name Ullr, right?"

Rem dodged Ullr's hand. Ullr shook his head as Rem appeared lounging in his palm. "I mean, I personally like the name. Ullr is the Norse god of winter, you know? I thought it was fitting." Rem gasped, "You're not a *girl,* are you?"

Ullr roared, smashing its hand into the ground. Rem hung upside down in front of Ullr's face. "Nah, you're too violent for a girl." Ullr opened his mouth and breathed a swath of frozen mist at Rem.

Ignis shook his head in wonder. "I wish our combination could be like that, Amber."

Amber nodded, "Me too, imagine how much power it would have!" Amber swooped low, meeting Bovi near the ground, "Portal's not too far!"

Bovi nodded. Cybele had her hands around his neck, "Careful Bovi! This ground's so unstable!" She yelped as a smiling Bovi cracked the ground under them, leaping forward.

Ignis gasped as Ullr charged for Bovi and Cybele. Bovi

yelped, bounding a hundred feet away, but Ullr was catching up.

Rem suddenly appeared in front of Ullr, "I said-"

Ullr swatted her away. Ignis gasped as she slammed into the Earth a mile away. Ullr brought a fist over his head.

Rem appeared on the ground in front of him, "*I said, STOP!*"

A golden-black shockwave blasted from Rem. To Ignis's surprise, the Seniorem Nix Reptans scuttled to a stop.

Rem pointed a finger at Ullr. "Now *you* listen here, *young man!*" She marched forward, Ullr taking steps back. Ignis watched in awe. "I do *not* appreciate being ignored! *Or* interrupted! If I have to tell you off again, I will *personally* kick whatever remains of your smart little *ass*, all the way to the North Pole! Got it?" Ignis's jaw dropped as Ullr nodded vigorously. Rem pointed towards the portal, "Now you are going to *go* to my friends, and you are *going* to *apologize* to them! *Do* you *hear me*?" Ullr nodded again. He slowly stepped in front of Cybele and Bovi.

Rem appeared next to them, huffing. Bovi said, "Umm."

Ullr stooped lower and opened its mouth. Ignis heard a sound like a toddler trying to speak. Rem said, "Latin will do."

Ullr scowled. Rem pointed a finger, "*Mister.*"

Ullr unmistakably, sighed. "*P-Paenitet.*"

Ignis saw a spear clatter from Cybele's hands. Bovi quickly picked it up.

Rem nodded, "Good. Now-"

They jumped as a roar filled the air. Rem said, "Oooh, it's *Aurgelmir.*" Ullr looked frightened and shuffled in place. Rem appeared on his shoulder, "Steady buddy." Rem glanced at the others, "Yo! You guys take Ullr and get out of here! Aurgelmir is coming!"

Amber dropped Ignis next to Cybele and Bovi.

Amber said, "I thought Ullr- the Seniorem Nix Reptans-wanted to kill us! And who the heck is *Aurgelmir*?"

Rem shook her head, "No, he's good, but *Aurgelmir* isn't! Get this baby boy outta here!"

Amber blinked, *"Baby... boy?"*

Rem smiled, "Yeah! Turns out he's lonely, and he likes us! Now go! Ullr, protect them!"

Ullr nodded and Rem disappeared from his shoulder. Ignis, Amber, Bovi, and Cybele ran after him as he crawled towards the portal.

Amber yelled, "Since *when* did Rem become a Fallen tamer?"

Ignis shrugged, "Gloria tamed the fire snake in October!"

Amber's eyes widened, "I thought she was joking! I wondered if she used him to steal my desserts! Oh, I am *so* grilling her after this!"

Ignis shook his head, this was totally *not* going to plan.

Ignis heard Bovi say, "Rem is a strange individual. She seems to know what's happening before it happens."

Ignis looked behind him, his legs almost gave out.

On the horizon, Ignis saw a Seniorem Nix Reptans charge Rem. It definitely didn't seem friendly. It was twice the size of Ullr and had six eyes on its head. Its arms were covered in large spikes of ice, and the claws on its hand could have supported a blimp. Its maw was hundreds of sharp ice teeth. Large stalactites hung from its jaw, while golden ice made large tusk-like teeth. One of Aurgelmir's eyes was scratched out. It was covered with scars and gaping wounds.

Amber gasped, "Aurgelmir doesn't look nice."

She jumped as Rem appeared next to her. "Yeah. Turns out Aurgelmir bullied little Ullr. Aurgelmir's an adult, so he defeated Ullr. The poor little guy ventured out to try to become stronger to get revenge." Rem patted Ullr on his head, "You don't need to Ullr, mama will protect you."

Rem disappeared, appearing half a mile in front of

Aurgelmir. She muttered, "I won't go easy on you, big boy." Rem took off her glasses and set them in her pocket.

Aurgelmir roared, crawling closer, shredding the ground in front of him and leaving the land behind him in ruins. Rem waited with her arms crossed. Aurgelmir stopped one hundred feet from Rem. He roared, the ice spikes lengthening, his eyes blazing a dark blue.

Rem scowled, "Step any closer and I'll annihilate you."

Ignis saw the portal in front of them, "There! Come on guys!"

Cybele yelped as Bovi jumped upwards, "I thought portals had to reset!"

Ignis shrugged, "So did I, but Rem said it was safe."

They reached the stone dais. Ignis looked behind him and his heart sank, "Wait... How the heck did she think Ullr was going to get through?"

Ullr absently scratched his head, and his eyes followed a bird in the sky.

Amber said, "Wait! Can't they do vortexes too?" Ullr tried to reach for the bird. Amber shouted, "Ullr!" Ullr flinched and set his hands on the ground. Amber said, "I need you to make a vortex!"

Ignis said, "Are you sure he'll understand?"

Amber ignored him, "Um, open a vortex wide enough for all of us. Connect it to the Fall Tree Valley! Do you know where that is?"

Ullr blinked and propped himself into a sitting position. He thought for a moment, then nodded. Amber said, "Then, take it away!"

Ullr nodded. He set his hand over the arch and covered it completely. Ignis gasped as a bright golden light blazed from Ullr's hand.

Amber groaned, "Oh, I forgot! An anchor is going to take a second!"

Ignis gasped, "Then we need to hold it for Glo- I mean Rem!"

Aurgelmir roared, slamming his fists against the ground, flinging the land in every direction. Rem landed on the ground, glowing with a faint gold light.

She said, "On second thought, if you turn away now, I won't destroy you."

Rem figured Aurgelmir found that funny. He smiled, coating his hands in ice. Rem flared her aura, and Aurgelmir hesitated. "Last warning. Turn back or die." Aurgelmir sneered, roared again, and charged Rem. Rem sighed, "Well, I tried to warn him."

She yelled, flew into the air, and rushed at Aurgelmir.

CHAPTER 15: GLORIA
Equilibrium Combination

Rem flared her aura. In a flash of green, her halo appeared over her head. A gentle chiming sound filled the air as golden wings formed behind her.

She caught Aurgelmir's hand in midair and a black shockwave blew the snow, and the surface of the ground, flattening every snow mound in the area. Rem disappeared in a golden flash and punched Aurgelmir in the jaw. Aurgelmir roared.

Rem shook her head, "Wow, strong jaw, big guy?" Her fist was covered in a golden-black light. She punched Aurgelmir in the face.

Rem smiled as he lurched back. He glowered at Rem with hate as he spat a bloody tooth from his mouth.

Rem smiled sheepishly, "Uhm."

Aurgelmir batted Rem aside and she crashed into a mountain a mile away. She groaned, dislodging herself from the mountain.

She smiled, "Ooh, idea!"

A dark shadow fell over Aurgelmir, he looked up as a mountain crumbled over him. Rem struck him across the face and smirked, dodging his swing. "Sorry to say dude, I won't let you hit me a-" Rem's face fell as Aurgelmir breathed frozen mist at her. She looked up in time to see Aurgelmir's hand appear, slamming her to the ground.

Rem grumbled, "Ok, now I'm mad." A strange chiming noise filled the air. Aurgelmir frowned, and an enormous black explosion threw him backwards.

Rem hovered over the crater, golden-black light formed intricate symbols on her arms. The green halo burned with a dark green light. Her shimmering wings released golden clouds of mist. Rem wiped blood from her lips. "Do your worst."

Aurgelmir broke through the snow and sat upward, a large bronze colored comet crackled in his hands. He roared and launched it at Rem. She yelled, charging, spun, gliding over top of the comet, then kicked Aurgelmir in the gut.

Aurgelmir collapsed to the ground sideways. Rem dodged an ice spear and punched one of Aurgelmir's eyes. Aurgelmir roared in pain, swinging at Rem. She dodged the strike, yelping as he lunged with the other hand. Rem smashed through the Antarctic floor, surged into the freezing ocean, and struck the bottom of the ocean floor.

Rem yelled and shot from the ocean floor, bursting through the ice. The water around her formed a delicate ice structure as she spun in midair. She yelled and kicked Aurgelmir in the face. The ice shattered, shards the size of buildings sliced Aurgelmir's skin.

Rem put her hands together, "*Sanctus tempestas!*" There was a bright flash of gold, and a black surge of light slammed into Aurgelmir.

Amber's jaw dropped, "Good lords above."

Ignis said, "How's... how's the portal going?" Ullr glanced at Ignis and made a strange, high-pitched noise.

Amber said, "Let's hope that means not too much longer!"

Rem panted and shook her head, groaning as Aurgelmir

rose from the trench.

Rem slapped a hand to her head. "Of course! I need more of Njord's magic." She raised her hands up, *"Fulmen aureum!"*

A gold flash of lightning struck Aurgelmir in the chest. He roared, throwing another ice comet at Rem. She yelped as Golden Ice skimmed her.

She yelled, *"Descendi!"* Hundreds of golden lightning strikes rained down. He roared, shielding his face with his hands. Rem yelled, the light intensified, and a large black explosion ripped from Aurgelmir.

Rem wiped sweat from her forehead, "Good. Now then-"

Aurgelmir lunged up, grabbed Rem out of the air, and threw her to the Earth below. Rem gasped for air, just as Aurgelmir formed ice spears, which he launched into the ground, crashing over top of her.

Amber gasped and covered her mouth with her hands.

Ignis yelled, "Come on, Rem!"

Amber said in a shaky voice, "Ignis, we-we need to go! We-" She gasped as Ignis rose from the ground. *"Forma eclipsis solis, the Second Sun."*

Amber looked away as a bright surge of fire exploded. She looked up at a blue streak shooting towards Aurgelmir. He hurtled sideways with a tremendous explosion.

Rem stared at a strange figure. Blue flames rolled off its shoulders. Its skin was blue lava and its eyes glared bright white. Rem smiled, "Are you the calvary? Sounds great! I'll help if you need me."

The figure smiled and shook its head.

Rem raised an eyebrow. "I'll standby." Rem saw the beast crawl over a nearby mountain.

Aurgelmir roared. Rem pointed. "He's a big bully. Light 'em up, please."

As the figure disappeared, she snapped her fingers, "Oh! It's the Second Sun! Ignis!"

Ignis was fuming as he appeared in front of Aurgelmir, "*Salve!*" Ignis roared, "*Vinci igni!*" A large wave of fire exploded.

Rem appeared over him, "*Sanctus coegi!*" A large spear of light struck Aurgelmir.

Ignis yelled, "*Maledictionem exorcismi!*" A bright white spear of fire pierced Aurgelmir's chest.

Aurgelmir roared, blasting a comet of ice. Ignis gasped, sounding like water touching a hot pan, and disappeared.

Reappearing, he pointed directly at Aurgelmir, "*Igneus iudicium!*" The entire mountain collapsed over them, as an explosion ripped into the sky.

Amber stood from the ground and frantically looked towards the horizon. She gasped as the mountain collapsed and the explosion tore into the sky. Two shockwaves slammed into her, throwing her hair straight back. She cried into the air, "Ignis! Gloria! Njord!" Cybele gripped her spear. Bovi stood on Ullr's hand, as he raised him over their heads.

Amber slumped to the ground, tears streamed down her face as she screamed, "No!" Amber set her face in her hands. Cybele and Bovi bowed their heads. Amber sobbed, not bothering to wipe the tears from her face. She took a rattling breath, screaming into the cold, quiet air. Amber gasped as a warm hand touched on her shoulder.

Amber looked up. Ignis stood over her. His skin was covered with burns and scrapes. His shirt was charred. One of his eyes was shut by a cut running through it. Amber couldn't hold back a final sob.

Ignis grinned, "Miss me?" Ignis winced as Amber threw herself into his arms, breaking into fresh tears.

Rem appeared next to Cybele. "The idiot used the last of his energy to destroy Aurgelmir. I was just able to save him." Rem stared at Amber as she hugged Ignis, who winced. "Ouch, careful."

Rem's eyes gleamed, "I wonder."

Amber let go of Ignis and sniffed. Her voice shook, "I-I thought you died! You *idiot!*" She broke into fresh tears. Ignis patted her hair awkwardly.

Rem took a breath and set a hand on Cybele's shoulder. "Right, I trust that you and Bovi will work hard to bring me back? It'll be a while, I don't want to be stuck in the void forever."

Cybele nodded, "Don't worry, we'll teach them everything we know."

Rem gestured to Ignis and Amber, "Them too, I hope?"

Cybele smiled, "Of course."

Rem added in a whisper, "Also, can one of you make a move before I return?"

Rem winked and disappeared in a green flash as Cybele spluttered. She glanced at Bovi, "Wha- You cannot be serious!"

Gloria and Njord appeared as a green ring faded around them. Gloria's hair was in a ponytail, with a green hair band holding it in place.

Gloria saw Amber, "Woah, what happened?"

Cybele, "Um, Rem and... I think Ignis killed Aurgelmir."

Gloria said, "Who?"

Cybele said, "A bigger and eviler version of him."

She gestured to Ullr with her head. Gloria and Njord yelped, "Woah!" Ullr smiled and waved at Gloria.

Amber saw Gloria and tackled her, still sobbing. Gloria said, "Hey there! I'm ok, watch the ribs, the ribs!"

Amber withdrew, sniffling, "N-Never do that again! Oh, I hated being here! I couldn't see you guys!"

Bovi dropped from Ullr's hand, "You made quite the fireworks."

Gloria said, "Did we?"

Amber wiped her face on her sleeve. Njord said, "We must depart. We are still participating in a war."

Gloria groaned. She preferred Amber crying all over them, rather than fighting an army.

She sighed, "Well, let's go kill monsters."

She turned to Cybele and Bovi, "Will you help us?"

Cybele nodded, "After busting us out of the capital, introducing us to your family, *and* saving my life? Oh yeah, we'll help."

Ullr smiled as a gigantic vortex opened in front of them.

Gloria said, "And...... what about him?"

Cybele said, "Ullr? He'll behave." Before Gloria could question, she shook her head. "Right. Come on people! Monsters to kill, families to help, and Lapsus to hurt!"

Amber collected herself and nodded. Together, they jumped through the swirling vortex.

Off in the frozen mountain, something writhed. A wound appeared in Aurgelmir's side, and a small Seniorem Nix Reptans, roughly the size of a human, scuttled from the hole.

Dux yelled, "*Scintilla creaturae!*" A blue ball of fire shot from his book, putting a hole in a Reptans. Dux squinted as Umbra Mortis killed another Furnace Fallen and ducked as an explosion rippled over his head. He yelled into the comms link, "Hey! Try not to kill me!"

Fornacem trilled in his ear, "Then dodge!"

Dux sighed, "Where the hell are you guys?" He flinched as a Reptans ran right past him. He laughed as he saw the monster army retreating, "Alright guys! We've got a few minutes! Let's have a- what the-?"

An enormous vortex swirled into existence in front of the Tree. Uncle Dux yelled in fright as he saw a Seniorem Nix Reptans surge forward. "HOLY- WHAT?" he stared as Gloria, Njord, Ignis, Amber, and two strangers appeared riding on the monster's head.

Dux heard Fornacem say, "Blow that to hell?"

Dux shouted, "No! It's the others! They're back!"

Uncle Dux ignored the confused voices from the communications and ran to the others. Gloria jumped down first and ran to hug Uncle Dux, quickly followed by Ignis.

Uncle Dux laughed, "You guys are ok! And-" He glanced at the Seniorem nix reptans, as well as the two Bestia waving at him. "And... you've got quite the story to tell.

It took an hour to tell the story. They sat around the dining table as Gloria and Njord told what happened, from the moment they left, to now. Ignis and Amber filled in their point of view. Gloria introduced Cybele and Bovi, who were surprised to receive very warm welcomes.

Uncle Dux shook Bovi's hand, "Man! This is great!"

Gloria said, "They want to help and said they'd even stay and help after the war!"

Bovi shook Dux's hand, "Bovi Bodacious, and this is Cybele Gratia."

Fornacem snorted, "Bodacious? Like Earth's most dangerous bull?"

Julia said, "Combination animarum, weaponry, guard skills, and personal protection, those will be excellent classes!"

Uncle Dux said, "Now! The moment I've been waiting for! A battle conference! With new members!" He gestured to Cybele and Bovi, who took empty chairs next to Ignis and Amber. Uncle Dux pointed to Njord, "We're surrounded by an anti-magic barrier! So far, we've discovered that we can do magic and elements as long as we use our auras. However, magic and elements are weakened by the barrier. There are fire monsters and ice monsters, all of them are magically enhanced, go."

Gloria smirked as Njord thought, "Well, processing your

information, I suggest we divide into teams. We should divide as equally as possible to maximize monster execution. If there are ten of us able to combat, then I-"

Another voice called from down the hall, "Eleven, actually." Arbor smiled as he entered the room, "I've got a serious bone to pick with a Seniorem Reptans." Arbor grinned at them, "Hello to new friends, and hello to my family."

Njord said, "Fornacem and Umbra Mortis will stay in their current positions. Fornacem will wreak havoc on the enemy from above. Umbra Mortis will orbit the valley, utilizing dark spells to keep the Fallen magicians distracted. They seem to be rather effective."

Fornacem and Umbra Mortis grinned.

Njord continued, "Gloria and I will focus upon fire monsters, as well as any Fallen magicians we may find. Ignis and Amber will focus upon the ice monsters, and any other Fallen magicians." They all seemed happy with this.

Njord then said, "Dux and Arthur? I suggest you both help where you feel it is needed. If a substantial threat occurs, focus your power there." Arthur rolled his eyes, Uncle Dux nodded. Njord said, "Julia, please continue to protect the students below." Julia nodded.

Njord finally turned to Bovi and Cybele. "You two should work together and execute every enemy. Do not hesitate to kill, they will not hesitate. If needed, use combination animarum." They nodded.

Uncle Dux said, "Oh I missed him."

Njord smiled, "There is an eighty seven percent chance that they are aware of our presence, therefore, they may send their entire army. Do not allow our teams to be overly separated. Are there any questions?"

Fornacem grinned, "How do you carry that brain around?"

Njord shook his head, and Gloria said, "What about

Ullr?"

Njord hesitated, "I suggest he causes as much destruction as possible. Uncle Dux will connect us with communication magic."

They got ready and paired up. Gloria patched the hole on the bottom of Ullr, so they wouldn't step in his poison. He seemed happy.

Amber forced Ignis to eat, provided happily by Arbor, and drink two bottles of water.

When Gloria asked why, she simply said, "Because he almost died."

"So did I."

"You were a combination. Ignis went in to *save* you two."

"Good excuse."

"*Right.*"

Gloria found Bovi talking to Cybele, "Listen Bele, I think we should save combination animarum. You can use your self-enhancing magic, and I can use mine."

Cybele was sharpening her spear. She nodded, "Sounds good."

Gloria nodded towards Bovi. Cybele said, "Um!"

Bovi suddenly halted, "Yes?"

Cybele blushed and looked at the ground, "Don't... Don't get killed."

Gloria smiled and nodded. Bovi blushed, "U-Um, yeah... you-you too."

At last, they stood in the valley. Gloria stared nervously at the moon which was partially an ugly red color. Black stars winked at Gloria from the sky.

After teaching Arbor the aura trick, he was able to reestablish the maze. Fornacem, Umbra Mortis, and Uncle Dux remade the traps, even in Arbor's maze. Gloria stood next to a nervous Njord, whose eyes were glowing. He remained silent when she asked if he was ok. Gloria looked past Njord, fifty feet to her right, Ignis was standing with Amber in their ready position. Amber stood with her sword drawn, talking animatedly to Ignis.

Gloria was nervous about the battle ahead of them. None knew what to expect, and yet, there was a feeling as though the entire valley was holding its breath. Gloria realized that since Arbor controlled the valley, it could have been.

Gloria jumped as Uncle Dux spoke, "Checking? Who's there?"

Gloria and Njord answered, "Here."

"Present."

Gloria heard Ignis, "We're here."

Amber said, "Hello Dux!"

Gloria heard Fornacem and Umbra Mortis, "Piss off."

Njord flinched, "Please be more cautious with your language."

Fornacem scoffed, "Bite me."

Cybele said, "Hello? I can hear you!"

Bovi grunted, "Bovi, reporting."

Arthur said, "Come on, I'm *right* next to you... *fine*, here."

Uncle Dux said, "Newcomers? Green flares mean they're in the field of traps, yellow is Arbor's maze, and after red, you'll see them. Exception of Fornacem and Umbra Mortis, kill whenever you see monsters. Oh, and everyone try to avoid Ullr. We don't want to scare him."

Gloria waited. After a few minutes Cybele said, "Ooh! Green over here!"

Uncle Dux said, "We got green too!"

Gloria flinched as silver forks of lightning shredded the valley, "Needless to say, Umbra Mortis and me are in action."

Njord muttered, correcting his grammar.

Gloria gasped as a green flare shot over her head, "We got

green!"

Uncle Dux said, "We got yellow."

Ignis and Amber said simultaneously, "Green."

Gloria took a nervous breath as Uncle Dux said, "Woah! Red! They're ice and fire crawlers!"

Gloria thought that *nothing* should have made it through Fornacem, Umbra Mortis, or the waves of traps. However, a red flare in front of her proved otherwise. "Red!"

Fire Reptans roared as they swarmed from the maze. Gloria saw Fallen magicians run forward. "I got left!"

She ran, jumped into the air, her aura bursting around her. She landed in the middle of the monsters. Gloria grinned and large ice spikes shot in all directions. Most of the Reptans were impaled and died instantly, but a few still lunged at Gloria.

Gloria sliced upwards, reducing one to ashes. She jumped on top of one, making ice spikes grow as she landed. It howled and fell into cinders. Gloria looked up and saw Njord fighting off five magicians. Njord ducked under a spell, and one of the magicians crooned, "I'll rip yer legs off, fry 'em up, and make calamari!"

Njord scowled, *"Really!"* He thrust his arms out, *"Kraken fluctus!"* A sharp wind knocked the magicians onto the ground. Njord huffed, "Just because you are participating in a war does *not* excuse you for poor manners!"

Gloria laughed.

They attacked in waves, Gloria gasping as ten Furnace Fallen roared from the maze. She ran at them, sending spears into two of them. She threw her hands forward, *"Angelus undam!"* A wave of gold light disintegrated the rest.

Njord said, "Be cautious when utilizing spells, you do not know when you will next be required to use one."

Njord and Gloria flinched as a loud roar sounded in the valley.

Njord replied grimly, "Such as that."

Gloria looked above the maze, a Seniorem Reptans charged at them, shredding straight through the traps and Arbor's maze. Gloria saw torn roots trailing from its back end, along with blackened organs pouring from it.

Gloria heard Uncle Dux say, "Gloria!"

Gloria nodded, "On it!" She nodded at Njord, and they leaped at the monster.

Gloria slid on the ground, under the monster. She sent a continuous burst of ice into its side before scrambling out of the way. The Seniorem Reptans roared, swiping at Gloria.

Gloria saw a black summoning circle blaze from Njord's hands, "*Tonitrua et fulgura!*"

Gloria covered her eyes as a bright yellow flash exploded in front of her. She uncovered her eyes and yelped, leaping over the monster's fist. She sent a few ice spears into its back, then landed cat-like in front of Njord. They nodded to each other and ran opposite directions as the monster blew fire.

Gloria shot ice over the fire quickly before it got out of control. Njord hit the Seniorem Reptans with another lightning bolt. Gloria leaped up at the monster, throwing an ice spear into its eye. The Seniorem Reptans roared, batting Gloria aside. Gloria pointed toward the rapidly approaching ground, and golden snow surged from her hands. She landed in it, cushioning her.

Gloria looked up to see Njord hit it with more lightning, flashing onto Gloria's burned retinas. Gloria gasped as the Seniorem Reptans narrowly missed his head, but Njord fell over. Gloria ran as it raised its fist and dove as it swung downward. She screamed, "*Angelus percutitur!*" A large golden spear shot from the ground and stabbed the Seniorem Reptans in the chest.

The monster roared, trying to dislodge itself from the ice. The ground shook as large roots tore up from the ground.

They wrapped the monster and yanked it into the ground, forcing the ice deeper into its chest. The monster roared one last time, and the light dimmed in its eyes. Gloria sighed as it broke into cinders.

Njord said, "May we have an intermission?"

Gloria replied, "I wish."

A crack of black lightning made Gloria think Umbra Mortis had accidentally fired at them. She looked up from the ground and found that she was very wrong.

With static covered arms, black teeth curled in a sneer, and purple spikes jutting from his arms, Lapsus leered at them. He walked leisurely towards them, black chains wrapped around his shoulders, making an X across his back.

Gloria whispered urgently into the comms link, "Somebody help! Lapsus is here!" No one replied.

Lapsus sneered, "So... you've sunk so low as to use *aura* magic..."

Gloria snarled, "And what are *you* doing?" She spat.

Lapsus grinned, "I do what I must. I see that you have *finally* thought the same way. Let's see Dux's best warriors in action, for the last time!" He raised his hand.

There was a red streak, and then Lapsus was yelling as black blood spurted from his shoulder. Gloria saw Amber and Ignis land beside her.

Gloria saw Amber and Ignis land beside them.

Gloria stood, cracking her knuckles, "So... what was that about the last time?"

Together, they attacked Lapsus in ferocious close combat. Amber swept in with her sword, barely missing him. Ignis shot fire spells, Gloria ice spears, and Njord kept him moving with lightning. Gloria saw him dodge Amber without looking, as though he knew she was there.

Lapsus scowled and whipped around to catch Gloria's ice spear, hurling it back. Amber swooped down and lifted Gloria.

Gloria gasped, "Woah! Why-" An army of Furnace Fallen tore through the maze. Gloria thrust her hands forward, "*Sanctus grail!*" A bright flash of gold surged towards them, freezing them in place. Amber swooped down, beheading them. Gloria kicked a stray head towards Lapsus, satisfied as she heard a loud *clunk*.

She landed on the ground. "Don't fly me off without my permission."

Lapsus yelled as Amber drug her blade across his back, "I will not be toyed with!" He roared, and a black wave of light blasted them.

Gloria saw Ignis gasp as he blasted into the sky to deal with Golden Guardians.

Njord, Amber, and Gloria stood. Lapsus sneered, "You could have lived, you know. But it's too late. I have already decided, you've sealed your fate. Your bodies will corrode as I slaughter your *beloved* students."

Njord's eyes glowed an angry green, "You will regret stating that."

Amber spun her sword, snarling.

Lapsus' chuckle grew into a bellowing laugh. He stopped as a gold comet caught his bad shoulder.

Gloria said, "Yo, freak, save the laughter for *after* you're licking your wounds in your army-less base."

Lapsus sneered, he roared, "Fight me if you dare!"

Amber, Gloria, and Njord jumped at him. He rolled over lightning, deflected silver streaks, and shattered golden spears. He was no more than a blur of darkness. Gloria tried to strike any part of him, but she couldn't see him.

Njord yelled, "*Tempestas percutiens!*"

Lapsus yelled as a surge of wind slammed him to the Earth twenty feet away. He struggled to rise, but lightning forced him to the ground. Amber drug her sword against the ground as she, Gloria, and Njord approached.

Lapsus laughed quietly. A dark plume of smoke drifted from his chest. "Can you shut up?" Gloria snarled.

Lapsus smiled, "Such a fiery spirit. He adores bravery." He laughed again, throwing his head back. Amber drove a foot into his gut. He gasped for breath, coughing blood.

Lapsus' head fell back onto the cold Earth, "You know... I wished to see her after all this time. My love, my family. I'm sorry I failed you."

Gloria hesitated. She whispered to Amber, "You think he's barking?"

Amber raised her sword, "No one could ever *love* that monster."

Lapsus grinned weakly, "You should thank me. What is to come... Only *I* know. And only *I* will be the one to decide the cataclysmic events. You'll see... People will suffer, just as I did. People will die... just as I did."

Gloria froze his hands to his sides and squatted next to him. She tried to speak through the communications, "Uncle Dux, we've got Lapsus. He's babbling nonsense." Static met Gloria's ear. Gloria said, "Uncle Dux? Where are you?"

Gloria spoke to Amber, "Can you get Uncle Dux? I want him to take care of *this* idiot." Amber nodded and with a strong gust of wind, she flew into the air.

Gloria glanced at Lapsus as he muttered, "I am my own destiny."

Njord and Gloria yelped as Lapsus' hand phased through the ice. He touched a finger to Gloria's head. He smiled weakly, "I hate to tear a family apart... but... Someone should feel my pain..."

As static pierced her eyes. Cackling laughter filled Gloria's ears, as well as a hiss. *No! Her destiny lies with me!* Gloria lost consciousness as she collapsed to the ground and the whispers filled her head with a cold, dark, emptiness.

Njord ripped Lapsus off Gloria as she collapsed to the

floor. He shook her, "Gloria? Gloria! Gloria! No... No!"

Lapsus whispered, "Death is a sweet sorrow... wouldn't you agree, fish?"

Njord grabbed Lapsus' shirt, "You! You restore her immediately! Or I will... I will..."

Lapsus smiled, "I cannot... does it hurt to feel utterly... powerless? To promise to protect someone you care for... only to watch them perish in your arms."

Lapsus cackled as Njord said nothing. Lightning crackled in the sky.

In the air above them, Fornacem thrusted his hand forward, he frowned as no lightning surged from the sky. "The hell?" He glanced at the sky as the clouds started to swirl. He flicked his hands. The sky didn't reply. He glanced down at Njord, "Huh. OH HELL!"

Amber appeared in a blast of wind, approaching Njord, "Hey Njord, what's... wrong?" Amber gasped, she appeared by Gloria's side.

Njord took a few paces back, "N-No... stay back!"

Amber ignored him, cradling Gloria's head, "Don't be dead." Amber set her head to Gloria's chest. She let out a sigh of relief and turned to Njord.

"Hey Njord! She's... Njord?"

A black and green light surrounded Njord. Strange markings blazed black on his arms. With a flash, his jeans ripped as he returned to his Cecaelian form. Lightning crackled through his hair.

Njord muttered, "N-No... stay back! I-I do not need you... stay back... you will not make this worse!"

Amber said, "N-Njord?"

Njord raised his head. Amber gasped, Njord's eyes were glowing solid black. A large black summoning circle burned around him. He grabbed at his hair, lightning flashed, and thunder rolled. Amber looked around as a salty wind nearly knocked her over. More lightning flashed.

Njord's shadow grew taller. Amber gasped as her vision followed Njord upward. She watched as Njord's shadow grew larger, covering her. It towered over her and kept crawling further and further. Njord's tentacles writhed, as though in pain, lightning crackling through his hair. Njord roared and the lightning flashed, accepting the royalty of its newfound leader.

CHAPTER 16: IGNIS
The Wrath of the Kraken Sorcerer

Ignis saw a swath of rogue Golden Guardians fly above. He gasped, shooting towards them, firing spears of fire. He fried a few, rolling in the air to avoid the carcasses. One exploded in front of him, and he flared his aura to avoid being covered in organs.

Ignis looked down and saw Gloria, Amber, and Njord fighting Lapsus. He was about to fly down when a Golden Guardian clamped its jaws on his pants leg. Ignis yelped, the Golden Guardian giving him whiplash. Ignis struggled upward, yelling in frustration. He kicked it in the face with his free foot. It grunted and dropped him. Ignis saw it coming for a second pass.

Ignis yelled, *"Ardeat!"* A comet of fire burned a hole through the monster. It groaned, bursting into gory chunks.

Ignis landed on the ground and let out a sigh of relief. He glanced at the others and saw Gloria unconscious on the ground in Amber's arms. Njord was pulling at his hair. Ignis ran as a flash of lightning lit up the valley.

Amber looked terrified, but not for Gloria. She was staring at Njord.

Ignis looked at Njord, "What... what the heck?"

Njord grew bigger, his tentacles plowing trenches around him. Amber grabbed Gloria and soared around the tree. Ignis watched Njord as he reached thirty feet tall. He growled like no monster Ignis had ever seen. He took a breath, making a deep rumble.

Amber shook Ignis's shoulder, "Ignis! What's happening? Njord muttered something about the Kraken Sorcerer. I think he thinks Gloria's..."

Ignis' heart leapt, "Is she?"

Amber shook her head, "No, just unconscious. But she... she..." Amber lost her voice as she looked over Ignis's shoulder.

Ignis turned to look behind him, his eyes widening, "Get Uncle Dux, now!"

Njord reached the height of the Tree itself, his shoulders passing the treetops. His tentacles writhed, each hundreds of feet long and thicker than a subway tunnel. Fifty feet from his body, black summoning circles appeared, making a hollow space between his tentacles. Fifty feet below the first set, the black summoning circles reappeared. Njord's tentacles shot through those, slamming into the ground. Blue light made five triangles above Njord's gargantuan head. Four were smaller, leading into a single large triangle, creating what looked to Ignis like a simplified crown. Njord's eyes blazed dark green. He stopped writhing.

The giant Njord raised his hand, as though to drop a microphone. A loud, familiar metallic noise filled the air.

Amber pointed towards the north peaks, "Look! *What* is that?"

Ignis saw a gleam of gold. Whatever it was, it slowly grew. Ignis's stomach plummeted, a golden trident raced to Njord. As it surged forward, the sound barrier broke. It kept growing, and growing, until... Ignis covered his ears as a loud *crash* nearly left him deaf. The trident slammed into Njord's palm, exactly his height.

Ignis felt a new power surge through his veins. He felt as though he had dropped the two hundred pounds from his shoulders that he never knew was there.

Amber gasped, "That's- That's Poseidon's trident! No other trident could have broken the barrier!"

They flinched as Fornacem appeared behind them, "That's not Poseidon's trident anymore."

Ignis whirled around, "What do you mean?" Ignis flinched. For the first time, as clear as day, Ignis saw fear shine in Fornacem's red eyes.

Fornacem said, "The trident is loyal to whoever rules the seas. And the ruler of the seas... will forever be... the Kraken Sorcerer."

Ignis gasped, "But! But that's Njord!"

Fornacem shook his head, "It's not Njord anymore. We need to get inside... Now!" Fornacem grabbed Ignis and Amber's shoulders. With a silver flash, Ignis found himself in the dining room. Amber lowered the unconscious Gloria on the table. Ignis and Amber raced to the window.

Njord scowled and waved the trident sideways. Black clouds swirled around the trident. With another silver flash, Fornacem appeared with the rest of Ignis's family.

Uncle Dux yelped when he saw Gloria, "What happened?"

Amber shook her head, "I don't know! Lapsus did something and she collapsed. She's alive, but Njord... Njord..."

Uncle Dux ran to the window, "*HOLY* SHIT!"

Ignis's eyes widened as the valley filled with water, a salty sea so dark, it appeared black. The sky's black clouds rose higher, flashed with bright lightning, and boomed with rolling thunder shaking the whole Tree. The water rose higher and higher, reaching the Kraken Sorcerer's waist.

Furnace Fallen, Ice Reptans, and other monsters were

briefly visible in the water which started to swirl around the Kraken Sorcerer. The monsters exploded into cinder as they drowned. Ignis saw Ullr crawl out of the water and disappear over the mountain peaks.

Uncle Dux slammed the windows shut, "FORNACEM! CALM THE SKIES!"

Fornacem shook his head, "I can't! They are no longer mine to control."

Uncle Dux bellowed over the thunder, "WHAT DO YOU MEAN YOU CAN'T?"

Fornacem yelled, "The Kraken Sorcerer is the lord of the skies and seas! He controls all storms and seas in existence."

Julia gasped audibly, "Is that... Is that Njord?"

Fornacem nodded, "It was, but now he's the Kraken Sorcerer."

Arthur's eyes focused on Njord, "What is that?"

Fornacem said, "The Kraken Sorcerer is the most ancient being in existence. Legend has it that in the beginning the Kraken Sorcerer lived in peace, the Earth covered in his ocean. But he grew lonely and decided to create life. He ripped a rift between Earth and the magical realm and created a land of sea creatures. Legends say after this, he drifted into a deep slumber for tens of thousands of years. As he slept, someone stole his trident to become the sea king."

Fornacem pointed out the window, "The Kraken Sorcerer awoke to find his trident missing and cursed all human life. They couldn't breathe in water or swim in his seas. If they dared, his sea creatures tore them apart. Ultimately, what you know as sea creatures today have descended from these early monsters.

Eventually his monsters recovered the trident and once again, he returned to slumber. Before he slept, he cursed the trident so that any who dared to touch it would be transformed into the very monsters tasked with guarding his treasure."

Lightning flashed, lining Fornacem's face in brutal glare. "Eventually, a sea creature risked the curse and stole the trident. But before the curse could take effect, a Cecaelia stole it back and returned it. As a reward, the Kraken Sorcerer bestowed his power on the Cecaelia. They became descendants of the Kraken Sorcerer.

Poseidon claimed the trident when he became the ruler of the sea, but as he was not Cecaelian, he was unable to achieve the Kraken Sorcerer's power. The king before Poseidon was none other than Oceanus Pacificus, who retired to raise a family. The power of the Kraken Sorcerer then fell onto the next descendent, little Njord Pacificus."

Ignis gasped as a deep roar rattled the Tree. Fornacem said, "The Kraken Sorcerer broke down *planets*, created *worlds*! He was nicknamed, Oceanum creatio, ocean creator, due to the strength of his power! Mortals wondered why they came from the seas. The Kraken Sorcerer leaked his magic onto Earth and created human life, that's how!"

Cybele gasped. Fornacem took a breath, "If we don't calm him down, he'll *destroy* this world! *None* can trump the Kraken Sorcerer. He is the true ruler of *all* seas and every realm!"

Julia and Amber gasped. "Fornacem said, "We need to calm him down! Now!"

Ignis said, "How do we do that?"

Fornacem said, "If he awoke by Gloria getting hurt, he needs to see that she is alright!"

Julia shook Gloria, "Gloria! Wake up! Please!" They froze as a quiet snore filled the silence.

Fornacem roared, "DAMN IT GIRL! WAKE UP OR YOU'LL HAVE KILLED US ALL!"

Uncle Dux pointed out the window. "We need to buy time! Amber! Ignis! Try to calm him down!"

Amber nodded, and Uncle Dux opened the window. A strong salty wind knocked everyone to the floor. The windows shattered as they smashed against the walls. Amber grabbed Ignis's hand, her voice was silent against the roar of the wind. "COME ON!"

Ignis allowed for Amber to fly, but they floated, not moving in the dining room. Amber closed her eyes and flapped her wings harder against the wind. Slowly they flew from the dining room and suddenly shot out the window. They were caught in the hurricane surrounding the valley. Impossibly, Amber grabbed the canopy of the Tree. She yelped as they slipped, then hauled Ignis up to the treetop.

Ignis held firmly onto the branches so as to not be thrown by the winds. Ignis looked down thousands of feet to where a Seniorem Reptans was drowning in black water. Ignis gasped as the Kraken Sorcerer raised his trident and brought it down on the Seniorem Reptans' throat. There was a colossal explosion, and a geyser shot skyward, soaking Ignis and Amber in cold salty water.

Amber shouted, her voice soft against the roar, "NJORD!"

Ignis bellowed, "NJORD!"

Ignis didn't hear himself in the wind. The Kraken Sorcerer turned to them. Ignis's stomach dropped as the giant face scowled. Ignis felt smaller than a toy soldier standing before the giant.

There was a deep rumble as though the very Earth spoke, "*Quis audet dedecus irae meae?*"

Ignis turned to Amber as she translated, "*Who dares the disgrace of my wrath.*" Amber bellowed at the gargantuan face, "IT'S US, NJORD! IT'S AMBER AND IGNIS! YOUR FRIENDS!"

The Kraken Sorcerer scowled deeper. Ignis's heart leapt into his throat as he saw three golden prongs glint in the rain.

"*Non habeo talis intentio.*" The Kraken Sorcerer boomed, "*Derelinquas me ad iram. Discedite!*"

Ignis felt a jolt in his stomach and suddenly surged backwards. He looked behind him, Amber had opened her wings, catching the wind. They swirled around the valley, giving Ignis motion sickness.

Ignis bellowed, "WHAT DID HE SAY?"

Amber bellowed back, "I HAVE NO SUCH INTENTION! FORSAKE ME TO ANGER! DEPART!"

Ignis bellowed, "HE SOUNDS LIKE NJORD!"

Amber bellowed, "WHAT?"

Ignis yelled so loud he felt as though his throat splintered, "HE SOUNDS LIKE NJORD!"

Amber gave a small yelp. Ignis yelled as she dived, a golden trident speeding after them.

"*Dixi discedere!*" A deep voice thundered. Amber twirled over the trident prongs, which were cracking with lightning. They made a deep, menacing, metallic whir as it swung through the air.

Amber said quietly, "We'll go."

Ignis saw her flap her wings and they shot into the dining room. They crashed through the window, slammed into the wall, and collapsed in a pile. Rain and wind roared as Uncle Dux ran for the broken shutters. Uncle Dux muttered a spell, and white barrier blocked the wind from the windows. Two inches of frigid water soaked the floors.

Julia muttered, "Oh my!"

Arthur shook Ignis's shoulders, "Ignis! Are you alright?"

Amber groaned, raising her head. "I have a headache." She muttered. Ignis groaned, and limped over, untangling himself from Amber.

Ignis shook his head, "He didn't recognize us. He tried to kill us."

Fornacem said, "Of course he did! We need someone close to him! Wake up Gloria!"

Arthur shook Gloria's shoulder, "Gloria! Wake up!"

Arbor appeared in the doorway, "He's breaking the entire

valley apart! If he gets any deeper, he'll kill the students!"

Fornacem shook his head, "They're just in the way! He'll sink to the center of the planet and shatter it to pieces! Move the room, then distract him!"

Arbor nodded and sunk into the floor. Ignis caught a glimpse outside.

Huge roots rose on every side of the Kraken Sorcerer. He bellowed, swiping his trident around him, and severed roots fell into the spinning sea. Ignis saw more appear. They bound him, tying tighter. The Kraken Sorcerer's eyes blazed bright and the roots exploded in such a shockwave that everyone was thrown to the floor.

Ignis saw the Kraken Sorcerer grab a root and pull it upward. Amber and a few others screamed as the room lurched.

Uncle Dux bellowed, "HE'LL UPROOT THE ENTIRE TREE! ARBOR, COME BACK!"

Ignis hung onto the wall, his legs over the hallway. He clambered onto the wall as a can of soup rolled by. The floor was at a steep seventy-five-degree angle. Ignis saw a root fly up, torn from the tree's bottom. Everyone screamed as the Tree lurched in the other direction.

Ignis felt the Tree vibrate and gasped as he saw even thicker roots entrap the Kraken Sorcerer. The roots groaned with the strain of holding him.

His eyes blazed brighter as he rumbled, *"Quis audet!"* There was a flash of green light and an explosion. The Kraken Sorcerer roared, leaving a painful ringing in Ignis's ears.

Arbor appeared in the dining room, "I can't hold him, it's taking all my power to keep the valley together!" His form was surrounded in a flowing bright green aura. Uncle Dux grunted. He had both hands on the wall of light, keeping the windows shut.

Fornacem said, "Wake up Gloria! Damn it!"

Arbor yelled, "INCOMING!"

The Tree rattled, as the Kraken Sorcerer slammed the end of his trident against its side. Everyone was flung to the walls. Roots managed to grow from the floors and furniture catching them. Ignis and Amber gasped as they seized their feet. Amber managed to grab Gloria's wrist.

The Kraken Sorcerer grabbed one of the roots, lifting it high over his head. Everyone howled as they tumbled towards the other wall. Bovi caught Cybele in his hands, kneeling against the wall.

The Kraken Sorcerer slowly raised his trident over his head. Uncle Dux yelled at Arbor, "DON'T LET THAT TRIDENT HIT THE GROUND!" Arbor nodded.

A single tree root, wider than a subway tunnel, caught the end of the trident. The Kraken Sorcerer scowled, "*Indignus es, fatum tuum accipere.*" He spun the trident, and a metallic whir filled the air. He rose it to the sky, "*Iram meam pati!*" Hundreds of black comets surged from the mountain peaks.

Uncle Dux said, "It's the enemy! They're fighting back!"

The Kraken Sorcerer thundered, "*Sentire meam potestatem!*"

Ignis's hair stood on end as a bright bolt of lightning struck the prongs of the trident. Lightning coursed through it and channeled into the maelstrom below. Ignis saw hundreds of waterspouts whirl from the sea. Monsters perished as explosions erupted in the storm. The Kraken Sorcerer roared, and a thousand forks of lightning sprung forth. Explosions littered the mountain tops. The lightning retreated into the trident. Fire rolled from the mountains. The Kraken Sorcerer roared as a single black comet exploded against his back.

The Kraken Sorcerer turned slowly as Lapsus roared, "THIS IS NOT WHAT I WAS PROMISED! I WAS PROMISED GLORY!"

The Kraken Sorcerer didn't flinch as a comet of darkness

exploded against his chest. He rumbled, *"Ibi non est... nulla gloria in tenebris"* and raised his trident over his head. It gave a metallic whir, glowing like magma.

The Kraken Sorcerer scowled, *"Metis quod seminas. Peristi in tenebris."* He threw his trident directly at Lapsus. Everyone gasped as the trident left his fingertips. There was a clap of thunder and the surge of lightning which followed turned night into day.

Lapsus yelled as the trident exploded over the mountain side. The entire south valley wall crumbled, and the trident flew back into the Kraken Sorcerer's hand.

Arbor ran next to Gloria, "I think I can channel my energy and wake her!"

Fornacem roared, "DO IT!"

The Kraken Sorcerer bellowed and plunged the trident into the roots of the Tree. Arbor's aura died, his eyes dimmed, and he fell to his hands and knees.

Uncle Dux yelled, "Arbor!"

Arbor muttered, "He struck a nerve, n-nothing I can't handle."

He shook, raising a trembling hand to Gloria's arm. A green glow flowed from his hand into Gloria. The Kraken Sorcerer roared tearing the trident from the roots. Arbor went limp, fell to the floor, and melted into the ground.

Gloria lurched upward with a gasp, as the Kraken Sorcerer roared again.

Arthur ran to her side, "Thank the lords! You must calm Njord down!"

Gloria looked around the ravaged room as everyone got to their feet. Amber and Ignis limped to her side. "Where... Where is he?"

Amber solemnly pointed outside. Gloria gasped.

The Kraken Sorcerer threw his arms wide. Intricate black symbols blazed across them. Hundreds of black summoning circles appeared around him. He roared, and they blasted lightning across the valley.

Gloria ran to the window, "What happened?"

Amber said, "Lapsus did something to you, Njord... I think Njord thought you... He suddenly turned into *that*."

Fornacem grabbed Gloria's shoulder, "It's the Kraken Sorcerer, if you don't calm his rage, he'll devastate the entire magical realm! Starting with us!"

Gloria gasped. Amber said, "Ignis and I will take you out there!" Gloria nodded.

Amber grabbed Gloria's one arm, and Ignis the other. Amber flapped her wings hard. Ignis blasted flames behind them. Together, they flew out the window.

Gloria screamed as she immediately looked down. She yelped as Amber and Ignis caught the tree tops. They crawled up the side and Ignis yelled as he slid ten feet before he caught another branch. They reached the top of the Tree, and Gloria struggled forward.

Gloria yelled, "NJORD!"

Ignis saw the Kraken Sorcerer freeze. He turned to face Gloria.

Ignis saw Gloria gasp, "Njord! It's me! I... I'm ok!"

Ignis gasped as the winds slowed. He looked down as the maelstrom slowed too. Entire trees fell into the sea, along with sections of mountain the size of city blocks.

The Kraken Sorcerer took a deep breath, "*Tu es... Gloria?*"

Amber gasped, "He said, *are you Gloria?*"

Gloria nodded, "Yes! It's me! I'm alright!"

The Kraken Sorcerer looked confused, like he was remembering something. He furrowed his eyebrows, lightning flashed in the distance, and thunder rolled quietly.

The Kraken Sorcerer said, "*Scio te.*"

Amber translated, "I know you."

Gloria said, "It's ok, Njord! You can calm down now! We're all alright!"

The Kraken Sorcerer closed his eyes. He snarled lightly and lightning flashed in the distance, "The- The seas rage in my domain. Can they establish peace?"

Gloria took a step forward. Amber and Ignis hesitatingly followed suit.

Gloria said, "You don't have to fight anymore, Njord! Come to us!"

The Kraken Sorcerer opened his eyes, "Are we..."

He snarled and the lightning flashed again. He took a breath, "Are we all right?"

Amber gasped. Gloria nodded, "Yes, Njord! We are all right."

The Kraken Sorcerer let out a breath. The seas flowed up his tentacles, disappearing into the summoning circles below his waist. The black clouds swirled above, whirling into a tornado, as they retreated into the trident. He set the butt of the trident gently onto the ground. His crown of light faded, as the Kraken Sorcerer shrunk in size, the trident mimicking.

Gloria turned to Amber. Ignis, Gloria, and Amber flew to the ground. It was slick with mud, uprooted trees, and boulders. Monster corpses littered the ground. Large cracks spread like spider webs from the center of the valley, wide enough to swallow vehicles. The sky became clear. The moon reappeared, in its ugly red. The red fell back, leaving a crescent shape of white moon.

The Kraken Sorcerer was now the size of Njord. He let out a sigh, and the crown over his head faded. The trident flew slowly into the air with a metallic whir. It flew upwards, stopping a hundred feet above them. There was a loud explosion as the trident broke the sound barrier. It raced north, to rejoin the king of the sea.

Gloria stopped in front of the Kraken Sorcerer. He looked

up, smiled, and the glow faded from his eyes. They were Njord's eyes. Njord shook his head, seeing Gloria, Ignis, and Amber.

"Er... what happened?" He yelped as Gloria tackled him in a hug. Njord and Gloria fell to the ground as Amber laughed in relief. Njord's eyes glowed green, like they did when he was nervous.

"Wha- Gloria! We are immersed in Earth! Restrain your excitement!"

Gloria grabbed the front of his shirt, "Don't ever scare me like that again!"

Njord nodded frantically, "Er- Yes, yes! I will not!"

Gloria hauled him from the ground. Together, they walked to the tree.

Uncle Dux tried his best to fix the room, but Arbor had not woken up. It took him, Arthur, and Bovi to push the table back into place. They found the chairs and set them around the table.

Uncle Dux filled Njord in on what happened. The more he told, the brighter his eyes glowed. He rested his head in his hands, staring at the table, shaking his head.

Gloria patted his back, "It's ok, Njord. We're all still here, right?"

Njord muttered, "I... I lost control... What if I had harmed you? I will never forgive myself."

Fornacem said, "Look at it this way. The Kraken Sorcerer absolutely *demolished* the army. Lapsus is surely dead, if not, he'd be extremely dumb to return. I mean sure... you almost killed us-"

Gloria and Julia both yelled, "Fornacem!"

Njord said miserably, "I almost killed Arbor. I almost killed Amber and Ignis. I am too dangerous to be in close proximity."

Gloria smacked his shoulder, "Don't speak like that! You sensed that we were in danger, so you did everything in your power to help. You know what I think? I think that you were very brave."

Gloria glared around the table, daring the first person to disagree with her. The surface below Njord's face glowed brighter.

Fornacem said, "As much as Njord did, there are still thousands of magicians out there. They sent out their entire swarm of monsters into the valley. The Fallen magicians may have escaped, but Njord killed every monster."

Njord shook his head. Fornacem said, "I've always been told, never provoke the Kraken Sorcerer."

Julia brought in supplies and said, "We should tend to our wounds before they return."

Ignis held up a familiar brown bottle. Amber looked away but yelped as Ignis appeared in front of her. "You got hurt in that battle! If we don't clean out monster wounds, you could get infected, or get curses!"

Gloria laughed as Ignis chased Amber down the hall.

Amber said, "I hate that stuff!"

Even Njord smiled as Ignis dragged her back into the dining room.

Ignis heard Cybele say, "I'm fine Bovi, it's just a bruise, it'll be fine!"

Bovi said, "And what about those? You heard them, if you don't clean them, they could get infected, or worse, cursed! I'm not taking that chance, and I won't let *you* take that chance." Bovi didn't wait for a response, he started wrapping Cybele's leg.

Ignis saw Gloria motion to Cybele, and she cleared her throat. "Thank you, Bovi. I really appreciate it."

Bovi blushed, "It... It's fine, someone... someone has to look out for you."

Uncle Dux spoke, "Alright people, they've run out of monsters, that's good. All we have to worry about are the magicians. Problem is, Arbor and Umbra Mortis are out of play. Arbor for... obvious reasons."

Njord stared at the floor. Uncle Dux said, "And Umbra Mortis used all his power to keep the valley together. He also managed to keep the storm from destroying the Celestial Forests and everything else within a hundred miles."

Cybele took a water bottle from Bovi with a quiet thanks.

Uncle Dux continued, "As we all know, the Blood Moon Curse will activate regardless. Soon, we will be forced to pull punches and spill no blood. Nothing sharp, no blades, swords, spears, the sort. Instead, try making blunt weapons, sticks, hammers, anything as long as it doesn't cut. The less blood spilled in the valley, the better. Maybe we will be lucky enough, and the Blood Moon Curse will pass by without a sacrifice."

Amber whimpered as Ignis pressed a cloth to her skin. Her wings slowly opened and closed as she squealed in pain. A bird flew from the canopy ceiling and out the doorless window.

Fornacem scoffed, "Wishful thinking."

Cybele said, "I've never used my bare hands before, but I'll keep my spear, in case I need it, right?"

Uncle Dux nodded, "Of course, use blades only if you're about to die. We all need to look out for each other."

Bovi said, "What magic will you use?"

Uncle Dux said, "Well, the barrier's shattered. We are free to use magic as we please. However, our enemy can as well."

Fornacem said, "We should discuss what spells we can't use."

Uncle Dux nodded, "Good idea. No weapon summoning, or elemental blades or points." Uncle Dux said, "Remember, Lapsus' goal was to cause the Blood Moon Curse to fall onto him. Knowing him, he'll start slaughtering his own army. Do everything in your power to keep him from achieving it. Even if that means preventing him from killing the enemy."

Fornacem said, "I mean, I could always teleport them high in the sky."

Uncle Dux shook his head, "And have them splatter into the valley? Definitely not."

Gloria said, "Ullr can teleport them to Earth, maybe Antarctica?"

Uncle Dux's face fell, "Oh, I forgot about him. Fornacem, can you see if you can coax him back into the valley? Tell him not to kill but send them to Antarctica."

Fornacem nodded. With a silver flash, he disappeared.

Uncle Dux continued, "Now, we have no idea what spells the Fallen magicians will use. So don't go easy on them."

Uncle Dux took a breath, "Remember, they want to *kill* you, in the most brutal way possible. They'll kill at the first opportunity. Do not give them that opportunity. Freeze them in ice or turn them to ash. Otherwise, bring unconscious enemies to Ullr to dispose of."

Everyone turned to Gloria as she said, "What about combination animarum?"

Uncle Dux shook his head, "It would be pointless to use it. As soon as the Blood Moon Curse starts, it will absorb magic worse than an anti-magic barrier. We can use our auras, but magic and spells may not work. The Elements, however, will. That means we'll be at a *huge* advantage, even when the curse kicks in. The enemy will most likely summon mortal weapons beforehand. Keep your distance, and *do not* spill any blood."

Cybele said, "No self-enhancing magic either?"

Uncle Dux shook his head, "Actually, that may work. But I don't think blades are a good idea."

Cybele said, "I have been training with the spear my whole life. I know how to spare my enemies. When the curse affects us, I will use my spear, but spill no blood."

Amber nodded, "Same with me, I can handle a sword." She yelped. Ignis ducked under one of her wings as they shot out.

Uncle Dux sighed, "Very well. Just know-"

There was a change in the moonlight and the air around them turned an ugly red. It carried the scent of copper. Uncle Dux's map disappeared into static.

Uncle Dux gasped, "What? It started early? That's impossible!"

There was an explosion outside the window. Everyone crowded onto the landing.

Hundreds of Fallen magicians yelled and called to them. Many held swords and shields. Others held rifles with swords and shields strapped to their backs. The warriors with the swords banged them against their shields. Another section of the army had black crystal chains wrapped around their arms. Others held torches of gruesome red flames.

Bovi forced Cybele to duck as a bullet ricocheted off the wall next to her.

Cybele resurfaced, "Thanks."

Uncle Dux grimaced, he said, "The invasion has begun. The army is out for blood."

Gloria said, "What do we do if we see Lapsus?"

Uncle Dux said, "Keep away from him. I have unfinished business to attend to with him. Njord, when I yell, assist me."

Njord's eyes glowed with a dark green light. He nodded, "With gratitude."

Uncle Dux said, "Alright, defend the tree!"

Uncle Dux grabbed a vine next to the landing and slid down the wall. Bovi scooped Cybele off the floor and leaped to the ground. Amber picked up Ignis, and they flew towards the battlegrounds.

Gloria glanced at the blood red moon and shook her head, as though clearing her thoughts. The moon leered, seeming to taunt her. It urged her forward. Gloria ignored it.

Gloria sighed and turned to Njord, "You ready?"

Njord nodded, "Affirmative."

Njord wrapped an arm around Gloria's waist and descended the vine.

The red moon glared over them all. With a black surge, the mark of the Blood Moon Curse appeared. It glared into the night air as static crackled around its profile.

CHAPTER 17: GLORIA
The Fall of the Angel

Gloria moved as soon as her feet met the Earth. The air was cold, and the ground was soft, as though gently inviting warm crimson to satisfy its hunger. Gloria glanced at the mark of the Blood Moon Curse above. The mark opened its mouth in a cruel silent laugh.

Uncle Dux, Arthur, Fornacem, Ullr, Cybele, Bovi, Amber, Ignis, Njord, and Gloria stood in a line as the army suddenly stopped. Lapsus staggered to the front of his army. He looked rough. Static was trickling from scrapes all over his body. He straightened his head and a loud crack sounded from his neck.

Uncle Dux said, "You should be dead."

"I die on my own time. I refuse to die by the hands of the *king* of *fish*." He sneered at Njord. "We outnumber you twenty to one. Give up now, you no longer have your precious *magic*."

Uncle Dux took a step forward, "We'll see about that, Lapsus."

Lapsus sneered. The mark of the Blood Moon Curse bellowed with laughter. Gloria heard a faint timpani drum pounding. The army leered at them as a gentle breeze carried a stray leaf across the grounds.

Lapsus and Uncle Dux roared at the same time, "ATTACK!"

All hell broke loose. Ullr charged into the crowd of magicians. Bovi tackled Cybele to avoid gunfire. Ignis and Amber rose into the sky launching fire into the army. Njord launched strands of lightning from black summoning circles.

Gloria made an ice shield as a Fallen magician swiped at her. His sword shattered against the ice. Gloria smacked him upside the head with an ice club. She ducked, rolled, and jumped over magicians as they stabbed at her.

Lapsus and Uncle Dux were locked in a ferocious aura duel. Comets of raw and dark magic shot around them. Spells flickered feebly, dying with a quiet hiss.

Njord shot lightning in every direction, striking ten magicians at once. "It is fortunate that I can utilize this magic. Otherwise, I would be of no help." He ducked under a sword swing, picking up the magician, and flinging them into the army.

Lapsus snarled, "It's a good thing I've been saving these." He gave a loud whistle, and the ground shook.

Uncle Dux yelled, "Incoming!"

Something broke the ground in front of Gloria. A large worm-like creature roared at her. It spit, and the grass hissed.

Gloria muttered darkly, "Oh, I *definitely* didn't miss you guys."

Earth wyverns broke the ground's surface, roaring and spitting at their targets.

Bovi leaped high over one and punched its jaw. The wyvern roared, as it slammed into the ground. Cybele passed Gloria in a green blur. She kicked a magician in the face, and he crumpled to the floor.

The wyvern roared at Gloria again. "Here we go." She ran away from it, the wyvern pursuing.

Gloria made an ice boulder and leaped off it. A strange emotion burned in the pit of her stomach. She made a spear in her hands. She slowed down as the wyvern opened its mouth in slow motion.

A chilling voice whispered in her ear, "*It is almost time, Angelo. Save your anger for now. I daresay you may need it later.*" The voice laughed, and static buzzed in Gloria's ears.

Gloria blinked, and her spear changed into a broad war hammer. She cracked it against the Wyvern's head. It roared, flailing awkwardly to the ground. It slithered like a snake, roaring at Gloria again. She glanced at the ice hammer in her hand, and it disappeared with a golden flash. *What was that?* Gloria thought.

She shook her head as the wyvern roared again and charged at her.

The Wyvern lunged at Gloria. She leaped over it, covered her fist in ice, and punched the Wyvern. Her hand ached, but she did damage. The wyvern snapped at her ankles and Gloria rolled away, breaking an ice club over its head.

Amber flew by overhead and kicked the wyvern in the head, it crashed to the ground. Gloria ran, screaming and broke an ice stick over its head. It twitched as Gloria brought the ice hammer to its neck. Gloria sighed as she heard a loud crack.

Off to Gloria's right, Ignis was firing volleys at the enemy. His image slowed down, and strangely Gloria smiled. The screams magnified in her ears as a buzzing static started and the world swirled. A voice whispered. *We enjoy watching them suffer... don't you?*

Gloria shook her head and ducked as a magician lunged at her. She cracked him in the head with ice. As he crumpled to the ground, Gloria's head spun.

What the heck was that, she thought wildly, *is the curse making me crazy?*

Another Wyvern surged from the ground in front of Gloria. It lunged at her. As she brought up a fist, she suddenly slowed down and looked at her hand. where a sharp ice blade crackled with intensity. Strange whispers filled her ears as she looked at the blade, imagining it soaked in blood. She shook her head and forced her hand up, the wyvern tearing by.

What was that? Gloria thought. She didn't know if monster blood would contribute to the curse. *Should I risk it?* Gloria shook her head, *better not.*

The wyvern spat at Gloria. She formed an ice barricade and the spit hissed as it splattered against the ice. As the wyvern slithered closer, Gloria yelled, exploding the barrier. She was relieved to see round ice chunks instead of spikes. The chunks showered the wyvern. It roared, collapsing to the ground. Gloria leaped up, forming a golden hue around her, and landed on the monster's throat with a loud *crunch*.

Gloria ducked under a spiraling spell of darkness. Lapsus had formed his aura, but it was completely static. It arced and hissed as it burned in the air. Uncle Dux's aura was a shimmering white light. The auras hissed as they made contact.

Uncle Dux dodged a blade of darkness and punched Lapsus in the jaw. Lapsus roared, swinging at Uncle Dux, but missing. Uncle Dux leaped over him, summoning an anvil. Lapsus snarled, and the anvil exploded. He whirled around as Uncle Dux punched him again.

Random spells shot out from them. When a dark spell hit a target, the unfortunate being instantly disintegrated. As spells of light hit a target, the victim was hurtled backwards twenty feet. Stars of white and black exploded around them, light clashing with dark. They continued to circle and clash again.

Amber swooped low, tucked her wings in, and set the flat of her blade on her knees. She crashed into a wyvern, crushing it with her momentum. Amber stood, wiping sweat from her forehead. She yelped as two wyverns lunged at her. She jumped upwards and the wyverns crashed into each other. They snarled at Amber and spat at her. She twirled and dodged as she flew higher.

Gloria saw a wyvern charge. She ran and dove into a nearby trench. She gasped for breath and jumped when she saw someone else there.

Gloria yelped, "Oh! Njord! You scared me!"

Njord sighed with relief, "And you as well."

They both watched as a wyvern flew over them. Amber grabbed it by the tail and threw it at nearby magicians.

Gloria said, "Are you feeling the effects of the curse?"

Njord nodded, "The curse will attempt to persuade us to shed blood. We must be strong, we are able to resist it."

Gloria said, "What's all happening?"

Njord said, "The curse will tempt us, as long as we do not shed blood, we do not need to worry. Lapsus is utilizing Fallen magicians and wyverns. They are using grade four imbued celestial steel. Do utilize caution when contacting the Fallen magician. The blades, I would theorize, are cursed with darkness. They will cause you to suffer tremendous pain."

Gloria shrugged, "Another day, eh?"

They flinched as a wyvern fell over their trench.

Njord said, "Please be careful."

Gloria, sensing genuine concern, smiled, "You too."

They leaped from the trench and Gloria saw Njord fire lightning at several magicians. Gloria rolled under a magician's legs and kicked her legs up hard. As she stood, the magician keeled over in pain. Gloria took him from his misery, dropping an ice block on his head.

See, Gloria thought huffily, *I am not a monster. I do not enjoy watching suffering.* A voice cackled in her head, and Gloria sighed, "This is beginning to get weary."

Gloria watched as Fornacem joined the battle. His insane smile stretched across his face. As he cackled, some of the enemies ran. He picked one up by the throat and threw him. Gloria's jaw dropped as the poor magician disappeared over the mountain peak.

Fornacem turned to Gloria, a mad gleam in his eye, "I feel like I'm playing in a children's sandbox." He plucked another magician and threw him, "Yeet!" Gloria shuddered as he bellowed in laughter and ran away.

Gloria shook her head, "He's a loose cannon." Gloria watched him bound towards Lapsus.

Fornacem yelled, "Put me in, coach!" Uncle Dux nodded, stepping back. Fornacem landed in front of Lapsus and advanced, cracking his knuckles.

Lapsus sneered, "Have you had your fun, immortal?"

Fornacem grinned, "Almost. All I have to do is *kick your ass.*"

Lapsus, "What are you without magic?"

Fornacem's smile wavered, "I am Fornacem Factorem!" He roared, "I made my peace *long* ago! You would do well not to dig up bones."

Lapsus smiled widely, "Have you? Then feel no fear as you face me!"

Lapsus' aura exploded around him. He bellowed and flew at Fornacem, who sidestepped easily. He yawned as Lapsus attacked again.

Fornacem said, "Quit embarrassing yourself. Your army is nearly gone. Another pass through by me, and you will fight alone."

Lapsus leaped again, Fornacem lodged a fist in Lapsus' stomach. If he wasn't holding his power back, Gloria thought Lapsus would have exploded. As it was, he fell to his knees and heaved. Fornacem looked down in disgust.

Fornacem said, "Lapsus... to be honest, I suspected you to betray me, straight from the beginning. You want to know *why* I didn't kill you then?" Fornacem grabbed Lapsus' hair, forcing him to look in his eye. Fornacem's eyes gleamed red, "I loved watching you suffer. You have been such a *pain* in the ass to me and to my family." He added hastily, "Now... Now that

I've got you in my clutches... I am going to be merciful... and end your *pathetic* suffering."

Lapsus groaned as Fornacem pulled his head back and snarled, "You... You really *are* a monster."

Fornacem smiled, "Damn proud too." Gloria gasped as Lapsus caught Fornacem's face with a spell.

Lapsus stood over him, shaking his head. "Sorry, Fornacem... But it's not you who will claim my life." Lapsus chanted, "*Aetherem nigrum voco. Nihil abiicias ad consumendum. Destruam et sequar te. Tactus mortis.*"

An orb of crackling static the size of marble shot Fornacem in the eye. The smile froze on Fornacem's face. Gloria gasped, as he fell to the ground.

Lapsus snarled, "Recover from that, then kill me, *you damn freak.*"

Amber appeared in a gust of wind, Ignis next to her. Cybele and Bovi gasped from behind Gloria. Arthur, Njord, and Uncle Dux rushed to Fornacem. Uncle Dux checked his pulse.

He gasped, "What... What did you do? *What* did you *do?*" Uncle Dux stood suddenly, his aura crackling loudly. Lapsus leered and a black symbol burned above his palm. Uncle Dux, Njord, and Arthur gasped when they saw it.

Lapsus, "Simple Dux Factorem... I've killed a god."

Everything slowed down as Lapsus pointed to Njord, "Now... I shall kill a child." Lapsus swiped his hand sideways. Arthur and Dux were blasted back. He pointed to Njord, "Know that you will die slowly and painfully. Just as you deserve, you half breed monster."

Gloria's breath froze in her lungs. She watched as Njord's eyes widened in fear. She watched everyone around her move... but they would be too late. In that moment, Gloria understood. A chilling voice whispered in her ear, *"Poor Angelo... they'll all be too late... as I'm sure you know..."* A single tear rolled freely down Gloria's face, reflecting the red moon above.

The voice sighed, "You can still *save* him *you know*... he's not *gone* yet... however, you must decide now, *Angelo*." Gloria heard the echoing screams of the damned, their souls charring in the pits of Hell.

The voice spoke in a false sympathy, "He cares for you... you know. He hasn't told you... and he's not going to... not for a while yet... We are a part of you, we can feel your heart throb with longing. You too will care for him, *more* than you do already, someday."

A blade of static descended towards Njord, who raised his hands over his eyes. Gloria gasped as she saw him look at her. The voices purred, *"Ooooh... how adorable...* he wishes for you to be his last sight. *How... sickeningly... touching..."*

Gloria glanced at her family. The voices said, "Your family... need not to suffer. Neither does your beloved friend. Time's ticking, *Angelo*. You will gain much, but you will lose much. Your memory will fade in the time in which you slumber. However, you will be free of us."

Voices hissed unintelligible whisperings.

The voice continued, "After... of course... one last visit... I *adore* blood, *Angelo*. I think you know what you must do..."

Gloria's hand curled in a fist and a red circle of light blazed in her eyes. The voice whispered, "I shall help you make this painless... Use your anger, *Angelo*. Let your wrath consume you. It will annihilate the enemy... Do not worry... your victims are already here."

A tall shadowy figure appeared in front of Gloria. Two purple eyes gleamed maliciously, he held a hand to Gloria, a blood red fire crackled in his palm.

Gloria stared at the demon, "Do we have a deal? *Angelo*?"

Gloria heard screams in her head, and a pleading voice, nearly lost in chaos. A loud buzzing made Gloria's ears bleed. Gloria's vision blackened. When she could see, her hand was held in the demon's ice-cold clutches.

The demon smiled, "Happy hunting, *Angelo*."

Gloria's vision was awash with red, and her body moved on its own.

Lapsus yelled as the blade sliced downwards. A gold flash nearly blinded him, the blade was smacked aside, where it shattered.

Lapsus gasped, taking a few steps back. An aura exploded around the figure, a dull bronze fading to blood red. The halo above her head burned red. Her shimmering gold wings opened a stained red. Her eyes were full of fire and blazing crimson. She pointed to Lapsus and snarled.

Lapsus threw his hand over his head, he yelled, "*T-Transportavit*! Attack!" Hundreds of magicians' auras burst to life and charged. The golden figure snarled and disappeared.

The Factorems backed away in horror as the mark of the Blood Moon Curse howled in laughter. Blades of bronze light flashed in the angel's hands. They whirled, hissing in the air. Skin tore, flesh ripped, and blood flew. The demonic creature lay waste to the Fallen army.

Uncle Dux gasped. Arthur said, "Dux, what is she doing?"

Uncle Dux shook his head, "The curse has consumed her. Everyone, stop her now!"

A golden flash flickered through the army, scarlet waves following. A red circle appeared on the creature's shoulder, blazing just left of its heart. The outline of a red crescent moon glared through stained cloth. Heads of victims flew up, to be sliced into pieces. Crimson victims splattered to the earth. The soil howling as it absorbed the fear and the copper taste of blood.

A white wall of light blazed in front of the golden demon. It snarled, slicing the wall in half. Dux appeared behind it, "Gloria! Snap out of it!" He yelped as a blade of stained gold shredded the ground next to him.

Don't worry Angelo... I always uphold my side of the bargain... I will not destroy your family... doesn't that sound swell? You are doing well, keep going, destroy the enemy.

Arthur spread his arms wide, and the golden demon hesitated. "It's us! Your family! Please stop this!"

The demon disappeared, sliding through the man's legs. Ice spikes shot from it, and many necks fell victim to a blood thirsty fate. Fallen magicians fell to the stained earth. One gasped, "Please... have... mercy..." There was a flash of gold, and scarlet danced onto the earth.

Amber flew in front of the monster, "Gloria! Stop! The enemy is retreating!"

The monster dodged the flying Dragonborn, bearing into another victim.

"*Yes,*" a voice crooned, "*Excellent, Angelo.*"

Two Bull Bestia surrounded the angel. Strong hands pinned her arms to her sides. She snarled as Cybele said, "Gloria! Wake up! You're falling to the curse!"

The angel snarled, kicking the Bestia in the face. It stepped onto the earth and flipped the other Bestia to the ground.

"*Don't worry Angelo... they will live.*"

The angel shot towards another magician, slicing him at the waist. What remained of the man tried to crawl, "Help! Somebody, help!" The angel beheaded the pitiful.

It shot forward to a crowd of magicians. A bronze flash entrapped them in a block of ice. The angel swung her hands, and the golden blade grew to the length and width of a bus. The angel roared, throwing it sideways. A blue flash deflected it from its victims.

Ignis appeared, "Gloria... please... don't make me hurt you. I know that you are still in there."

The voice cackled, "*He may be right, Angelo... but you are mine for the time being!"*

The angel roared, unloading the blade, swinging it sideways. Ignis kicked the blade up. He flew forward and kicked the angel in the stomach. The blade broke. The angel stumbled shakily to its feet.

Amber turned frantically to Dux, "What's wrong with her?"

Uncle Dux shook his head, "The curse has corrupted her! It- It's like some form of control, something is controlling her."

Amber gasped, "Not... Not the *curse*?"

Dux nodded grimly, "The curse has taken her."

The angel screamed and hundreds of ice spikes flew at Ignis. He dodged, ducked, and yelped as one sliced his leg. He fell to the floor and looked up to see the angel smiling. It flicked his head and he fell unconscious to the ground.

A static vision blurred the angel. It held seven blurred figures. The figure in the center smiled widely, "Excellent, you are almost there *Angelo*. Keep going, and you shall be rewarded."

The angel screamed, and the ice containing the magicians rattled. The walls sunk into the earth. The screams and pleads were silenced. The angel took a step forward, a green light glowed behind her. It turned around, blood dripping from its hands. Njord took a steady breath, his eyes were glowing brightly.

He said, "Gloria... you helped me... now let me help you." He held out a hand, "You do not need to do this... please, come back to us, come back to me."

The angel hesitated, a feeling of uncertainty stabbed at a beating heart.

The voice scoffed, "He must really care for you to rival *me*. No matter, it will be done quickly. Don't worry, *Angelo*, he'll survive."

The light in the angel's eyes blazed brighter. She

screamed, hands covering her eyes. The golden blades appeared. She lowered her hands and crimson liquid dripped from her face. She snarled and lunged.

Njord dodged the first swing. The angel screamed, swinging again.

Njord said, "Please Gloria. Come back to us. We need you. We love you."

The angel groaned; its vision burned with static. The voice scoffed, "Don't worry, *Angelo*, it won't hurt for long."

The angel screamed, an inhuman sound, and lunged again.

Njord threw out his arms and caught the angel. Embracing her, he spoke in a shaky voice. "You cannot leave me, Gloria. I did not have the time to tell you how grateful I am to have you. I wanted to tell you on Earth, I... that I cared for you, deeper than you may realize. I do not care if you do not return my feelings! Answer me! Tell me that you are there!"

The angel groaned, blood red images flashed through its mind.

Njord muttered, "Captains' log... she has lost her memory... I had attempted to inform her of my feelings... but she had forgotten. She has changed, however, I feel the same... What should I do?"

The memory crackled and the voice said, "No! That is far in the future! After I have succeeded!"

Another memory blazed behind the angel's eyes. Julia said, "Don't worry, Gloria... change is perfectly normal. It's a part of life. Humans evolved, they changed for the better!"

The memory buzzed. The voice said, "Only I may reveal fate, and that is what this is... yes... I am helping you achieve your destiny. It is your fate!"

An image flashed. The angel gasped. She saw Njord holding her. Tears spilled from their eyes. He cared for her... he wanted to help her... he was holding her... as though he cared immensely.

The image shifted, a Njord in a colored shirt smiled from a desk.

A stranger's voice said, "How he thinks when talking to me, that book, and what he's writing about me!" The Njord smiled shiftily, "Fortunately, Njord would be glad that you forget. If that makes you feel better."

For some reason it didn't, it made the angel's heart ache. She wanted to remember. She didn't want to forget. She wanted to know why she hurt. Why did she feel pain? She hurt in battle. She hurt in her dreams. This was different... Why did she hurt? She doesn't understand... She must understand... It hurts. It hurts so much. Why can't she ask, why does she hurt so much?

The angel took a ragged breath and red tears spilled from her eyes.

The voice purred, "Aww, I'm sorry *Angelo*. You will be blind to his feelings again. And you cannot return them. You will have to forget. Don't worry, *Angelo*, one day, you will understand your feelings, and you just might be able to return them. Until then, hold blindly to his heart."

The angel screamed. She tore from Njord, ducking under his arm. Blades of gold burned in her hands and stained tears trickled from her face. Death... a red death was purged from innocent veins. Screams were silenced, pleas, ignored, and mercy... mercy had perished long ago.

"No!" Gloria screamed and pounded on bars of static. She watched through red eyes, unable to control, unable to unhear, and unable to feel. Gloria fell to her knees. Tears fell from her eyes, "Please! I don't want to do this! I don't want to forget! Please don't let me forget!"

A red light blazed under Gloria. An infinite red abyss gaped below the cage. Roars, screams, groans, and inhuman noises flooded from the pit. The pit whispered something

Gloria couldn't hear. There was a quiet clank, and the cage slowly lowered, closer to the infinite pit.

Gloria screamed, "Please! Somebody, help! Anybody! Please help me!" She sobbed, collapsing to the floor of the cage. Her tears flowing into the red abyss below her.

A golden light flared weakly in front of Gloria. She gasped. The glowing figure from her dreams. The pure halo, the golden wings reached out to her.

Gloria gasped and reached her arms through the bars. The inches fell away and Gloria touched a cold surface. The angelic figure disappeared. She stared into a red mirror.

Gloria sat alone in a cage of static. Blood drenched her clothes. Her arms were soaked in it. Her tears turned red as they fell from her face.

Gloria gasped and fell to the cage floor. She sobbed as the cold compressed around her. A memory flickered. Njord's voice, "Captains' log... It is approximately five weeks until... *Valentine's Day*. Umbra Mortis forced me to sleep. I now predict that this may have been necessary."

Gloria gasped, she slowly looked up into the memory. Njord scratched his head. He looked tired. His tie was crooked, and he wore a stained shirt. "Gloria still has not awoken. Neither has Fornacem. I... I do not understand the mortal ritual of Valentine's Day... However, Amber informed me I required a valentine."

Njord blushed, "Someone I cherish... Amber hoped I would ask Gloria... She has not awoken, however... I wonder what she would say."

Gloria screamed, "I will Njord! I will be your Valentine!"

Njord sighed, "Day fifty-two... following the Blood Moon Curse. Gloria... please... wake up."

Another warm memory flashed. Gloria could see her surroundings. She was lying in what looked like her bed. Njord was sitting, writing in a small black notebook. He yawned, brushing a feather from his shoulder, writing. "Captains' log. It has been a week since Gloria fell ill, and a week into my research. Dux claims she should have awoken by now. The fact that she has not... No! I refuse to believe that! She still produces a pulse! She is alive!"

Gloria shook her head. *I don't remember these, are they mine?*

Gloria gasped as a voice cackled around her, "I know what it may seem, but... fate is what *will* happen... is it not? I think *you* are smart enough to connect the dots..."

Was this from the future? Was Gloria to be ensnared in this wretched fate? A cold cackling answered her question.

The memory shifted. Njord looked worse. His tie was loose, his shirt buttoned incorrectly. He had bags under his eyes.

Njord yawned, "The others are beginning to grow worrisome... I realized that the only facilities that I have visited in three weeks are the bathroom, my office, and this room. They beg me to quit my research, to sleep. However, I refuse. No matter how much I may require, I promised I would not rest until I discover what is plaguing Gloria." Njord flinched as he drifted to sleep. He shook his head, "My research shows no relevant information. The Blood Moon Curse is rarely recognized, however, no victim has ever fallen into slumber for this long."

Gloria gasped as another memory flashed. Njord looked worse. He was missing his tie, severely unlike him. Both his eyes were glowing, though one was brighter than the other. His head was resting in his hands. He sighed, "Day... day seventy... I... I have prided myself in seeking knowledge. And yet..."

Gloria felt fresh tears roll down her face. Njord looked up, his eyes were red and bloodshot, he had tears welling in his eyes. He shook his head, "I... I wish to deny my logic for the first time... I am ignoring the fact that it has never led me astray. Gloria has been asleep for so long... Fornacem has awoken. He is suffering, but he is ok... Why?"

Njord threw the notebook to the floor. His voice shook, "What must I do? What must I do to hear her laugh? What must I give to see her smile one more time? I would give anything! Do whatever I must-" His voice broke, and he sank to his knees, "I... I am nearing the end of my road. I... I do not wish to give up."

Gloria gasped as Njord stared into her eyes, "Whatever lord I must ask... I beseech you... give Gloria back."

A cold voice said, "There... can't have you descending into madness, *Angelo*. Here is your happiness, until you are reunited with them. Humans have their determination, use these memories until they fade. Fight for your life, *Angelo*."

The angel flinched as she found herself kneeling in a blood soaked field. The smell of lavender burned in her nose. It looked at its hands, dried blood to her elbows. It lowered them and stared into the red moon. It cackled at the angel and roared with laughter at its fate.

The angel chuckled, then it froze and screamed, a loud, demonic sound. It tore blood afresh from its throat, but still it screamed. Its body lay surrounded by red death. It screamed still. Anger poured from every fiber of its being. As it roared, dark liquid fell from its stained fingertips, and crimson fell to the earth.

A red light filled the angel's vision. The moon called. The light became brighter. The angel fell.

Njord slid to the ground, "Gloria!"

He set his head against her chest and cried out in relief, "She- She is alive! She is alive!" He whipped around seeing somber faces.

Dux Factorem said, "I don't believe it. She may live, but the curse took her. It stole her from us. She is trapped in the trance until it is done with her."

Arthur said frantically, "There... there must be *something* we can do Dux! A-A spell, or... or a relic! Anything, please!"

He stopped suddenly, as tears rolled from Dux's eyes, "It's too late Arthur... the curse took her... now... all we can do is wait... and hope..."

CHAPTER 18: GLORIA
The Seven Deadly Sins Converge

Gloria gasped in wonder as she looked around, surrounded by what seemed like a forest, but instead of trees and color, there was only static. The static took the shape of trees and bushes everywhere she looked. She stood on the brink of a crackling abyss. In front was a small village, stone buildings with clay tiled roofing. Most of the windows were dark, like the sky. Moonlight shimmered on the smooth surface of a lake.

Gloria heard a shuffling. Two figures were sitting in the grass behind tall bushes, covered in black shadows. Gloria saw purple eyes gleam from the figure on the right. It spoke, "Do you feel it Satan? There is suffering like I've never seen before in this village. It's almost overpowering. It tastes *divine*."

Red eyes glowed from the second figure and a gruff voice said, "Aye, but why the hell did yeh bring me here? Knowin' yeh, yeh'll make bags of it."

Purple eyes purred, "Oh, come on Satan. You're the best backup I could ask for. Beelzebub would have gone insane smelling the suffering. Asmodeus will fill her pants with all these humans."

Satan scowled, "I don' wan' teh hear that, yeh moran. Feck, whatever, les' just crack on."

Gloria watched them stand and shove through the bushes. They were tall, two foot taller than she was. She followed and jumped in surprise at the tail, sleek and red like a rat's, hanging behind the figure named Satan. Just as fast as Gloria saw it, it was covered in shadow.

Gloria watched as they passed two humans. Priests, she thought. They were dressed in black clothes with closed collars. The shadowy figures must have been invisible, as neither man noticed them.

Purple eyes glittered, the figure smiled, and the shadow on its face parted, revealing pointed teeth. It brushed its finger against the back of one priest's neck. The man whirled around, looking past the dark figures, but said nothing.

The second priest tapped his shoulder, "Alright there, Alexander?"

Alexander said, "I... I felt a dark presence. It was strong, dark, and evil... the most satanic aura that I've ever felt."

The second priest shook his head, "You must be imagining things. Come on, we need to get back, it's late." The priest hesitated but nodded and followed the other.

Satan smacked the back of purple eyes head, "What are yeh thinkin', yeh fecker? Are yeh a moran, *Lucifer*?"

Lucifer chuckled, "Sorry, Satan. Couldn't resist."

Satan shook his head, "And yeh worried 'bout *Asmodues*."

The two continued, stopping at a rundown building, two stories tall, with stone bricked walls. Tall torches flickered in a cold wind. The lights were on inside and Gloria heard drunken voices singing.

Satan growled, "A feckin' manky ass *guild*?"

Lucifer nodded, "It would appear so."

They strode through large wooden doors, Gloria hastily following in their wake. She saw large men in the guild holding pitchers and sloping drinks on the floor and themselves. Many were dancing. The music seemed to come from the air. Gloria saw a wizard playing cards with a nun in a corner.

Satan snarled, "Manky langers."

They walked to the corner where a door was concealed in a shadow behind the stairs. Lucifer smiled, "*Here*, through this door then." They slipped through the door, down creaking stairs, into a cold, dark basement.

As her eyes adjusted, Gloria found herself in a room where a single flickering lantern hung from a frayed rope. The ground was scratched and faded wood, the walls cracked stone brick.

Gloria looked up as a creak sounded from the wood ceiling. A ripped and stained, old blue sofa sat in front of her. A coffee table with a missing leg carried a bloodied knife, a single empty mug, and many empty black bottles. A small recording device crackled from the table.

Gloria approached the couch slowly and gasped. A young Fornacem sat on the sofa. He looked horrid, his face covered in stubble, his hair a mess, and his clothes stained in blood. He was dressed in scratched pants, and a gray shirt. Half a wooden shield leaned against the couch. His red eyes were bloodshot. His unmoving stare made him appear dead.

Gloria saw a shift from the shadows and two maroon eyes gleamed. A voice purred, "Hello, human." Satan appeared behind Fornacem. The figures flanked him, though he made no movement, nor acknowledged them.

Satan scowled, "Manky langer. Why are we here, Lucifer? He's suffered enough, hasn't he?"

Lucifer's grin wavered. "Look at me, human."

Fornacem slowly gazed into Lucifer's eyes. His smile stretched across his face as his eyes filled with ink, and he began to chant in a demonic language. The shadows disguising them fell away and Gloria realized they were demons. Fornacem looked away.

The shadows returned and Lucifer scowled, reared back and smacked Fornacem across the face. Deep gashes appeared, but still Fornacem said nothing.

Lucifer snarled, "No one ignores me." He snapped his fingers and chains appeared from the shadows. They flew through the air, curling around Fornacem like snakes.

Lucifer leered at Fornacem, "Do you know who I am, human?"

Fornacem stared into his eyes and spoke in a monotone voice, "I do not know, and I do not care."

Lucifer snarled, "Don't pretend to be devoid of knowledge! I am Lucifer! The Sin of Pride! The Fallen angel! The angel of death! Is *any* of this ringing a bell?"

Fornacem didn't move, "Do what you must, demon."

The fires in the lanterns flickered. The device on the table crackled with static.

Lucifer said, "Do what I must? I could drag you into Hell. I could peel the flesh from your bones. I could let your soul burn for eternity."

Satan set a hand on Lucifer's shoulder, "Easy mate."

They stared in shock as Fornacem chuckled, then reared his head back and roared with a dry laughter. Lucifer smacked him across the face, "You dare laugh in the face of a demon? I am a true monster."

Fornacem stared into his face, blood mixing with tears. He took a shuddering breath. "You claim to be a *monster*? There is no torture great enough to cause me pain. You can never make me suffer like they have. You could never make me feel as they made me feel. There is no greater hell than the one that I live. My life... My pathetic life... *That* is my hell, and I must live with my sins and mistakes for eternity. All will wither and rot before me, and still, I will not perish. I will suffer long after everything is dust."

Fornacem smiled, "You think you are a monster? You

know *nothing,* demon. Monsters are not beneath beds, or haunting nightmares. They do not kill or roar in the night." Fornacem shook his head. "True monsters walk among you. They live next to you. They stretch a false smile across their face before digging a blade in your shoulder."

The demons backed a step away, "They wear a mask of stone none can see through. They took my soul to hell and back already. My heart is cold and petrified; my soul is dark. The day my soul is dragged into the darkest pit of Hell would be a fresh breath of life. My suffering could end, my madness could rest. There would be no better Heaven than Hell."

The demons said nothing. They were stunned into silence.

Satan shook his head, "He's *mad,* leave 'im be."

Lucifer scowled. He snapped, and the chains dissolved. "Listen here mortal. I enjoy suffering. But *you...* you make me *sick.* I will keep my eye on you, Fornacem Factorem. May your suffering appease me or suffer my undying wrath."

Fornacem said nothing. Lucifer scoffed and swept from the room, disintegrating into the shadows. The chains faded away, and Fornacem fell to the couch. Satan shook his head, following Lucifer into the shadows.

Fornacem shook and slammed his fist against the ground. "You are correct of course. Why didn't I see it before?" He raised his head; a crazed smile strained his face. "I will have my revenge! For too long have I been meek. I will take no more from those *damn* heroes! I will have my vengeance!"

Fornacem stood shakily and the wounds on his face slowly closed. "They will see their blood on the floor, as I laugh. I will destroy them and see their hearts destroyed, as was mine. They think I'm weak? I will show them a monster."

He grabbed the knife from the table and stared at its glint of silver. He roared with laughter and stabbed the blade into his eye.

◆ ◆ ◆

Gloria's head spun. She opened her eyes but saw only darkness. Whispers floated around her. She groaned, and they grew silent. A hand fell over her shoulder. A deep, smooth voice spoke. "*Surgere.*"

Gloria felt a shock surge through her. She yelped, and a grinning face came into view, magenta eyes, teeth pointed like sharks, and long horns curled from combed black hair. As her vision cleared, more of the creature came into view. He wore a black suit and a blood red tie.

Gloria tried to move, realizing she was tied to a simple steel chair. Who dares entrap her? She shook her head; the alien thought fled. The demon held onto the chair back with his hand.

He grinned, pushing the chair. "Hello." The demon smiled. "Welcome to our abode."

Gloria looked around at the large circular room with seven large windows in what seemed to be a makeshift lounge. Outside the windows, cramped buildings could be seen, flames danced on the horizon. Sofas, chairs, and a TV were scattered across the room. An ashtray billowed smoke from a coffee table.

Gloria said, "Where am I?"

A female voice purred from behind her, "Oooh, isn't she *darling?*"

A familiar gruff voice said, "Shut it, *Asmodeus.*"

The demon in front of her sighed. "Now, now, you'll be introduced in a second." The demon grinned, "You're in Hell." It waved his hand, "Sorry, that sounds worse than it is."

A bored voice said, "You're going to scare her, Lucifer."

An angry voice yelled, "Shut it yeh…"

Lucifer laughed, "Ladies, gentlemen, are we not *civilized* demons?" He winked at Gloria, "And angel, if you may." The demon continued, "Before you ask, plead, weep, *no*, you're not dead."

Gloria said, "What... What happened?"

Lucifer smiled, "Well, I took control of your body and forced you to take the Blood Moon Curse."

Gloria gasped; six sets of laughter cackled around her.

Lucifer smiled, "More on that in a second, a few demons are *dying* to meet you."

A shape elbowed Lucifer out of the way, a very young, very attractive woman. Her blue eyes sparkled. Choking perfume made Gloria light-headed. Two small horns poked through white hair. Her hourglass shape would turn the heads of most men. She wore a black leather dress so tight that Gloria would have never worn it. It was covered in tears showing an uncomfortable amount of skin. Several rings glinted from her clawed fingers. A halo tattoo graced her upper thigh.

An uncomfortable warmth flared in Gloria's chest. The demon curled a finger under her chin. "Oooh, she is even more *divine* in person. Makes me just want to eat her up."

Lucifer shoved her out of the way, "No you're not, she's mine. Remember, Asmodeus?"

Asmodeus made an inappropriate gesture, involving her middle and pointer finger in a V shape in front of her chin.

Another demon shoved forward. Shorter than the others, they wore a dirty shirt, with ragged pants and their horns seemed too large for their head. They had green eyes.

They smiled, "Oh, I wish I was young again. What beautiful eyes-"

Lucifer leaned over the top of him, resting his elbows between his horns, "Gold, I know."

Another figure appeared over Gloria's shoulder, far skinnier than the other demons, but slightly taller. Gloria saw a jaw full of silver teeth. Gold chains hung from the various pockets of their sleek suit. Gloria thought how much the metal would be worth before shaking her head.

The demon smiled, "Did someone say gold?" Pure yellow eyes gleamed, "Ahh, yes, what shining eyes."

Asmodeus shoved him aside, "Move Mammon, I wanna look!"

Mammon scowled, "You had your peek, slut!"

The familiar angry voice yelled over all of them. Gloria realized it was a strong Irish accent, "Feck off! The lot of yeh! Let me take a gander."

A large scowling demon appeared over Asmodeus' shoulder. They wore a gray golf cap, low over dark red eyes. It towered over the other demons by at least a foot and was almost twice as wide. They looked strong enough to break a marble column with their bare hands. Large horns curled off its head. It sported a red shirt tucked into black dress pants. A chain replaced a belt. Large red wings sprouted from their back in addition to a sleek tail, like a rat's.

The demon nodded, "She's a fine thing, int' she?"

Gloria snarled, "Untie me! I'll kill you all!"

The large demon smiled. Lucifer said, "Your influence, Satan."

Satan scowled, "Oi! *Belphegor!* Get over here yeh manky feck! Come an' gawk"

Gloria heard a groan from her right, "Settle down *Satan.* It's too early to yell."

Satan scowled, "Fix yeh puss, yeh holy show."

Gloria shook her head, "It's just a nightmare. It's not real." Gloria gasped as she sprawled to the floor. She looked up and saw Lucifer grin.

"Boo."

Gloria yelped and stumbled backward into a pair of thick legs. Satan growled at her, "How ya doin' lassie?" She leapt to her feet only to run into another demon. A chill ran up her spine as a demon breathed down her neck.

Asmodeus ran a finger down Gloria's back, "I *love* humans, can I keep this one?"

Gloria whirled around. Asmodeus folded a twenty-dollar bill in her fingers, and to Gloria's shock, stuck it down the collar of her shirt. Gloria made a noise of indignancy and made to slap the demon.

She giggled, disappearing into a choking cloud of blue. Mammon hung from the roof, snatched the twenty from Gloria's front.

Lucifer flicked it from his finger, "Now, come on, you'll offend her." He glanced over his shoulder, "Restrain yourself, Asmodeus."

Gloria whirled around and stumbled into a lounge chair. Twelve eyes gleamed at Gloria. "B-Back! Get back!" To her surprise, a comet of ice shot from her hands.

Lucifer ducked, "My! Feisty! You heard her folks, back off, let her take a moment."

Gloria shook her head, "Why- Why am I here?"

Lucifer chuckled, "Because you achieved the Blood Moon Curse, my dear."

Gloria said, "Wait, who are you?"

Lucifer grinned, "Lucifer, pride if you may."

Gloria gasped, "Like... Like the Sin? I thought Lucifer and Satan were the same thing?"

Lucifer scoffed, "Stupid humans..... I suppose you've never read The Lanterne of Light, I will make a note to get you a copy."

Asmodeus gave a dazzling smile, "Lust, Asmodeus, you can call me *whatever* you like, love."

Mammon dropped from the ceiling, "Mammon at your services, Greed if you please."

He flinched as Satan knocked the side of his head, "For *payment*, yeh gombeen." He huffed, glaring at Gloria, "Satan, Wrath. An' yeh can eff off as well."

The small demon appeared in between Satan's legs, "Leviathan, Envy."

The last demon appeared from Lucifer's left. He rubbed his sky blue eyes, his eyes were drooping. He wore a wrinkled shirt, and baggy pants. Small horns were visible just above his ears. He yawned, "Belphegor, Sloth."

Gloria glanced over his shoulder, "If I... If you're the... the-"

Lucifer suggested, "The Seven Deadly Sins? The Seven Capital Sins? The Cardinal Sins? We go by a few..."

Gloria said, "Then where's the seventh? Gluttony or something?"

Lucifer sighed, "Unfortunately, he's stuck half formed in the magical realm, in your *sock drawer*."

Gloria said, "What am I doing here?"

Lucifer smiled, "Because you drew blood! You slaughtered your enemy ruthlessly." He shrugged, "With my help of course."

Gloria said, "What... What are you going to do to me?"

Asmodeus squealed, "She is too *cute*! Can I *please* keep her?"

Lucifer scowled, "We all know what *you* would do with her."

Satan lit a cigar with a burst of flame from his finger, "Aye, horny feckin' hag."

Asmodeus snarled, "*Nobody* calls me a hag!"

Satan puffed his cigar. "Doesn' help that yeh're the age o' the dawn a man."

Lucifer smoothly stepped in between the demons as Asmodeus marched towards Satan.

Lucifer chuckled, "We're getting off topic." Asmodeus snarled as Satan flipped her off. Lucifer glanced at Gloria, "Now, we Sins *love* humans, this is true. But we mainly love *blood*." He plucked a cigar from Satan's pocket, "Humans, let's be honest, will *always* sin. They sin from the moment they are born, wanting what the other has, or plotting revenge."

Lucifer twirled the cigar in long fingers. "What are you doing here? Simple, I wanted to tell you about your... *conditions.*"

Gloria stared, "What conditions?"

Lucifer smiled. He flicked the cigar back to Satan, "The conditions of which you fell to the Blood Moon Curse. And of course, what you'll become."

Gloria's heart raced. She felt light-headed, like leaning over the edge of a cliff.

She stammered, "N-No, I couldn't have, I-I would never."

Asmodeus giggled from behind her hands, "I said the same."

Lucifer waved a hand, "Now, I always know when to strike. I know human weakness."

Satan scowled, "Aye. Sadistic feck."

Lucifer shook his head, "Humans are *always* the same. Too predictable *not* to have fun with. If someone, or something, you cared for was in danger... I knew you'd do *anything* to help."

Asmodeus moaned from the corner. "*Love*, it's a bittersweet thing. But Lucifer... How did you know? Wasn't that farther up in... *fate*?"

Lucifer shook his head, "Well, technically it was, but I had a suspicion for the future."

Mammon smiled, "Flip of the old coin?"

Lucifer smiled, "You were always a gambler, Mammon."

Gloria said, "Wait! What do you mean, what will I become?"

Lucifer laughed and strolled to Gloria. "*Still* haven't figured it out? *Angelo?*" He smiled, "As they say, you've done a deal with the *devil*." He turned away, "Of course, there are a few complications, which I hope you can endure of course."

Gloria shook her head, "What-"

Satan snarled, "Jesus, Mary, an' Joseph! Leg it already!"

Lucifer smiled, walking slowly towards Gloria, "You are, I am sure, aware of the Blood Moon Curse?" Gloria hesitated. Lucifer continued, "You humans have sort of predicted what it does. It does *not* change you into a demon."

Satan said, "Naw."

Lucifer said, "It *can* create demonic power. A simple human can become a demon since they fall for sin. In humans with magic, things get more *interesting*." Lucifer's eyes gleamed, "For magicians, it bestows upon them power from which they are descended."

Gloria watched Lucifer pace. He smiled, "What happens during a Blood Moon Curse? The moon collects blood and gives it to the sins. Humans have sinned. As time wore on humans became more aggressive." Lucifer continued, "Some of the worse despots in history, Hitler, Mussolini, Stalin. The curse requires the blood of many. During war, it sometimes adds up, but the politics are exhausting."

Lucifer sighed, "*Anyways*, why *are* you here? Good question. After all, *you* didn't draw a summoning circle, *you* didn't have the thirst to kill, and *you* most *certainly* didn't want to."

Gloria said, "Then... then why am I here? Why did I suffer the curse?"

Lucifer held up a finger, "Why are you *suffering*, you're under the curse right now, be thankful we're speeding up your evolution."

Gloria's head spun, she suddenly felt sick, "Evolution?"

Lucifer smiled, "Which brings me to my next topic. *I* forced you into killing countless human lives. I *certainly* didn't want you to turn into a demon."

Lucifer walked slowly towards Gloria, "So... *Why* did I bring you here? *Why* are the seven deadly sins *themselves* bothering to meet you? *Why?*" Lucifer smiled, his magenta eyes flashing, "Simple, *you* are an interesting human, Gloria Factorem. Even *Asmodeus*, surprising as it may seem, has grown, well, *obsessive* over you."

Satan spoke from the couch, "Damn melter, yeh're bein' *generous.*"

Lucifer said, "Well, she is what she is, the incarnation of Lust, after all."

Lucifer smiled, setting his hands on either side of the chair, "Now then... What will befall *you*? Gloria?"

Gloria realized she was trembling. Lucifer shook his head, "*Ooh*, am I *scaring* you? *Terribly* sorry." He looked thoughtful, "Where was I? Right. What will become of you? Now that you've successfully fallen for the Blood Moon Curse? Well... you aren't a demon... Do you know *why*?"

He released the arms as the chair and circled Gloria as she began to think. "Let me give you a small hint." He appeared in front of her, "What do you think when you hear *Hell*? A place of damnation? Fiery pits of eternal suffering? Well, sometimes.

You see... There are only *two* afterlives." He hesitated, "Well, most people believe that. But yes, Heaven and Hell. Hell is the place where sinners go. Sinners become unfit for Heaven, so they come to Hell. Mostly because they're too prideful to admit sins. Think of Heaven as... um... oh! Think of Heaven as the *Harvard* of the afterlife. You have to avoid sin your *whole life*? Well, no wonder people end up in Hell.

Anyway, Heaven and Hell, they are opposing ideas, right? Red and fiery, white and pure, think on this.... angels and demons...opposites, hmm?" Lucifer said, "Well, demons were depicted with *fire*. If angels are opposites of demons, then what is the opposite of fire?"

Gloria hesitated. Mammon said, "Ooh! I know!"

Satan smacked the back of his head, "Yeh haven' a bloody

notion! Yeh feckin' chancer!"

Lucifer said, "*Ice*. Yes, the magic race of mortals believed that the Golden Ice was used by angels, and the Flames of Destruction by demons."

Asmodeus giggled. Satan scoffed, "The right *morans*."

Lucifer ignored them, "So, through the power of belief, it became true. Long story short, fire users were thought to be the image of devils. While ice users, the image of angels."

Gloria swallowed. Her heart raced faster.

Lucifer took a slightly more menacing tone, "What does that mean? *Angelo*? If you're not a demon...then you are an *angel*." Lucifer shrugged, "Well, you will be the most unique angel of your kind. Almost like a mortal archangel, really. You'll have the proper figure, golden wings, oh, be sure to keep track of your halo. If you break or lose it, you will be extremely uncomfortable. It can regenerate, just so you know." Lucifer hesitated, "Oh yeah, you won't remember any of this. Guess there's no point telling you."

The Sins stood and began edging closer to Gloria. Asmodeus giggled. Satan grinned. Mammon dragged Belphegor from his chair, and Leviathan leaped into the front. They surrounded Gloria. She trembled and tried forming her aura, but only a cold mist plumed from her hands.

Lucifer smiled, "Well, I think you should have a wonderful evolution."

Asmodeus moaned as Lucifer raised a hand to Gloria's head. "Wait, Lucy! Am I *ever* going to see her again?"

Lucifer rolled his eyes, "*Yes*, Asmodeus, you'll see her again."

Gloria yelped, "Wait! What do you mean by that? What do you mean *you'll see me again*?"

Lucifer looked slightly surprised. He snorted, and the demons roared with laughter. Even Belphegor was laughing. Lucifer said, "I suppose there's no harm telling you. In a year or so, let's just say... there will be *hell* to pay... and us Sins will be *glad* to join the fun!"

Asmodeus wined, "Is she gonna forget me?"

Lucifer sighed, "*Yes,* Asmodeus, she *has* to. It's the *deal.*"

Gloria gasped, "Wait! Why do I have to forget? I don't want to forget!"

Asmodeus smiled, "*Awww,* how cute! You humans are *so cute!*"

Lucifer hesitated, "Well, I suppose we can't send her off without a proper explanation. I suppose she *will* forget...what the hell."

Lucifer glanced at Gloria, "Right, a few words then. First, I assure you that you *will* survive your slumber. Many perished, but they were not like you."

Satan muttered, "Aye."

Lucifer said, "Second, you will be forced into a three-month nightmare that began in early November. You'll wake up a little over a week before Valentine's Day."

Asmodeus smiled, "Oh... How *enticing,* romance before horrendous disasters!"

Lucifer said, "Now, since I'm so *nice,* I'll allow you to hold onto a few pathetic memories to keep you sane. I daresay you will face a horrible fate when you awake."

The demons crowded around, and Lucifer rested a finger on Gloria's head. As her head filled with a red fog, Lucifer spoke. "I grant thee power beyond your dreams, *Angelo,* but at a heavy price. You fell to Sin, and now... you'll pay the price."

Gloria felt a searing pain cover her body, as though a million red hot needles pressed against her. It was pain beyond what Gloria had ever felt. Before she could scream, her sight went dark, and she fell to the ground.

Asmodeus peered worryingly over Satan's shoulder, "Oooh, is she going to be alright Lucy?"

Satan shrugged her off, Lucifer smiled, "She'll be fine."

Satan growled, "Aye, I don' know Lucifer... looks banjaxed teh me. Wasn' she sayin' shit bout' the future?"

Lucifer nodded, "A *strange* effect. Memories from a future that has yet to come to pass. Emotions from the future... strange."

A red halo flared over Gloria's head. It faded into a dull red and a bright golden speck of light circled within the halo. Gloria shifted restlessly, as though having a bad dream.

Lucifer smiled, "Well, it's different for everyone of course. Needless to say, we will be seeing each other again, *real* soon."

Mammon scowled, "Not another curse?"

Lucifer shook his head, "No, Mammon... there's more blood to come... far more than the moon will hold. We'll be there to... help things along."

A dark shadow blackened the room. Twelve eyes blazed briefly and were lost in the cold, black abyss.

CHAPTER 19: IGNIS
The Demon with Lavender Eyes

Ignis stared at the moon as it shifted. The mark of the Blood Moon Curse exploded, scattering black stars into the skies. The moon remained red as a faint hissing filled the night air. An intoxicating smell of lavender burned in Ignis's nose. The grass in the entire valley was painted red. Ignis and everyone else ran to Gloria's side.

Njord turned to Uncle Dux, "She- She still has a pulse! She cannot be..."

Uncle Dux set a finger against Gloria's neck and sighed with relief, "Thank the lords, she's alive. But I shudder to think about what will happen to her."

Ignis said, "What's going to happen?"

Everyone gasped as a red light flared above Gloria's head. A red halo blazed. A red light slowly orbited inside the halo. Gloria shifted restlessly, as though experiencing a night terror.

Arthur glanced around, "Where is Fornacem. He should know about this."

Ignis glanced around, he pointed, "There."

Ignis and Uncle Dux ran to his side. Uncle Dux froze, "*What* the hell?"

Fornacem's eyes were wide open. One red eye started blankly into the air. The other eye was filled with a crackling static which arced and hissed. The static fluctuated, and Fornacem jumped, as though shocked. He muttered under his breath and smiled suddenly but didn't move.

Uncle Dux shook his head, "What happened? Is this some kind of twisted curse?" He looked behind him, "Hey, Bovi? Can you help us?"

Bovi walked over. Uncle Dux said, "Let's... Let's just carry them inside for now, alright?" Bovi nodded. He threw Fornacem over his shoulder easily.

They walked over to Gloria. Amber and Cybele lifted her.

Njord appeared by her side. "Is she alright? What is going to happen? What do we do?"

Uncle Dux shrugged helplessly, "We can't do anything to oppose the Blood Moon Curse. The one person who might have knowledge of this is unable to tell us anything."

Njord said, "What of Umbra Mortis?"

Uncle Dux said, "I don't know. We'll ask right away."

Everyone froze as Gloria muttered in her sleep. The halo brightened, and Gloria whimpered.

The door creaked as Uncle Dux pushed it open. It took a while to carry Gloria up the stairs, and into the dining room. They set her on a chair and sat in silence. Bovi set Fornacem onto another chair. After what seemed like an hour, Umbra Mortis appeared by Ignis's side.

Umbra Mortis smiled, "How are my little mortals doing?"

Uncle Dux stood suddenly, "You! Tell us what's wrong with Gloria!"

Umbra Mortis glanced at Gloria, "My, my, indeed." He appeared next to her, felt her head, and poked the red halo.

There was a blinding red flash, and a small explosion. Umbra Mortis was blasted to the other side of the room, he groaned, and fell to the ground. "Son of a *bitch,* that hurt!"

Uncle Dux said, "Well?"

Umbra Mortis dusted himself off, "Obviously, she's been tricked into the Blood Moon Curse."

Uncle Dux said, "What do you mean?"

"Throughout the millennia it has always been the same. Some poor human is fighting a war too big for them. They get in a tough spot and *lookie here!* They freak the hell out and destroy the enemy."

Julia said, "But... Gloria would never do that."

Umbra Mortis continued, "Neither would most people. However, the Seven Deadly Sins connect with this curse." He sat unsuspended in the air, "It's always the same... as they say, history repeats itself. The Sins tempt the poor person into making a deal. They fall along the same categories. They give brief power to the individual and kill for them. So, they achieve the Blood Moon Curse."

Julia gasped, Arthur said, "So you mean to say that Gloria is possessed?"

Umbra Mortis shook his head, "Let me finish. There are a few things off about this curse."

Uncle Dux said, "Like what?"

Umber Mortis continued, "Well, first, Gloria didn't make a blood circle. She didn't connect her life to the moon. She didn't want to kill, but she was selected anyway. *Why?* Why was she selected? She didn't do anything to contribute to the curse! They were her enemies, sure, but they sure as hell weren't innocent!"

Arthur said, "But, didn't she kill those people?"

Umbra Mortis said, "No, she was possessed; she wasn't in control."

Uncle Dux said, "What else?"

"Don't you see? Gloria was chosen *personally*. The Seven Deadly Sins collaborated, plotted, and altered the system themselves. They spied on Gloria, spoke to Gloria, and tricked

Gloria *personally.*"

Uncle Dux shook his head, "What does that mean?"

Umbra Mortis said, "The Seven Deadly Sins *themselves* took interest in a mortal! Something that has *never* happened before! Another thing-" He pointed to the halo hovering above Gloria's head, "What is this? A *halo*? Demons don't have halos. Why would the worst demons in all of creation bestow *heavenly* power?"

Arthur said, "Is she going to survive?"

"Uncertain, there is always the chance of death, insanity, brain implosion. What *I'm* wondering? What is *with* this protection?" Umbra Mortis fired a small spell at the halo. The spell stopped in midair, a tendril of red electricity arched from the halo and ricocheted back, striking Umbra Mortis.

He shook his head, "That's demon magic. Why is *demon* magic protecting something that wears a *halo*? This is a unique case. Possibly the first in a new class."

Uncle Dux said, "But will she *live*?"

Umbra Mortis said, "She will evolve in her slumber, with such power protecting her. It's hard to tell when she will wake up, or what she will evolve into, if she *survives.*"

Njord sat in silence. His eyes blazed fiercely. He suddenly stood, "I will commence research. I beseech all of you to not bother me."

Julia caught his arm, "What are you going to do?"

Njord avoided her eyes, "I will discover what troubles Gloria. No matter what it takes."

Arthur stood in front of him, "Njord. I should have told you sooner... I'm sorry for how I've treated you. You're a good person, and I was wrong to ever think otherwise."

Njord nodded, "Thank you..." With that, he disappeared into the hallway.

Uncle Dux said, "Now, what about Fornacem?"

Umbra Mortis glanced at him. "*WOAH!*" He shoved Bovi

away. "ARE YOU ALL STUPID? WHY DID YOU TOUCH HIM?"

Uncle Dux said, "What's wrong?"

Umbra Mortis said, "He has been struck with *cursed creation*. A spell designed to obliterate any target it strikes. It corrodes the magicules in the target and sends their being back to the first phase of creation. *What remains.*" Umbra Mortis said, "Who touched him? WHO?"

Bovi said, "I carried him up here."

Uncle Dux said, "His hand smacked my face while we were carrying him up the stairs."

Umbra Mortis grabbed Bovi's arm, "Oh, this is bad." He appeared inches from Uncle Dux's face. "This must have been Lapsus' *ace* card. You both have already been infected." Umbra Mortis pointed at Uncle Dux's face.

Ignis saw a small patch of static appear on Uncle Dux's face. It crackled, and Uncle Dux groaned, reaching towards his face.

Umbra Mortis caught his hand, "Don't touch! You'll spread it faster!"

Ignis glanced at Bovi. Large patches of static were spreading up his arm and along his shoulder. He waved his arm as though trying to shake off an animal. Tendrils of static arched from his arm, hissing in the air. They spread from his hand and arm. Bovi groaned and fell to his knee.

Cybele gasped, "Bovi!" She ran to his side.

Umbra Mortis appeared in front of her. "Don't touch him!" He pointed, "*Translatio, passiva.*" The static stopped growing and froze in place.

Bovi sighed, "Thank you."

Uncle Dux said, "What did you... do..." He collapsed to the floor. Everyone gasped. Umbra Mortis said, "Oops." and teleported next to Dux and touched his face, "*Translatio, passiva.*" He shook his head.

Arthur said, "What did you do? What happened?"

Umbra Mortis waved his hand. Bovi's arm flashed and appeared in a sling.

Umbra Mortis snapped his fingers and Uncle Dux disappeared. "Dux is in the infirmary, no one touches him unless they wish to die a painful death. I've neutralized the curses on them. I did not get rid of them, nor am I able to do so."

Cybele said, "Why did Bovi stay awake?"

"Bestia are naturally stronger than humans. So, they are more resistant to curses. We need to get rid of this curse immediately."

Arthur said, "How do we do that?"

Umbra Mortis shook his head, "I don't know. I'm telling you what I do know. Now, who was the first struck?"

Arthur said, "Fornacem."

Umbra Mortis said, "Directly? Or was he touched?"

Arthur said, "Direct."

Umbra Mortis ran his hands through his hair, "I'm too old for this... We can't do anything for now."

Arthur said, "*What?*"

Umbra Mortis said, "The curse invades the mind, traveling through the mind is a grade A *shit show*. We're in *no* condition to travel through the mind. Especially not *Fornacem's* mind."

Arthur said, "What do we do to cure the curse?"

Umbra Mortis scowled, "I just said! We need to kill the curse at the source. But we can't do that!" He pointed at Bovi, "You can go about as normal, if your arm hurts, find me." Umbra Mortis sighed.

Ignis said, "Now what?"

Umbra Mortis said, "The curse will slowly spread. And we can't do *squat* because if any of us were to travel into Fornacem's mind, we'd die. Dux is already in phase two, Fornacem is suffering phase four. He is only still alive because he's immortal. If anyone finds static on themself, find me immediately."

Ignis said, "How come you can touch it, and why isn't it affecting you?"

Umbra Mortis said, "I'm made of that. There's nothing more it could take from me."

Ignis said, "How come you know so much about it? What happened to you?"

Umbra Mortis said nothing. "Do not ask me that ever again."

Ignis sighed. Bovi occasionally winced as the static on his arm hissed. Amber sat next to Ignis with a sigh. Ignis grabbed a brown bottle from the table.

Amber groaned, "Do you enjoy that? Fine, get it over with."

Arthur said, "Well, we have dealt with the army... now we have other problems. Dux is out of action until further notice, Fornacem too. Gloria is suffering from the curse and won't wake up for who knows how long. We must wait as the infection slowly spreads from Fornacem."

Amber muffled a yelp. Ignis said, "What if we contact the other kingdoms?"

Arthur shook his head, "Can't, none of us know magic like that. Only Dux really did."

Julia said, "What do we do, Arthur?"

Arthur shook his head, "I... I don't know... The best that we can do is wait until one of them wakes up. We'll clean up around here and make things more livable."

They halfheartedly adjourned. Ignis followed Amber to the other room. They repaired the main rooms as best they could. They decided to leave the children underground until further notice. They didn't answer them on when they could come up. They didn't know.

◆ ◆ ◆

Ignis sat with Amber on the canopy of the tree and watched the sun set behind the valley.

Amber sighed, "It's been almost three weeks and Gloria hasn't woken up yet."

Ignis said, "Don't worry, she'll pull through. She's tough." They sat in silence. Ignis said, "Remember how mad she got when we eavesdropped on her?"

Amber smiled weakly, "Or when we started a pillow fight that lasted until midnight?" They chuckled. Amber said, "Are you worried about Njord?"

Ignis hesitated, Njord hadn't slept in days. He visited Gloria every day after dinner, then disappeared into his office. Each time Ignis saw him, he looked worse. Julia suggested he should rest, but he refused.

Ignis said, "We'll all feel better when the others wake up. Arbor's alright, right?"

Amber said, "If you call half his nervous system shredded alright?"

Ignis said, "Well, he says that he is."

Amber rested her head on her arms. Her eyes reflected the sun's light. "I miss Gloria. I want her to wake up."

Ignis nodded, "All we can do is hope."

Amber said, "Arthur has been almost as restless as Njord. He's traveled all over, hasn't he?"

Ignis nodded, "The Capital, the Behemoth Capital, the Kingdom of Hydro, even the Saharan Kingdom. He couldn't get meetings with the kings, or your dad."

Amber said, "And... Umbra Mortis?"

Ignis said, "I think he's mad at me. He hasn't spoken to me."

They fell silent as the sun disappeared behind the valley.

Amber said, "What about Lapsus? He's still alive. What is he plotting?"

Ignis said, "There's nothing we can do. We don't know where he is, and we don't know what he's planning. He hit us hard with something we weren't expecting."

Amber huffed, "Looking to be a very merry Christmas, huh?"

Ignis said, "Well, it's a little over a week 'til then. Maybe they'll wake up, and we can find Lapsus and beat him up."

Amber scoffed, "That would be a Christmas miracle."

Ignis said, "Well, Arthur said that Uncle Dux has improved. A strike to the face is still dangerous though. My dad says we should try to act as normal as possible."

Amber smiled, "Our friends are on the brink of death, our enemy could strike at any moment, and we have no idea what to do about it. On the other hand, happy holidays!"

Ignis snorted. Amber looked at him, "I planted a few mistletoes."

Ignis smiled, "A few? That's generous. You put them over *every* doorway, and every chair. You *do* realize what they mean, right?"

Amber snickered, "*Of course.*" She said, "I can't believe that we can still teach the students."

Ignis nodded. They had cleaned the classrooms and started teaching. Julia substituted for Gloria's class, and Arthur for Njord's. Arbor substituted for Uncle Dux. With Bovi and Cybele there, they were able to open new classes. They both were remarkably surprised the students were anxious to learn from them.

Ignis stood, "We should probably visit Gloria."

Amber stood and stretched. Ignis pushed one of her wings out of the way as he walked to the edge of the canopy. He stretched his arms up and yelped as Amber flew over him, grabbing his hands. With a gust of wind, they flew over the end of the canopy. They flew through the window and into the dining room. They started down the hallway, passing Bovi and Cybele.

Bovi held a notebook and Cybele a few books and notebooks in her arms. Bovi pointed to a page, "We should make a note of that. I think it would be a good idea to review self-defense."

Cybele said, "Go easy Bovi, you're still hurt."

Bovi raised his arm, it was still covered in static, but it hadn't progressed further. It would randomly pulse, disintegrating what was in that hand.

Bovi shook his head, "I... I'm fine Bele. They said that I won't infect anyone else. What's most annoying is how I randomly disintegrate things." As if on cue, the static on his arm pulsed, and the notebook disintegrated.

Cybele pulled another notebook from her stack, "I made copies."

Bovi smiled, "Thanks." They disappeared into their classroom.

Ignis knocked and entered Gloria's room. A few flowers in vases surrounded her bed. Gloria lay sleeping in it. She was surrounded in a faint red light. A couple fireflies flew near her head. Amber tapped Ignis's shoulder and pointed to the side of her bed.

Njord was sleeping in a chair, a pencil in one hand, and a small black notebook in the other. His reading glasses were askew. Ignis gently tapped his shoulder.

Njord opened his eyes, lurching awake, "How long was I asleep?" He shoved his book into his shirt pocket, and ran from the room, tripping on a bed leg.

Amber sighed, "Poor boy. He feels like he needs to help."

Ignis said, "Well, better to be doing something."

They sat in chairs next to Gloria. She was breathing heavily, as though still experiencing a nightmare. She whimpered, the red halo crackled, sending red tendrils of light circling.

Ignis said, "We're trying our best to keep the academy going, Gloria."

Amber said, "I don't know if she can hear us."

Ignis said, "Well, just in case." Ignis said, "Cybele and Bovi are fitting in well as teachers. Uncle Dux is making progress. Arbor is awake. Fornacem is starting to stir."

Amber said, "Um, I don't know if seizures count."

Ignis said, "Well, Umbra Mortis said that it was progress."

Amber said, "When things calm down, we'll have Christmas for you. Um, whenever that is I mean. We can have a snowball fight in Antarctica or something."

They sighed. Ignis said, "I remember when they formed Rem. We destroyed Aurgelmir."

Amber sighed, "Don't mention that; bad memories." They chuckled.

Ignis said, "Well... we still haven't had any word from anyone. Aunt Dottie is ok. Amber hasn't had word from her dad, but we're making progress. According to Umbra Mortis, Uncle Dux should wake up soon. But, if we don't figure out something, the curse will spread into the valley."

Amber blew a raspberry, "Such a stressful situation."

They fell silent. Gloria whimpered and shifted in her bed. Ignis and Amber gasped. Gloria's skin glowed. She floated a few inches off of the bed. Black stars winked around her, slowly orbiting her body. The light spinning in the halo spun slightly faster.

Amber said, "Um... does that count as *progress*?"

Ignis said, "Yeah, I would say so."

They ran to get Umbra Mortis. He followed them into Gloria's room and observed Gloria, floating around her to see every angle. He fetched everyone and they stood in front of the bed.

Umbra Mortis said, "Right, Gloria is now in phase two of the curse. This is preparation for evolution. She is surrounded by layers of magic, anything interrupting the process now will be disintegrated. This phase usually happens a few hours or a day after the curse settles. Not three weeks."

Arthur said, "So... What does that mean?"

Umbra Mortis said, "Well. The magic protecting Gloria is very strong. Meaning that the curse is still setting some sort of power into her. Judging by how long it took to achieve this phase, she won't wake up any time this month."

Everyone gasped. Arthur said, "Not this... month?"

Umbra Mortis said, "No."

Njord swayed, "I have researched the Blood Moon Curse... There are no similar situations to this if one was documented at all."

Umbra Mortis said, "Right. This evolution is unique."

They glanced at Gloria as she muttered in her sleep.

Umbra Mortis said, "She's still alive. Unfortunately, we don't know how much longer she will suffer the curse. I can try something." He slowly approached Gloria and gently set his hand to her head.

The black stars froze in place and a small shockwave rippled through the room. A tall figure emerged from the red halo in a black suit, with a blood red tie, and two horns curled over its head. A sleek red tail and two red wings sprouted from the figure. Two purple eyes flared. They opened their mouth in a wide smile.

The figure bowed, "Hello, mortals." He winked at Umbra Mortis, "And immortals." He stood straight up, "No need to fear. I come in peace. I am Lucifer, the Sin of Pride, the Fallen angel, the angel of death."

Julia whimpered. Umbra Mortis said, "What do you want, demon?"

Lucifer appeared behind Amber. She yelped as he laughed. Lucifer said, "Simple, I wish to speak with you..." He reappeared by the bed and ran a finger across Gloria's face. She whimpered in her sleep.

Arthur roared, "Don't touch her!"

Lucifer retracted his finger, "*Arthur*, is it? Keep your tongue in check. Or I'll rip it out. I come to bring good news. Gloria is a third of the way through her evolution! How exciting!"

He interrupted Njord as he opened his mouth, "Honestly, you mortals are *so* fragile. One hit with cursed creation, and oh... you fall ill." He chuckled. Ignis felt his fist curl. Lucifer smiled at him, "Oh? Is that Wrath I feel? Hmm, typical, all you humans do is sin. Nevertheless, I will share my message." He smiled, "You may not believe me, I do not care. But... the only way to stop the curse is traveling through the mind and stamping it at the source."

Umbra Mortis said, "And where may that be?"

Lucifer cackled, "Don't act like you don't know! You must travel through the mind of a mad man, Fornacem..."

Julia said, "... That's unheard of! The mind is treacherous!"

Lucifer nodded, "Unfortunately, that is true. You will all die otherwise. Fortunately, there is an easier way to navigate."

Lucifer smiled, "Why... power of course... but... *divinity* also helps a bit, hmm."

Arthur scowled, "None of us are of divine blood *or* power!"

Lucifer looked genuinely shocked, "*Never*, in my lifetime have I seen an Elementalist decline divine blood." He looked thoughtful. "And now I feel bad for not telling you anything! Oh... what a conundrum."

Arthur said, "What do you mean?"

Lucifer sighed, "The others will give me *hell* if I tell you anything... Oh... *I* know." He strode to Gloria's wardrobe and opened the bottom drawer. He plucked a sock from the bottom and pulled out a black orb.

The orb glowed brightly as Lucifer held it. Lucifer smiled, "Now, now Beelzebub... I've got you." He chuckled and slipped the orb into his pocket. He strode over to the Factorems, "Right. As payment for returning Beelzebub to me... I will tell you *one* crucial thing that you should do." Lucifer glanced around the room, "Agreed? Satan? Asmodeus? Excellent."

Lucifer sat upon the foot of Gloria's bed, "Right. You are correct. For now, you are unable to act. Once again, you are waiting for the angel."

Arthur said, "What?"

Lucifer said, "You cannot act until Gloria awakes." His purple eyes gleamed, "Sorry. if she wakes, that is... Your only option is to travel into that broken mind. Trudge through insane memories, and not *die* in the process. It *is* a major setback of course... however, no one here wishes to join me in *Hell*, do they?"

No one spoke. Lucifer said, "As I thought. The curse will continue to spread." He pointed to Bovi, "Don't worry, you'll live as long as you distance yourself from Fornacem, until the time comes, that is."

Ignis said, "Tell us what we must do!"

Lucifer smiled, "Oh... those are desperate words, sort of demanding... Thanks, Satan. Oh well." Lucifer said, "Unless Gloria dies... very possible by the way... I recommend sending your strongest warriors to kill the curse. When the time comes, of course." Lucifer said, "Well, I suppose most will be able to go."

He pointed to Arthur, Julia, Arbor, and Umbra Mortis, "If any of you were to go, you would die. Therefore..."

He gestured to Ignis, Amber, Cybele, Bovi, Njord, and

Gloria, "The rest must try. One with the curse already." He glanced at Bovi. "All remains possible, as long as Gloria doesn't die in her sleep."

He plucked the halo from the top of Gloria's head. It burned brighter, giving off a slow-moving black smoke. Gloria whimpered and shifted in her sleep.

Lucifer observed the halo, "Hmm... excellent work if I do say so myself. I suppose I should speed things along."

He snapped his fingers and the red-light surrounding Gloria faded, along with the black stars. Gloria fell back to the bed. The halo turned dark, resembling a stone ring. Lucifer sighed, snapping his fingers again.

The halo blazed with a bright golden light, making a quiet chiming noise. Lucifer sneered as his hand started smoking. He set the halo over Gloria's head and let go. It stayed suspended in the air.

Lucifer shook his hand, "Damn, that powerful already?"

Arthur said, "What did you do?"

Lucifer said, "I shaved off a month for you. I also rushed the halo along, it should heal her if anything bad occurs. Don't touch it unless you wish Gloria to die." Lucifer sighed, "Well, I've overstayed my welcome, as per usual. I bid thee adieu."

A wall of flames flared from the wall. Black iron gates rose from the fire. Lucifer opened one of the doors.

Arthur said, "Wait! Why are you helping us?"

Lucifer smiled and turned slowly to Arthur, "Helping is generous. I am simply keeping to my... that is to say, the interests of the Sins. Promise the Sins blood and... well, we just *might* help. If there is something to gain, then why not?" He grinned, his smile stretching inhumanly across his face, "There is worse to come, and more blood to spill. Luckily, you'll have the Sins to help you... you'll need it, regardless."

He disappeared into the flames, "Tell Fornacem I said hello, and that I told him so, from the Sins, with love!"

He cackled, and a wave of fire exploded from the gates. They disappeared into the fire. There was a loud hiss, and he was gone.

Njord said stiffly, "I must commence my research... Now including the mind as a study." He disappeared from the room.

Arthur said, "I'm going to... Um... yeah." He left the room as well, Julia following.

Cybele turned to Bovi, "We should help Njord. The Mind, this doesn't sound good."

Bovi said, "*There is worse to come, and more blood to spill...* What does that mean?" Bovi turned to Cybele, "Let's do that. We need to help now more than ever." They left, the door snapping shut behind them.

Amber sighed, leaning against Gloria's bed, "Well, the Sin of Pride visits us, tells us worse is to happen, and takes one of our strongest weapons. Travel through the mind, eh? Sounds like fun."

Ignis said, "That's *if* Gloria wakes up. It sounds like the curse will spread. We need to be careful not to do anything stupid until she wakes up."

Amber smiled, "Well, stupid or not, we'll do it."

Ignis noticed Amber was shaking and biting her lip. Her wings were flapping, if ever so slightly. He rested a hand to her shoulder, "Look... I know that you are scared. I am too. I'm terrified... But we have to stick together, we have to be strong... for Gloria. And if she... no... *when* she wakes up... we'll be ready, and we'll do everything we can to stop this curse, and defeat Lapsus."

Tears welled in Amber's eyes, she burst into tears, flinging herself onto Ignis's shoulder, "I'm s-so scared Ignis! The Sins, the Curse, the Mind, what will we do? What if we fail?"

"We won't fail as long as we have each other's backs. I won't let anything hurt us."

Amber sniffed and looked into his eyes, "You'll protect us? Cybele and Bovi? And Njord? Gloria?"

Ignis nodded, "Of course."

Amber wiped her eyes. "Promise me you won't leave me alone. When the time comes, don't abandon me."

Ignis laughed, "Of course I won't! Who is going to help you clean your wounds? I know *you* sure as heck won't."

Amber gave a dry laugh. Ignis smiled, "Speaking of... Where did *that one* come from?"

Amber smiled, "What one?"

Ignis raised a brown bottle. Amber laughed and flew out the window. Ignis ran to the balcony, "Get over here, you!" He laughed and flew out the window as a fiery blue comet.

A gentle stillness rested over the room and a breeze rustled Gloria's hair. Leaves covering the ceiling. The halo made a quiet chiming noise, flipping once over Gloria's head. There was a flash of gold and a single pure white feather fell to the bed.

She shifted in her sleep and large objects fell to the floor on either side of the bed. They shuffled as Gloria shifted in her sleep. They rose once and fell, sending a weak gust of wind around the room. The halo dimmed and made another chime. The two objects moved onto the bed and another feather fell to the floor as they disappeared.

The halo brightened again, and a golden light began spinning inside it. A gentle breeze swirled in the room carrying pure white feathers.

CHAPTER 20
Peccatum Superbiae

Fornacem stood in an empty field, wild lavender plants as far as the eye could see. They brushed against his shins in a gentle breeze. The world was devoid of color. Fornacem looked at his hands. He was wounded, but his blood was dull gray. The only color in the world was the blooming lavender. The clouds passed before a white colorless sun.

Fornacem looked around, *"What* the *hell."* Fornacem sighed and started walking. He trudged down a small hill, making his way to the taller hill in front of him.

"Lavender, it *had* to be lavender, didn't it?" Fornacem reached the top of the hill. He noticed a figure at the bottom sitting on a withered blue sofa, with a battered coffee table in front of him. A small square recording device was lying face down on the table. The figure was looking into the distance.

"What's *this*?" Fornacem trudged to the bottom of the hill and stood in front of the figure.

The figure was grubby. They seemed young; however, the abundance of gray hair gave an older appearance. They wore a dress shirt, tucked into belted slacks. They wore no shoes, nor socks. Their clothes were worn, and ragged. Fornacem realized this figure was in color. The dark gray hair was mingled with coarse gray and white. They had eyes the color of cold steel.

The figure smiled, "Hello, old friend."

Fornacem pointed a finger, "*You're* not Cane! He would *never* leave Lyncoln by himself, and where's Vulpes without Lyncoln? They're *always* together. Cane would *never* leave his house, without *Wolfsbane*, I might add."

Cane smiled, "Well, I'm not technically Cane. However, for the time being, I can be him, if it makes you feel better." The image buzzed with static, and two more figures appeared.

The first captured the likeness of the man next to him, the same hair, and eyes. Except this boy wore suspenders with his pants. A small black bottle was in his left pocket. The boy seemed about twelve. He stood at the level of Fornacem's chest.

The second figure was female, around the same age, several inches shorter than the boy. She had brilliant curly red hair that brushed her shoulders. She had a small nose, with large brown eyes. She wore large welding goggles just above her eyes. She wore a small navy-blue coverall that almost entirely covered her hands. The sleeves of the coveralls were folded back several times. A large blue bandana was tied loosely around her neck. There was an adjustable wrench in her front pocket, and a screwdriver in her back pocket. Two small, pointed ears stood tall from her hair. A large red tail twitched in the grass behind her. The girl smiled shiftily. Fornacem scoffed, he was staring at a Fox Bestia.

Fornacem sighed, "Oh yeah? Just as I remember them? Hey Lyncoln, hey Vulpes."

The boy and girl waved. Lyncoln said, "You remembered my name this time?"

Fornacem groaned, "Oh shut it, temperamental."

Vulpes said, "Hey now! You best be nice before I knock your teeth out with my adjustable!" She waved her wrench threateningly.

Fornacem scoffed, "That sounds like her. Whatever." A

chair appeared in front of him. He sat in it, as Cane gestured.

Fornacem waited a moment, "Where the hell am I?"

Cane sighed, "Well… you have been hurt, Fortem."

Fornacem's eye twitched, "Don't call me that." There was silence for a moment.

"You were struck by what seems to be cursed creation-"

Fornacem groaned, "Hate that shit!"

Cane continued, "Do you have any idea *why* you may be here?" Fornacem crossed his arms. Cane continued, "You are entrapped in your mind, are you not?"

Fornacem scoffed, leaning his chair back on two legs, "What makes you say that *buddy*?"

Cane gestured around him, "You stand in a field of *lavender*, speaking with the image of your old friend, his son, and his friend. You see no color, besides the flowers, the children and me."

Fornacem rolled his eyes, "So?" A gentle breeze shifted the flowers and Fornacem heard a faint voice screaming.

Cane said, "Well, a little more proof then?"

A square of static appeared in front of Fornacem, and a voice echoed from it, "You shouldn't have come here! Not on the full moon!"

There was a sarcastic scoff, "C'mon Cane! I can't miss your boy's birthday! The big one zero! You don't turn ten every day. Besides, Vulpes has been bothering me about it for two *weeks* now. She made me give in when she almost tricked me into drinking oil… *twice*."

A voice muttered, "That Vulpes… fine, come in! And be quick! Hello Vulpes, yes you too-"

Fornacem waved the static away, "Alright, alright! I get it."

Cane said, "You have come here to repent and mourn, Fortem. Something that you have refused to do for almost half of a millennium."

Lyncoln said, "You need to admit to your feelings!"

Vulpes said, "Stop running!"

Fornacem let his chair fall to the ground, "To hell with repenting! And mourning! They make you weak! They show your enemy how vulnerable you are!"

Cane tilted his head sideways, "Are you *not* weak? Fortem?"

Another breeze shoved lavender into Fornacem's nose. He stood suddenly, "Screw you. I say that knowing *none* of you all are real. I'm getting out of here."

Cane sighed, "You may travel to the next hill. You will only find me. You may wander to the edge of this world; you will still find me. In other words, you will not get rid of me. And you will not continue until you face me. Until then, go ahead. Wander for eternity. I have nothing else to do. And I am *extremely* patient."

Fornacem was silent. He sat slowly back in the chair. Cane continued, "Now… Why are you seeing me? Why are you denying your pain?"

Fornacem said, "I feel no pain."

Cane said, "You *do.* You may be immortal, but you are still human."

Fornacem scowled, "There's nothing human left in me. I may as well be a monster."

Cane waved to the children, and they disappeared. Cane leaned forward, "And yet, you are human. You have no fangs, no claws-"

Fornacem said, "Is *that* what a monster is now? Fangs? Claws?"

Cane said, "Is it?" Cane continued, "I mean pain that is not visible, Fortem. You have walked with an invisible knife in your shoulder for a long time."

Fornacem gasped in pain, as a burning sensation flared in his back. He reached back and felt a hilt lodged in his shoulder. He gritted his teeth, "I-I've moved on. It's in the past."

Cane said, "It may be. But you felt Wrath. You craved revenge, and you got it. That is why you claim it is gone. Is it not?"

Fornacem snarled and yanked the knife from his back. He stabbed it into the table, "Watch it."

The light glinted in the knife, momentarily blinding Fornacem. When he could see, a new figure was sitting there.

She had long curly brown hair and green eyes. She wore simple leather armor, with an empty sword sheath on her back. Her neck was crooked, as though someone had broken it.

Fornacem stood and took a few steps back, "No... you're dead."

The figure nodded, "Because of you."

Fornacem shouted suddenly, "AXEL BETRAYED ME! *YOU* BETRAYED ME! YOU ALL BELONG IN HELL! WHAT DID *YOU* EVER DO FOR ME, *PATI*?"

Tears welled in Pati's eyes, "I only tried to do the right thing... you didn't understand. I didn't understand. For that... I truly am sorry Fortem. But why? *Why* did you kill me?"

A voice whispered in Fornacem's ear. *That's life, that's what all the people say.*

Fornacem shook his head, "Piss off-"

Pati said, "You didn't have to. If you had only told me what was wrong... I would have helped you."

Fornacem roared, "I AM A MONSTER! THE LIKES OF YOU WOULD NEVER *DARE* HELP A MONSTER! YOU DIDN'T KNOW WHAT I'VE DONE, OR WHAT I WAS! AND NEITHER DID I KNOW WHAT YOU WOULD BECOME!" Fornacem took a deep breath.

You're riding high in April, shot down in May.

Fornacem ripped the knife from the table and stabbed it into his eye.

Pati shook her head, "You can't avoid me forever."

Fornacem tore the knife from his eye, "WHAT THE HELL ARE YOU?"

Pati smiled, "Humility."

Humility disappeared. "I have been waiting for this opportunity for *centuries*, Fornacem. I am the bane of Pride. You have shoved your emotions and your pain away. They tore from their shackles and surround you. What will you do?"

Fornacem groaned, "PISS OFF!"

But I know I'm gonna change that tune. When I'm back on top, back on top in June. I said, that's life.

Humility said, "Answer us. You cannot escape."

Fornacem roared. A silver explosion ripped from him. A shockwave blasted, the sky turned black, and ashes fell. The lavender plants charred and disintegrated.

Fornacem fell to his knees, taking a deep breath.

Humility said, "Better. Observe what you have done. The innocent lives that were purged by your doing. Your mother. Your father. Fortis? Quinn? You still have emotion. You still have pain. Why do you struggle to deny this? Sins can be forgiven. Is this why you fear death? You fear burning in Hell for eternity?"

A streak of liquid fell from Fornacem's face, "Hell is a grace, more than I deserve for my sin. I just... I didn't want to leave her. I knew not what lay after death. I was scared of losing her. I was scared of living without her."

Fortem looked up, Quinn rested a hand on his shoulder, "I still wait for you. In the afterlife, my soul wanders the abyss before Heaven's gates. I still wait. For you to walk to me, for you to smile, and embrace me in your arms."

"Please... stop." Fortem croaked.

Humility said, "She still waits to this moment. Her heart holds you still."

"She... She was the only one..."

Humility nodded, "She was. She was the only one who

loved you. And the only one whom *you* loved, Fortem. Your desire to reunite with her was strong enough to trigger a war. Many perished by your hands, but you only wished to be by her side."

Humility whispered in Fortem's ear, "You want to know something? She *still* loves you. She never lost hope. Her feelings never changed. She forgave you for your sins. Not only because she loves you, but because she knew that you cared for her. She only regrets leaving you behind to suffer."

Fortem raised his head, "No! She didn't leave me! I... I ended her life! Please-"

The spirit of Quinn wrapped her arms around him. Tears fell silently from her face.

Humility said, "You regret what you did. Don't you?"

Fortem croaked, "Yes."

Humility said, "You wish that you could undo what was done."

Fortem nodded, "I do."

The world around Fornacem faded. The hills lost to darkness. He stood in darkness with Humility, and with Quinn.

"You can repent, Fortem. Because you *are* human." Quinn hugged Fortem tighter, Humility said, "Continue to repent, continue to mourn, continue to forgive. May your sins rest in peace. And may you live on in peace."

Humility faded into the darkness.

Quinn whispered, "I love you Fortem. Like you, I could never move on." She gave a dry chuckle, "There's our flaw, huh?" She sighed, "I will wait for you always, Fortem. I will continue to wait. I will finally feel again, the moment we are reunited. As will you. We move into a bright tomorrow. We will have our time, wait a little longer."

Fortem nodded, "I will always wait for you... my love."

Quinn smiled, and slowly faded into the darkness.

Fortem tried to grasp her tighter as she disappeared. He let his hands fall as colorless despair fell around him. He remained in darkness, clutching himself for warmth.

Each time I find myself flat on my face. I pick myself up and get back in the race. That's life.

Fortem repents in a cold eternal darkness. Unable to feel, unable to forget, unable to die. A voice whispers in his head. *To feel is to live, to live is to feel. You are human, my love. You are human, remember this, for as long as you live.*

A shaky voice trembled from Fortem's lips, *"Why... Why can't I die?"*

He collapsed to the ground as the cold abyss constricted around him. Once broken memories drifted around him in fragments. They slowly placed themselves together around him, another voice spoke.

"Hello! My name is Pati, this is Axel, we're heroes of this town... what's your name?"

"Why?"

Fortem lay there, unable to feel, unable to forget, and unable to die. Another memory drifted around him, a cold voice whispered.

"Know your place, you freak. You will never be human like us. You will forever be a slimy, disgusting monster."

A silver flash echoed from the memory, and the voice fell silent.

A crackling recording spoke in a warbling voice, *"I've been a puppet, a pauper, a pirate, a poet, a pawn and a king, I've been up and down, and over, and out, and I know one thing. Each time I find myself layin' flat on my face, I just pick myself up and get back in the race! That's life."*

Fortem shuddered, "Living... sucks." He sat up as the ground below him turned into clear water. An endless black abyss swirled below the water. Fortem swirled the water's surface, "Well... I've been dealing with bullshit for a millennia... I guess I can deal with this a little longer."

That's life and I can't deny it. Many times, I thought of cutting out, but my heart won't buy it. But if there's nothing shaking, come this here July...

He sighed, falling flat on his back, the water splashing under him, "Suppose I'm supposed to lie here and relive this sh- ah, my lovely memories?"

A gentle breeze blew through the world. A voice whispered, *"That's life!"*

Fortem sang along with the voice, *"Myyy myyyyy."*

In a compressing darkness, a cold wind stirred. A purple vortex swirled above the ground. A corpse flew through the vortex and splattered against the ground. The corpse made a gurgling noise, twitched, and a mangled arm snapped back into place.

Lapsus groaned as he stood. He set an arm onto a desk, heaving himself to his feet. He coughed, wiping blood off his desk. He snatched one of the liquor bottles off the top of his desk and sat heavily in his chair, wincing as he peeled off soaked bandages.

Lapsus said, "I hate possession. Wasn't necessary to kill the Bestia, or the children." He threw a bandage into a nearby waste bin, "So I do my job? *Bull.* All it's doing right now is getting me killed. Turning me into even more of a monster, way more than I bargained for."

Lapsus downed the liquid in one gulp, smashing the bottle against the floor. The door creaked open.

Atom said, "E-Er, sir? He requests a visit."

Lapsus waved a hand, "Yeah, yeah, I got it." The door groaned shut.

Lapsus took a moment and heaved himself from his chair. He followed a steel hallway into the main hangar. Most of the cages were empty. There were no workers milling about the hangar. Mangled monster corpses were visible in very few cages. Lapsus entered through a black door. A chilled voice spoke.

"Failure... *why* am I not surprised?"

Lapsus gritted his teeth, "In time, my lord, you will rise."

The voice whispered, "Do you know what it feels like not to have a body? To possess *filth* such as yourself in order to get *anything* done. I have granted you a brief and pitiful immortality. You cannot escape me. How does it feel to never receive the relief of death? Is it more than you dreamed of? No fate is worse than death, right? To never exist again, to truly perish. You should be grateful that I bestowed such a power unto you."

Lapsus remained silent. The voice continued, "And yet... with all my efforts, I still didn't manage to achieve the curse. How annoying those Factorems prove to be. However, all is not lost... why is that, Nigel?"

Lapsus said, "They have cursed creation in their midst and one of their family has fallen to the curse."

The voice chuckled, "*Yes* of course. They do not have enough strength to protect themselves. If we had an army, I would finish them off. Instead, we will remain patient, and... we will make me whole."

Lapsus said, "My lord, how will we achieve that?"

The voice purred, "*Regnum Vetitum.* A realm where we should have started... a land of pure evil, murder, and darkness. There... I will regain my body, and my strength, if only a fraction."

Lapsus said, "My lord, how will we reach... Regnum Vetitum?"

The voice said, "They are weak. We will reforge the portal to the Regnum Vetitum. We will reclaim its dark treasures, reform our army, then strike while they are scattered. There are dark forces that lie waiting in Regnum Vetitum... waiting to extract their revenge. They will be only too happy to help us. I'm sure they will oblige."

Lapsus said, "My lord... they have one who has achieved the curse. The Sins have abandoned us-"

The voice yelled, "Who's fault is that? Who lost Gluttony *and* Wrath? Your incompetence makes me grow weary, Nigel. As for the curse... if the girl lives, then no matter... they will still remain scattered as they enter a shattered mind. She will never master her newfound power in time."

Lapsus said, "What if they somehow succeed? What if they interfere again?"

The voice crooned, "They will. That is for certain, our priority is to create my vessel, then our forces. When the time is ripe, we will strike. The Factorem family will be born anew, as their corrupted descendants are purged. I will bring the Factorem family glory, since they are the eldest in this realm."

The voice sighed, "For now... find the portal to Regnum Vetitum. Discover what it needs to open. Rally the Fallen here. Should you be interfered with, send their essence to what remains... Do not make me fix your mistakes again, Nigel. I daresay that your heart... she cannot handle much more madness."

Lapsus' fist clenched. He nodded stiffly.

The voice said, "I will be glorified... I will be overlord of this realm, as I so rightfully deserve. It is my birthright. That pesky immortal will rue the day he killed me. I will extract my revenge. Resorting to possession, how irksome. Leave me, Nigel. Allow me to think."

Lapsus nodded and left the room at a brisk pace.

The voice sighed, "Why has thou abandoned me, Pride? Wrath? Have I not served thee well? I shall be the lord of my dreams, my destiny will come to pass, and all will kneel before the most powerful being in all of creation."

Lapsus breathed heavily, shaking his head, "Glory... Where is *my* Glory? When will I receive my promise? I will play along for now, *no one* threatens my family."

The words of the Kraken Sorcerer echoed in his mind, "*There is no glory in darkness... You reap what you sow, you perished in darkness.*"

Lapsus paced down the hall, threw open his office door, and slammed it shut behind him. His hands shook as he sat in his chair. He looked at his hands, coated in blood. The scent of copper and lavender burned in his nose. He sighed, picking up a phone, "Atom, find me every book you can about Forgotten Portals, Regnum Vetitum, and the creatures that live within. Thank you."

He set the phone back on the desk and opened a drawer, pulling out a thick stack of photos. They were bound in a small red cloth. His hands shook as he unwrapped it.

A voice echoed in his mind, "Your daughter grows afraid in my clutches... supply her with something to occupy her. Her crying makes me want to end her pitiful life."

Lapsus turned over a crude crayon drawing, there were three figures in the picture. One captured the likeness of the man staring blankly into its depths, with his dark hair, and shadowed eyes. Next to him was a much smaller figure, her hair reaching her waist, her hand holding the man's. The girl held hands with another figure with long hair and caring blue eyes.

There was a shaky message written on the picture. *We love you daddy! Please do not lose hope!* Some of the letters were backwards and a few words were misspelled. Lapsus took a rattling breath as he held the picture.

"I made the wrong choice... I know that now. I promise, my love, I will break free from this, and we will run away. We will continue to run until we can't be harmed. First... I must bide my time and wait for the right moment. Then I will destroy my enemy and rejoin you."

The door opened. Lapsus quickly shoved the pictures into his desk, wiping his sleeve against his face.

Atom appeared with a large stack of books, "Um... here you are."

He placed the books onto Lapsus' desk, "We have *Regnum Vetitum, Dark Portals, What Lies in the Darkness,* and *The History of Regnum Vetitum.*"

Atom turned to leave. "Atom."

Atom froze, "U-Um... yes sir?"

Lapsus said slowly, "If... if there was something here that... that thought of opposing the lord... you... you wouldn't say anything... right?"

Atom's eyes narrowed, "U-Um... is this a trick question?"

Lapsus shook his head, Atom said, "Um... no... I would not."

Lapsus exhaled, "You may leave now."

Atom hesitated. He shook his head and left the office. Lapsus opened *What lies in the Darkness.* He looked at the first page, cringed, and slammed the book shut. "Good lord." He took a moment and opened the book again.

"Why do I have to see these monsters? These are horrible." He shut the book, opening *Dark Portals,* "Let's see, the Land of Blood, no... the dark giants? Nope. Ah, Regnum Vetitum. Location... unknown, great. Wait... *only the words of a dark elf may reveal the location of the portal to Regnum Vetitum.* Dark elves?"

Lapsus opened *What lies in the Darkness,* "Dark elves, creatures that live in abandoned elf villages, prefer places of carnage." Lapsus scratched his head, "Weaknesses, light spells, angel magic, and deity prowess. Intrigued by dark relics, curses, weaponry. If one wishes to speak with these creatures, be of dark blood, bring dark relics." Lapsus sighed, "Now I have to find dark relics?"

Lapsus ran his fingers through his hair and a pain flared

in his side. He heard a loud crackle, and a patch of static buzzed his side. He took a shaky breath and picked up his phone, "Atom, find books for dark relics and elf history. Schedule an appointment for- yeah, him... thanks."

Lapsus set the phone on the desk, leaned back in his chair, and sighed, "I really hate myself. Just thought you ought to know." He chuckled, "Now *I'm* going crazy."

An angry voice said, "Oh? Are yeh now? Yeh can at least clean in here, yeh manky feck."

Lapsus leaped from his chair. Two blood red eyes glared at him from the corner. Satan took a step forward, his long legs clearing half the room, his horns scraping the top of the ceiling, cement dusted his shoulders.

Satan puffed on a large cigar, "Howya doin?"

***

Weary, that was the word imprinted upon Umbra Mortis's mind for a month now. The air turned colder, and snow began to fall upon the Fall Leaf Valley. Those badgering mortals *always* crawl to Umbra Mortis whenever they have a problem. *Oh, he's immortal, and ancient, he'll solve all our problems!* How *irritating*.

Umbra Mortis scoffed, he walked along the empty halls, at least the students weren't running rampant. Those mortals *were* smartening up, however.

Umbra Mortis watched them train. The Dragonborn and the Boy, they were training with the Bestia for combination animarum. They spent *hours* in the training room. In the span of a month, Umbra Mortis was surprised to see that they were making progress.

Umbra Mortis remembered an invisibility spell he used to use. He opened the door to the training room. The two Bestia were standing a few feet from Amber and Ignis.

Umbra Mortis absently glanced at the male Bestia... *What* was his *name*? Right, it was *Bovi*. Umbra Mortis made sure the Bestia didn't die from cursed creation. He did not know the Bestia well, but Cybele was always kind to him.

Bovi spoke to Amber and Ignis, "Alright, remember, accept equilibrium, you both will have to work together. Feel the connection, then hold onto the feeling. If all goes well, the equilibrium will take over. An equilibrium combination will heed desires from both your minds, as well as its own thoughts. It's a little complicated, but once you achieve it, you'll understand it."

Cybele said, "It'll become natural after you achieve it. Don't worry if you don't get it on the first try. You just need to be in the proper mindset."

Ignis and Amber simultaneously pulled out two small green orbs. Umbra Mortis smiled as the orbs glowed. A ring of green fire blazed around them. Amber and Ignis simultaneously said, "Simul!"

Nothing happened, Umbra Mortis cackled silently. Cybele said, "Don't worry, just try it a-" There was a bright flash of green light and a crackling explosion blasted Umbra Mortis backwards. There was a loud roar, a wave of green, and a new figure stood in the ring of green fire.

Taller than Ignis and Amber by a few inches, they had blue hair, with green ends. They wore dark blue jeans, and clean cowboy boots. They wore a leather jacket over a black shirt, and dark aviator sunglasses. A scar ran along the figure's jaw, but they also wore a smile. There was a spiked choker around the figure's neck, as well as a fire pendant. Two large blue wings, two curled horns, and a spiked tail sprouted from the back.

The figure smiled. The glasses and jacket disappeared in a green flash. The figure stretched. *"Finally!* I thought I'd *never* leave the void! I was half formed the first time those two combined." The figure's voice was much deeper than Ignis's.

Cybele's jaw dropped, "Wha- That's excellent! That... is that equilibrium?"

The figure smiled and pointed a finger gun at Cybele, "Um... I... I *think* so?" The figure thought a minute. "It's... still a *little* off, but I have most of it down. I have a name anyway."

Bovi said, "What... what is it?"

The figure smiled, "It's *Spiritus Inferni,* but I kinda like the name *Loki,* I mean, he's considered the Norse lord of fire... *yeah...* we'll go with *Loki.* Yeah! I *really* like that!" Loki laughed, two blue wings unfolded from his back, green fire rolled slowly from his form.

Umbra Mortis smiled, "*Oh,* he's *strong.*"

Loki smiled wickedly, "Why not take this for a spin?"

Cybele and Bovi took nervous steps backwards, "Wait... Easy you two..."

Bovi said, "Bele, we should take cover." They both yelped as an aura exploded around Loki. It was an acidic green, outlined in dark purple. Small yellow stars winked within the aura.

Loki said, "Who wants to go a round?"

Umbra Mortis chuckled. The mortals were steadily getting stronger. They would need all the power that they could get. If Lucifer was correct, they would have to travel through Fornacem's mind to kill the curse.

Well... *if* Gloria ever wakes up... Umbra Mortis walked into Njord's office, papers littered the floor. Books lie open scattered along the floor, and Njord didn't bother to fix his ties. In Umbra Mortis's opinion, he was starting to crack.

Njord staggered towards the other desk, slipped on a few papers, and fell to the floor. He stood, "Next book... the answer must be in the next book..."

Umbra Mortis doesn't usually take pity, but Njord had been getting worse. He muttered a spell and Njord collapsed to the floor. A quiet snore drifted through the air.

Umbra Mortis slipped into Gloria's room. She still lay in her bed, through Umbra Mortis's instruction, only Arthur and

Julia were allowed to enter. Who knew how the others would react to the state Gloria was in?

The halo chimed faintly, and Umbra Mortis's skin started to burn whenever he entered the room. The halo was beginning to repel him.

Finally, he came into Fornacem's room. Fornacem lay in his bed, occasionally convulsing. He would suddenly smile and burst into laughter with such intensity that he would choke. Umbra Mortis stood next to Fornacem.

"At the time... we are hurt... the enemy will take the opportunity to reforge their forces and supplies. Who knows what that will look like when they return from the shit show called your mind?"

Fornacem said nothing. He smiled and static formed on his right eye. The static was retreating from everywhere else. Umbra Mortis supposed his immortality was starting to take effect.

"Well, you'll be awake soon enough. But the curse still won't die. We need a plan, Fornacem." To Umbra Mortis surprise, Fornacem lurched upwards.

"GOOD LORD! I THOUGHT I'D *NEVER* LEAVE THERE! IF I HAVE TO SMELL A LAVENDER PLANT *ONE MORE TIME*, I'M STARTING ANOTHER WAR!" Fornacem stopped suddenly and turned to Umbra Mortis, "*Sup?*"

Umbra Mortis crossed his arms, "One immortal to another, *speed up* the healing factor next time."

Fornacem shrugged, "Apparently the curse corrupted that feature a bit."

Umbra Mortis smiled, "Ah, *that's* why it took so long."

Fornacem stood from the bed and smiled as the static on his eye crackled, "*That* stings... alright, how we holding?"

Umbra Mortis said, "Oh... Gloria fell to the Curse. Bovi and Dux have cursed creation."

Fornacem said, "Badass to the first, shit to the second.

Ah, right, I should call a few favors, those memories have got me thinking. We need more hands around here..." The immortal made a silver ball in his hands, "Right, to Cane, Lyncoln, and Vulpes..."

ABOUT THE AUTHOR

L. Wolfram

L.Wolfram enjoys reading enough to annoy those around him, as well as chess, and various outdoor activities. No different than many others during the pandemic, the author found himself stuck in the house, surrounded by books he had read numerous times. Given this incentive, he decided the world could use something different and new, and so decided to tell a different story. Though it was slow, and he hadn't the slightest bit of experience, worlds formed in his mind. They spiraled, grew, and took color, branching into something more than ever expected.

CHRONICLES CATACLYSM

Series description:

The Chronicles Cataclysm follows the journey of siblings, Gloria and Ignis Factorem, on their adventures in the Realm of Magic. Born in the Mortal Real, they have lived a quiet life until the magic awakening within them pulls them into the family business. This is a journey of enlightenment and growth, as they come to terms with the good and bad in their family history. The brother and sister form new friendships and allies as they seek to understand their new reality and the new players that inhabit it. Just who can they trust and how do they save the Realm of Magic from cataclysmic downfall?

The Next Great Wakening

Book 1 in the Chronicles Cataclym series, The Next Great Awakening begins the story of siblings Gloria and Ignis Factorem.

The Blood Moon Curse

This book

Elements Of Madness

Coming in the 2nd half of 2022

Made in United States
Orlando, FL
07 May 2022